Advance Acclaim for Flood

"*Flood* is a supernatural journey into a world that is only evil all the time and must be saved by God's merciful judgment. A soul-searching, heart-rending, deeply satisfying story. McPherson taps our imaginations to consider what Noah, his family, and their lives might have been like before the Flood. Many of my questions about Genesis 5–9 now have a place to rest in this well-researched fiction."

—Mesu Andrews, ECPA Book of the Year award-winning author of *Love Amid Ashes*

"A tale as enjoyable as it is immersive. With *Flood*, Brennan McPherson proves himself worthy of telling a story as old as time in a bold and fresh way."

—Billy Coffey, critically acclaimed author of *When Mockingbirds Sing*

"How do you take a centuries-old story and put a new spin on it, inviting readers into an evocative world they thought they already knew? Brennan McPherson figured out the way. *Flood* will entertain you, yes, but also take you deep into your soul and make you ponder both the vastness and the intimacy of God."

—James L. Rubart, Christy Book of the Year award-winning author of *The Five Times I Met Myself*

FLOOD

The Story of Noah and the Family Who
Raised Him

BRENNAN S. MCPHERSON

FLOOD

The Story of Noah and the Family Who Raised Him

Copyright © 2017 by Brennan S. McPherson

ISBN: 978-0-692-95353-2 (softcover)

ASIN: B075RCDZ47

Published by McPherson Publishing

Sparta, WI, USA

Scripture quotations are from the ESV® Bible (The Holy Bible, English Standard Version®), copyright © 2001 by Crossway, a publishing ministry of Good News Publishers. Used by permission. All rights reserved.

Cover design by Josh Meyer Photography and Design

Edited by Natalie Hanemann, NatalieHanemannEditing.com

Author's Note

The Fall of Man series is a group of stand-alone novels based on the book of Genesis. They are historical fantasies I wrote to explore the deeper themes woven throughout the Bible. This has caused confusion, so I hope the following explanation will help clarify my intent.

Flood is based on the story of Noah and the worldwide flood that destroyed nearly all life on our planet. Any novel based on such an ancient, true story is necessarily speculative in nature. So, I decided to embrace a more fantastic interpretation to establish distance between the story and our preconceptions, which so often blind us to the message behind the words.

Some of the preconceptions include the idea that Noah was mocked for his belief in an impending flood, or that it never rained before the Flood, or that Noah and his family were the only ones who labored to build the ark. You won't find these ideas in the Bible. They're as much fantasy as the novel in your hands.

Our knowledge of ancient Israel (or Rome, Egypt, etc.) is bolstered by archaeological, textual, and social studies. However, any evidence of the pre-Flood world would have been destroyed in that catastrophic event. The text of Genesis 5–9 is all we're left with that remains reliable.

Many have disbelieved a worldwide flood possible, but

modern science has shown many of these doubts ill-founded. I have included a section at the end of this book that details the research used in recounting the cataclysm, along with links to an academic essay on how it might have happened.

Genesis 4 contains some lineage leading up to Noah's story, and describes how only a few generations away from Adam, mankind invented agriculture, animal husbandry, musical instruments such as the lyre and pipe, bronze and iron forging, and the concept of the city. Based on both this and the Bible's claim that people in this time period lived to be over nine hundred years old, we can be certain that by the time the Flood took place, an advanced and unique culture had developed, and cities had spread across the face of the earth.

If you are interested in feeling the depth of emotion these ancient people might have felt, and in having your ideas of this monumental event challenged or deepened, *Flood* might be the right book for you.

I've come to believe it's healthful for us to ponder the mysteries of God, yet not to take too seriously our belief of what isn't explicitly stated.

One more note before you go: if you want to download two free e-books, get new release alerts, and have a devotional sent to your inbox every Saturday morning, go to brennanmcpherson.com and sign up!

Prologue

At the dawn of Time were Three who were One. Creator, Spirit, and Word.

As the Spirit hovered over the formless waters, the Creator stretched out his hand, bidding the Word to begin an eternal Music that brought light and form to the universe.

Empty space shifted and became solid. Matter rose green from the elements, and the Spirit breathed into the green matter life but not awareness, and ordained that it should bear seed and spread across the earth suspended in the darkness amidst countless masses of flame and shadow.

Afterward the Creator brought forth creatures not bound by root and soil. They held awareness but lacked will. Governed by the personalities imbued, they spread and multiplied.

The lights were divided, as were the waters, and the seasons. The earth crawled with life given dimension amidst light and shadow. Dew condensed and fell, sprinkling the ground with the scent of life. And the Creator saw that it was good.

But the Creator's vision was yet incomplete, for the most beautiful themes of the Music still roamed the halls of Timelessness. So the Creator descended and walked the fields, gazing at all he had done in so short a span of Time.

He dipped, grabbed a handful of soil, and said to the Word and the Spirit, "Let us make man in our image, after our likeness. And let them have dominion over all living things." So the Creator made man and woman in his image, and said to them, "Be fruitful and multiply, subdue the world and have dominion."

But the man and woman were not satisfied with dominion. They wanted to transcend the boundaries the Creator constructed for them.

They grasped fruit too high for their arms to reach, and ate what they should not have eaten. They became aware of a second Music, of darkness amidst the Light, and they aligned themselves with that second Music, and death entered their forms.

However, even this faltering of steps was planned in the first Music that would sweep up the faltering into a melody more beautiful than any other. The Creator told the man and woman of this coming theme in the first Music, of a babe to issue from the woman's womb—of the one who would be the undoing of death.

The man and woman traveled on and bore two boys. Yet neither was the babe to come, for the elder murdered the younger, and birthed within himself an Abomination bent on twisting humankind to evil purposes.

The Abomination knew of the babe to come, and sought to prevent its arrival. The Abomination grew and festered, and brought others of its kind into the world, spreading ruin and darkness.

Hope faltered in the hearts of men, and it seemed for a time that the Light of the first Music might be eclipsed by the darkness of the second.

But there were other legends. Whispers passed down by those faithful to the Old Way. That before the promised babe would come another child, a foreshadowing of the one to come. A herald of righteousness who would see a burning world quenched.

And he would be called Noah, for through him God would bring rest to the world.

PART I

The Mother and the Father

"Lamech . . . fathered a son and called his name Noah, saying, 'Out of the ground that the LORD has cursed, this one shall bring us relief from our work and from the painful toil of our hands.'"
—Genesis 5:28–29

Chapter 1

Adah straightened to match her father's stare. "Tell me why I cannot choose whom I might marry."

Father ducked past the central beam that held their farmhouse aloft and stepped near. "Because I will not have you dishonor the family by marrying a fool." His head tipped like a boulder on cliff shoulders, and Adah waited for what would surely come tumbling out of his mouth.

"Irad," Mother warned as she stood against the wall kneading dough on the only table in their living room. Her shadow stretched double in the light of the candles that burned on the opposite side of the room, the flickering silhouette mirroring Adah's father in size and shape.

"Lenah," Father mocked, not looking from Adah. "Don't say my name like an obscenity. Our daughter is throwing away our lives, the labor of our ancestors. The stress will be the death of me."

Mother dusted her hands so the dough wouldn't stick. "You are fine." The table's legs danced on the packed dirt floor as the weight shifted.

Father's face darkened as he turned. "I spent the last month lying in bed coughing blood." He thrust a finger toward Adah. "And what has she done? Learned from that vagabond how to chisel symbols into clay?"

Adah's shoulders tensed. "He has a name, if you would only care enough to remember it. I chose to better my future. The furthest you can think is next spring."

Father laughed. "Did you drain our wineskins with that mouth of yours? The early frost killed half our crop, and if you would have been anywhere you *should* have been, we could have saved twice as much from the second frost already descending."

"Stop shaming her." Mother rested one hand on the table, the other on her hip. "You know as well as I do you refused her offer to help harvest weeks ago."

Father slapped the beam. "I didn't need her help weeks ago!"

"If you would have but told me," Adah said and remembered finding Father when he first caught sick—clawing his throat and wheezing. Since childhood, she had thought him indomitable, but seeing him too weak to breathe had opened her eyes to a new reality. Even now, months later, he could handle only half the workload as before.

"Look what you've done," Mother said. "Her face is pale. And she's shaking, the poor thing."

Father sat on a stool beside the candles and rubbed his face with a callused hand. "I trust Jubal. Jubal is a good man. I just want my daughter to be with a good man."

"I know." Mother crossed to him and rubbed his shoulders, dusting his tunic with flour. "She knows."

Adah's fingernails bit her palms like clutched cinders. "Good is not enough."

"She wants to be free"—Father glanced up—"like some wild animal in the forest. But she is no deer. She cannot run off with every charismatic foreigner who wafts through our village. My heart tells me that vagrant she's fallen for is a coward. And what will they say?" He flicked his hands as if to cleanse them. "She must marry a man like Jubal and stop this foolishness before she throws away our dignity."

"I hate him," Adah said, and her insides shook.

Mother squeezed her arm. "Now, dear, you don't hate Jubal."

"I will care for the farm," Adah said. "You claim I'm more

knowledgeable about farming than any man you've met. Yet now I'm not enough?" Cold breath burned Adah's nostrils.

Father frowned. "A woman may do a man's work for a day, but not a lifetime. Do you not think of shame?"

Embers spread through Adah's chest. "You've taught me nothing else."

Father glanced at Mother, who shook her head, crossed to the table, and squashed the dough with renewed vigor.

"The farm may thrive under your ownership," Father said. "But when you die, all your labor will be choked by weeds. You need children, and to have children you need a man. How many times must I say it?"

"Explain to me how choosing my own husband is anything but fair," Adah said.

"I do not ask you to understand. Only to obey. Do you really think I would let you marry that fool? His hands have known as much work as an infant's."

"What she asks is fair," Mother said.

Father's brow creased like freshly plowed fields. "Our daughter is fiery enough without you tossing her kindling."

"You can afford to give her what she asks for," Mother continued.

"And you can afford to keep silent."

"This isn't about—"

Adah skirted them to the door, threw it wide, and exited the house. The air was crisp and opaque. Shadows bled from the fog rolling over the tilled farmland toward the forest rearing like a host of spears, ice-tipped and glittering. The mountains loomed beyond, crowned white to match their weaponry.

Adah found a hatchet lodged in a stump and heard Father's voice rising against Mother's. She took up the hatchet, returned, and set her back to the door as they noticed what she held.

"Hand it over," Father said.

"You taught me I could be anything I wanted."

"Give me the tool." He stepped forward, but Mother stopped him by the arm. He glanced back. Set his jaw.

"If I were a boy," Adah continued, "our struggle would be over. So why not let me be what you always wanted?"

"You don't know what you're saying," Mother said.

"I'm no fool," Adah said. "I hear the intent behind your words louder than what you speak." She chilled her voice until it was colder than the iron in her hands. "You're ashamed I wasn't born a boy, that you have no heir, no legacy. So you wish to trade me to gain one." She smiled humorlessly. "Barter the worth of my womanhood for the benefit of your pride."

Father's eyes flashed like glowing sickles, and Mother spoke before Father could. "You're upset. We understand."

But they didn't. They couldn't. Not unless she showed them. Before they could say anything more, she grasped her hair into a thick tail and, as Mother cried out, sliced it through, letting it fall to the ground.

Mother blinked and knelt to grasp at the hair on the floor. "This has been growing since you were a babe."

Father let a breath grate his teeth. "You should have let me take the hatchet."

Mother lifted a fistful of hair. "You think that would have made a difference? She's forced your hand, you old fool. No man would dare marry her now, save the one you call a vagabond."

Father turned toward Adah. "Nothing in this world has made me more infuriated than you." He approached, his voice and gaze sharper than obsidian. "But I would take you over five sons. You've no right to claim I wouldn't."

Adah dropped the hatchet and balled her hands into fists. Mother rolled the severed hair between her hands, grimaced, and let it fall. Adah closed her eyes in preparation for what might come next. She had experienced it all too often—the harshness of Father's voice as he shrunk her actions to shameful little things.

But Father stepped near, embraced her, and kissed her forehead instead.

Her breath stumbled on the edge of a sob, though she managed to maintain her composure for she knew these tactics too. Father would humble himself to elevate his rebellious daughter to something more elegant—to anything but what she was.

She stiffened to show him she was no fool, not anymore. But her throat ached, and in truth, what good would resisting do?

Her stomach knotted with the realization that part of her, the part that really was still small and weak, wanted his tenderness, wanted to hug her father and weep into his shoulder and tell him she was sorry she couldn't be what he wanted.

She scowled and blinked burning eyes.

Father inhaled as if to speak, but five knocks at the door silenced them.

The three turned, and the knocks returned, followed by a voice muffled past the pitched wood. "Open, in the name of the God-King."

Mother said, "What?"

"Hush," Father said, and stared until the knocks became pounding. "Who beats my door at such a time?"

"Messengers of the God-King." The voice was deep, throaty. "Open the door."

Father turned toward Adah, sweat glistening across the bridge of his nose. "Hurry," he whispered, "to the cellar. Do not—"

"They have no right to be here, don't let them in," Mother said.

"You speak of what you don't understand. If—"

"Open the door!" The voice came louder.

"Men such as these do not abide being made to wait." Father's eyes grew hard. "Go. These are foreigners."

Mother started to protest, but Father cut her off. "Their king has been visiting our city since midway last season. I fear more than inconvenience in this nightly visit."

Mother frowned, grabbed Adah's arm, and urged her back.

"No," Adah said.

Mother jerked her close. "Enough."

Adah set her jaw and dug her feet in, but after an insistent shove from Mother, a furious gesture from Father, and more violent pounding on the door, she allowed herself to be marched into the other room.

The cellar door was heavy on its hinges, and Mother eased it open, careful not to let it creak. When it was wide enough for

Adah to slip through, Mother pushed her in, and Adah tripped and caught herself on the skinned lamb hanging from chain hooks anchored in the cellar's ceiling. She twisted around, glared, and wiped the blood on her dress.

"Hush," Mother said, and pressed the door shut.

All was dark. She reached for shelves but failed to find them. Her belly tingled and she felt uneasy. Chains swayed and jangled as she crouched and hugged her knees. Blood dripped to cold puddles. Wind buffeted the house, bending it minutely, beating moisture from wood. She could hear each beam settling slowly, the weight of their bulk pressing into the earth.

If her parents thought they could continue treating her like this, they were mistaken. However, Father had never ordered her into the cellar before. Something was wrong, that much she knew.

Deep voices. She wished she could hear what they said, but the walls were too thick.

Her head spun. She pressed her hands to the floor to steady herself. An insect scurried up a wall, and she turned toward it, eyes straining.

Father's voice overwhelmed the others, warm and powerful at once. The voices grew. Adah's breaths came and went like the tide, shallower with each pulse.

Father yelled, a scream tore the air, and the house shook. Adah twisted, her shoulder knocking pots off the shelves. The pots shattered on the floor, spilling spices and pungent oils. Her trembling hands reached for a broken shard. She found one, gripped it hard, struggled to her feet, flung the door wide, and sprang into the light.

There, in the entryway, lay two strange men. Blood seeped from the corners of their mouths. Though Adah had never seen a dead body, they lay disturbingly motionless. Father leaned against the wall beside the open door, holding the hatchet. Mother shut and barred the entrance as Father pressed his back to the door and slid to his seat.

Adah trembled, staring at the motionless men. "What happened?"

Father cursed. "They saw the hair. The hair! They wanted

you, Adah. Do you hear me? Thought we were trying to trick them, make them think you were a boy. Gods protect us."

"Why did they come here?" Adah said.

Father offered a glance that said more than words could. "This is not the first house they visited."

Mother stood with a knife in her hand and wildness in her green eyes. Adah looked at the men and noticed curved horns sprouting from their skulls. The horns were so foreign her mind hadn't let her see them upon first glance.

From outside came muffled shouts. Adah's skin tingled and her face chilled. She closed her eyes, hoping it was all a dream. But as she opened her eyes, everything remained.

There came more pounding and new demands. Father leaned against the door and stared at the bodies. Mother wrapped her arm around Adah, who stood examining the knife clutched in Mother's hand, and the pottery shard in her own.

Mother said, "Do you hear that?"

Father moaned, tested his wounded arm, and grimaced.

"We need to clean that wound," Adah said, her voice high and brittle. "If we don't—"

Mother chopped the air. "Listen!"

There it was. Crackling. Popping. A low drone.

"They've set fire to the house," Father said.

Adah searched for signs of the flames, closed her eyes, and kneeled, holding her head in her hands. "This is all a dream. I'm going to wake up now."

"Something must have gone wrong," Father said. "We knew they were a warlike people . . . but this? I fear our sovereign is dead."

"Wake up now," Adah said. "Wake up!"

"Stop, Adah!" Mother turned to Father. "We can't just wait here in the entryway. Why not run? Or hide in the cellar? Irad, what is happening?"

"The cellar won't save us. They're waiting outside, likely listening to us now. My grandfather didn't build this house cheaply, like the others. The wood is thick and strong. It will take longer to burn, and will look worse than the others while remaining safe. We wait until we can no longer. Then we run. But not yet." He closed his eyes. "Not too soon."

"You're betting our lives on your grandfather's woodcraft."

Father did not respond.

"Gods help us." Mother paced.

Flames crept through cracks and licked the ceiling. Fire spread and rippled, danced and shifted, filling the house with black fumes.

Adah's head spun. She bent to her hands and knees. Sheets of flame rolled and snapped. She opened her eyes against the heat and saw the horned men aflame and her father leaning against the door—a final island in a sea of red. His face was pale and his good hand clasped his throat. His other lay limp on the floor as he coughed in the smoke.

Mother found Adah's arm, and they shuffled to the door. Father's body blocked it. They rolled him to the side, unbarred the door, and pulled it open.

Burning air tossed them back. Adah's hair crackled, and she yelled and smothered it with her arms. She looked up. Flames poured in from the edges of the doorway as if the world had been pitched on its side and down was in and up was out.

Mother hauled Father through the doorway, then pulled him smoking across the yard and slapped at the flames. Adah struggled to her feet and hobbled out, feeling a burst of wind across her shoulders.

A voice sounded behind and to her left. She turned.

Strange men tossed a net over her and she tumbled to the ground, enmeshed. Mother screamed and ran to her aid, but the men kicked her to the ground. Father crawled toward them with sickle eyes brandished, but they laughed at him.

"Stop!" Adah said. "Leave them alone!"

She watched the polished surface of their horns reflecting the red and black of her burning home until the wooden end of a spear slammed into her temple and she succumbed to the relief of emptiness.

Chapter 2

L amech found the girl facedown in the dirt between the stones that marked the turn to the stream. The snow-capped mountains held little kindness for wanderers. It was hard terrain, even for wild animals.

Goats with shaggy coats and pointed horns danced like ghosts across gaps in the cliffside. Hawks preyed on shrews hiding among thistles and skeleton shrubs.

But a woman?

Since a child, Lamech had seen but the few who brought him and his father supplies every season. Even then they were men. Not women.

Never women.

And never had he seen anyone travel to the peak so late in the season in anything less than thick furs. She wore a thin dress and mud-covered sandals that looked more appropriate for ceremony. But she was still breathing, her chest slowly rising and falling.

How had she gotten here?

He tried to still the uneasiness that surely reddened his cheeks, but part of him wanted to indulge the rush, let it fill his chest, fingertips, and toes, and tingle the top of his head.

Father would be angry. He often spoke of how they didn't need a woman to be happy. But Father repeated the biggest lies most often, and seeing her broken body gnawed by frostbite and crumpled like sagebrush—how could he leave her?

It made him think of Mother's frailness in her final days, though that was nearly all he could recall. The rest had been lost like a mural wind-beaten and crumbled with age. Even though he had no idea who this woman was, or why she was here, he couldn't let her suffer the same fate.

He bent close, eased her onto her side, tested her limbs, and studied her face.

Her eyes fluttered open, and she grunted and twisted away. He hushed her and tried to keep her from moving as he had with the wounded sparrow he'd nursed back to health. "I'm not trying to hurt you," he said, but she struck him in the chest hard enough to push him off-balance, and he fell.

She slid away, cradling her ribs, and covered her mouth and coughed, wetness crackling in her chest. She pulled her hand away dappled with blood.

He sat up and narrowed his eyes as the light shimmered across the red on her fingers.

She looked away and wiped her hand on her silk dress, which looked as if it had once been a rich purple, though now it was tattered and stained.

He stood and stepped back. "Are you sick?"

"Leave me alone."

She had obviously been beaten, so perhaps the sickness that stole Mother had nothing to do with it. A slave with an abusive master could conceivably flee up a mountain in thin clothing and sandals.

But not in a purple silk dress.

He swallowed. "I'm sorry I scared you. I pass these rocks every day to find the stream. Are you thirsty? Hungry?"

She flared her nostrils and glared at him as if she expected him to stab her at any moment.

"If you doubt my intentions, your distrust is misplaced. I will not harm you." He waited and listened to her silence amidst the wind whistling through the rocky pass. She was injured, and if she resisted him, attempting to care for her would only risk greater harm.

But he couldn't help his curiosity. Couldn't imagine how a young woman could end up alone at the top of a mountain.

At the top of *his* mountain.

Still . . . he could not force her.

He turned and said, "I pray you find your way."

He walked away slowly, and had nearly made it around the bend when he thought he heard her speak. The sound was so faint he thought it could be leaves rustling in the wind. He held his breath and listened.

"Wait . . ."

He turned.

Tears clung to the woman's cheeks. "Please. I've been alone for so long."

He returned slowly, foreign emotions churning inside his chest. He thought of her wounds, of the pain she must have endured to arrive in such a state. Of his mother laid pale and lifeless on a grassy knoll. "What happened to you?"

She shook her head. "I can't speak of it." Her tears moistened the ground.

"I wasn't trying to hurt you," he said. "You could come back with me, warm yourself, dry your clothes, eat and drink, and rest under shelter."

She nodded like one thinking of far-off days. "A moment," she whispered. "Can we just rest a moment, first?"

He rubbed his face, nodded, and sat to wait until she was ready. Wounded as she was, movement was likely painful. But she could not wait forever. The marks of frost damage on the tips of her fingers were proof enough.

Chapter 3

A dah awoke with the smell of her burning home still fresh in her mind. She knelt alone in a bamboo cage that smelled of blood and urine, and the cage rocked and bucked. Ahead and behind were cages like hers atop wheeled platforms pulled by yoked bulls. Inside the cages were bound women lit by the moon's star-pricked cape.

Where were her parents?

Closest was a young girl she recognized from down the valley. Alvaretta, a farmer's daughter. She lay on her side. Knees tucked to her chest. Rope around her neck. Clothed in swelling bruises.

Adah shut her eyes, clenched her teeth, and felt a rush of heat. A sickness churned her stomach. The darkness made the moans and startled breaths from those around her grow more disturbing. Had all these women—*so many*—been taken from their homes? Thrown into cages like animals?

Like Adah.

She reached to comfort the girl, but found her wrists tied to the cage with hemp rope. She stretched against her bonds, jerked, kicked, and threw herself side to side, but the bonds held, and the skin of her wrists was rubbed raw.

She rested, her breaths coming short and quick. The wagons

and women seemed strangely false. As if at any moment she could step through the bars, stand in the weeds, and watch the procession disappear into the dust kicked up by wheels.

Instead, she knelt shaking for hours. Wind stung her skin. Grasses bowed as they passed. Dust eddies danced across the road and broke themselves upon the wagons. Little breaths come and gone, as if from Father's lips.

She couldn't stop seeing every crease in his face. Every red line running across his smoke-burnt eyes. He had protected her when danger came near. He had been injured protecting her.

So how could this cage be real?

She blinked to clear the blur from her vision as the procession crested a hill and descended toward a walled city. Inside the city rose narrow buildings, and roads wove like veins toward a black tower in the center. A tower she had seen only once in her life. But once was enough to prove Father's fears true.

Their sovereign had been murdered, and the foreigners with horns had taken the city.

An orange glow grew as they neared burning pyres outside the city gates. Beside the fires were hastily built wooden platforms. Emaciated men stood upon them and threw bound bundles atop the pyres. As the procession passed, she watched the heat burst the bundles' bindings and twist what remained inside.

She gazed past the snapping flames to one of the men on a platform. The shackle on his leg clanged as he turned and tossed another bundle on the fire. He nodded at her. She nodded back and glanced at the burning bundle.

Her breath stopped. That was no bundle. It was a person.

She thought of Father's hands clenched against the pain of the flames burning their home, and reached uselessly for the bars, screaming his name, though she knew the man in the flames was not her father.

The procession moved through the gates, and Adah fell back and watched the bars of her cage fade from orange to gray. They passed tall buildings with slatted windows, and Adah twisted, searching for the family she knew she would not find.

All she wanted was to see them crouching amidst the shadows. To hear their voices argue, to bear Father's scorn, to suffer Mother's chastisement. Instead, she watched dirty orphans run the alleyways and dart around corners.

The wagons wound through an open courtyard of slippery cobbles. Past meat vendors and bins filled with rotting vegetables that peddlers tried to shove into the hands of nightly passersby. Soldiers stood clustered in little groups, staring at peasants as if searching for a reason to test their proficiency. Women with matted hair clutched babies swaddled in brown sheets and sent furtive glances toward the soldiers. Finally the soldiers and the women also disappeared, replaced by the endless drone of wooden wheels riding the cobbles, and the burning torches of a city whose pulse beat hardest in the shadow places.

Adah had thought some of those they passed would have offered comfort, but none even glanced their direction. Not the peddlers, not the soldiers, not the mothers. She wondered if it was because they were ashamed.

The alley opened and ahead loomed the tower lit by moonlight. The snake of wagons turned, and she caught sight of their driver and the horns atop his head. The man jumped down, halted the procession, and stood at attention. From the tower's side came a line of soldiers who opened the cages and broke the captives' bonds. They went down the line, freeing and corralling them into neat lines. The ones who didn't obey were beaten. The ones who still couldn't rise were cut open on the cobbles.

Two soldiers in metal shirts opened Adah's cage and cut her bonds. She tried to jump down but nearly fell with the pain and stiffness in her legs. Soldiers stood clustered here and there.

Beyond them, open alleyways.

A woman near Adah threw herself to the ground and rolled under the carts. The soldiers cursed and grabbed for her. Two women ahead wrenched one of the soldier's weapons away and ran him through.

The rest saw their opportunity and seized it. The captives and guards struggled against each other, and the two women who managed to seize a weapon were themselves cut down while Adah stood forgotten, staring at those open alleyways.

Her breath caught, and her face chilled. *Where do they lead?*

She glanced back. The two closest soldiers dragged the woman out from under the carts and ended her before leaving to beat the mob into submission.

Adah bit her cheek, tightened her fists, and readied herself to dash for the open alleyway.

She froze. She'd forgotten the driver. Her neck hair rose as she turned. The driver stood with a bow in his hand, watching her from afar. Smiling.

She inhaled and flexed her stomach to ward away sudden nausea. The captives had submitted, and one of the guards noticed Adah and jerked her forward.

She stepped in line and lost all sensation in her legs. As the driver lit torches, Adah clenched her teeth and grabbed her hand hard enough to hurt.

Had she thrown away her only chance at freedom? Her father had given his life to protect her, and she had just stood there.

One of the girls stumbled over a prone body, and as Adah passed, she couldn't help but stare at her empty, open eyes, wondering if hers would soon look the same.

The driver guided them toward a cellar door in the tower's side, unlocked it, and flung it wide. Men in black hoods held flickering torches. The driver greeted them and waved his captives inside.

The hooded men led them down endless clammy corridors. They turned through a passageway and passed four doors. Then came more staircases, and more turns, until Adah's mind spun.

When they stopped, the soldiers pressed them into little rooms with iron bars and slick floors. Adah was second to last. They tried fitting her in with a group of other women, then decided it was too full and placed her and the last woman in a cell all their own.

Adah's companion collapsed and became so still Adah thought her dead.

The soldiers locked the doors and left with torches in hand, submerging the women in darkness as cold and heavy as a mountain lake.

Adah thought of the smile on the driver's face. As moisture dripped on her shoulders, she thought of the dead women and shivered.

Chapter 4

Lamech waited two hours in near complete silence until the girl finally decided to follow him. Father once said that silence is a balm for the wounded. Lamech thought it close enough to the truth, for words often erupted from inner violence, but a man calm in silence was a man at peace with the world.

"Slow down," she said.

He turned, and she was farther back than he thought. "Sorry," he said. Lamech swore his legs had never felt more eager. Several times before they arrived, he turned back to see her too far behind. After they made it, he brought her into his and Father's second hut, where Lamech had taken to spending his nights.

He hated to admit that she would soon become an uncomfortable topic.

"Father won't be happy," he said.

"Why?"

He paused. "He doesn't like women."

"Then I don't like *him*," she said.

"Don't say that until you've met him."

"Well, any man who can dislike someone he's never met is a fool. I already know I don't want to meet him."

Lamech shook his head, but no words came. He reached and began pulling her dress back, but she struck his hand away.

"What are you doing?" Her voice shook, and her eyes burned.

He frowned and felt his cheeks flush. "Your clothes are wet, and you have frostbite. If you don't get into dry clothes, your skin will start to decay. I'm sorry. I'm not used to having a woman around. It's been—" He swallowed. "A long time."

She studied him. "I'll change myself. Look away. Better yet, go out until I tell you I'm ready. Where's the fresh clothing?"

"I still have to get it."

The silence thickened as she glanced toward the doorway.

He rubbed his jaw, angry at himself for being so foolish. She was muddling his thoughts. "Please . . ." He almost said *trust* but realized that word was too thorny for—what did she say her name was? "Be patient with me. I know this is a strange situation for you. It is strange for me as well. No one ever comes here. These mountains are perilous, even for those who know them well. I could hardly believe I found you alive."

The wordless pause returned, and she tossed a distrustful glare into it.

He listened to the scrape of her breath and the thump of his heart until they blended together, forming something greater. Something beautiful that recalled Mother's matted hair and, for the first time in years, the warmth of her hand on his arm as she whispered of love with a voice ravaged by illness.

The girl's clothing rustled, and he looked up. She still stared with green eyes aflame. "If you try to do anything to me," her voice shook, "I will kill you."

He rubbed his chest to warm the frost that spread there. "I would deserve it." His hands grew clammy. "My name is Lamech."

She nodded.

He opened his mouth. Closed it, nodded, and left to find fresh clothing.

Just outside the door, Lamech stopped so suddenly that he nearly fell.

His father, Methuselah, stood with arms crossed and gray

eyes glittering beneath thick, speckled brows. "I know what you're thinking," Father said, his voice like gnarled brush scraping rock, "but it was a mistake to bring her here."

Lamech felt a sudden rush of nausea and said, "I couldn't—"

Father stopped him with a raised hand. "I know, son. We've lived together too long for me not to. But it's time we spoke."

Lamech followed his father into the brush until they came to that familiar tree stunted by altitude and lack of moisture. It was smaller than he remembered, and today the clouds cleared the peak that jutted like a spear about to tear them open.

Father crouched, knees popping as he leaned into the branches. Lamech knelt beside him. The last time they'd visited the tree, Father lectured him about what it meant to be a man. But today Lamech had done what any man should. "How have I displeased you?" Lamech said.

"I still think of your mother," Father said, and Lamech felt that old fissure throb. "After all these years, I still wonder what she would say to comfort me. How she would speak or sing while doing chores . . ." Father looked down. "I thought I could protect her. Keep her with me. That's why I brought you up here when she took sick. As I nursed her, I tended the fantasy that somehow I was strong enough to hold on. Still, after all these years, I can't seem to let go."

Lamech looked at the horizon and remembered Mother's blue eyes had reddened like the sky behind the setting sun. "I heard her voice today," Lamech said. "Do you ever?"

Father shook his head. "I've been too long in the pain. I remember what she said, but not the quality of how she said it."

Lamech stared at the roots of the tree grappling the stones beneath it. "Is it too much to believe we can heal?"

Father exhaled hard, and his brows bristled. "I've seen this day coming since the moment your mother was taken." His eyes grew wet, and his voice thickened. "You're the last piece of her left in this world. If I let you go . . ."

So this was why they came to the tree. Lamech shook his head. "Nothing could take me away."

Father observed him long. Gray eyes flitting over his features.

"I've not been a good father. Whatever happens before the end, you deserve to hear that."

"What has gotten into you?"

"Change, son. Don't ask me to explain it. I've been feeling something growing these past months. Been having strange dreams. And now the sense is undeniable. That girl brought something with her. Or maybe something brought her. Either way, I believe that it's time for you to make the very choice I've kept you from making all these years."

"I'm not going to leave," Lamech said.

"You only say that because I've never let you know better. I've laid bonds on you and called them love. But I knew. I still know. If you stay, I think you will be fighting something greater than yourself. Greater than either of us."

Lamech shifted and crossed his legs. He never remembered Father speaking like this before, and he fought to still the shaking in his hands.

Father placed a hand on Lamech's shoulder. "Whatever happens, choose without regard for my loneliness. My heart tells me some profound sorrow is coming. Only remember when the day comes that the right decision can sometimes be more difficult than death." His gray eyes flashed. "Don't misunderstand me—I still don't believe in your grandfather's God. Not after he broke our family. But lately I've been feeling something growing. Some heartbeat, some rhythm in the fluttering of birds' wings and the scurrying of insects. It seems to me like some great Music, and more and more I find myself wondering if maybe there are forces in the world that we do not understand. Things we've never imagined. Now, after that girl's arrival and the shifting of the world beneath these old feet, I wonder if you'll be given the chance to rise and meet them."

Father squeezed Lamech's shoulder, struggled to stand, and braced his bad leg to make it up the rough path. He paused a moment, as if listening, then said, "I've long watched you tend to any life that comes your way. But now I wonder if maybe it's deeper than that. Maybe it's just who you are. A protector. And that's what I most fear."

Lamech felt his father's words slip behind his ribs and strike at his heart. Though he'd never explicitly thought it before, his father's words resonated with the very marrow of his bones.

But as he opened his mouth to tell his father, "Yes! That's exactly right! That's who I am," the sound dried in his throat.

Because if what his father said was true, maybe the comfortable life he'd known all these years really would be brought to an end by the arrival of the girl and the destiny she brought.

Chapter 5

I t could have been days or weeks before the eunuchs visited Adah's prison, for the endless dark shifted her thoughts like shadows in a forest. The light of their torches burned Adah's eyes, and she heard them toss balls of rice on the stone floor of the cell and ladle water into her bowl. She was shaking so badly she didn't trust herself to lift the bowl, so instead she dipped and sucked up the liquid.

Her companion still hadn't moved, and that made her hate the men who had imprisoned them even more. She envisioned them standing against the darkness of her cell, an army of faceless soldiers with black eyes and horns.

When the eunuchs came a second time with more food and water, they removed her companion's body. Adah was able to eat this time, but her stomach pained her.

"Please," Adah said. "Put me with the others."

The eunuchs didn't answer. She pressed her face against the bars and said, "Let me out."

A fat eunuch turned and lowered his torch, a set of keys jangling at his waist. "You think you deserve freedom?" The corner of his mouth lifted, mocking, and his voice was high and rough like that of an old woman too many years over an open fire.

"Help me," she said, keeping her thoughts on the keys and her eyes on the eunuch.

"Why? You're nothing but a tool. And we will use you until no use is left. Then you, too, will burn on the pyres, and nothing will be left save ashes and the scent of death on the wind." The eunuch leaned close until his fat, smiling face pressed against the bars. Sweat dripped off his cheeks down the iron, and the crackling heat of flames carried his stench into her face. "You're nothing. Naked, pathetic, weak. Perhaps I should bring a mirror so you can see how disgusting you've become. Stripped of niceties. How does it feel?"

He cackled, shooting spittle onto her face and sending a burning down the length of her arms. Her fingers curled to claws, and as he turned away, she clutched the ring of keys on his garment and pulled him against the bars. He cried out, dropped his torch, slapped her hands, and said, "Let go of me, wench!"

She held on, trying to rip the keys from his garment. He shoved his hand through the bars and grabbed her throat. She coughed as his hand tightened and she released the keys, grabbed his arm with both of hers, and threw her full weight against it in the wrong direction against the bar.

The eunuch screamed as the others fumbled with their keys. "Get her!" The eunuch wept. "My arm—it's broken!"

A key sunk home and rolled tumblers. The eunuchs swung the door wide, threw aside their cloaks, and withdrew bamboo rods. The back of Adah's ears burned with anticipation as she spun. Moments later came the first blow to the side of her head. She cried out and guarded her head with her arms.

The fat eunuch wept. "She ruined it. Kill her!"

They beat and kicked her, and she screamed and cursed and tried to strike back, but a boot smashed her side, and she felt bone snap. The pain stole her breath and sent her to the floor. They continued beating her until the violence faded to weary breaths and desperate swallows. Seemingly satisfied with what they had done, the eunuchs left, taking their wounded companion with them.

Tears wetted Adah's face. "Let me out," she whispered, but

the effort sent pain. She lay still, breathing as shallow as possible. But the burning in her chest made it hard not to weep. "Let me out."

The darkness returned heavy, and in the prolonged absence of light, finding any anchor for her thoughts became increasingly difficult. All sensations—from the throbbing in her torso to the bitter burn of anger—coiled inside until she thought she might burst.

She closed her eyes and let the darkness recede to dreams, but even there she found no rest. Black horns glistened in the light of her burning home. She could not rise for the netting thrown across her, and she kicked at the devil forms and managed to push them into the flames. Their bodies caught fire, and their screams rose like sparks to the sky until she saw their white silhouettes smoldering in her eyelids.

She awoke, shuddering with the chilled-sweat feel of her underground prison, and shut her eyes on the darkness to see their burning figures again—the only light in a hole under the earth. She would escape this pit and find the men who crushed her family and destroyed her home, and throw them on their own pyres.

Or die trying.

Chapter 6

Father went to milk the goats while Lamech retrieved two spare tunics and returned to the hut where he'd left the girl. She sat shivering, and her voice was sharp as he entered. "You said you would be right back."

He tossed her one of the tunics and hung the other on a peg in the wall. "Father wanted to talk."

She fingered the fabric. "Will he let me stay?"

"Do you want to?"

She pursed her lips and cleared her throat. "Can you step out while I change?"

Lamech exited and leaned against the outer wall of the hut. After she groaned and sucked air through her teeth, he said, "Are you well?"

"Do I sound well?"

"I can help," he said.

"If you step foot in here, you will never walk again. Owe!"

Lamech suppressed a chuckle.

"Very well, I'm finished. But I'm thirsty. Do you have any water?"

Lamech rubbed his eyes. "I was on my way to grab some when I found you."

"So that means you don't?"

"That means I don't," he said.

A pause. "Can you get some? I don't think I'm in any shape to walk right now."

"It will take a while. Is there anything else you need before I leave?"

"Do you have any food?"

"No. We mountain dwellers eat only air and dirt."

Silence.

He cleared his throat. "We should have some cheese. I'll grab it before I retrieve water." He brought her freshly strained goat cheese in a clay bowl, but as he entered and saw her dressed in that simple tunic, he stopped. He hadn't expected her to look so vibrant, her green eyes like emeralds amidst tendrils of black hair dusty and wind tossed.

"What?" she said.

"Nothing." He handed her the bowl, and she stared at the wet white lumps. "It's freshly strained. Go ahead. It's good."

She placed a small piece in her mouth. Her eyes widened and she shoved more in until her cheeks bulged.

"Slow down, you'll make yourself sick."

"Water," she said through a mouthful and waved him off.

"All right, but slow down."

She grunted and took another mouthful.

Lamech grabbed an empty pail and walked the pathway to the stream. He had made this trip nearly every day for years and stopped at the crest to gaze down the mountainside. But this time all he could think of was the girl's severe, disapproving expression, and the momentary tenderness she had displayed when he found her in the mountain pass.

What sorrow had Father foreseen in her? What could she have brought with her besides the thrill in his chest and the memories of his mother that he'd thought lost?

He arrived at the stream, scooped the water, and began waddling home. When he returned, he found her waiting with her hands folded in her lap and the bowl set by the doorway, seemingly licked clean.

He dipped the bowl in the water and handed it to her. She drank it dry, leaned against the wall, and sighed. She held her waist as if it pained her, but he knew better than to try to tend her wounds again without permission.

"Why do you live in these mountains?" she said.

"You wouldn't believe me if I told you."

"You seem quite sure of yourself."

Lamech frowned. "I know only how strange the story is."

She shrugged. "If I decide I don't believe you, at least your story might entertain me."

He paused and searched her expression for any hit of humor, but could not find any. She goaded him with a quirked eyebrow, and he looked away. "In the mountain pass, you said you couldn't think of what had happened to you. Couldn't speak of it."

"Maybe if you tell me your story, I will tell you mine," she said.

"Maybe?"

"If you think you deserve more, then keep to yourself, and I will do the same."

Lamech pursed his lips and sat with legs crossed. "Fine. I will share my story. But you are a hard woman. I was only trying to make conversation." He paused and waited for her to rebuff him. When she didn't, he tipped his head and searched his memory. "It began with my grandfather, Enoch. He had a habit of walking for days talking to himself. Everyone had accepted his strangeness as harmless until—"

"Who do you mean by 'everyone'? Your family?"

Lamech paused, cleared his throat. "They and the rest of the village we lived in." He lifted his eyebrows to make sure she understood.

She waved him on.

"My grandfather gathered everyone in our village and preached about a judgment that his God was bringing."

"What god was it?"

"I don't know," he said. "He never called him by any name."

"Strange," she said, and furrowed her brow.

Lamech cleared his throat. "We thought he had gone mad with age, but—"

"The sickness was real?"

"Would you stop interrupting?"

"I wouldn't have to if you would just be clearer," she said.

"I am being clear." He could feel tension build in his temples.

"So, the sickness struck?"

Lamech nodded. "That same week. I remember my father carrying bodies out of huts. Women, children . . . infants." He looked down, his voice becoming a whisper. "We burned them."

The girl leaned forward. "What kind of sickness was it?"

"Those infected would cough so much blood they would drown."

She paled and nodded, waving him on.

"My mother . . ." He paused. ". . . became ill, along with my younger brothers and sisters. The leader of our village built buildings for the sick at the foot of the mountain to keep it from spreading. But when Father led the rest of my family to the mountain, he brought me with so we could remain a family. He didn't believe we would catch it, for we had been taking care of my mother and siblings for some time. He also didn't believe the sickness would take them."

"Was he right?"

"We never became sick," he said. "But they didn't survive." Then he shook his head and rubbed his throat, feeling that familiar strangling sensation.

"How old were you?"

"Young."

"I'm sorry."

"It's been many years. But still I find it hard to talk of."

After a moment, the girl said, "I think my father had that same sickness. It took many I loved. My father was one of the lucky ones. Well, until—" She waved as if to dismiss her thoughts. "How did your father react?"

"He believed my grandfather was the cause of the sickness, so he confronted him and demanded he give his wife back."

"What did your grandfather do?"

"He said the sickness was only the beginning. My father cursed him to die, but Grandfather replied, 'Man cannot kill who God has chosen to work his pleasing and perfect will. A child is coming who will bring relief to humanity through the earth. But I have been faithful. I have walked with God. Now, as God promised, he is snatching me away from this cursed generation.' And he reached toward the sky and disappeared like smoke on the wind."

She raised her eyebrows. "What?"

"I told you my story was strange. Had I not seen him disappear with my own eyes, I wouldn't have believed it. But from that day forward, the village believed my family cursed."

"I see . . ."

"They wanted no more of Enoch's God or his judgment. It didn't matter that my mother was a victim, or that my father disdained my grandfather—we were still his *family*."

She pinched her bottom lip and stared at the wall as if in deep thought. "Did they try to hurt you?"

"They feared more punishment, so they commanded us to remain in the mountains. Once every season, they agreed to send someone from the village with supplies to a marker of black rocks. That's the only reason we've been able to survive here these many years."

She glanced at him with wide eyes, then looked at the hut as if seeing it for the first time. "Why didn't you just go live in another village?"

"Father never wanted to."

"And you?"

Lamech shrugged.

"Not even once?"

"Where would we go? I've known nothing but mountains and silence, and my mother and siblings are buried here. For Father and me both, no other place would have felt like home. Besides, if Grandfather spoke truth, maybe the world beyond these mountains is worth missing."

The girl stared at the packed dirt beneath them. At length she nodded and whispered, "Maybe."

Lamech stood, brushed himself off, and said, "Enough *entertainment*. The sun is setting. Would you like anything else before I retire? I'll grab you bedding yet."

She shook her head, and Lamech turned to leave, but she

caught him by the arm. He looked down and saw that same transparency she had shown in the mountain pass.

"My name is Adah."

Lamech nodded and smiled.

This time, she returned it.

Chapter 7

When the torches returned the third time, there were four men. Three were eunuchs and one had horns like the ones who had burned her home, though his head was deformed. He had two faces, between which ran a gulley like a long scar. The skin of both faces was cinched tight as if burned years ago. The mouth on the left emitted a nervous chuckle, and its eyes danced independently. The other face's lips were pressed together as if tasting something sour, its eyes methodical and penetrating.

A particularly small, boyish eunuch dipped his head and said, "Three prisoners died, Lord Tubal."

"This one attacked one of your servants," said the tallest eunuch, who Adah recognized as one of the two who beat her.

Tubal's left face chuckled. The right face imbibed Adah's figure and said, "Disgusting. What did you do to her? Bring it and one other as tribute." The left face gurgled and the right face continued, "When you return the leftovers, I shall visit."

"Yes, Lord Tubal."

"Beautiful decision, Lord Tubal."

"What else might be expected, Lord Tubal?"

"Fools," Tubal said. "Hasten. Your Lord Tubal grows . . ." The left face moaned and the right continued, "Thirsty for healthy ones. More. We need more! Beautiful ones with exotic eyes and perfect skin. Always the skin." His sharp eyes impaled Adah. "Hideous. Does no one listen to my instruction? Get it out of my sight."

Adah's face grew hot, and she attempted to cover herself.

"What else, Lord Tubal?"

"Could we ever expect our Lord Tubal to accept imperfection?"

Tubal's left face chuckled. "Yes. You could. And you do." Tubal approached the tallest eunuch, the one who had beaten her, and cupped his cheek. "Look at me."

The eunuch hesitated.

Tubal's left face cackled, and the eunuch glanced up, gaze darting from face to face as if he were unsure which to look at.

"Oh," Tubal said, "are you confused?"

The eunuch paled. "No, Lord Tubal."

"Castrated one—does such a one find our instruction complicated?"

"No, Lord Tubal."

"Does it like bruised skin? Is that why it beat the woman?" Tubal's left face was laughing. Voice rising in pitch as if dragged up a hill.

The eunuch looked away, sweat dripping down his face. "As you say, beauty is of primary—"

Tubal ended the eunuch with a knife. "When next you bring such women, you will consider death a kindness. Bring the tribute and send for me when you finish."

The remaining two eunuchs bowed and unlocked Adah's cell.

Tubal departed, his cackles echoing through the labyrinth.

The eunuchs entered and tried to lift her, but she cried out in pain. After they got her to her feet, she realized she could walk so long as they didn't urge her too quickly forward.

She cradled her torso and shuffled where directed. The impulse to hobble into the dark to find freedom burned at the back of her mind, but she quickly extinguished it. Maybe she would have tried if uninjured, but she needed clothing, food, knowledge of her surroundings, and likely the attention of an herbalist.

"Where are you taking me?" she said.

The boyish eunuch unlocked the other cell and ushered a sickly girl out while the thicker, squat eunuch clenched Adah's arm. After the boyish eunuch closed the door and urged the sickly girl forward, the other prodded Adah on. They turned left, then right, were told to hurry, then to stop.

Adah glanced over her shoulder.

"Keep your eyes forward," said the squat eunuch in his throaty, high voice.

She obeyed as they argued about which turns to take. Ahead was a strange opening that looked like a hole in the floor. "What is that?"

The squat eunuch chuckled. "One of the many places you might have fallen had you run off on your own."

She felt the strange compulsion to steal his torch and toss it over the edge to watch the flames flicker as they fell. "What's at the bottom?"

"Death. And may it teach you to listen. There is only one exit from the labyrinth, and the way changes daily."

"Changes?" She turned again, only to be slapped by the squat eunuch.

That high, husky laugh. "Won't live long in the service of the God-King behaving like that. You're a stupid one, aren't you? No wonder they beat you."

Her fingertips tingled. If what they said was true, escape would be infinitely more difficult. But if they were bringing her above where others could see her, maybe she would have another chance to escape.

She glanced at her companion. The girl swayed as if sleep-walking. Adah nearly asked if she was all right, but the squat eunuch jammed his palm into her back, bringing enough pain to wipe her mind blank.

"Ah," the boyish eunuch said, and extinguished his torch. The other did the same, and they pulled the women up a stair-case in the dark.

Movement was much more difficult without the aid of the light, but with the eunuchs' help, she stayed upright.

They stopped and listened as the squat one patted the wall as if searching for a handle.

"Keep them closed," the boyish eunuch whispered, his breath hot in her ear.

A door swung open and the light on the other side nearly threw Adah to her knees. She cried out and pressed her palms to her eyes. The eunuchs jerked them forward. She tried removing her hands from her eyes, but the world seemed brighter than the sun.

The eunuchs led her by the arm. By touch and sound she recognized that they were passing through a cobbled courtyard and narrow alleys. She kept her eyes closed as they entered a building and passed open doorways, finally stopping in stale silence.

The eunuchs' breathing grew heavy, and they retreated.

"Wait——" She reached for them and groaned at the pain that shot through her chest.

But they were gone.

Chapter 8

The next day Lamech was allowed to tend Adah's broken ribs and make herbal tinctures to aid her healing. He couldn't deny she was beautiful, but she had awoken something in him far more potent than attraction. He felt a narrowing of focus, as if she were the only reason for every event that had happened in his life. He told Father of this, but Father only frowned and told him to retrieve more water for their meal.

Most of the time that Lamech and Adah spent together was in silence. Every so often she would ask him questions about what he was doing, and he would explain. After he told her how he had begun inventing new varieties of goat cheese, she said, "You and my father would have had much to converse about." But her voice failed as her eyes dimmed and turned toward images only she could see.

Judging by how she referred to her father, he dared not ask to know more. Instead, he shrugged and said, "The mountains are unforgiving. And solitude is a great teacher. When I was young, I had no toys, no one to play with, no distractions except the shapes of nature and the creeping pace of change. I tried my hand at gardening, building, fire-making, foraging, hunting, goat herding, trapping, and anything else I could think of."

She turned toward him, the light in her eyes returning. "How successful were you in what you tried?"

"Successful enough to survive."

And they continued to survive in the ensuing weeks, until Adah's broken bones were mostly mended and she could move without much pain.

...

Nearly two months after finding Adah in the mountain pass, he found her sitting on a boulder outside their hut, watching the sunrise bleed to blue. He joined her to let the familiar silence pass between them, but as he sat, she said, "What was your mother like?"

The question struck him like a splash of cold water. "I . . . she was . . ."

"You can't remember, can you?"

He stared at his own feet. "At times, when I'm with you, I remember how her hand felt on my shoulder, or how her voice sounded before the sickness took her."

Adah nodded. "All I remember of my parents is the sound of their screams." Tears shone on Adah's face. "Why is that?"

"I don't know."

Her knuckles grew white. "Sometimes, when I wake in the night, I think I see him bending over me, blocking out the stars."

"Who?"

"The devil who took my family from me," she said.

"Have you been sleeping outside, that you see the stars?"

"No . . ."

"Then you see only a phantom, a dream," he said.

"Before I left, he said he would find me. That no matter where I ran, he would kill me." Her voice fell to a whisper. "He can't find me, can he? How could he find me?"

Lamech scooted closer and said, "No one has followed you. That was me who found you on the road. Remember?"

After a while, she turned away from him, and when she spoke again, her voice was cold. "The last conversation I had with my parents was filled with bitter words."

Lamech said nothing. He knew they were dancing on the outskirts of a great pain, and feared that any words he might speak would break the spell the coming twilight had placed upon her.

"My father wished me to wed a man he considered acceptable. But I found the man contemptible, and had said as much many times. He didn't listen. He never listened. So I cut my hair to make myself too ugly for a man to wed." She dipped her head and her voice shook. "I was trying to hurt him, but he only wanted good for me. Now . . . I can never tell him how sorry I am."

Lamech reached his arm around her, and she spun toward him and pressed her face to his chest, nearly knocking him backward.

"Promise me that you'll never leave," she said.

"I promise," Lamech said, blinking and angling forward to regain his balance.

She turned to face him. "Why do I feel like you're going to leave anyway?"

Lamech squinted down at her and shook his head. He just wanted them to stop speaking, to regain that familiar silence so truth could remain unmolested by words. But as she glanced back to the fading sun, he looked at her face in profile and felt a stirring in his abdomen. He turned her chin back to him, leaned down, and kissed her. She pulled away as if he had burned her and brought a hand to her lips.

His throat went cold and he steadied himself with a palm against the rock. His face warmed with heat, and he turned away.

But she grabbed the back of his neck and pressed her lips into his with such passion he lost his breath. After, they held each other until the moon shone overhead, casting a silver glow about them.

...

That evening, after an hour spent debating Father, Lamech stood with his arm outstretched over Adah's. Father said the invocation that bound man to woman and tied their wrists with a grapevine.

They spent their first night together learning what it meant to become one. And as the excitement of the day blended into the peacefulness of night, Lamech drifted to sleep tangled in the smell of her hair and the warmth of her touch.

He awoke to her prodding him. "He's here," she said. "He's blocking out the stars!"

Lamech looked at the thatched ceiling and pressed her face into his neck. "Hush. You are only dreaming."

After she fell back asleep, he remained awake, staring at the open doorway. Twice before morning he thought he saw the glint of eyes like silver stars set into a lightless moon.

Dreams, he told himself. *Only dreams.*

Chapter 9

Adah opened her eyes like a newborn, painfully overwhelmed by every line and color. Before her spread a vast hall, its floor made of multicolored granite slabs polished to a glassy shine. Narrow windows lined the walls, sending diagonal shafts of sunlight to the floor. Emerald chandeliers burned high above, coloring the pillars a sickly green.

Ahead sat whom she assumed was the God-King in an iron throne atop a staircase. He stood and descended toward them.

Adah glanced at her companion. The girl was sweating and shaking. Her skin sallow. Mucus dribbling from her nose. "Are you all right?" Adah said and reached for her.

The girl shifted away, lips shaking over crooked teeth. "Don't touch me."

Enormous horns adorned the God-King's head and twisted two entire revolutions before ending in black spines that pointed toward the ceiling. She wondered at how such unnatural protrusions could seem so normal paired with his full, balanced lips, strong nose, and dark skin devoid of blemishes.

He moved nimbly in his leather tunic and silk gown embroidered with concentric patterns. From his neck to midway down his chest lay bare skin, more than enough to make a spectacle of his physique. A gold chain clutched a teardrop emerald against his skin, and his black hair flowed long past his shoulders—

though his most striking feature was his set of luminous, silver eyes.

Her pulse hastened as he neared and stopped, and the knowledge of her nakedness warmed her skin like the flames in the chandeliers above. She fought the impulse to cover herself as she stared at his feet, bare on the granite, wanting to look up but fearing what she might feel.

I hate this man. I want nothing to do with him.

But she could not deny that he was beautiful. In fact, if her mind weren't so muddled, she would be confident he was more beautiful and terrible than any man she had seen.

"What is your name?" the God-King said, his voice thick and low.

"Nalla," the sickly girl said.

Adah glanced at her companion, whose eyes glowed with fever.

"Not you," the God-King said.

Adah flicked her gaze toward him. Her face rushed with heat as he stepped close and she looked toward the floor, fists clenched, lips tight against her teeth.

He touched her neck. "Tell me your name."

She dug her fingernails into her palms. "Adah."

He caressed her cheek, and sweat dripped down her forehead. "A beautiful name. Certainly not because you deserve it."

Her face warmed as he stepped to Nalla and kissed her full on the lips. Nalla clutched him to keep from falling, and Adah grimaced and looked toward the windows, feeling another rush of heat. How had she allowed this man to affect her? All she wanted was to be taken from this place.

But why would he favor Nalla over Adah? As much as she desired to be gone, the idea rankled her. Was she really so ugly? Nalla had scabs around her mouth. Her skin was pale and thin as cracked vellum. Her body smelled foul. Her features unattractive even without the layers of grime and sickness.

Others had found Adah beautiful. Even now, the memory of the way the young men in the village looked at her seemed proof enough.

"Pick me," Nalla said.

"You?" The God-King eyed the sickly girl.

"You know I'm better than *her*."

Adah bit her tongue to stifle a bitter laugh and rolled on the balls of her feet, for she knew the girl was only terrified, wanting anything but to go back to the endless dark of that dungeon.

"*Hmm* . . . Eunuch!"

The boyish eunuch returned and bowed.

"I have made my choice," the God-King said. "Take this one back to the labyrinth. And don't let me *ever* see her again."

The eunuch bowed again. "Understood." He grabbed Adah by the arm and pulled.

She jerked out of his grasp. "Wait, what are you doing?"

The eunuch bowed and said in a low voice, "Come now, the God-King has chosen."

The God-King whispered into Nalla's ear. She shivered, and he braced her to keep her from collapsing as they walked toward his throne, their feet brushing the dusty floor.

"No," Adah said. "That's not right. Disgusting figure?"

"Come," the eunuch said. "Follow me."

The thought of returning to her cold black cell made smashing her head on the stone sound more attractive. "How could he choose her over me?" Everything was wrong. She was in a foreign place, stolen from her family, stripped of all possessions, beaten by strangers, and now rejected by a demon.

Now, before her, stood a eunuch whose face was both lined with age and populated with a boy's facial hair. "Come, I must take you back to the labyrinth," he said with the voice of a woman.

She bent to one knee and fought back tears, nausea rising like a certain tide. She retched, and tears sprang from her eyes, for the pain in her ribs was excruciating. The eunuch brushed her hair from her face and whispered, "Quiet yourself. Do you want the others to hear? And look at the mess you've made."

On the night she had been brought to the city, all had been bright. Her home had become a cage when it should have been tilled fields. And now the eunuch's soft hand rubbed circles on her back when all she had been shown was brutality. He cooed to her and fixed her hair, then called for servants to mop the mess while he led her in a new direction.

The thought struck her weakened mind that he was taking her back a new way because the entrance had changed. Then she realized she must stall him to gain time to discover a way to escape. She looked at his soft features and realized he hadn't chastised her for talking like the others. "What is your name?" she said.

The eunuch stopped to let a cart pass. "I am a nameless servant of the God-King." He urged her faster forward.

She felt a moment of panic and scrambled for more words to delay him. "I came to this city once when I was a little girl, long before the God-King came."

The eunuch said nothing, only continued rushing her, and she resisted as much as the pain would allow.

"My father was a man of influence. He led a group of farmers whose lands stretched for miles, and together they fed half this city."

The eunuch nodded absently.

"I am no maid spinning tales."

"I believe you," he said. "But we must hurry. We took longer than we should have in the throne room. Tubal will not be happy."

Adah dug her feet in so that he had to pull her forward. She searched the alleyways. "The king brought my father and me to the tower. Back then I thought it was beautiful in the sunlight." Sentries stood atop buildings with bows in hand, scanning the alleyways. She frowned. Escape during daytime would be much more difficult. "But that was before it was turned into a haven for devils. What have you done to our king?"

The eunuch stopped and glanced at her, his expression hardening. "He is dead. Along with the kings of the other kingdoms my master now rules."

Adah nodded and searched the eunuch's eyes. "Do you enjoy it?"

"You hate me," the eunuch said. "But if you don't stop trying to distract me so you can find a way to escape, you will taste pain like you've never imagined." He turned and led her harshly through a narrow alleyway partially blocked by a broken cart.

"Why do you threaten me?"

"It's not a threat," the eunuch said. "It's a warning that not all the God-King's servants are like me. A different law governs those who find themselves trapped in the labyrinth."

"Who built the labyrinth?"

"Tubal oversaw its construction over the last eight years," he said. "You might think you can escape from it, but you will only die if you try."

"Ah," she said. "I see. Offer help to neighboring kingdoms. Build for them. Share with them. Then kill their king and rule them with fear."

"Fear keeps all of us in place," he said in a low voice. "Even those who think themselves free." A dark shape moved in the alley beside the tower, and the eunuch's face hardened as he shoved her along. Fear spread its fingers down her scalp as the eunuch glanced around and whispered without moving his lips, "Do not speak. Do not move. Do nothing but follow my lead without hesitation."

She stared at him and breathed quicker to douse the cinders in her chest. He opened the door in the side of the tower and the blackness repelled her. She thought of bolting. Of striking him in the throat and sprinting away. But it was too late to sprint for freedom; too late to do anything but follow the eunuch back into the labyrinth.

He jerked her forward, and she stumbled inside the cool, dark chamber. He closed the door behind them and slid her into a side corridor. After several turns, he opened a wooden door and began pulling her up a narrow, dimly lit staircase.

"Where are we going?"

"Hush!" He turned, and the flames of the torches seemed to burn behind his lamp-like eyes. "Do you wish to die?"

"Of course not," she said.

"Then listen to me, and do what I tell you."

"Why?" Adah steadied herself against the stone wall to lessen the discomfort in her wounded torso.

"Because you have no other choice. If the God-King had

ordered me to slit your throat in the throne room, I wouldn't have hesitated."

"Then why didn't you?"

"Because you have found favor in the eyes of the God-King."

"He rejected me."

"Fool! If he had chosen you as tribute, you would have had your heart cut out of your chest while it was still beating."

The breath in Adah's lungs congealed. "But Nala, she was . . ."

"She is dead. And unless you want to join her, after we exit the labyrinth, you will listen to every word I say. There are many ears amidst the servants of the God-King, and not all of them hold similar allegiance. There has been a secret uprising among the God-King's servants. A select few seek to usurp him, and they would kill you on sight if allowed. Obey me and you may yet live."

Chapter 10

Ten months after Lamech and Adah married, Adah's pregnant belly grew so large that she spent most of her days lying in their hut while Lamech worked to prepare the way for their soon-to-be-born child. Adah's energy level had decreased the past two weeks, and her hips began to ache, keeping both of them awake through the night. Though it was midday, Adah needed rest, so Lamech let her sleep while he left to milk the goats.

Lamech was finishing when Father approached and said, "Did you dream last night?"

Lamech glanced up. "I dream every night."

Father shifted. "Tell me what you dreamed."

"Something bothering you?" Lamech lifted the pale of milk and patted the goat on the behind.

"Just tell me what you dreamed, and in as much detail as possible," Father said.

Lamech searched Father's eyes, noting his serious expression. "All right." He searched his memory. "I remember being high in the branches of a tree, guiding clouds between mountains with a shepherd's hook so the jagged peaks didn't gouge them open and drown the villagers below."

Father paled visibly, grabbing at his beard.

"What's wrong?"

"Come quickly," Father said. "And say nothing to Adah."

"She's asleep," Lamech said as he followed Father into his thatched hut. After entering, Father fiddled with the door covering and peered out suspiciously. Lamech set down the milk and said, "She laid down not half an hour ago. I'd be surprised if she awoke so soon."

"Good. I don't think it would be healthy for her to hear what I have to tell you. It might make the baby come early."

Lamech's eyes narrowed. "Well? Get on with it, then, if it's so serious."

Father faced him, took a deep breath, and said, "I dreamed the same dream as you."

Lamech waited for more, but when none was offered, he shrugged. "Certainly that must be common enough."

Father shook his head. "You don't understand. I dreamed of you shepherding the clouds, but that's not all. Afterward, when I thought I had awoken, I found myself lying on the ground peering up at the stars."

"Again, how is that significant?"

Father pointed at the thatched roof. "How could I wake to stars if I fell asleep in my hut?"

"By walking outside in your sleep, I suppose."

Father shook his head. "If only that could be true!" He paced, his feet sweeping the woven bed coverings, the whip of his cloak setting the candle flames fluttering. "Afterward, I awoke here. I am certain that I was lying here the whole time."

"Fine. What was wrong with the stars?"

"Nothing," Father said. "However, as I was studying their alignment, a dark shape bent close, blocking those to the east. At that moment I felt the most profound sense of foreboding—the same sense I felt the day you brought Adah home, only ten-fold stronger. And the shadow said, 'Ask your son what he dreamed last night.' Immediately I awoke, sweating."

Lamech remembered the dreams Adah had confided to him just before they had bound themselves to each other, and shivered as if a cup of stream water had been poured down his back.

"Has Adah ever told you where she came from?" Father's

eyes seemed to bulge as he crept toward Lamech. "How she came to be in the mountains?"

Lamech took a step back. "Never in much detail. It is difficult for her to speak of it, and I never felt it appropriate to pressure her for more information. I do know she was held captive and beaten."

Father nodded. "Did you really dream about the clouds?"

Lamech felt impatience lodge in the base of his throat. "I am no liar."

Father chewed his cheek. "Yes . . . I believe you. Only, it feels as though pieces of the world are falling into position, though for what purpose I cannot foretell. I think—I fear—that your grandfather is a part of it."

"Enoch?" Lamech remembered his grandfather's voice, and the shimmering left in the air after he disappeared . . .

If the dreams and Enoch's prophecy of coming judgment were connected to Adah's past . . . but how could they be? Lamech, too, could feel something changing, but along with it came a cold anxiety, a swelling pressure.

It felt like mother's lifeless skin.

He turned away.

"I know, son," Father said. "But what of the dreams?"

"We must have talked of clouds and mountains the night before." The lump in Lamech's throat burned hotter and hotter.

"We didn't."

"You just don't remember it." Lamech turned to leave, but Father grabbed his shoulder and twisted him back. Lamech pushed him away, fingertips prickling. "You're mad. You're mad like Grandfather."

Father's left eye twitched, and his voice fell to a whisper as his tangled hair fell forward. "Maybe. Maybe, son."

Lamech gritted his teeth.

"Have you never dreamed that you woke to the stars?"

"No," Lamech said, and turned to leave. This time Father did nothing to stop him.

After Lamech brought the goat milk to the larder, he returned to Adah and shook her. She moaned and turned away.

"I need to ask you a question. Just promise you won't grow alarmed."

"I promise," she mumbled, and pulled the covers over her head.

"Do you still dream of the stars?"

A pause. The covers slid down. "What did you say?"

"Do you still dream about the stars?" Lamech deliberately watched the dust flecks floating through the sunlit doorway to avoid her stare.

"Why do you ask?" Suspicion marked her voice.

He nodded. He was a fool for waking her. For asking at all. He patted her leg. "Just try to get more sleep. You need it."

He rose and left to walk the mountain paths alone.

Chapter 11

The eunuch brought Adah to a richly furnished room with wooden cabinets filled with silk gowns. Red, blue, black, and white, embroidered with intricate designs, glittering with beads and overlaid with gold. Incense burned, sending fragrant breath to the ceiling, for the first time illuminating just how foul Adah's body smelled after so many days of captivity.

The eunuch rushed ahead and opened a door, allowing richly dressed servants to enter. Adah grabbed at the gowns to cover herself, but the eunuch said, "They are going to bathe you."

They ushered her dazed into the next room, where a tub sat filled with steaming water. They helped her inside, and despite her fear, she let the water lap her skin. As they scrubbed her with jasmine petals dipped in lye, she shivered and gazed at their stolid expressions. They brushed soft fingers through her hair and treated her with startling gentleness.

The eunuch smiled that boyish, innocent smile. "Enjoying yourself?"

She narrowed her eyes, wondering how to respond.

In the pause, the eunuch's expression shifted to something like horror, and he rushed to the tub and backhanded one of the servants. "Make her comfortable!"

He raised his hand to strike again, but Adah caught his arm, and cried out at the pain in her injured abdomen. "No. They are treating me well."

The smile returned. "What troubles you, then?"

She chewed her lip. "Why are you doing this?"

He gripped her shoulder and dug a fingernail into her skin. She almost cried out, but saw his smile and the meaningful tip of his head.

"We treat all our guests with such honor," he said.

He wants me to play along, to avoid letting on to the servants that I have no idea why I'm here.

She glanced at the servants to make sure they weren't looking. They bustled about mixing soaps and mopping the excess water they had spilled. She met the eunuch's gaze and nodded, then sank into the water and let the servants finish.

Afterward, they helped her out, and the eunuch guided her back to the dressing room and shut the door.

The eunuch opened cabinets and showed her hundreds of dresses. He babbled incessantly, explaining each dress's design and purpose. "This purple—see how it is dark enough to be the color of clotted blood? The God-King's chemists have raised a species of sea snail and daily stick a needle in their flesh." He smiled at her disgusted expression. "When the sea snails feel threatened, they secrete a protective mucus from within their fist-shaped shell. The purple is so deep it is said to be blood drawn from the heart of the God-King himself. Here, try it on, feel how light and cool the material is."

She hesitated, but he lifted it over her head and helped her slip her arms through. It fell past her curves and she paused, feeling strange in such luxury after days of brutality. He clucked his tongue and brought her to the tall mirror against the wall.

She touched her hand to her mouth to stifle a gasp because the image in the reflection couldn't be her. The dress shimmered strangely, enhancing her good features and somehow replacing what she lacked, even bringing color to her pale, bruised complexion.

The eunuch smiled. "It is perfect. Is it not?"

"Perfect," she breathed. "But for what?" She turned and

carefully slid her palms down her hips. "What are you preparing me for?"

The eunuch dipped close, smile flashing. "You have been given the opportunity to dine with the God-King."

Her eyes hardened. "But—"

He gripped her hand hard enough to make her wince, saying in a low voice, "A rare opportunity few would rebuff."

She paused, thinking of the doorway to the bathroom. She nodded and, when the eunuch turned, threw a glance toward the doorway, but she saw no cracks or holes through which anyone could be watching.

What, in the name of the gods, was happening?

The eunuch hung a delicate silver necklace around her neck, and slipped thin rings on her fingers, until both hands glittered and clinked.

He stepped behind and braided her hair, forming one tress into a spiraling circlet, while the rest he formed into a pattern that fell past her shoulders and both defied the mind and drew the eyes.

Adah watched in the mirror, enraptured by how the dark powder he applied to her upper eyelids seemed to make her eyes flash. He lifted one foot at a time to slip on leather sandals with carved ivory clasps.

"Now you are ready," he said, and bowed, offering her his hand.

"Have you always served in the labyrinth?"

The eunuch went about cleaning up the excess materials, apparently not worried anyone might overhear. "I became a eunuch at a very young age. The labyrinth has only existed for a short time. Like most eunuchs, I've attended to myriad duties, the majority related to tending the God-King's concubines."

"So that's how you know how to . . ."

"To make you beautiful? Simple tricks that only enhance the features you already have." He offered his hand, and she laid her fingers in his and let him lead her through another door, down several corridors, to a large table set with silk tablecloth and glimmering silverware.

The eunuch sat her at the far end and scooted her chair in

until her chest touched the table. She grabbed her thumb in her lap, wiped the sweat from her palm, and tried to still her bouncing leg.

The eunuch bent and whispered, a smile in his voice, "The God-King will join you shortly."

Chapter 12

A week after Lamech and his father dreamed the same dream, Lamech exited his hut to a rose-colored sky and his father staring at the pile of rocks marking where supplies were dropped every season. He approached and waited for Father to speak. Instead, Father bent, knees popping, callused fingers scraping the stones. His brow furrowed, gray eyes squinting. His black hair was more unkempt than usual, and when he finally spoke, it was in a raspy whisper. "They're not coming."

Lamech's jaw hung as he breathed the cold mountain air and looked down the empty pathway. He had been so distracted by Adah and her expanding belly that he hadn't given their supplies any thought.

"In all these years, they've never been late," Father said.

"Something must have happened."

"Of course something happened." Father stood. "But what? And why?"

Lamech dug at the packed earth with his toes, ignoring Father's weighty gaze. "Maybe they forgot."

Father buried his face in his arm and coughed long and hard. "They don't forget."

"Are you sick?"

"It's nothing." Father scratched his nose and rested his hands on his hips. "We've used up our supplies. We need grain, firewood, herbs, salt, rope, and new tools to replace the broken ones. I can't carry all that up the mountain."

Lamech picked a skeletal twig out from amongst the rocks and cracked it in half. "Adah would never make the journey."

"No." Father grabbed a black stone from the pile. "Still. Our needs remain." He coughed again, and used the porous stone to dab the mucus from the corner of his mouth.

"I can't leave her," Lamech said, and continued breaking the twigs into smaller halves.

"You're her husband."

"You don't understand," Lamech said. "I promised her I wouldn't leave."

"If no one brings us supplies, you might have no choice," Father said.

Lamech tossed the fragments to the wind.

Father gauged him. "Did I ever tell you the last thing I said to your mother before she died?"

"I'm in no mood for a lecture," he said.

"When have I ever cared for your moods?"

Lamech glared down the pathway, refusing to look into those gray eyes.

"Will you let me go to the grave unheard?" Father continued.

"I'm not stopping you," Lamech said.

Father coughed and slapped at his chest, taking a moment to recover. "I told her I wouldn't let her die."

"What does that have to do with anything?" He saw the twinkle in Father's eye and looked away.

"Sometimes we speak out of ignorance," Father said. "That's forgivable. What matters is that we act out of conviction." Father laid a hand on Lamech's shoulder. "When the time comes, you'll know what to do. And you'll do it. Promise or not."

Lamech shrugged his hand away and let his father's words spill cold and bitter. "Do as you say and not as you do?"

When Father spoke again, his voice sounded small and distant. "I am no more than a shadow in the mountains. I've never wanted you to be like me." He hobbled away, leaving Lamech standing in the mountain wind, fighting tears.

Chapter 13

The God-King entered ceremoniously with female servants caressing him and pouring wine into a goblet from a weathered wineskin. The liquid splattered the God-King's white undergarment, and he lifted the goblet to his lips, letting it slosh over the rim and drench his chest. He slammed the cup on the table, and the female servants cowered and giggled.

"Leave," he said. Their feathered headpieces bobbed out of sight. He smiled, his teeth red, his silver eyes and black horns more unnerving than before. "Thank you for joining me."

Adah picked at the bloody dirt beneath her fingernails.

"I'd like to formally welcome you to my kingdom." The God-King motioned with his hand to indicate the room and beyond. "Have you enjoyed yourself?"

Adah bent her fingernail back.

A smirk tipped the corner of the God-King's mouth, and words poured like droplets in a dark cave. "Does my company not satisfy you? Does my food not please you? How about the adornments I've given you? Or your beautification by my eunuch?"

Adah's hands shook in her lap. Her forehead burned, and her mind darkened with the memory of the smoke in Father's eyes. She stared at the God-King as if doing so were an act of violence.

He pushed back his chair and paced, the flesh of his feet sweeping the floor. "Do you feel superior? Too beautiful to grace the hall of the God-King?"

"No."

He smiled. "Then what?"

"You murdered my parents."

The smirk widened. "Come now," he said. "You're a grown woman. Do you really still need your mother and father to enjoy dinner with a man?"

She jumped up, knocking the chair over. Her body shook, and she gripped a knife. The light of the flames of the torches along the walls flickered across its dull edge.

"Ah . . ." His teeth glinted.

She held her breath as he slid toward her like a tiger. She willed the arm holding the knife to stab, but could not move, for his silver, predatory gaze held her immobilized. He swiped the knife from her hand and replaced it with his own fingers. His eyes hovered above her and seemed to grow into twin moons blacking out her surroundings.

"Have you never thought," he said, "about how strange it is that we have bodies? That we are flesh, blood, and bone?" He leaned forward until his lips nearly touched hers, bending her wrist until she cried out. "We are so easily crushed. Thrown away. Burned. And yet . . . something remains, does it not? After the body dies, what of the soul? The vapor, the essence of a person? Where does it go?"

Adah's fingers curled around his, digging into his hand as she imagined seizing the knife again. But she could barely breathe, for his words had lodged themselves in her throat.

"I'm going to let you in on a secret," he said. "Something I've not told anyone else in many a century."

He released her wrist and leaned in until his breath kissed her ear. "I am not like you. You were born in your body, but me? I was born a vapor on the wind, aimless, thirsty for the blood that pumps in your veins. And as was planned in the halls of Timelessness, I formed this body with the wisdom of the Watchers, and the help of a woman like you, pulling it on as a skintight robe. If you picked up that knife and stabbed me, you may be able to destroy this body. But you would never destroy me. I would only come back to haunt you in your dreams. And eventually, after I found another body, I would have my way with you."

He released her, and she jerked away. But all she could think of was the way his breath had warmed her skin. Though he smelled perfumed, she felt dirtied by his touch.

He turned and said, "Follow me."

She obeyed, feeling drawn like an empty boat tied to a galley. He led her down a hallway through a door to what appeared to be his private bedchamber. The eunuch stood guard outside, and after she and the God-King entered, he shut and barred the door.

Adah watched as he crossed to a table and took a sip from a bowl of what looked like blood. "To do what we desire, we need bodies. But we can neither mate with you, nor do what we must without first becoming like you. And the terrible truth is that we then become bound. Now I must drink, and drink, and drink, or die." He smiled again. "But so long as I have a steady supply of blood, this body will continue as it has these past two thousand years. And by inhabiting this body, I have been given a gift. The ability to change children while they are still in the womb, to craft them into receptacles fit to receive my brethren, the spirits of the Watchers."

Adah took in the room. Hanging curtains, wooden arches over the bed from which hung white sheets that blew in the breeze from the narrow windows at either end of the room. Several tables held silver flasks and wooden bowls, but she saw no utensils. No weapons. No means of escape save jumping to her death.

"Now that I have been gifting the Watchers with bodies fit to receive them, they reward me by plotting my assassination. They want control." He steadied himself against the table, his fingernails scraping the wood. He turned, silver eyes glowing. "Oh, they know it wouldn't last long. But they are hungry. All their thought is bent on it."

Adah cleared her throat and said, "Why should I care about the squabbles of demons?"

"I'm not the one who killed your family," he said.

"You might as well be."

Another smile. "Maybe." He slipped his hand into his pocket. "I know what burns within you."

Adah's feet flexed as the silken dress rippled cold against her legs.

"The one who plots against me is the same who burned your village and murdered your parents. He sought to start the war prematurely to make me look the fool, because he thinks he's unlocked the secret that might replace my gifting. Do you not want revenge?"

"Why involve me? Why not just kill him, if you're so powerful?"

"I could have him swinging by his neck from the city gates," he said. "But what of the others? Many follow him and rely on him and the abominable machines he's invented to run the city. He's begun to convince the others that they might not need me. I must make an illustration of him." He chuckled at her expression. "Yes, you hate me, but you will do this for me: you will murder my servant, the one who calls himself *Lord* Tubal."

Adah remembered the demon's double face, heard his breathy laughter, felt his gluttonous eyes, and thought of her parents, of the price she'd paid that could never be returned. Indeed, she wanted nothing more than to murder Tubal, but how could she justify helping the God-King? "You ask a great thing of me."

"Revenge is no little reward," he said, and for the first time she thought she saw a flair of anger in those cold, silver eyes.

She straightened. "If I do this for you, I would want the freedom to leave this place, to go where I will, to live the rest of my years in peace."

"I grant it. What else?"

She blinked. What else could she want? She could ask for food, but it would likely be poisoned. She could ask for a servant to follow her, but how could she trust anyone who served such a demon? "Promise on your life."

A smirk. "Of course." He pulled a small wooden box from his tunic, opened the lid, and retrieved a tiny, sharp object. "Take this and hide it in the palm of your hand. Careful. Do not let it prick your skin. It is hollow. Filled with deadly poison. After you return to your cell, Tubal will visit. When he does, you will press this needle through his flesh, take his keys, and escape your cell. But you will not free the other women." He gripped her chin and she met his eyes. "If you free the other women, I will know. You may think you could disobey me, but I promise that there is no place on earth that you could go where I could not find you. Do you understand?"

Adah pulled away, nostrils flared. "I understand."

"I will order the western aqueducts emptied for one day, and one day only. The entrance to the aqueduct is near your cell. If the aqueduct is full, you will be drowned in the current. But when you find the aqueduct dry, you will know the God-King has done as he said. That he has granted you life as only God can."

Chapter 14

Lamech awakened the next day, rolled out of bed, and left Adah to check the stone marker. It stood as before, dark and deserted, and Father was nowhere to be seen. Since Lamech was a child, Father had woken before sunrise, but the sun was already climbing the axis.

He ducked into Father's hut and found him lying under the covers, head tangled in sweat-soaked hair. He knelt and shook his shoulder. "Father? Are you awake?" He felt Father's forehead with the back of his hand, and parted his eyelids to bloodshot white. He tapped his cheek. "Wake up."

Father grimaced, moaned, and rolled his head.

Lamech stood, unsure what to do. Father was feverish and they had no supplies. They had used up the last of the herbs that could be used to resist a fever, and Lamech could no longer hope for help. Worst of all, Adah was due to give birth at any moment. And he had promised he would never leave her for fear of the dreams that pursued them like shadows from her darkened past.

Lamech pressed his palms to his eyes and sucked at the air through bared teeth. He had to get supplies. But it would likely take him half a day to walk down the mountain, and at least an entire day to make it back with supplies. If he didn't explain to Adah where he was going, she would think he had abandoned her. What if she wandered down the mountainside to find him? She was too far along to journey the brittle cliffsides without an experienced hand to guide her.

But what would she say when he explained himself? Her dreams hadn't stopped, and she would resent him for breaking his promise.

He kicked the leg of a table and pain shot up his leg. He coughed, cradled his foot, and wiped the wetness that flooded his eyes. He felt like a fool for crying, but he hadn't left the mountains in years, and the way Father laid unresponsive reminded him of Mother's pallid skin. Worse, the help they had relied on all these years had suddenly disappeared. And to help his father, he would likely need to betray his promise to Adah.

He observed the thatched ceiling and wished it were the stars. At least then maybe they could help him chart some middle way. But he could no longer trust the stars.

He exited Father's hut, returned to Adah, and shook her gently. She smiled and said, "Hello, love."

He sat cross-legged, but his voice was like the dry hiss of wool rubbing wood. "We need to talk."

She pushed herself upright, struggling with the awkwardness of her belly. Her green eyes grew concerned, and she brushed her hair behind her ears. "What's wrong?"

"Father's not feeling well. I found him this morning in bed. He's feverish and won't wake. I don't know what to do."

"What do you mean?" Her voice sparked with suspicion. "Why not make an herbal compress?"

Lamech paused, wondering if he should continue.

Fool, he thought. *You've gone too far to turn back now.*

"When the time comes, you'll know what to do. And you'll do it."

Adah was staring at his shaking hands. He clasped them, swallowed the stone in his throat, and said, "We have no more herbs. I hadn't told you because I didn't want to worry you. But—"

"Won't someone bring more soon?"

He shook his head. "Not this time."

She twisted the covers, tossed them away, and leaned forward. "What do you mean, 'Not this time'?"

"They should have been here weeks ago." His face warmed as he avoided her calculating gaze so it would no longer addle his mind. "They've never been late. Not in all these years. We could wait and hope they're on their way, but . . ."

"But what?" She frowned and winced, holding her belly as the baby kicked.

"I do not think I'm willing to risk it with Father the way that he is." Lamech stood and paced so his legs would stop threatening to move on their own. "It reminds me of . . . of my mother." He chanced a glance in time to see Adah's gaze darken.

"What do you propose we do?"

"You must stay here while I descend the mountain, gather the necessary supplies, and bring them back to take care of Father before his sickness progresses."

"How long will that take?" Her eyes glowed like copper in a fire.

"Half a day down, maybe a day back," he said and shrugged away the prickling sensation rippling down his shoulders.

"No. Absolutely not." She steadied herself with one hand and placed the other on her belly as she struggled to stand.

He crossed to help her up. "Adah, I—"

"You promised." Her chin shook, and she quieted. "You promised you wouldn't leave. You knew. That's why you held this from me."

His insides dropped as if thrown from the cliff. "I had no idea how sick Father was."

She pushed him away. "What if he is watching? What if he made your Father sick to lead you away so he could have me alone and do what he wants?" Now she was rubbing slender fingers through her hair.

"If the man you fear could have crept into our encampment, poisoned Father's food or drink, and been gone again before anyone noticed, why would he not have just killed us long ago? Why would he wait?"

"Because he would want me to know. That's the way he would want it." Adah's lips thinned until they nearly disappeared. Tears grew between her eyelids, and a moan escaped her throat.

Lamech stepped forward, but the coverings twisted around his ankle, and he kicked them away. "Your dreams are nothing but an extension of your fears. I am going to leave, and nothing will happen. You will just be alone for a while. And then I'll return and treat Father, and the baby will come and we will live a happy life together!"

Adah twisted with hands clasped around her belly and eyes shining red. "Stop yelling at me. My father used to do that and I hate it."

"I'm not yelling at you!"

She pressed her hands over her ears and said, "Go."

He blinked as his face warmed. "What?"

"Leave!" She thrust her finger toward the door.

He stood shaking. Fingers clamping to fists. "I didn't mean to—"

"Just go!" Her voice made him jump.

He shut his mouth, turned, and staggered out the doorway.

He cut through the mountain brush between paths not so much thinking of his destination as of his desire to get away. He cycled through their conversation, searching for what went wrong. They had never fought. Not since they bound themselves to each other.

Perhaps that was why his thoughts were so blurred. Why his breaths came so shallow and constricted.

She could be so difficult. So determined. Yet that was what he most loved about her. It was what he had seen the day he found her. Proof that she could lift him outside of himself.

And lift him she had.

An unfamiliar male voice came from just around the corner and broke his thoughts. "Bloody business back in the village. Lost twelve of our own."

Lamech slipped on the gravel, landing hard on his back and rolling into the brush to avoid being seen.

"What was that?" Footsteps scuffed, stopped.

Lamech held his breath, belly flat to the earth. He couldn't see whoever had spoken, but if any part of him was exposed . . .

He glanced down and thought he saw his legs covered by thick branches. His pulse washed his ears and black spots threatened his vision.

"You heard something?" said a second voice.

"Yes," said the first with no small amount of irritation.

"It hardly matters," said a third. "The God-King expects us in a fortnight. We're already behind schedule. We can't risk losing more time."

"What if it's one of them?" said the first. "Following us?"

"If it shows its face, run it through," said the third.

Footsteps continued up the mountain. Lamech closed his eyes and stole several quiet breaths, clearing his mind. Bloody business in the village? Lost twelve of their own? The God-King? These were not men bringing supplies, and if they continued up the path they were on, they would be headed right toward Adah.

Lamech pressed his temple to the ground and wiped sand from his lips, grimacing at the metallic smell of mountain dust. If they so much as looked at her . . .

He couldn't hear their footsteps anymore, but what if the first one had been overly cautious? He could never match more than one without surprise on his side, so he waited and hoped against hope that they had all moved on.

He filled his mind with the peaceful rise and fall of Adah's shoulders, and the subtle movement of the innocent babe inside her, then rose to a crouched position and crawled up the mountain, skirting the pathway to avoid being seen.

A yell erupted behind him, sending cold shocks down his neck. He turned just in time to see a figure vaulting over a pile of rocks. Lamech burst into a sprint up the mountainside, throwing his arms as he climbed, slipping on loose rocks.

Desperate scuffing sounded closer and closer. He glanced behind and saw the man's face red between what looked to be curved, black horns sprouting from his skull. The man was well-conditioned to have such endurance so high up the mountain. Even after years of acclimation, Lamech realized he couldn't outrun him. So he grabbed a large jagged stone and spun around, using the momentum of his turn to force the projectile into the man's face. The man dipped to the left and the rock hit his right horn, toppling him toward the cliff edge two body-lengths away.

Lamech sprinted down and leapt into the air, his foot colliding with the man's midsection, throwing him farther backward, arms and legs flailing for a hold. The man's lower half disappeared over the edge, then his upper half, finally his horns.

But the momentum sent Lamech sliding toward the cliff too. With dust flying and stones skipping, he twisted onto his belly and grabbed at a gray bush that flashed by, but the roots gave and he slid farther. He dug his fingernails into dirt and scraped them against stone as he slowed to a stop, his legs dangling over the edge.

He belly-crawled until fully back on solid ground, and after taking several breaths to calm the spinning of his vision, he twisted back to peer over the edge. The man's motionless body lay broken amidst pieces of shattered horn.

Lamech struggled to his feet, beat his legs to stop the tremors, and hurried home as quickly as he could.

Chapter 15

Adah sat cross-legged in the darkness of her cell, clutching the shaft of the needle. It seemed days before torchlight warmed the way, but as the light grew, she smiled, wiped her face, and slipped the needle against her left palm, careful not to prick her skin.

First came the chuckling, followed by footsteps and heavy, wet breaths. Tubal was alone, and he came close and raised the torch to toss the glow about her features. Horns shone atop his head, and a smile sat crooked on his left face. "Rejected, eh? Not good enough for the God-King?" Tubal laughed as he unlocked the door with a set of iron keys dangling from his belt. He swung open the gate and stepped in. "You'll be good enough for what I have planned, won't you?"

She shot to her feet and dashed toward him holding her empty right fist high to divert his gaze from her left. Tubal screeched with delight and caught her wrist, but she kicked at his groin and swung her left hand in to stab with the needle. He sidestepped, kneed her in the stomach, and palmed her to the ground. She wheezed, rolled away, and fumbled with the needle, nearly losing it.

Her ears adjusted to the shift of his feet as she tried to rise, but already his arms grappled her with terrifying strength, his laugh ringing in her ears. "A fighter! I love the fighters!"

She screamed and twisted, but he threw her against the wall, knocking the breath from her chest. She wheezed on the ground and clutched her broken ribs, tears sliding down her face.

He approached, grabbed her by the throat, and raised her off the ground. His hand squeezed tighter, and she felt as if she had been tossed into a well that's lid was slowly closing, blocking out all sight and sensation.

Finally, as her mind fell into darkness, she swung her body from left to right, hoping the needle was still clenched tight in her fingers, for she could feel nothing but the pressure behind her eyes.

Then the pain returned, and with it a roaring noise, as if the earth were on fire. She perceived that she was lying on the ground, and that Tubal towered over her, bent and blurry. There was a terrible noise like a thousand oceans scraping the depths of the earth, so loud that it threatened to split her from ear to ear.

She coughed, realized her palms were pressed to her ears, and saw Tubal collapse, convulsing. The needle was partially embedded in his shoulder, and its slender shape gleamed in the firelight.

"What did you do to me?" he screamed.

The world came into focus, and the stone edges of her cell fell back into place. She pushed herself to her knees, crying out with the pain of it.

Tubal was convulsing and lay in a pool of what looked like blood. He no longer made any noise but the rustling of cloth and skin against stone.

She sat for several minutes breathing. Watching.

His body went stiff, and the light of the torch continued, even as the red pool threatened it with extinction. She crossed to him on hands and knees and worked the torch from his grip, coaxing the flames back by feeding them with bits of his clothing.

She tipped her head and held the torch between her teeth so her hands were freed to tear the keys from his tunic. But there, beside the keys, hung a vial of oil useful for refilling lanterns.

She removed the stopper, poured the liquid over Tubal's body, removed the keys, and lit his body on fire.

For several moments she watched the demon crackle and glow, and couldn't help but think the burning she felt in her abdomen was a cleansing. But as she walked into the dark corridor and heard the startled gasps of the other women, her satisfaction turned to dread.

She turned and saw them huddled together, a mass of bruised skin. Eyes gleaming like wild animals stripped of fur and starved to skeletal forms.

"Help us," they whispered. First one, then several, then all of them, crowding against the bars, arms reaching, voices rising.

How could she leave them? Even if it meant her death, how could she bow to the same cruelty that brought her here, a slave in a dark hole in the ground? She was no better than these women, no more deserving of life, of freedom.

The flames still crackled across Tubal's body, and the burning in her abdomen returned like an inferno. Now she thought she saw the God-King's intentions with clarity. He had promised to never harm her, and maybe he would have remained true to his word. But even if he never touched her, what greater damage could he do than to pressure her to abandon her own? To betray not just her sisters, but herself?

He had threatened her with death, and offered her what she craved. Before this moment, she thought that would be enough to keep her from daring to disobey. But now that she saw the women watching her in the dim light, she couldn't imagine leaving them in such hellish, dark captivity.

Not to save herself. Not for anything.

The keys jangled in her hand as she walked to the cells, unlocking them one by one. She motioned to the women in the dim light, and they issued past her shaking, tentative. "Thank you," they whispered, and some threw their arms around her, weeping, kissing her, though after realizing how injured she was, they stopped.

"We have little time," she said. "Follow me to the aquifer. It will be empty, but not for long."

She led them to the hole in the ground, then held up her hand to stop them. "I will jump first."

She handed over the torch, sat on the edge, and took a few shallow breaths, gazing into the abyss below. The women shifted on their feet, and their breaths seem to fill the entire labyrinth, echoing on and on.

Closing her eyes, Adah pushed herself over the edge. Wind rushed past, whipping her hair, and for a moment she imagined that the God-King had lied. That she was rushing to meet violent water, to be bashed against stone and carried along, drowned in dark water.

But even as her mind said, *So be it!* her feet met solid ground, and she collapsed. Pain exploded through her abdomen, and for several long moments she lay hovering on the edge of consciousness, moaning. Finally, she rolled to her back and looked up at the light flickering against the women's pale faces above.

"It's safe!" she rasped, and the women, one by one, began to drop.

When Adah finally made it back to her feet with the help of the others, she looked down the aquifer and far in the distance saw a prick of light, like a star in the night sky. Together, with her arms draped for support over two of the starved women, they turned from the darkness to walk toward the light.

Chapter 16

A s Lamech reached the plateau, a blast of cold wind
separated the huts from the narrow pathway beyond,
followed by Adah's scream and a frenetic throbbing in
the soil. The mountain shook and boulders tumbled, and as the
shaking stilled, Lamech bounded forward, retrieved a bronze
cooking rod from the toppled fire pit, and grabbed a handful of
ashes in his left hand.

The tarp over Adah's door had been slashed, and the roof
sat askew from the quake. As Lamech rushed inside he saw three
shapes. Another scream erupted from the smallest shape with its
back against the wall.

"Adah!" Lamech said, and she glanced toward him. One of
the other dark shapes dashed toward her, but she swung a small
knife, forcing it back.

Now the other two shapes turned toward Lamech, and he
saw they, too, had what looked to be horns on their heads.

"Lamech! It's them!" Her voice tore as if she had set her
knife to it.

The horned devils moved quickly, but not quick enough.
The one on the right was closest, but Lamech stepped right, saw
the demon adjust, and so he slid left, slamming the cooking rod
into the side of his neck, sending him sprawling.

The other jumped a small table, but Lamech tossed the

ashes into his eyes. He cried out as Lamech shifted and struck the devil in the back of the head.

"Lamech!" Adah said, and he whipped around. The first one had recovered and had hold of Adah's arm. She stabbed him with the small knife, but he growled and wrenched the weapon away, pinning her arms to her sides and pressing the blade to her throat.

"Drop the rod," the devil said with a glint of teeth and a hiss of breath.

But Lamech would not drop the rod.

Sweat dripped down the devil's face, and one of his black horns pressed against Adah's head. "Drop it or I will kill her and the baby both."

Lamech hoped Father had somehow awoken. But if he hadn't come by now, he was either more ill than Lamech thought, or already dead.

His grip tightened. What if these men had come for some reason other than murder?

The devil smiled, stuck out his tongue, and dragged it across Adah's cheek.

Lamech sprinted forward, but the man kneed Adah in the stomach, threw her away, and fled for the door. Adah shrieked and rolled as Lamech caught his ankle, pulling him to the ground. The devil twisted, and Lamech punched him in the stomach. The demon kicked Lamech in the shoulder and twisted away, leaping up faster than he thought possible. He stumbled after, rushing out into the mountain pass just as he saw the devil taking off down the mountain road.

Lamech grabbed the cooking rod laying on the ground and followed. But after rounding two bends, he saw no one and came to a stop, chest heaving for air. The devil couldn't have made it so far in such a short time. He had to be here somewhere.

Lamech slid forward slowly, eyes shifting from side to side. The devil burst from the brush, head down, horns aimed toward Lamech's midsection. Lamech jumped back and smashed the rod into one horn, sending splinters flying.

He slid back and swiped grit from his cheek as the attacker

tumbled to the ground. Lamech bounded toward him before he had time to recover, smashing first his left knee, then his right.

"Mercy," the devil said. "Have mercy!"

"Mercy?" Lamech screamed.

He shook with pain. "You won't kill me. I know what kind of man you are."

"You do?" Lamech loomed over the monster. "No one touches my family." He lifted the rod, and the creature screamed and turned to crawl away, but Lamech beat him until he stopped moving, then beyond, screaming with each strike.

But he felt no satisfaction. Only an empty horror. And as the bronze rod fell from his hands, he turned, shaking, and ran back to the hut to find Adah.

She lay in the dark, and he cradled her and pulled back her dress. A dark bruise had begun forming across the length of her swollen belly, and she was sitting in blood.

He pressed his hand against her cold cheek. She sucked at the air, and tears drew flesh-colored streaks through the red on her face. "Our baby," she said, and cried out, arcing her back. "It's coming."

Lamech held his wife in a pool of blood as she screamed with each sudden, strong contraction. But he could do nothing to stop it now.

Three hours later, pale from exhaustion, their son exited her womb, followed immediately by a bag of tissue and a fountain of blood. Lamech lifted their son and cut the cord with the small knife Adah had fought with. He then turned the boy over, searching for wounds. The boy wailed, but Lamech found no injuries, so he laid him on Adah's chest to suckle.

Adah wept silently, eyes glazed, blood continuing to issue from her womb. "Noah," she whispered. "Our relief from the struggle."

Lamech's spine felt immersed in ice water. "Yes," he said, "he will be our joy." Tears blurred his vision and choked his words as he grabbed her trembling, cold hand and kissed it.

"He will be the voice to a world"—she swallowed hard —"filled with violence. A righteous man among those whose thoughts are only evil."

"Hush," Lamech said, and kissed her cheek and forehead, then pulled her to his chest. "I love you," he said. "I love you." Over and over, he repeated it.

She reached up and laid her hand against his cheek. "I love you too." She smiled. Her eyes, which had before been so dim, were now clear. "I will always love you."

"Stay." The words caught in his throat, and he sobbed and kissed her. "Promise you won't leave. Promise like you made me promise!"

Now she was crying, too, and she shook her head. "I'm not angry. I was never angry. Not at you. Only them."

He nodded and kissed her on the lips. "I'll mend you. We'll be together." But that, too, was a lie. And he knew it.

Lamech had promised he would take care of her, but even then he had known he would fail.

He was just like Father.

Noah cooed, clenched his fists, and softly beat Adah's breast. Adah reached up and placed a shaking finger in his hand. He seized it and wailed, snorting and sucking for breath. Adah breathed sharply and stilled. Noah's gums gleamed in the dim light as he screamed for comfort, food, sleep.

Lamech lifted Noah off Adah's motionless chest and let him clutch his finger as he kissed his wife's tear-soaked eyelids. He rocked Noah to sleep, weeping beside her until at last darkness fell and he slept with Noah in his lap and Adah's cold hand in his.

But instead of finding empty sleep slumped beside his dead wife with his child in hand, a dark dream penetrated his mind. In the dream, he lay flat on the cold, dusty ground. Above and immeasurably distant hung cold, white stars in a strange arrangement. Like flint, they sparked in him a near manic desire to study them, as if his life depended on his understanding their alignment.

Then came a sweeping darkness that blocked out the stars to the east, and a voice warm at his neck. "We do not have much Time," said the voice, "for he is near, and my presence disturbs the Waters. You have endured the deepest pain imaginable, and though I wish it were not so, now is the moment when most is asked of you."

Lamech tried to speak, to move, to do anything in response, but failed.

"I am sorry," the voice continued, breath tickling Lamech's neck as if it were behind him, though he knew nothing but dirt pressed his back. "But I could not risk you disturbing the Waters so soon, so I cannot allow you to speak. When some time has passed, I'll find you again and show you the way you must take. But for now, you must simply flee the mountain and enter the village you grew up in. There you will find a woman to suckle the boy. Be cautious, for the Abomination hunts your child, and it is closer than you—" The voice stopped and the shadow turned. Footsteps approached, and a chill deeper than any Lamech had felt pricked from his head to his toes. Then, as Lamech felt deadly fingers clutch the hem of his garment, he heard the voice cry out, and felt a rush of air pushing him through the darkness into the light.

He awoke gasping, pressed Noah to his chest, and abandoned his dead wife to find his father. For his wife would never now warm their child with tender fingers, nor use her hands to rock him to sleep, nor apply her kisses to the pains of boyhood. And if the dream was true, he must flee as soon as he could. Noah needed food, and Lamech had none to offer. And so, just as the voice suggested, he would need to find someone who could suckle him.

Tears fell down his cheeks and neck. Dear God, how could he so love a child he had only known for moments? But he could let himself think of nothing else. Because he could not bear the thought of her ruddy skin gone pale. Could not think of her blood splattered across the stone. The sound of her spirit riding her final breath. He tugged at the neck of his tunic, but found it already slack.

Father was still in his hut, motionless but alive. This time he awoke when Lamech shook him. And as Lamech told him in tears what happened, Father said roughly, "I am sorry, my son. Alas, the choice is here. The world is burning. I see it with my waking eyes. A wall of flames rolling over us. And that babe stands against it all, the crux upon which the world has been balanced. If he dies, so do we all. Protect him as you tried to protect her."

Lamech returned to Adah, swaddled Noah and set him down to weep, then went to bury his wife. As the sun rose, there came a clanging and chorus of angry voices. Lamech snatched Noah and gave him his knuckle to suck to quiet his cries, only barely slipping down the mountainside in time.

He turned to look back. A giant of a man stood at the cliff edge, looking toward the horizon, head adorned with yellow horns and yellow eyes, dressed as a soldier, one arm missing. Others bustled behind the giant, and Lamech saw the glow of flames as his home was burned.

Lamech sped down the mountain, for the first time feeling released. Compelled. Never before had he felt love like he felt for Noah. Warm and swaddled in muslin, flesh of his flesh and bone of his bone. In Noah, Adah lived. The blood she spilled still pulsing in the infant's wrists. A final gift. A consuming blaze that drove him down the mountain, through the forest, and into the deserted village destroyed by fire.

Protect him, Father had said. That, he would do. But first, Noah needed to survive his first week without his mother . . . *find a woman to suckle the boy*, the voice had said.

And so he would.

PART II

The Devil and the Child

"The Nephilim were on the earth in those days, and also afterward, when the sons of God came in to the daughters of man and they bore children to them. These were the mighty men who were of old, the men of renown."
—Genesis 6:4

Chapter 17

The God-King sat in his hastily cast, iron throne, his hands glistening with sweat, the distant sensation of the fabric he tried to grab hold of still echoing in the skin of his fingers.

After centuries of thinking the man dead, the God-King had caught him interfering again. He was certain, for no one else had ever cast such a disturbance over the Waters.

True, the disturbance had been subtler, and had he not been studying the Waters, perhaps he would have missed it entirely.

But that was the most disturbing part. How long had the fool been moving under his nose? It made him thirsty.

He stood, walked to the entrance of his tent, and tossed the covering wide. "Eunuch," he said, and the boyish eunuch slipped out of the shadows, bowing low, subservient. "Fetch Berubbal."

The eunuch bowed a second time, turned, and disappeared down the corridor. The God-King returned, closed the door, and sat.

A quarter sundial later, the massive general entered and knelt before the throne, a colossus shadowing the iron seat. "For what does the God-King desire my presence?" Berubbal's voice shook the room like distant thunder.

The God-King noted the giant's features. Yellow horns

above yellow eyes downcast. One arm missing. As tall as three men. Filled with a spirit more bloodthirsty than any of its brothers. Berubbal was one the God-King was glad to have in his service. After all, those with the strongest appetites might be controlled through their addictions.

"Berubbal," the God-King said. "You begin to enjoy your assignment too much. Should I retract the authority I gave you?"

Those yellow eyes flickered. "I don't know what you speak about."

"After I commanded you to find the girl, Adah, you challenged my decision to let her go to begin with."

Berubbal paused longer than expected. "The God-King spies on me now, as well."

"I have too much to care for now that you've helped me conquer a third of the known world. I would be a fool not to spy on my enemies, even more so not to spy on my friends."

"You finally found one?"

The God-King smiled. "You, of course. That's why I brought you here to listen to a story. And then, perhaps, to answer a question."

A nod of ascent, for how could he refuse the God-King?

He paced and said, "Years ago, when the world was still covered in the dew of creation, my Father was there, coiled amidst the branches of Eden, where he brought the first man and woman to the knowledge of good and evil. However, after that initial success, our Enemy made a covenant with the woman."

"I know," Berubbal said. "We all do."

The Abomination smiled. "But there is much you do not know. Yes, you know that the Enemy promised the seed of the woman's womb would crush my Father's head. But we also know that Eve's children failed to do as the Enemy promised. Indeed, in his wisdom, my Father saw fit to use the woman's firstborn, Cain, as the conduit for my birth. And what a sweet victory that was, though short-lived."

"Get on with it," Berubbal said, his voice little more than a growl.

"Are you so incapable of mastering yourself that you cannot endure a minute without speaking?"

Berubbal ground his teeth together.

"The prophecy is about to be fulfilled," the God-King said.

"You seem sure of yourself," Berubbal said.

"I am as sure of this as of anything else."

"How?"

"I am able to see with more than just eyes," the God-King said. "I can also see the shadows of things that have happened and what yet will come to be. Some are unclear. Others are bright as day."

"You've seen this coming savior?"

"I've seen Adah giving birth to a child who holds the weight of our futures on his shoulders," the God-King said.

"And yet you let her go," Berubbal said.

The God-King met Berubbal's yellow gaze. "Are you going to make me deal with you as I did Tubal?"

Another pause. "I am still useful."

"You were hardly able to find the girl, as commanded," the God-King said.

"She is dead, and we captured the old man they lived with. He calls himself Methuselah. Apparently, he's the grandfather of the child you speak of."

"The little foresight you showed in not killing the old man is the only reason you still breathe. Further prove your usefulness by listening to the rest of my story."

The God-King waited. Berubbal said nothing.

"Good. Already you learn." The God-King clasped his hands behind his back. "I not only know what might come to be, but also what impact our decisions could have on the future. I am as attached to my father's designs as a scarlet thread is woven through a tapestry. Indeed, I cannot be removed without unraveling it altogether—and let that give you pause where it did not Tubal. Though I see only in part, I can follow the tapestry's course well enough to be certain that at particular intervals certain actions would mean disaster. And this woman —this girl who bore the child who might destroy us—she could not have been killed before birthing that child."

"How is that possible?" Berubbal said, a grin edging the corner of his mouth.

"The Enemy is a cunning weaver at the loom." The God-King returned to his throne and sat, leaning to one side and lifting a leg over the opposite armrest.

"So, we must stand idle while this savior crushes us underfoot?"

"Of course not. We could do little to her, and less to her child. But what of *their* choices? What if they corrupted their own way?"

Berubbal's eyes flashed.

"Have you never thought of why my father has given you the chance to come live in human skin? It is precisely to help me corrupt the human race so that the true Savior might never come. Men are simple. Pressure them with violence or fear of death and they will destroy themselves. If the potential Savior corrupts his way, the world might be damned, and we may seal our dominance. For if we pervert their seed, no Savior will ever come."

"But the Savior is here already."

"Only a foreshadowing. And if he fails, we will have succeeded. The rules are subtle—and clearly beyond you—but my father is certain he understands them, as am I. You forget that my father was closest in the Enemy's company before taking up the second Music."

"No," Berubbal said, "I have not forgotten."

"Then your body clouds your judgment. I have the ability to twist humanity beyond recognition, to give you a receptacle by corrupting humanity so far that no Savior might be born from a human womb. But it might only be done if we first convince them to corrupt their way. If we can succeed in this task, we might have the earth as birthright, as should have been in the beginning."

Berubbal nodded.

The God-King waved his hand in annoyance. "It didn't work on the woman. She was supposed to let the others die. Instead, she sacrificed herself to save them. But hope is not gone, for the seeds of bitterness are sown in loss, and we must patiently tend those seeds until the roots grow strong through the child." The God-King thought of Cain, who first brought him life, for that man also had been a tender of root and soil.

"So, Berubbal. What do you choose?"

Berubbal studied his own fingernails covered with dried blood. "I choose patience. For now."

Chapter 18

Noah slept in Lamech's arms during the journey down the mountainside. Several times Lamech slipped and nearly fell, and Noah jerked awake and cried until Lamech pacified him.

Noah had eaten nothing and already seemed to be losing weight. Each time he awoke, he cried longer and harder, until his voice was hoarse.

They were running out of time, and Lamech knew to do nothing but search the village for help. As he approached, his breath quieted and his gaze rolled side to side. Sweat stuck his clothes to his body despite the chill of the wind, and his muscles twitched and ached.

Buildings slumped like burnt bodies, and the smell of ash and singed hair hung like a fog. Half-destroyed goods stuck out of piles of rubble in the marketplace. Tattered pieces of clothing blew across the roads while linens flittered, caught in collapsed windows.

From the way the men climbing the mountain spoke, it seemed there had been survivors. What if some of the enemy soldiers were still here, waiting for stragglers to return to search the rubble for lost loved ones and possessions?

Noah cooed and stretched in Lamech's arms. His eyes fluttering open. His lower lip jutted, and he began wailing, eyes pouring tears.

"Hush!" Lamech said, sticking his knuckle in Noah's mouth. "You're all right."

But Noah would not take his knuckle. He continued crying, tears soaking Lamech's tunic.

Lamech searched the rubble for a place to hide, then dashed to the edge and ducked under an arch of a partially collapsed bathhouse.

As Noah stopped wailing and began sucking loudly at his finger, there came footsteps. Lamech held his breath and turned Noah into him to muffle his noises.

Stealthy and quick, a small figure rushed by the entrance, then peeked inside. It was a woman with hair cut short like a man's, and a bundle oddly strapped to her chest. She must not have seen them in the shadows, for she squinted and slipped farther in.

"Are you alone?" Lamech said.

The woman cursed, turned, and ran.

"Wait!" he said and took off after her, feet slipping on the loose rubble. He followed the sound of her footsteps through the alleys until he lost track.

Stopping, he listened to his pulse pounding louder than his feet. He willed the wind and his heart and the fluttering leaves to stop so that he could figure out in which direction the woman ran.

But Noah was wailing again from being jarred on the way, and for the first time since Adah died, Lamech realized the full weight of all he had lost. His limbs felt leaden, and the knowledge of the days that lay ahead stretched like an endless road, bleak and desolate.

How could he keep Noah alive without Adah? How could he ever be whole?

He kissed Noah's forehead. "It's okay. It's okay. You don't need to cry anymore. Everything's going to be all right." But the more he spoke, the tighter his throat became, until he could speak no more, and his body shook.

A formidable-sized shadow slid into view, and Lamech

jumped and readied himself to dash away. But it was the woman.

They stood watching each other. Gauging.

She adjusted the bundle on her chest, and a tiny hand shot out from the fabric, followed by a coo.

Excitement spread down his forearms and his fingers twitched. "You," he said, "you have a baby?"

She lifted a hand to block her child from view, but already Lamech wondered of all that had brought him to this moment. His grandfather's prophecies. The sickness that struck his family. Their flight to the mountain. Mother's death. Adah's arrival. A love grown softly, swiftly. Father's dreams, then his own. And the attack in the mountains, Adah's death, and the words she and Father spoke over Noah while hovering with eyes to see beyond death's doorstep and life still enough to speak of what they found.

Whether Lamech's unshakeable trust in that moment was foolish or not, what could he do but believe that the woman in front of him had been born to meet Noah's needs?

"My son," he said. "He was just born in the mountains. My wife, she . . . didn't make it. I . . ." But the rest was lost in an ache so deep he thought he would be torn apart.

"He needs food?" the woman said, voice hesitant.

"We were attacked by men . . . with horns."

"Why should I trust you?" She looked around, gazing down alleys that he still remembered, however dimly.

"I grew up here. My father took me into the mountains after my mother became ill. We lost her. We've lived in the mountains all these years."

Her eyes narrowed.

"Please," he said, "I don't know how to convince you." He looked at Noah, who cooed in his arms, eyes red and puffy from crying. "He needs help I can't offer."

He felt a burning anger at the men who had so twisted his world. What right did they have to tear families apart and burn villages? It was they who had sown the distrust that now grew in the woman's eyes.

Surely a mother could not leave an infant to die.

"Set him down," she said.

Lamech paused, wondering whether he really could trust her.

But what other choice did he have? If he offended the woman and she refused to take Noah, what hope was left? He could die in a day without food.

Could Lamech really hope to find another woman to suckle him in such a short time?

He placed Noah on the ground and motioned toward him, fighting every instinct that commanded him to pick his child up.

The woman stepped forward. "Back up," she said.

If he stepped away, she could do anything she wanted. Of course, Noah would also die without her.

He took a deep breath and shifted back several paces.

The woman kept her gaze on him as she approached, dipped, and lifted Noah from the ground, holding him in one arm while her other slipped into her tunic. "I will take care of this child," she said. "But you must leave. If you follow me, I will know. And I will kill him." Her hand slipped out of her tunic, clutching a bejeweled dagger.

Lamech cried out and jumped toward her, but the woman yelled, "Stop!" and brought the tip of the blade within a finger's width of Noah's neck.

Ice flooded his limbs, and he resisted the temptation to strike himself.

Fool!

He glared at her and said through gritted teeth, "I will kill you if you hurt him."

"You might be twice my size," the woman said, "but I have a weapon, and you do not, and I have just agreed to save your child's life."

"For what purpose?"

"To do what you could not," she said. "Do you agree?"

How could he? He needed Noah just as much as Noah needed the woman. A mother, no less, already gifted with the ability to produce milk.

And a knife poised to destroy him! Adah, forgive me if this ends badly.

"You will not hurt my child," he said.

"Not if you do as I say. You ask me to sacrifice much, and I agree to do so. But I must ensure my own child's safety." She nodded toward the baby strapped to her chest. "You understand?"

He nodded absently, mind racing for alternatives.

"Very well," she said. She backed away slowly, not taking her gaze from him, nor the blade from Noah's neck.

Lamech stood motionless, watching until she disappeared.

Then he sprinted after her.

PART III

The Woman and the Man

"Now the earth was corrupt in God's sight, and the earth was filled with violence. And God saw the earth, and behold, it was corrupt, for all flesh had corrupted their way on the earth."
—Genesis 6:11–12

Chapter 19

Elina knew the man would follow. She believed he was the father from the beginning, but couldn't be too cautious. She had seen evil men use infants for diabolical purposes too often to trust a stranger in a war-torn land.

Every so often she caught glimpses of him stealthily following the trail she'd left. Broken branches, footprints, and soiled wrappings from when Jade or the boy would need to be cleaned.

Part of her was disgusted with herself for toying with him. But the time it had afforded her to examine him was precious. No true father would abandon his child. Likewise, no true father would let his baby starve. The truth of what kind of man he was could only be deciphered safely through observing the consistency of his actions from afar. Even then, she wasn't sure she could handle traveling alongside him.

The burn of the memories had waned the past year, but she didn't think they'd ever truly disappear.

Some scars healed too dark.

And so she waited. And watched. He hadn't intentionally given himself away yet, which showed restraint and care for his child's well-being. But how long could he hold out?

How long would I hold out?

"Forever," she whispered as she gazed at Jade asleep in her lap.

The boy was beside her, but awake. His gray eyes searched the sky, drawn to the brightness yet clenched against the cloud cover transmuting the sun's gold to silver. Hills rolled toward the forest to the south, and as she ate the little bread and fruit left in her bag, she wondered about him.

He was too young to smile. Possibly only days old, judging by how small he was. What stroke of fate had brought him to her, she did not know. But for his sake, she was glad. If what the father said was true, the boy likely would have died by the next sunrise without food and care. She could only imagine how desperate the man had to have been. And how surprised he'd been to find her.

Not nearly as surprised as he'd be if he found out who she really was, and what she'd done.

The boy stuck his tongue out and moved his arms and legs in a restless, random pattern. She scooped him up.

"Are you hungry?"

She brought him to her breast and he latched and drank his fill. Within minutes, milk drunk and satisfied, he fell asleep.

She tucked Jade back into the wrap she had tied around her torso, drank the last of the water from her wineskin, and picked up the boy to continue their journey.

She had traveled south toward the forest because the horned devils had come from the north. No reasoning firmer than fear of brutality and bitter cold drove her, for winter was closing in, and finding food would be of great concern.

No one seemed to know where the men with horns came from, but all agreed they were the most evil race to walk the earth.

Rumor of the devils' savage brutality had spread wide. They slaughtered everything they touched. They drank their victims' blood like wine. They burned everything that came under their possession. Soon, if allowed to continue, some claimed the entire world would be laid waste.

She looked at the children. Male and female. A perfect pair with nothing but light behind their crystal eyes.

If only the entire world could be like them. If only these two babes were the last people left, and the world could begin anew.

What did the boy's father think of her? Was he thankful for her service? Angered by her distrust?

Or was he what she most feared when she lay in the darkness with two sleeping infants?

As she stepped over a fallen log patched with moss and crumbling with rot, a thick cord snaked around her ankle and yanked her leg sideways with such force she thought it had been torn off. Thin sheets of metal crashed together as her head and shoulders smashed the ground, knocking her breath away. She managed to keep hold of the boy as her leg was hauled into the air, and Jade remained strapped to her chest.

Elina blinked away the shadows and spots that threatened to overcome her as she swung through the air and the metal sheets clanged. She could only barely make out the infants' faces reddening as the blood rushed to their heads, but they were squealing.

Hurried footsteps sounded, followed by whistles and harsh laughter.

"We caught ourselves something this time, brother," said the first voice.

"Tonight will be a night to remember," said a second in low tones, as if savoring a dessert.

Elina swung and glimpsed two men in soiled clothing before spinning away again. One small and thin. The other thick and shaggy.

She made certain she could hold both babies in place with one hand, then used the other to feel for her dagger. Her eyes widened and her insides chilled.

The dagger was gone.

The first man cursed loudly and sucked air through his teeth. "She's holding a baby!"

"Babies," said the second.

"I can count," said the first.

"Do you have a problem with infants?"

There was a pause. "An infant?"

"Why not, little brother?" said the deeper voice. "The world is burning."

She had promised herself it would never happen again, but as she swung, only gaining momentary glimpses of her surroundings, it felt as if the world were falling under a heavy shadow, and the air was being pulled from her chest.

"Quick, let her down before she drops the children," the deeper voice said.

"Hand me the knife," said the younger.

Clothing rustled, and footsteps sounded close to the tree. She dropped about a foot, the rope rubbing bark as she was let down in jerky movements. Finally her shoulders touched the ground, and the darkness faded slowly from her vision.

The man sawed the rope until it snapped, dropping her legs to the ground.

She moaned and looked at her ankle. It was badly swollen, and the skin was bleeding. Then she remembered the dagger and tried to find it. Something hard dug into her shoulder, and she shifted subtly, felt a prick.

Was it the dagger? Had it dropped out of her tunic as she was hauled into the air?

The men approached and grabbed her by her head. She clutched Jade and the boy to her chest, screaming as they dragged her by her hair.

It was too late. She had lost her opportunity. And now they would all die for it.

Chapter 20

Lamech stared at the dagger in the dirt and momentarily feared the woman had caught him following. Had she left the dagger to tell him in which direction to find his dead son?

Of course, that would be insane. Even as the thought sped his pulse, he realized the dagger must have been left here by accident—which wasn't much better, seeing that she was supposed to be taking care of Noah.

He knelt to get a better look at the weapon. It was unmarked by blood, so she hadn't used it to fight anyone—or to stab Noah.

But he couldn't think of why she would leave it behind. It was the most useful tool she could carry. And she was too intelligent to purposefully part with her only means of defending herself.

Was it a message? A sign of trust?

Strange way to show it. Better that she met him face-to-face with the weapon still in hand.

He walked his gaze in the direction the dagger pointed, then reexamined his surroundings. There were several trees, a few patches of disturbed dirt he would have to get a better look at, a vine—his back tensed.

That was no vine.

He approached and examined a length of rope slung over a

branch, finding it looped at one end and frayed at the other as if sawn through. Its length had been fed through several sheets of metal.

If Lamech knew anything about surviving in the wilderness, he would call this a trap. But why would the woman drop her dagger near . . .

He swept the dagger up off the ground, sheathed it in his tunic, and ran to the patches of disturbed dirt.

Large footprints. None small enough to be left by the woman.

He stood, clutching his throbbing head.

Right there, between two trees and snaking around a set of deciduous bushes, was a trail. It looked as though something heavy had been dragged away. As he neared it, a yell echoed through the trees, sending birds fluttering and leaves rustling.

He crouched low, brought the dagger out, and followed the trail into the brush, struggling to keep his breathing under control.

Chapter 21

Elina continued clutching Jade and the boy, who were now fussing, moving their limbs with surprising strength.

"I'll go first," said the second, deeper voice as they let her drop.

"Right," said the younger.

The bigger man smirked, his dull eyes set into a slippery face like black stones in a puddle. Over his shoulder, the younger one rubbed his hands together. The breeze bent the trees over them, casting shifting shadows over their faces.

"Are you ready, girl?" the man said.

She tried to twist away, but he ripped Jade and the boy out of her grasp. She screamed as he tossed them and smashed his palm against the side of Elina's head, nearly blacking out her vision.

Jade and the boy wailed.

Spit flew from the man's mouth as he commanded the children to quiet, raising his hand to smack the boy. But as his fist fell, he arched backward and screamed, sending echoes reverberating through the forest. His eyes rolled back, and his breath crackled in his throat as he flopped to the ground, legs crumpled beneath him.

The younger man stepped over him, glancing down and

retrieving a knife from the back of the older man's neck before cleaning it off on his tunic.

For a moment, Elina felt a rush of hope. The younger man had attacked his own brother. Had it been because of what the brute planned to do with Jade and the boy?

But even as she thought this, the dull smile that spread across his sweating face revealed different motives. He gripped her clothing with long fingers, trying to tear it.

She punched him in the throat, and he coughed and struck her back. Then, as he tried to step over her, she thrust her knee into his groin, sending him sprawling.

She tried to get up, but the pain in her ankle sent her back to the ground. Her injury was worse than she first thought. He crawled toward her, angry breath throwing bits of sandy dirt. He clutched her hair in one hand, the knife in the other.

"I'm going to bleed you like I bled my brother."

A shadow rushed toward them, and the man looked up, managing a yell just before the blurred flash collided with him, sending him tumbling.

Elina scrambled back, recognizing the boy's father atop her attacker with her family heirloom dagger in his hand.

But the other man had a knife, too, and he was fumbling with it, trying to get a good grip as he held the father's knife-hand at bay.

"Watch out!" Elina said.

The father caught sight of the knife just in time to dodge the attacker's wild slash.

Her hand found a stone, and as the attacker scrambled up, she hopped behind him, careful not to put weight on her bad ankle. She was almost there when her foot snapped a branch, and the attacker spun, giving the father time to close in and stab him in the shoulder.

The man cried out and dropped the knife, clutching his wounded arm while Elina smashed the rock into his skull. His eyes went blank as he hit the ground, motionless.

The boy's father stepped over him and slit his throat, then stood straight, chest heaving, face splattered with red. He dropped the dagger and scooped up his wailing son. Tears shone on his cheeks as he hushed and comforted his infant boy, cradling him close, violent hands shaking with attempted tenderness.

Elina found Jade, picked her up, made sure she didn't have any obvious injuries, and began nursing her. This distracted Jade from the pain of any bruises or sprained muscles she might have sustained, and she stopped crying, looking up at Elina's face with watery eyes.

A relative silence followed, broken only by each other's heavy breaths and whispered words of comfort.

When at last she looked at the man, she found him watching. A spear of panic struck her, and she struggled to suppress the urge to hide. But there was no helping it now.

"Are you all right?" he said. "Did they touch you?"

She shook her head. "I am fine. Thank you." But her voice was wooden, and she knew it.

He nodded, fresh tears pooling in his eyes. "I'm sorry." His voice was constricted with emotion.

She stood and tried to walk away to escape the emotions that chilled her, but the pain in her ankle was excruciating. She stood, balancing on her good leg, breathing heavily, feeling blackness dance at the edge of her vision.

She could not show weakness. It was bad enough that he had found her in so desperate a situation.

She took one full step down on her wounded ankle and crumpled into a heap, eyes flashing wide to a world gone empty.

Chapter 22

The woman fell straight back with her baby in her arms. Though her unconscious body absorbed most of the jar, the baby jammed its nose against her chest and wailed as a fine trickle of blood trailed down its lips.

Lamech didn't really know how to help them, so with Noah fussing in his arms, he paced and waited, glancing at the baby from time to time to make sure it could still breathe, though it was crying hard enough to assure him.

Lamech shifted Noah to the crook of his arm, then knelt and retrieved the woman's dagger with his right hand, cleaning the blood off on the grass.

The attacker had died with his eyes open, something Lamech found deeply disturbing. Even more disturbing was the thought that Lamech had been the one to end him.

In only a few short days, he had killed four men with brutal abandon. He never wanted to harm anyone, so how could this have happened?

He turned away, so the man was no longer within view, and finished cleaning the dagger. After dropping it beside the woman, he sat rocking Noah to sleep.

The woman's child still wailed, and eventually the woman moaned and her eyes fluttered open. She rolled forward and repositioned her baby. "Hush, Jade," she said as she cleaned the baby's face off. "I'm sorry, hush."

She tried to get up and nearly fell again, so Lamech caught her by the arm.

She turned on him, screaming and thrusting him away. "Don't touch me!"

"What's wrong with you?" he said.

The noise and movement woke Noah. Lamech looked down at the fresh tears growing in his son's eyes, that little gummy mouth opened wide.

The woman cradled Jade and began feeding her again in an attempt to calm her, but Jade refused to eat. "It doesn't matter. Just stay away from me."

"No, I can't stay away," he said. "Not after what just happened."

"You can, and you will," she said.

"I'm not leaving Noah alone again."

"He won't be alone in my arms."

"Those men nearly killed him. They nearly killed you!"

"You think I don't know that?" She whipped toward him. "I know!" Her face softened, but the calm in her voice seemed forced as she said, "The danger is passed. I will take your child again, and we will continue as before. You may follow, but only from a distance."

"You're not thinking clearly," Lamech said.

Her voice smoldered. "Oh, I'm thinking clearly."

"You took one step on that wounded ankle and collapsed. You couldn't make it half a mile in such a state."

"I will be more careful," she said.

"It won't help."

She tried to stand again, and failed.

Lamech sighed and stepped toward her.

"Stay back," she said. "I'm warning you."

"Or what?" He reached down and pulled her up by the arm.

She yelled and swung at him. His eyes caught the glint of the blade in her hand too late, and he jumped back as the blade sliced through his tunic and nicked his shoulder, drawing blood.

He stared at her in disbelief, then stepped back, guarding Noah.

She brandished the dagger and bared her teeth. "Touch me again, and I'll kill you both."

Heat flooded Lamech's arms, and he kicked her wounded ankle, dashed forward, clutched her wrist and twisted hard, forcing a cry from her throat and the dagger from her hand. As the weapon dropped, he kicked it aside, tossed her back, and said, "Don't you ever threaten my son again."

She screamed and wept, back arching on the ground.

Lamech felt the blood drain from his face. "What are you—?"

"Stop, it hurts!" She groaned and convulsed, and Jade rolled off her into the grass, crying again as her mother screeched.

Lamech swooped in and snatched Jade away before stepping back to observe the woman thrashing, screaming, and groaning.

After several long moments, she settled to quiet cries, and eventually to sleep. Lamech paced for nearly an hour after she quieted, trying to still the shaking in his limbs and the questions in his mind.

The woman was insane. He shouldn't have harmed her, of course, but what right did she have to threaten him?

He sighed. No more or less reason than he had to hurt her. The only difference—and he continued to believe the difference significant—was that he knew his own reasons, and they made sense, while he could barely come close to inventing a compelling reason for her actions.

He could not trust her. She was intelligent and articulate, yet struggled with some sickness.

Could there be a reason more solid than insanity? If not, they were in trouble, because they needed her.

As the sun settled, exhaustion weighed heavy on his shoulders, and he laid with both children a healthy distance from the woman, thinking of Adah, of her fire and kindness.

She, too, was intelligent and could be unpredictable, and sometimes piercingly perceptive. How could he not be reminded of her? How could he not think of the time they had spent together? And of how it all ended in the pall of her skin, the warmth of her blood, and the chill of her words in his ears.

He pressed hot tears from his eyes, feeling contorted emotions smoldering just beneath his skin. He longed to rip his chest open, if only to pour them out.

But for as long as he lived, he knew he would remember the silence and terrible isolation that washed over him in the wake of her final breath. And after . . .

The dream. The same dream his father and Adah had dreamt. Only his had been slightly different—the words the shadow spoke meant only for him.

The dream hadn't felt like any he'd ever experienced. Instead it seemed as if he had been extracted from his body and placed on the ground of another world.

Adah and Methuselah had both mentioned the stars in their dreams, as well. Was there something significant about them?

He stared up at the sky as stars blinked awake in the absence of the sun. The moon rose low and thin, a curved slash in a black tunic.

Something was happening. Something deeper than a father and mother trying to find a way to survive with their children in the wilderness.

He felt the layers of reality peeling away, as if revealing something hidden below the surface of the ground beneath and the sky above. Indeed, as exhaustion made drunk his mind, he wondered if the moon peeking through the sky were the slit of a great eye. Could the moon, perhaps, be the shadow watching him from beyond the veil?

And then he closed his eyes and was there again in that strange land, lying alone. Exposed.

The stars were wrong, and the shadow hovered just outside the realm of his vision.

"You've done well to find the woman," the voice said, "but more danger now awaits you. The Abomination found me—I risked too much too soon. It hunts you, and I fear your only choice is to run."

"But the woman," Lamech said, and was surprised at how his voice echoed on and on.

"Hush," the voice said, "I know! She is injured, but speak no more. I must go, and much sooner than hoped. But before I go, I warn you to move, and to continue moving. Stay nowhere overlong. Everything depends on it."

And then the voice was gone, and the stars melted back to the sky he knew—the same sky he'd studied as a boy in the mountains.

Chapter 23

Elina awoke shivering in the middle of the night. She had told herself it would never happen again, and yet it had. Worst of all, the man had seen.

Surely he would never trust her again. Not after glimpsing her wounds. He had already shown a great propensity for intrusiveness, and she couldn't keep the truth from him for long.

Yet I will keep it for as long as I may.

To let another know what had happened was more shame than she could bear. Yet, despite herself, she felt a distant thankfulness that the man had protected Jade.

Just . . . why did he have to be a man?

"Because a man is what I need," she whispered. Only, what one needed and what one could bear were hardly ever the same. After so long, it was hard to believe anything could bridge the gap.

What a terrible mystery the soul could be. That one could live for thirty years and still not understand the depths of its complexity, the visceral reactions that erupted from schisms delved by dark memories of nights long passed. Some days the pain throbbed so deep she thought she would burst.

She only wanted to forget. To watch Jade grow unmarred by the wounds that held she herself chained.

But she could not leave that precious boy. Noah, his father called him. Beautiful. Innocent. Perfect.

Everything she wished men could be.

Why would the father not trust her with the child and leave? Did he not realize his presence was what made her ill?

Yet even as the stars bowed their lesser crowns to the greater light that issued from beneath the horizon like bloodstained gold, she knew all her thoughts were aimless. The acrimony she aimed at him changed nothing.

The helplessness she felt to escape the chains that bound her to those two evenings nearly a year and a half ago did not diminish the equally powerful instinct that compelled her to keep the boy alive.

The man awoke not long after the sky brightened, but said nothing. He only sat and gazed at Noah and Jade, who remained sleeping. All of them were exhausted from the past days. Traveling was hard on such young children. And beyond travel, they had been brutalized.

When Jade finally woke, the father approached Elina with Jade in his arms as if presenting a peace offering.

Elina accepted her child and fed her. Then, as she held Jade and rocked her to sleep, she noticed the father holding Noah, trying to calm him as he grew fussy. The father did not act as if he expected her to feed or comfort his child. He merely did what any father could. Which wasn't much.

"Give him to me," Elina said, her voice no longer wooden.

The father gazed at her long. Brown eyes glowing in the shade of the forest.

"He is hungry," Elina said.

"You are sure?"

Elina nodded and waited.

He lifted Noah, walked to her, and offered him hesitantly.

Elina avoided his gaze as she took Noah and began nursing him.

Silent tears fell from Elina's face, but if the father saw, he ignored them. When at last Noah drank his fill, the father said, "I will be back," and disappeared into the forest.

Hours crept by. Elina listened to the winds and watched the

sunlight trickle through the sparse canopy. Pure white clouds flecked the sky above and moved slowly from east to west. The infants woke periodically to eat. Afterward she cleaned their bottoms, and both returned to sleep.

Hunger gnawed at her stomach, and she knew that if she did not find more food soon, she would lose her milk, and the children would be endangered. But with her ankle wounded the way it was, she could do nothing but wait for the man to return. So she waited and breathed the slow rot of undergrowth that she could not eat.

The father returned as the sky darkened once more. He held a long shaft of wood crudely carved in a strange manner, and he handed it to her and said, "Place the carved portion beneath your shoulder and use the wood in place of your wounded leg. You may walk this way, but I expect you will have trouble using both the wood and holding the children. I will follow behind carrying Noah at what you deem a comfortable distance while you carry Jade."

Elina looked into his eyes, and though the unnamable terror remained, she felt a momentary stab of gratefulness. "Thank you," she said.

He nodded, took Noah, and returned to where he'd slept the previous night. "We must restart our journey tomorrow." He built a fire with small twigs and dry underbrush, coaxing the fire large enough to toss warmth across her shoulders.

She laid and slept fitfully, falling in and out of nightmares. Each time she awoke, she saw the man sitting beside the fire, facing outward toward the darkness. When drowsiness caused her to fail to recognize him, her breath rushed, and she clutched at the clothing across her chest. Then she remembered, and the fear was replaced by another fleeting stab of thankfulness.

Chapter 24

L amech sat before the fire, eyes and ears scanning the night. Nearly an hour earlier, he heard the howling of wolves, but it was impossible to determine how many there were. He could hear paws scraping brush, noses nudging piles of leaves and twigs. Or at least he thought he could.

Regardless, whatever animals were out there refused to come close enough to be seen. Though Lamech had no more than a dagger, no beast could know that. And so he sat and watched for what he could not see, thinking of the woman, Noah, and Jade mere spans away.

They had made a silent treatise: he would respect her and she would keep Noah alive. They had come to this under-standing without need for explanation. Indeed, silence had once again given him the clarity to find the path to peace.

That and several hours alone in the forest.

The reason he hadn't seen the solution was that it had been too simple. All the woman longed for was safety.

He had seen the feral fear in her eyes before she cut him. But she was a paradox. Resisting the very man who offered what she most craved.

How could he have understood it was *he* she feared? And yet, maddeningly, he had proven to himself that was the only answer. He didn't understand why, only that it was true. Because he had done the one thing he thought might release the tension, and by doing so risked everything.

He had entrusted her with Noah, then left long enough for her mind to clear, returning with a gift that offered her the independence she craved. She had accepted both, and the wildness in her eyes had disappeared, leaving only a distant sorrow in its wake.

He still feared the madness that had overtaken her when he wrenched the knife from her, but he believed the madness overcame her for some knowable reason. He would watch her, and limit the time she spent holding Noah.

And he would do everything in his power to avoid triggering the madness again.

He was thankful for her service. Enduring his presence obviously strained her, and that made her offer to care for Noah seem noble.

At the same time, he did not like that she was hiding something from him. And did motherly instinct drive her, or was it something else? Something dark?

He feared for Noah, and dared trust the woman only so far as he must. He had enough to worry about with the dreams. He distrusted them, as well, but mostly he distrusted stagnation.

And so he was caught. He must move, but to move meant to obey the shadow in his dreams. The voice had wanted him with the woman, but as soon as Noah was old enough, he planned to part ways with her and move into the deep wilderness.

Until then, they were bound to each other. She could not survive alone in the wilderness. She was wounded, and madmen were laying traps, and wolves roved the countryside, likely emboldened by the recent destruction of local villages.

Noah would not survive without a woman to feed him, not for his first year, at least. Indeed, even if Lamech did find another woman who might care for Noah, trusting the next might prove a greater risk than staying with the woman whose fears he'd at least partially begun to understand.

The woman inhaled, and her clothing rustled as she twisted to look at him. She had done so five times already. The first two times, he had looked into her eyes and seen that same animal fear. Then, as lucidity dawned, the fear waned, and she closed her eyes and returned to sleep.

He wondered how long she had been wandering the wilderness alone, caring for Jade, who was old enough to hold her head up without aid. That meant that Jade was nearly two seasons older than Noah.

Could she have survived the wilderness for so long? Doubtful. Especially after seeing the traps those men had laid. The woman was intelligent, and no stranger to violence. But the dangers one encountered in the wilderness were beyond what intelligence could overcome.

She was likely savvy at foraging for food, but a nursing mother could spend her whole existence in the wilderness just trying to gather enough to support her and her child. Then what of protection? Shelter? Clothing? Illness?

No, it seemed more likely she had become a shadow in local villages, stealing food, taking shelter and sleeping where she could, always moving, always searching. To walk the wilderness alone was a death wish. To walk the wilderness alone with an infant was insanity.

And yet here they rested with two infants.

Lamech gazed up at the stars, just barely visible through the sparse canopy, and wondered what Adah might say if she were still alive. Would she urge him to live in a nearby village and hope for safety?

He opened his mouth and whispered the words she might say, *"Those men were the same who attacked my village. I grew up on the far side of the mountains, and they had come from even farther away. If they attacked villages on this side of the mountains, they have only grown more powerful."*

"Yes," he would respond, "but how might I diminish the risk?"

"Travel as far south as you can," she would say, *"the woman was right in attempting that. But you will not make it far. You will soon need shelter. You will need to find a village."*

"We could make it many miles."

"Where will you find water? Food? Shelter to weather storms and the

change of seasons? Noah is too small to handle so much. Find a village, bide your time, raise him to be strong.”

"Too much risk."

"You and I both know there's more risk in loneliness.”

"That doesn't take away the risk of remaining static."

"Never stay too long in one village. Gather word of danger, of the machinations of war. Collect supplies. Work if you must. When you retrieve what you need, move before any become too familiar with you.”

"You speak with a harder voice than before."

"That is because there is no breath left in these lungs. I am hard earth tossed through the refiner's fire and beaten to a deadly gleam. War will make weapons of us all—yes, even little Noah, if you are not careful. You love who I was, but I am her no longer.”

Tears trailed down Lamech's face into the corners of his mouth. He was gasping for air, clutching the dagger so hard his knuckles ached. "Then who are you?"

"A ghost of your memory.”

"I love you," he whispered. "I miss you. And I love you."

"I love you too.”

Chapter 25

E lina woke to nearly inaudible footsteps and lifted her head to scan the wooded thicket for what caused the sound.

There, not five paces away, a dwarf deer stared through wedge-shaped pupils. The animal seemed statuesque until it flicked its ear and flared velvet nostrils.

Elina lay back, and the deer moved on, foraging, letting her drink the distant birdsong and countless leaves clashing like cymbals. In the glow of restfulness, she imagined the swirling colors, sounds, and smells as part of some great Music whose roots stretched down to the center of all things, to the Beginning. The thought put her in a mind to hold Jade, to look at her, to see the freshness of new life once more.

She turned to reach for her, but did not find her. Glancing around, she found the boy and the father were gone. The remnants of the previous night's fire had been extinguished, and the smell of burning wood lingered acrid and sharp.

Sudden, quick breaths scraped her throat. She pressed her lips to her teeth and hurled herself up, scaring the deer away. She forgot she'd harmed her leg, and as she stepped down, pain threw her to her knees and bade her clutch the skin above her ankle. She bit her lip and closed her eyes.

Recovering, she looked for her dagger, but that, too, was gone.

Of course, how could she have forgotten the way he wrenched it from her? She glared at the red marks still pressed into her flesh and clenched her hands into fists, coughing at the pricking sensation in her throat.

She would kill him. She would stalk him in the night and . . .

Sobs overwhelmed her. She gritted her teeth and screamed, striking the ground.

"What are you doing?"

The man's voice made her twist and nearly fall. He stood amidst green ferns with both babes in his arms. They were cooing happily, and the dagger hung from his belt. His expression was wary.

She hid her face and sniffed away the moisture.

"Did you hear me?" he said.

"Give me my child back." She was surprised to hear so much bitterness in her voice.

He paused a moment. "They were fussing. I walked the forest to keep them calm and let you sleep. I found berries, wild carrots, and asparagus." He pulled out a sack, untied it, and dumped its contents at her feet.

She motioned toward the baby, not taking her eyes from the food, or her mind from the ache in her stomach. "Give me my baby. Now."

He seemed to gauge her, then stepped forward and offered Jade. Elina cradled Jade while inspecting the berries and tasting a few. After days of bland food, they were painfully flavorful. The skin burst between her teeth, sending sour shocks across her tongue while the sweetness warmed her chest. She closed her eyes and ate several more, savoring the lingering buzz in her mouth.

The man paced, gently swaying Noah. He seemed offended by her harshness. But what had he expected, taking Jade from her like that?

He said, "Do you remember the destroyed village where I found you?"

"Where I found you," she corrected, and popped another berry in her mouth.

"Were you there when . . . ?"

"When what?"

"When it was attacked?"

"Of course not," she lied.

"Oh . . ."

An awkward pause ensued, but she avoided his gaze and kept eating. She tried the asparagus, which was woody and slightly bitter.

"We were lucky," he said.

She glanced up, went back to chewing.

"We won't always find so much food in the wilds," he said. "We can't expect to continue this way."

"Of course we can."

"We need supplies," he said. "Even water might become scarce if we continue. We should find a village and gather supplies first. We could use wineskins, a length of rope, a tarred leather cloak large enough to cover us in storms—"

"What's your name?" she said.

"What?"

"Your name. You never told me."

"Oh. Lamech."

"Lamech." She smiled. "You are a burden. Not my leader. I choose where I want to go. You may visit any village you'd like, but I will not stop to wait for you. You may go off to search the woods for food, but you will not take Jade from me. And you will give back what you stole."

His face tightened and his eyebrows crouched. "I stole nothing."

Elina's voice rose. "The dagger. It belongs to my family. I want it back. If you refuse, Noah will go hungry."

"You really think you could fight someone off with a ruined ankle and an infant?" He shook his head and returned to pacing to keep Noah satisfied. "Besides, if you don't feed Noah, I could just leave you as I found you." He motioned to the wood tool he crafted her.

She took a deep breath, another handful of berries, and tried to ignore him.

"There's a village close-by," he said. "I stumbled upon it yesterday."

"What's your point?" she said.

"Look—" He knelt, and she couldn't help glancing at her dagger in his belt. "You need help. Rest. You can't continue wounded as you are. You have no food left."

"How do you—"

"I checked your bag while you slept last night," he said.

"A thief and a spy. Perhaps I've misjudged you."

"You seem to be enjoying the food I brought." He picked up a dirt-encrusted wild carrot and tossed it toward her.

She tossed it back. "I could return what I've eaten." She stuck two fingers into the back of her mouth.

He laughed. "When I first saw you, I couldn't understand why you were alone." He paused. "Now I think I do."

"Mock all you wish," she said. "But stay out here long enough and you'll be the same."

"Why? What have you seen?"

She turned away.

"Why haven't you asked me of my past?" he said.

"Because I don't care," she said.

"I'm trying to help you."

"What if I don't want your help?" She was yelling now, and Jade fussed in response.

"You do."

She stared at him, wanting nothing more than to slap that smug, innocent expression off his face.

But he was right, and she hated him for it.

"I know the struggle this has caused you," he continued.

"You don't know anything."

"Maybe not. But I want to know. Not to disrespect you, of course—"

"You've already done that."

"Never my intention," he said.

"Then what was?"

"All my life, I thought I was comfortable with loneliness. But now . . ." He shook his head. "I keep dreaming of it. Of my wife's last moment. Over and over. It's terrible enough to be forced to relive the moment. Even worse to wake and find the nightmare holds true. I can't bear it any longer."

"I can't help you," she said.

He looked away, cheeks reddening. "I know."

"And you can't help me."

He shook his head.

She played with Jade's wisp-thin hair, black against brown. Noah was beginning to fuss as well, so she motioned for Lamech to give him to her. He obeyed, and returned to pacing as she fed him.

"Tomorrow, we should go to the village," he said. "I won't leave Noah, and despite my threats, I couldn't bring myself to leave you."

"It's not safe."

"Of course not," he said. "But neither is being out here. What would have happened to you yesterday if I hadn't—"

"Don't," she said, her voice harsh again.

He nodded. "We will have to lodge together."

"Never."

"In private, I will stay away from you, but they must think we are married so they will not try to use you." He flipped the dagger out of his tunic and offered it to her again. "If I don't honor you in every way, I won't stop you from retaliating."

She looked into his eyes, and though the unnamable terror remained at the edges of her awareness, suppressed just enough to keep hysteria at bay, the man's total and utter sincerity stabbed through it, more unnerving than anything else.

He offered her safety, but could it really be as he proposed? What motives lurked beneath the surface of his expression? He knew more than he let on, and manipulated people easier than most while feigning ignorance in a way that made her struggle to question his sincerity.

Of course, he was right. They could not stay out in the wilds without replenishing supplies. And she was injured.

But what would it cost her? What if she could not keep the madness suppressed? What would happen if they were confined

to a small room when it struck? Too close for him to get away?
To ensure Jade's safety?

He was still looking at her. Patient, immovable, and innocent
as a boulder.

"I'll decide tomorrow," she said, and hid the dagger in the
folds of her clothing.

Lamech nodded and left, he said, to gather materials to
make a fire and roast their vegetables.

Chapter 26

The night was a symphony of crackling flames and howling wolves. Two straight days of wakefulness had drained Lamech dry, and though every moment was a fight to clear his thoughts, he could not sleep for the wolves.

Beyond the wolves lurked the dreams. As long as he remained steadfast, the stars shone in their proper place above, predictable clusters of white around a moon sickle sharp.

Despite the heat of the flames, bursts of wind pierced his tunic like spears, and he could just begin to see his breath in the air. It was enough to shock him awake.

Elina had found little enough sleep waking through the night to feed and care for Noah and Jade. And though she would not look at him, he no longer seemed the target of her bitterness.

Despite Elina's periodic madness and paranoia, they had been forced together by forces beyond them. He couldn't help thinking of Father's words under the stunted tree in the mountains.

After their discussion earlier, she had eaten the roasted vegetables in comparative silence before retiring with Jade.

Lamech stretched his back and wondered how night had the power to darken the mind and strengthen desire. When the sun hung high, its light beat back the memories. But at night, with nothing to focus on but the movement of flames, the images of

Adah's last moments came back with near as much force as any nightmare.

He stood and began walking a circle around the fire. For what gain had the men attacked his home and destroyed his family? Could it be as the voice implied, and Adah feared?

Had her enemy finally found her?

He shook his head and released clenched fingers. Elina woke, sat up, and stared at him. He wiped cold sweat from his forehead, watched it glisten on his fingers, and continued walking, searching the shadows for movement.

Elina did not speak, but he knew what she was thinking. They needed the safety of a village more than either felt comfortable admitting.

The problem was that he didn't trust her. And she didn't trust him.

Regardless, they needed each other.

Elina said, "You will call me your sister when we go to the village."

Lamech rubbed his itching eyes. "It won't help."

"I don't care. It's what you'll say. Fight me and I may yet change my mind."

"I won't," he said, because he knew it wouldn't help. Sometimes, she reminded him very much of Adah. But he refused to think of her any longer.

"I'm thirsty," she said.

"There are a few berries left."

"No water?"

"None," he said.

"Then let me eat a bit and we can move before the sun rises."

Lamech nodded and offered to take both Noah and Jade so she could prepare herself for travel. To his surprise, she handed Jade to him with relief, and finished the berries before preparing the body wrap she carried Jade in.

Lamech passed Jade back to her, helped her adjust the wrap, offered her the walking stick, and helped her stand.

He led the way with Noah in his arms. It took several hours

at Elina's hobbling pace, but the walking stick worked surprisingly well.

Finally, they found the village, a small cluster of well-hidden buildings. No large roads led through it, but smoke rose from small chimneys, and women sat with children offering curious glances.

A few buildings had been built into the thick branches of gophar trees, and ladders hung low leading up into them. There was a blacksmith, an herbalist, foresters, carpenters, hunters, tanners, and potters bustling about from shop to shop and home to home. Toward the center, an inn of pitched wood and tarred thatch sat beside a small but busy marketplace with men and women yelling pricing for vegetables and wares.

"They've not found this place," she said.

"You mean . . . ?"

A nod. "The devils from beyond the mountains. They've laid waste to more communities than you could imagine."

"Why do they attack?" he said.

"I don't know if anyone knows. They're not like normal men. They drink blood like wine."

Lamech thought of the way the one had begged for mercy after dragging his tongue across Adah's cheek. He dug his nails into his palm. "You've seen them do this?"

Elina ignored him and motioned toward a woman standing in front of a pottery house. The woman's hands were caked with clay and stained with dye. She nodded a curt greeting.

"Excuse me," Elina said, and smiled. "Do you know of a place my brother and I could stay? We're journeying south and I hurt my ankle. We're in no rush, and can work for our keep."

The woman's eyes narrowed slightly after glancing at Noah and Jade. "We don't need any more refugees."

Lamech stepped forward. "I lived many years in the mountains. I have some skill as an herbalist and gatherer. I know the uses of plants many have not seen, and how to cultivate and cross them. Perhaps I could speak with the herbalist?"

The woman turned and sat at a potter's wheel, wetting her hands and coaxing a spinning hunk of clay. "We don't want your kind. Leave."

Elina approached, her voice quiet. "You deny shelter to infants?"

The woman ignored her, brought the clay walls up, then out.

Lamech grabbed Elina's arm, and she spun around, hand flashing toward the dagger until she noticed the look in his eyes. He let go. "Come," he whispered. "She doesn't want us, but others might."

They left the potter at her wheel and continued through the village. Lamech thought to go to the herbalist, for that was where his skill lay. Elina brought them instead to a hunters' lodge.

Skinned animals hung from hooks, and hides from racks. A young boy mopped blood, and two men stood over a table counting silver pieces and scratching marks on a stone.

Elina stepped toward the two men, who glanced at her, curious.

She withdrew her dagger, stabbed it into the table so that its ornate hilt stood upright, then removed a carbuncle ring from her right hand and dropped it on the table beside the dagger. The taller man inspected both and frowned.

"My brother and I need lodging," Elina said, her voice calm and direct. "The woman, a potter"—she pointed and the men looked, glanced at each other, back toward Elina—"denied us and our infants."

"Elina," Lamech said, but she held her hand up to silence him.

"Where can we stay?"

The hunters stared for a moment, and the boy stopped mopping. The taller man swept the silver coins into his hand and deposited them in a satchel at his waist. He motioned toward the boy, who bowed and escaped into a back room before the man leaned forward and spoke in a hesitant voice. "The inn is perfectly suitable for anyone. Just because a woman says you're not welcome doesn't mean anything. She's a simple woman, and she fears the Others. The devils with horns."

"How much does it cost to stay at the inn?" Elina said.

The taller man paled a bit. When he didn't answer, the other said, "Three bronze coins per day."

The taller man stuck his hand into his satchel and retrieved two silver coins. Elina stretched out her hand, and the man dropped the coins and returned to his work.

Elina said, "Thank you," retrieved her dagger, and replaced the ring on her right index finger. She turned and hobbled away, Lamech following.

Lamech's face tightened. "What did you just do?"

"No time for questions." She continued hobbling toward the inn.

"You knew those men," Lamech said, catching up with her.

"No. I didn't. Now keep your mouth sealed so we can get to our room without problem." She seemed nervous, so Lamech relented, and they entered the inn, which was warmed by a crackling hearth fire, and lit by many candles.

Men and women passed drinks and stories over low tables as Elina found the innkeeper, passed him a silver coin and said, "Three weeks for my brother and me." The man nodded, glanced at the infants and their crumpled clothing, and gestured toward a room down the hall on the left.

After they entered their room and shut the door, Elina lay on the bed and said, "Tomorrow, we talk. Right now, we rest." Lamech opened his mouth to protest, but Elina said, "Remember who holds the dagger."

Lamech sighed, found a space on the floor, laid down, and despite his curiosity, closed his eyes and finally slept.

This time, he did not dream of the stars.

Chapter 27

Elina woke to Lamech snoring. When at last he opened his eyes, it was nearly midday. She could see the slow machinations as he worked through yesterday's memories. He sat up and crossed his legs, expectant.

"I thought of not telling you," Elina said. "But after what you did . . . thank you."

He nodded.

She could not admit she needed him, however true. But if they stayed together long enough, he should know. It would be better that she told him and they parted ways now than in the wilds. Besides, there were others in a town such as this that she could enlist as companions.

So why stay?

Because this one is special.

Special?

I hate and fear him as other men, but there is something else.

You're lonely. Desperate. Eager.

I don't desire sex.

Then what?

"Elina?" he said.

"Yes," she said. "Just gathering my thoughts." She removed her carbuncle ring and handed it to him. "Notice the matching serpents. They are family heirlooms. The ring and dagger of my house."

"What do they mean?"

"That I am my father's daughter," she said.

He glanced at the ring. "What did your family do?"

She watched the rays of light enter the window and bleed across the floor. "They were hunters."

Lamech's eyebrows crouched. "In the hunters' lodge, the man who gave you two silver pieces looked fearful."

"As he should," Elina said.

"You said you did not know him."

"We did not hunt animals," she said.

"Then what did you hunt?"

"Men."

"Oh," he said.

The simplicity of his statement drove a cold laugh from her. "Yes, come to my father with a sizable enough gift, and we would pursue the mark until the end."

Lamech took this in, nodded, then brushed the dust from his tunic.

She stood and hobbled to the window to feel the warmth of the sun on her legs, but the light seemed sapped of substance. "Do you understand nothing? My family butchered people."

"Not just your family," Lamech said. "You mean yourself, don't you?"

Her breathing sped.

"I saw it in your eyes days ago. The same feeling I had when I killed your attacker."

"Then why did you trust me?"

"I didn't," he said.

She whipped around, eyes twitching. "Tell me why you stayed."

"You have no reason to be angry with me."

"I have every reason to be angry with you."

"Name one."

She eyed the serpent on the dagger's hilt. One to threaten, the other to strike. "Because," she said.

"Do you hate yourself?"

A deadly chill seeped into her fingers. Her vision narrowed and for all the fire that sparked in her words, her voice lay distant and cold. "I hate only the ones who . . ."

"Do you want to tell me what happened?"

She laughed, snatched back the ring and dagger, and held them aloft in the light. "Don't you get it? This is all that's left of the house of Zillah. This, and——" She motioned to Jade.

Lamech nodded. Frown deepening.

"Stop nodding," she said, but the room blurred and her throat ached. She looked away and wiped her face on her sleeve. When she looked up, his eyes were red and filled with tears. "Why are you crying?" she said.

"I'm sorry," he whispered as intimately as if he had kissed her.

She stood on her good leg, balancing one hand on the wall, clutching the dagger and ring in the other. "How could you be sorry? You don't know what it's like. I was happy, until they ruined it. A man like you could never understand what that was like."

Lamech stood, and for the first time since she attacked him, she saw anger in his eyes. "What do you know of me?"

She turned away. "It doesn't matter. I've told you what you wanted to know. Go figure out if this village has all the supplies we need, and let me rest."

He waited a moment, as if weighing whether to speak his mind. Of course, as before, he knew she was still hiding things. Then, with one last infuriating nod, he left.

As soon as the door closed, Elina collapsed and wept until her breaths failed and she choked. Jade and Noah's cries were little anchors for her soul. All she wanted was to drift beyond the horizon, into the darkness past which the sun only set. Instead, she wiped her eyes, caught her breath, and scooted toward them.

As she lifted Jade, her daughter looked up with eyes of gray so pure that they struck a furrow through her soul, and all her anger poured out. After Jade drank her fill, she tended Noah, whose little body was hardly half the size of Jade's.

Then she laid them beside her and stared out the window as they slept, thinking of Lamech's face glistening with tears.

Chapter 28

As demanded, Lamech left Elina and locked the door behind him. He pressed his back to the wall and listened to Elina weeping quietly. He wondered if he should stay to make sure she didn't hurt the children. But after Jade woke and cooed, Elina seemed to feed her and the cries slowly dissipated.

Lamech knew he would have to spend more time apart from Elina while she cared for Noah in the future, so he made up his mind to trust that the madness would not return. Risks were inherent, and he couldn't deny that she had cared for Noah. Indeed, if not for her, his child would have already died.

So he walked the halls, trying to keep from worrying about his son. He noted the thud of pewter goblets on oaken tables, the slow scrape of feet over dirt-encrusted floors, and the earthen smells of men and fire.

He was thankful his soiled garb matched the travelers at the inn, for it kept their eyes from roaming his appearance too frequently. But the heat of the hearth made the room stifling, so he made his way toward the exit.

He stepped outside and the air lightened. The sun hung roughly midway through its course, and most of the villagers worked carrying goods, hoeing gardens, slicing meat, bundling herbs and wheat. The kind of labor that leaves one exhausted and satisfied. He could see it in their faces. A sense of quiet purpose in simple lives. It was so quaint as to make the smell of his burning home a distant memory.

But he knew that what evil now swept the lands was a truth as undeniable as Adah's absence.

As he made his way toward the edge of town, he let his thoughts stumble toward Elina. She hadn't needed to tell him of her family history. So why had she?

In part, it seemed clear her admission had been designed to push him away, and when that failed she had lashed out—as cornered animals often did. But there was something else. Some lingering hope in her words, in the way she studied his reaction.

"I was happy, but they ruined it."

Maybe she was totally insane, but he thought it unlikely. There was too much life behind her eyes. Too much pain. Too much that he recognized in himself.

What would she do when he returned? Would she act as if they had never even spoken? He thought it likely, for she seemed ashamed of herself.

But Lamech understood now that the terror of loneliness was the truest of pains, and she was in the deepest throes of isolation. What else would have forced her to admit murder?

Of course, she hadn't told him everything. But he wondered if she would ever fully voice what harm she'd endured. He hoped she would. Because he would try to help her bear it. He would be there for her.

He would . . .

He stopped himself, feeling a sudden rush of warmth to his face. What was he thinking? Adah was gone, and their vows had been made in life for life, but even still, it seemed perverse to think of intimacy with another.

Even more, he wondered if he and Elina could ever be more than acquaintances.

Why not?

"Because," Elina had said. Because of the pain. Because of the impossible gulf between them. Because of shame and guilt and brokenness.

Why must he ever long for what could never be? For his mother, for Adah, and now for Elina's friendship.

The herbalist's home stood before him, and he realized he had been standing in front of it for several moments, drawing the attention of a girl holding a basket of flowers. She ducked inside as he glanced her way and followed after, pushing aside the heavy curtain guarding the entryway.

The air inside was pungent with crushed herbs. Several young men and women ground dried burdock, chicory root, and rosemary with mortar and pestle. Too absorbed in their work to worry about a traveler in soiled clothing. They paid him no heed as he explored the shop.

Braided garlic and clusters of medicinal flowers hung from racks. Strange smelling powders sat in clay jars arranged neatly on shelves against the walls. The floors were remarkably clean, seemingly swept daily to keep the molds away. And there were no windows. Nothing to let sunlight in. Even the doorway was protected with a long covering, and the only light came from seemingly hundreds of slouching candles placed haphazardly throughout the rooms. The shop spoke on a primal level, as if inviting him to a feast.

"Do you need help identifying what you need?" said a hoarse, female voice. He turned, saw an old crow of a woman leaning on a walking stick. Back bent, eyes bulging between snarled raven hair, nose and ears overgrown with age. A wry smile played at her lips, and her fingers moved deftly over the knots of her walking stick.

"No," Lamech said. "I was just admiring your shop."

"Admiring?" She laughed, though it turned to a wheezing cough. "In my eight hundred and fifty years, not a one has admired my shop. You want free gifts from Granny, eh? Thought to bribe me with flattery?"

Her age staggered him. If she spoke truth, the knowledge she could have of herbalism would be far beyond anything he had ever encountered. "I would like to work for you," he said. "Though I don't know how long I can stay before having to move on."

She turned those bulging eyes on him, and pressed her lips

together until her smile appeared no more than an extension of her wrinkles. She snatched a jar off the counter, thrust a hand inside, retrieved dark berries, and crushed them between her fingers. "Tell me," she said, wafting the scent toward him. "What are these, where do they grow, and what is their primary purpose?"

The astringent aroma of juniper leapt through him, conjuring images of dwarf shrubs clinging to hillsides, pale blue and silver green grown from bone branches. "They are juniper berries, and they grow where moisture is little and height is great. You ask of their primary purpose?"

Her bulging eyes widened as she bent toward him.

"They increase the expulsion of water," he finished.

"Urination," the woman corrected, and nodded with an appraising look. "What brings a mountain dweller here?"

"Knowing juniper doesn't mean I'm from the mountains. How do you—"

"Don't ask Granny questions. Just answer hers. And follow me while you're at it. You interrupted my preparation of extracts."

He followed her into a dark room more pungent than the last. The scents of sweetness and bitterness mixed to form a web riding his breaths in and out. The thought gave him the strange sensation that he was connected, somehow, to the countless visitors who had already walked through the dark hovel.

The woman crossed to a hand-crank press, where dripped a lemon-scented oil from green leaves. She continued her work, bottling the extract in a tiny clay jar that she sealed with wax. "So?" she croaked. "Answer my question."

"What brought me? Death, I suppose."

"Ah, Death. Our infernal enemy. Some say he is greater than the herbalist's craft, but they are wrong. He only continues because the Almighty has offered him power over man."

Lamech squinted at the strange reference.

"Yes," she continued, "we ourselves gave Death power over us when we chose to worship ourselves over the Almighty."

"Who is the Almighty?"

She turned those bulging eyes on him. "The Weaver of body

and spirit. The One who strung every vein through every leaf
we use to staunch the wound and heal the mind." She turned
back to the little vial she'd filled. "This is lemon balm, a green
herb that grows throughout our forest. It is used to calm the
spirit of those who endure much."

"I would buy it from you," Lamech said, "if I had money.
But I have none to spare."

"Yes, yes, you want to work for your goodies. And why not?
You know more than most, Granny can see. Oh, yes, she can
see. You've a talent for the craft, eh? Fancy yourself learned. But
you know little in comparison. I would teach you, yes. But for
how long? There is a darkness before and behind. You stand in
the midst of shadowy flames that burn and burn and burn. You
have come to the oasis to quench the heat only a moment. And
sooner than you think, you must return to the path you follow.
Whither it goes, no one knows."

He stepped back. "I did not come here for an oracle."

"I have seen you before. Yes, many times. Many times."

"I came for a job," he said. "If you will not give it, then I
would rather leave."

"Do you not long for answers? Is that not the deeper reason
why you came here? To find some way through the wilderness?"

Lamech's mouth dried, and he thought it might be
because the moisture in his body had been transferred to his
palms.

"The Weaver makes webs of dreams. Cold visions from
heights above. Many meanings deciphered by those who love
him."

"You speak in riddles."

"Not riddles. Poetry. We who love the Almighty love all that
is beautiful." She smirked. "Which excludes me, I know. I made
peace with that centuries ago. But the Almighty is beautiful
enough to cover my ugliness, for he has made all the world
beautiful in its time. Seasons come and seasons go, and the earth
he formed grows and withers and buds and blooms. I just
happen to be withering, though you hold one who buds." She
nodded at him, those bulging eyes seeming to bore into him,
understanding more than he felt comfortable allowing. "Yes,

these words speak to you, for your pursuer is not far, and he seeks to force you into isolation!"

"Someone follows me?"

"The Almighty knows all, but chooses a select few to enact his will. Sometimes," she narrowed her eyes, "they don't even know that they have been chosen." Her eyes widened, and she bent as if someone was whispering in her ear. When she spoke again, it was in a shaky whisper. "Dreams. He has given you dreams of a darkness coming to separate us from the constellations—to separate us from the promise of the Savior who would deliver us." She made a sign he assumed meant to ward off evil, and Lamech stepped back, feeling a prickling across his neck and shoulders.

She started rocking, expression strained, worried. "There is a heaviness borne on the shoulders of the little one. Until he is old enough to bear it, you must bear that heaviness for him. That is your purpose. The child, the boy, he will bring relief to us through the earth. He will quench the burning, burning, burning!" Her arms reached into the air, and the smoke from the candles seemed to curl around her outstretched fingers.

Lamech was shaking, attempting to form words.

"Go," she said, straightening. "Flee! They are coming! They have sensed us!" Now she screeched. "The devils! They're coming to stamp us out!"

She thrust him away, and he turned and stumbled out of the room, nearly knocking over the flower girl. "Sorry," he muttered, and exited the herbalist's shop to dash for the inn, wanting only to see Noah, get away from the herbalist, and hide himself from her piercing gaze.

From those terrible, knowing eyes.

Chapter 29

Elina rested her hand on the dagger as Lamech returned and locked the door behind him, his face covered in a sheen of sweat, gaze skittering around the room.

"What's wrong?" she said.

He ran his fingers through his hair. "Nothing, I—" He caught sight of Noah, crossed to him, kissed his forehead, and felt his little fists.

"Stop," she said. "You're making me anxious. Where have you been?"

"I was walking through the village," he said. "I visited the herbalist's shop."

"You don't need a job now that we have money." She held up the silver coin, more than enough to purchase the supplies they needed.

"I desired training, not money," he said. "It would be a waste to spend our money on what I can gather myself. I have skill as an herbalist, but I do not know the plants in this region as well as I'd like. I wanted to learn of their make and usage, and how to find them. The mushrooms worry me most. They can be deadly."

"Did you find the herbalist?"

"A crone. An old crone," he said, and readjusted Noah. "Tried to fill my head with nonsense."

His actions and words held a disturbing furtiveness. She gathered Jade in her arms and scooted against the wall, careful of her wounded ankle. "How about the market?"

"What?"

"Did you visit the market? Do they have what we need?"

"Oh," he said. "I forgot."

"We have no food."

"Right. I'll request some from the innkeeper." He left, and Elina stared at the knots in the wood until he returned with bread, sausage, and wine. They ate their fill, and Elina tossed the leftover sausage into her bag, leaning back to rest.

Lamech did not look at her, but seemed intent on the window, as if drawn to the light. Noah sat in his lap, and when the boy grew fussy, Lamech paced. "Do those shutters lock?"

"I believe so."

"Take Noah for a moment." He handed the boy to her. Juggling two infants still felt awkward, but she held him and watched as Lamech closed the shutters and tried the lock. They bent as he pressed his shoulder into them, and he frowned.

"They are built to withstand pressure from the outside, not the inside," she said.

"Could not someone work a hook underneath the shutters and pull them free while standing outside?"

"Why do you care?"

"I just want to keep us safe," he said. "I think I will go to the market before it grows dark. Maybe see if I can't haggle for supplies." He held out his hand for the silver coin, and Elina examined him, wondering whether she should offer the money. It felt risky, somehow.

He waved his hand, hurrying her along, and she knew she could wait no longer. She handed him a silver coin, and the brush of his fingers against hers made her stiffen.

She forced a smile and said, "Leave the door unlocked. I'd like to breathe the air outside."

Lamech shook his head. "I think you should rest." He grabbed her bag, and she thought she saw him toss something into the bag, though she assumed it was the coin. "The quicker you can recover, the quicker we can continue."

"The hearth, then, to warm me." She willed herself from staring at the bag—the bag that held her family's dagger—her only weapon.

He stared at her for several moments. "Rest would be best." He shut the door and locked it, taking the dagger with him.

Her hand still tingled where he'd touched her. She rubbed it, furrowed her brow, and looked down.

Her ring was gone.

Chapter 30

As Lamech leapt the final step of the inn to the packed earth beyond, the sun threw red overhead, and the wind carried the scent of blood and leather from nearby butchers. His body shook as the herbalist's words echoed through his mind.

How could he explain to Elina the old crone's mystic words and private meanings?

He didn't believe some transcendent force could have followed them, so the only reason he could think they might be in danger was that Elina had risked revealing her identity to extort money from the hunters. It had been dangerous, and though he hated the idea of deceiving her, he felt certain taking her ring and dagger was necessary.

Because if the hunters were why the crone claimed danger, they would likely need Elina's family seals to prove she had tried to steal from them. If they called the village guard to try to get their money back, they would find no proof that she had claimed to be anything but a mother with two infants.

But Lamech had more to worry about. At the least, they needed a leather satchel, a thin, tarred covering, enough food to last a week, water skins, a hatchet, flint, and two sets of heavier sandals before they fled. He found the marketplace soon enough, bought the necessary items, trading silver for copper for wood for goods, and returned heavy laden to find the window of their room open. He crossed to it, peered inside, found the room empty and the door open, and felt his pulse pound.

He had locked the door, hadn't he? Now the memory was clouded. But as he jumped through the window, he found the door had been forced.

His breaths came sharp and deep. He gazed at the surroundings for signs of footprints, struggle. There was nothing —nothing but the door.

It didn't make sense. If their room had been attacked, there must have been a struggle. But there was no evidence of one. In fact, it seemed nearly as if Elina had . . .

Of course! He pressed his palms into his eyes and sucked at the air. She was a man-hunter. The only reason he had been able to track her before was because she had wanted him to track her. If she truly had left, she would only want him to think she had been attacked to give her enough time to get away on her wounded ankle. And wherever she was, she had Noah.

He wanted to throw his new hatchet into the throat of that old crone who had made him paranoid. It was her fault that—

Wait. The old crone. If she really could see the future, perhaps she knew where Elina was.

He vaulted the windowsill and sprinted toward the herbalist's home, passing the potter who glared before returning to her work, and the empty hunters' lodge. The rest became a blur until he arrived and took the steps three per stride, bursting through the door to startled workers.

His chest heaved, and he swallowed and said, "The herbalist. Where is she?"

The teenager who'd brought flowers earlier pointed toward the back room and backed away, expression pallid. Lamech took a deep breath, laid his hands across his face, and tried to still the shaking.

The workers were staring, but he waved them away. "I'm fine. Thank you. You can go back to your duties. I just need to ask the herbalist something."

"She doesn't like being interrupted," the young girl said, tone suspicious.

"That's fine, I just need a moment." He left them for the darkened room of candle-flame and herb scents, but instead of finding the old woman bent over her work, he nearly stumbled into a cloaked man stooping over a crumpled heap on the floor. The man turned, and two eyes shone momentarily in the dark before the figure dashed past him out the doorway.

"Hey!" Lamech called. "Stop!" He tried to grab the man's cloak and just missed as the man sprinted past. The workers saw him as a shadow flitting like a bat out of the shop. They looked again at Lamech.

Lamech returned to the herbalist's room, adjusted the bag of supplies on his shoulder, took a candle from a stand, and lowered it to illuminate the shape on the floor.

Orange light flickered over short legs, a thick torso, then the bird-bright eyes of the herbalist.

They were open—and motionless.

He backed away and dropped the candle just as one of the male workers entered the room. The worker lowered a light and knelt beside the herbalist, touching her chest. He turned to Lamech with a red face. "Did you do this?"

"No," Lamech said. "It was . . ." He pointed at the exit, but the worker stood and clutched Lamech's wrist.

"It wasn't me. I—" But the man was not listening, and Lamech didn't have time. Each moment was another step away from Noah.

He snatched a jar within reach and smashed it over the worker's head. The man cried out and fell back, knocking down a stack of shelving.

Lamech leapt through the doorway and out of the shop, sprinting back toward the inn and pulling the hatchet from his bag.

He heard yelling back at the shop, but he was gone before anyone could think to follow. He tore through the village, passing huddles of merchants arguing over prices and stolen goods, and the rest of the homes and shops.

Upon returning to the inn, he entered the dank interior, spotted the innkeeper behind the small table beside the hearth, and grabbed his garment by the fist. "The woman I was with. Did you see her?"

"Of course," he said, stuttering, eyes flittering toward the hatchet.

"Where is she?"

"I make it my business not to ask travelers where they're going."

"What do you remember seeing?"

Sweat dripped into the innkeeper's eye and he blinked hard and shook his head. "I've been busy caring for guests. I saw her leave with her two infants, and one of the men from the village."

Lamech's grip tightened. "The boy is my son. Where was she going? Who was she with?"

"One of the hunters, but I swear, she didn't speak to me! I thought she was off to meet you."

Lamech thrust the innkeeper back, slipped the hatchet into his belt, and turned for the doorway just as two large men wearing leather protection entered, followed by one of the hunters, who pointed at Lamech. "That's him." The guards nodded and approached.

Lamech's stomach dropped as he realized Elina had not fled at all. She had been arrested. He threw a glance toward the windows but knew it was too late to run. He needed Noah, and he wouldn't get Noah back by attempting to flee. Lamech said, "What's going on?"

The first guard clapped Lamech's wrists and crossed them while the other tied them together.

"What have I done, that you bind me?"

"Quiet," said the darker of the two. "We'll see soon enough."

The hunter followed the guards who led Lamech outside. It only took a few moments for Lamech's eyes to register another set of guards holding Elina, whose wrists were bound. Jade and Noah were gone.

"Where are our children?" Lamech said, and began fighting the viselike hands on his shoulders.

"They are safe, for now," said the hunter, sneering.

"I demand to know what my family is being accused of," Lamech said.

"Don't, Lamech," Elina said, eyes warning.

The hunter laughed. "As if you don't know." He pointed. "The bag, check it and you will find the weapon, every bit of proof you need to know these are the ones."

One of the guards slipped Lamech's bag off his shoulder and began rummaging through it as Lamech's mind ran through the events of the past few minutes. The empty room, the cloaked man standing over the dead herbalist.

Sweat matted the hunter's hair and beaded across his skin.

Lamech said, "You're trying to accuse me of murdering the herbalist?"

The hunter's eyes flashed, and his smile widened. "I didn't say anything about the herbalist, so how would you—"

"Because I just found her dead in her shop at the feet of a man in a black cloak."

The hunter's smile dulled. "Convenient story. Might I ask what were you doing there?"

"Ask the workers," Lamech said. "They saw the man flee just after I entered the herbalist's room." Perhaps it had been his workmate. The hunters' lodge *had* been empty when he passed it to go to the herbalist's.

"Here it is," said the guard rummaging through Lamech's bag. He pulled his fist out of the bag and held up the dagger. "And the ring too."

"Give them here," said the largest man, who seemed to be a soldier, for he wore a sword at his side.

The guard offered the soldier the dagger and the jeweled ring, and the soldier held them up in the light, examining their make. "For once, Jamal," the soldier said, "you speak truth."

The hunter smiled and shook his head. "When have I ever done otherwise, Kellin?"

"Accusing innocents of murder is a serious crime," Kellin said. "One we hope no one ever commits in this village. I had every reason to doubt you, but this—I must admit, it is significant."

"And my money," Jamal said. "I want back the money they stole."

Kellin held up his hand. "I have not heard back from my guard on whether the woman is dead. Even if she is, his presence at the herbalist's home does not prove a crime. This knife bears no markings, no proof of being used."

"What does that matter?" Jamal asked. "It proves who they are. Would you trust known murderers over me?"

Kellin circled Lamech, examining his clothing. "No blood on his bag. No freshly splattered clothing. If he murdered the herbalist moments ago, he's the cleanest murderer I've encountered. And the infants bother me. What reasons could push a man and woman with young infants to murder an herbalist?"

"Clearly the infants are meant to conceal their motives in moments like these," Jamal said, and his expression darkened.

Another guard came running, out of breath. "It's true. The herbalist is dead. The workers found her just after this man here"—he indicated Lamech—"visited her in the back room. He fled moments after, and struck one of the workers unconscious."

"Hah! You see?" Jamal said.

Kellin addressed the newcomer. "Mahalel, how long ago did they say this man fled?"

"Only moments before I arrived at the herbalist's shop. He had only just made it out of sight, otherwise I would have pursued him."

Kellin stared at Mahalel. "Did you touch her body?"

"What?"

"Did you feel the dead woman's skin?"

"Well, yes. I had to make sure she had not merely fainted."

"And?"

"I am absolutely certain she was dead."

"How did you know?"

"She was cold!"

Kellin grew quiet and after a moment's thought said, "Mahalel," and pointed at the hunter.

Mahalel drew his eyebrows together and cocked his head. "You are sure?"

"No," Kellin said. "And that is precisely why we must."

Mahalel nodded and grabbed Jamal, twisting his wrists as a second guard approached with rope to bind him.

"Wait," Jamal said. "What are you doing?"

"None of this is to my liking," Kellin said, "but do you not think it strange that the herbalist's body was cold? This supposed murderer's garb and weapon are clean, and yet he only just visited the herbalist's home."

"He killed her hours ago!" Jamal said, his face reddening.

"The workers only just found her body moments ago. You knew of the murder earlier," Kellin continued. "Why? What reason did you have to be at the herbalist's home?"

Lamech recalled the image of the man in black and realized he had not seen a weapon. Perhaps the man had killed her at some more convenient time and dragged her body through a back entrance to where it might have been found at the opportune time. But whoever had done it had lingered too long, and Lamech had found him.

"I can't believe you'd trust assassins over me!"

"I don't," Kellin said. "But I will find out who is responsible —of that you can be certain. I may have been sent only a few months ago to help protect this village from the expansion of the war, but I have not spent my days with eyes closed and ears stopped."

Jamal's face seemed ready to melt, or tear.

Piercing screams echoed across the village, reverberating off the mud-brick buildings, whipping everyone's heads. People yelled, and iron clanged against iron.

"What is it now?" Kellin said, but as the words leapt from his mouth, a woman screamed, "The devils! They've come for us!"

All the color drained from Kellin's face, and his mouth twitched. He tossed Elina's ring and dagger and said, "Forget the prisoners. We fight or die. Mahalel, gather everyone you can find capable of holding a weapon and join me. Enosh, make sure the innocents are barricaded in the safest of places. Go!"

The guards scattered, and as Elina's support disappeared and she was forced to put weight on her wounded ankle, she crumpled to the ground. Jamal's eyes locked on Elina, and as the guards disappeared, Jamal made for her. Lamech loped after, attempting to stop him, but Jamal reached Elina first.

Lamech nearly cried out to warn her, but like a bolt of lightning, Elina twisted around and thrust her good heel into Jamal's nose. Before Lamech fully realized what was happening, Jamal clutched at his face with bound hands. Elina delivered a final blow into the center of his chest, and he crumpled in an unconscious heap, blood trickling from his nostrils.

It took a moment for Lamech's shock to wane as Elina grabbed her knife from the ground and awkwardly sawed off her bindings.

Then he remembered. "Noah and Jade. Where are they?"

"The potter is caring for them." Elina's voice was cold and precise, and Lamech was happier than ever to know they fought for the same goal. She motioned for him to lower his hands, and she cut his bindings. "If we don't go soon, they'll likely barricade themselves beyond our reach. I can't believe the devils are actually here."

Lamech grabbed his bag, swung it around his neck, and draped one of Elina's arms around his shoulders. He felt a sickening weight in his gut at the thought that the herbalist's oracle had been true, that she had died as a result of her own vision.

Is that why she had been so afraid? Had she known she would die?

"Is your walking stick there?"

"No," Elina said.

"We'll find something for you."

"Is that why you stole my ring?"

He nodded.

She did not respond, but he knew by the temperature of her silence that she understood and appreciated what he had done.

In that moment, he determined never to tell her about his dreams, or the potential prophecy that hung over Noah. He could not admit that staying with Elina could endanger her. And yet, if what he'd been told about Noah was true, it very likely would.

From behind came startled yells and the sickening sounds of

battle. Even still, as they made their way to the potter's house, Lamech couldn't stop himself from thinking of Elina's arm draped over his shoulder, and her slender hands, strong when pressed, yet in appearance, so lovely.

Excitement stabbed his chest, but when he saw her unyielding expression, the excitement gave way to shame. How could he think of such things when Noah lay in the arms of another?

My boy. I'm coming for you!

Rounding a corner, they saw the open doorway of the potter's home, but as they entered, it was silent. They checked every room, but the home was empty.

Panic struck as they exited and checked the next home, finding that empty too.

The guards had done their job, and the women and children had responded faster than Lamech thought possible. Then again, these people had lived on the edge of fear, even receiving soldiers to help prepare for war.

As Lamech helped Elina hobble to the third home, the potter peered out from behind a slatted window and motioned them inside.

"Quick, you fools!" she said.

A door opened and Lamech helped Elina inside.

The potter closed the slats over the window and shut the door behind them, blocking most of the daylight. Lamech noticed myriad shapes moving through the shadows. A huddle of woman gathered, their bodies blocking the light from candles around the room. A few children stared wide-eyed at the strangers, and as his eyes adjusted, he saw the potter approach, holding Jade.

She offered the girl to Lamech, but he shook his head and said, "Jade is Elina's daughter. Please, where is my son? Where is Noah?"

"Noah? A strange name for times such as these," the potter said, her eyes every bit as shrewd as they had been when they first met. "It means 'relief from the struggle,' yes?"

Lamech nodded.

"My cousin is feeding him in the other room," she said.

Lamech closed his eyes and felt relief flood his throat. "Thank you," he said. "And thank her too."

"As soon as she is done feeding the boy, you will leave," the potter said. "Immediately. I do not care where you go, or whether you are wounded." She glared at Elina. "I knew when you first came that you would bring the Others upon us."

Lamech thought of the dreams and the herbalist's prophetic words. "We will go. We never intended harm. But for our children, we would stay and fight with you."

The potter nodded, though her expression remained hard. "But you are not childless."

"No," Elina said. "We are not."

Elina reached for Jade with her free arm, and the potter passed her. She sat on Elina's forearm and clung to her neck with red, puffy eyes.

Lamech wrung his hands, trying to keep from entering the next room to snatch Noah and hold him close. It didn't matter if she had treated him with more tenderness than he had yet been shown. All he could think of was his son in the hands of a stranger, and he vowed to never let it happen again.

Even as he knew he ever failed to keep his vows.

Chapter 31

The God-King bent forward on hands and knees just outside the village Noah and Lamech had stayed in, his mind split between waking reality and the ever-flowing Waters of Time. He could sense Noah in that spiritual plane, a massive weight lifting the Waters like a fallen moon.

As his soldiers entered the village, the pressure lessened. He closed his eyes, wiped away the half-images, and sighed. The family was fleeing, just as he needed them to.

As soon as he felt the boy's father connect with that old herbalist, the strands of the Light Bringer's glorious future immediately had begun to unravel.

How could he have known the woman was a follower of the Old Way?

Now he would need to double his search for the faithful, because if any of them were allowed too much time with the boy, everything would collapse. He would kill them all. He would slaughter them and drip their blood upon the walls of every home.

But for the time being, his plan had succeeded. All that was left was to keep the strange little family moving. Keep the fear of death always in their minds, so that they would never become moored in true community.

The roots of bitterness would grow strong in Noah. The

God-King would force the boy into isolation. He would destroy every one of his relationships. He would tear Noah down until there was nothing left.

And then, at the end of all things, he would strike.

"I will not fail you, Father," the God-King said. "I will not fail."

Chapter 32

With one arm still draped around Lamech, Elina held Jade close in the darkened room filled with the scent of dusty bodies and molded thatch. She drank the warmth of her daughter's clammy fingers against her neck and thought back to before Jade was born.

After failing to terminate the child her own brother had forced to grow within her, she had murdered him and the rest of the men who'd stood complicit.

As she watched her belly grow, she had thought only of the destruction of her body and the prison-like weight her child would be.

But the moment Jade erupted from her covered in blood and screaming for comfort, her dread of life had been replaced by something else. Something dense and transcendent.

What a mystery that to care for her own flesh, it need first be taken out from her.

Now Jade was a mighty weight indeed. No longer a prison chain, but rather an anchor.

Hold me down, she thought. *Hold fast, and never let go.*

At length, the woman caring for Noah entered and offered the boy to his father, but Lamech shook his head and said, "I want nothing more than to hold my child. But Elina needs help to bear her weight. Her ankle is still injured."

The potter nodded, disappeared into the next room, and to Elina's surprise, returned with the very tool Lamech had crafted for her. Elina let go of Lamech and leaned on the crutch, letting Lamech tie the wrap around her torso and slide Jade inside. Finally, he took hold of Noah, and his body relaxed. "Thank you," Lamech said, and the woman bowed.

After an awkward silence, Lamech turned to leave, and Elina followed.

After exiting, they turned south and made their way out of the village as quickly as Elina's pace allowed. They went deeper through the forest, where trees and dense brush blocked the sounds of battle in the village. Darkness settled and they traveled on. Their bodies ached with exhaustion, but they both knew that to stop would have fatal consequences.

Finally, the sun rose on the next day, and they hobbled on. Their pace was much slower, and they broke for Elina to feed the children and eat and drink. They exited the woods, climbed hills, traversed valleys, and plowed their way through long grasses in myriad prairies.

Night fell a second time, and they settled next to each other in the dark, too afraid to light a fire in the open yet too exhausted to continue.

Elina felt no more fear of Lamech, and no longer begrudged his touch. They warmed each other, for the night was deadly cold, and they held their children close. As the night rolled on, she listened to him cry, and joined him.

Elina knew Jade's life would be bettered by the company of this man and his son. Though the pain of her past still held her enthralled, in what little way she could, she'd grown to love Lamech and Noah, and to think of the four of them as a strange sort of family.

Lamech seemed to feel the same, for when Jade cried in the night, he picked her up and rocked her, hushing her and whispering tenderly about how loved and safe she was.

Weeks passed into months as they traveled, scavenging food and continuing south. Fall blended into winter, and winter into spring.

Jade and Noah grew larger, stronger. They babbled, and

eventually began speaking. Travel became difficult as the two grew heavier. But Lamech and Elina managed as best they could.

At times, they were forced to pass through villages and barter for goods by offering labor or what little materials they could scavenge.

Lamech gathered herbs as he found them. These he tied and hung from his shoulder to dry as they moved. When they entered towns, he would sell the most valuable for simpler necessities.

Sometimes, Lamech would work an entire day for food or supplies. A few times, the children became ill, and passed their sickness to Lamech and Elina. But never again did they spend a night in a village, for everywhere they went came rumors of horrific violence. Ever they seemed only just in front of the tide of war, and so they continued.

Elina still, at times, felt an aversion toward Lamech's presence, but believed now that fate had bound them together. They agreed that to brave the world without the other would likely mean death for their children, and so they cleaved to one other, for they trusted no one else.

As Noah grew older, he started asking questions that made Lamech uncomfortable. "Why do we always have to be moving? Why can't we live in homes like everyone else?"

Lamech and Elina explained how the world was filled with evil, and that they needed to live separate from the Others so that they could be different, so that they could be good. People in villages were not safe because the Others knew where to find them. And when the Others found you, they took everything.

As the years rolled by, their needs grew. Elina and Lamech talked often of finding some place to settle, but the farther they traveled, the more villages they found, so they never felt comfortable.

But as Noah neared the end of his first decade of life, they ventured into a land completely untouched by humans, and settled in a quiet valley using stolen and bartered goods. Lamech built a shelter and a garden, and they lived there for some time.

It was a quiet, patient life, filled with the longing for former years, and an anxiety for the morrow.

In all those long years, no dreams came to Lamech, but every so often, as he hovered between sleep and wakefulness, he would think he saw eyes glinting in the night, and feel a stab of fear. Each time he opened his eyes, he found his fears unfounded.

Each time but for one.

PART IV

The Father and the Son

"Jesus, when he began his ministry, was about thirty years of age, being the son (as was supposed) of Joseph, the son of Heli . . . the son of Noah, the son of Lamech, the son of Methuselah, the son of Enoch . . . the son of Seth, the son of Adam, the son of God."
—Luke 3:23, 36–38

Chapter 33

The day before their home was discovered, Lamech stood beneath the thatched awning watching Noah and Jade chase each other around the outskirts of their garden.

Noah was trying to catch her, but Jade was a head taller, and quicker. When Noah perceived that his pursuit was hopeless, he slowed to a stop.

Jade glanced back and said, "You're quitting again?"

Noah scowled. "Say anything and you won't walk another day."

Jade laughed and propped her hands on her hips. "If only you could catch me. Why don't you go sit on a log until you grow roots? At least then you could run a little faster."

"That's it!" Noah picked up a stone and dashed after her.

She ran, laughing harder. As Noah tossed the stone, she dove and screamed, "Help! Noah's trying to kill me again!"

Elina appeared beside Lamech and leaned against one of the pillars that held their home aloft. "How long before Noah grows clever enough to avoid her prodding?"

"A man's pride is hard to let go of," Lamech said.

Jade was rolling on the ground, laughing while Noah walked toward the line of trees.

"He always quits when he doesn't get his way," Elina said.

"He is twelve years old. He should have grown out of that by now."

"But he always tries again," Lamech said. "He's tenacious."

"Stubborn, more like it," Elina said. "Sometimes I think you two couldn't be more different."

Lamech shrugged. "He takes after his mother."

Jade jogged toward them. "Mother, did you see that? He tried to kill me while you just stood there."

Elina swatted Jade on the shoulder and said, "There's nothing funny about death."

"I'm not joking. If he ever caught me?" She feigned choking herself and glanced at Lamech. "Why is Noah always so angry?"

"Of all people to ask that question," Elina said, and shook her head. "Stop teasing him."

Jade sighed. "He's such a bore. All he wants to do is talk about plants and making things."

Lamech smirked. "And all you want to do is talk about how superior you are."

Jade propped her fists on her hips and widened her stance, smiling. "Not my fault he can't accept the truth."

Elina pressed her palms against Jade's cheeks. "Go entertain yourself. And please, whatever you do, stop bothering him."

"Fine," Jade said, and ran off, picking up a stick and whacking everything within reach.

"I need to check on the vegetables," Lamech said. "I thought I saw some molehills yesterday."

Elina nodded as Lamech strolled into the sunlight toward the eastern end of the garden. All about them lay the quiet of the forest they called home. The wind in the leaves sounded a million whispers, and birds and little animals hopped from branch to branch. Amidst these noises lay nothing but the tranquility he had known and loved in the mountains.

Before his high home had been burned, he'd gone to the mountain pass nearly every day to look out on the world and conjure some sense of permanency. In those moments, he could convince himself that the world was sublime. Now, in this copse, he frequently sensed the same.

As he approached the root vegetables, he clucked his tongue as he found some of his crop raided by the vile creatures. He returned to the fire, fetched live coals on the flat of a hoe, and dumped them into the holes, surveying the rest of the garden on his way.

Some of the seeds had sprouted. Beans, radishes, and carrots. Others still slept beneath little mounds. He loosened the topsoil, watered his future harvest, and returned to Elina in the shade of their shelter.

The weather this far south was warmer than that atop the mountain, and the growing season twice as long. The only disadvantage was the summer heat. But for the stream a moment's walk from their shelter, the sun would have been all but impossible to keep up with. As it was, they had kept their vegetables from burning, and eaten enough to survive. Still, subsistence had hardened the skin of his hands.

Elina was mending clothing, and Lamech approached and tapped her shoulder.

"Yes?" she said.

"How long has it been?"

"You asked me that a week ago."

"Then tell me again." He leaned against the wall.

"It will be six years this summer since we saw another person."

Six years. It felt like yesterday . . . and also like a lifetime. Strange how time could become so distorted in one's mind. He knew that one could have solitude yet not feel lonely, and also feel lonely while surrounded by others. He and Elina could tolerate both. It was the children he feared for.

"Stop worrying," Elina said.

"I'm not worrying," Lamech said.

"You're staring at the wall as if it were a dead animal."

Lamech sniffed and breathed deeply. In the many years since Noah was born, Lamech had shifted from worrying about the danger Elina posed to the danger others posed. He had set off Elina's madness only one other time when he woke in the middle of the night and accidentally kicked her as he padded around trying to look for Noah.

After she recovered, he said, "What do you experience when that madness sets in?"

"The memories," she said. "Of how they touched me."

Those few words had been the final nudge he needed to do away with his worry that Elina might harm them. However, in its absence, a void seemed to erupt, and worries he'd never contemplated seemed to pool there and fester.

He wanted to find Noah, to see what he was doing since Jade angered him.

He left Elina to her work, and it didn't take long, for Noah hadn't gone deep into the woods. The boy was breaking branches and stripping them of bark while huddled over a little shape he'd formed from a round stone and sticks. It seemed he was making a doll, binding the limbs to the body and forming clothing with the bark.

Lamech pulled back before Noah saw, and returned home. Since a young boy, Noah had been a gifted creative. He could draw anyone's likeness in the dust with a stick. He could tell enthralling stories that stole your breath. No matter his vision, he could bring his ideas to reality in more ways than one.

Lamech was proud of him. But Noah's temperament troubled him. Something burned behind the boy's eyes. At times, when Lamech gazed into them, he thought he caught sight of Adah's blood-dappled reflection, and the flames that had consumed their home all those years ago.

But that could only be his imagination, for Noah knew nothing of Adah or their past. Lamech had been unwilling to speak of their loss for he knew all too well the pain and damage of losing his mother. He preferred to keep the past where it belonged, lest the truth wound Noah similarly.

He had hoped it would be enough for Noah to be near Elina and Jade, but Noah connected deeply with neither. They cared for one another, of course, but the connection built on blood possessed an intimacy Elina and Jade could never match. They did not understand Noah as Lamech did, and always Noah seemed in search of what they could not provide.

So Noah grew angry and pulled away to tinker with sticks and stones, or to draw in the dust. Jade mocked him to hide that she resented he chose sticks and stones over her. Elina maintained her distance, and Lamech turned his focus toward keeping them safe and fed.

Just like his father in the mountains. Was he cursing his own child to the same fate that had embittered him toward Methuselah?

When Lamech returned to their shelter, the sun was dipping, and he barely had time to rebuild the fire before retiring. Noah returned as late as he dared, and hid the mannequin beneath his bedding. Jade was already asleep, and Elina rested upright in the corner.

Lamech lay, but as sleep approached, the back of his neck tingled, and he fought the urge to check if something was watching them. It had been long since he'd feared they would be found in the wilderness. They had labored to find the perfect spot, secluded yet surrounded by rich vegetation and wildlife. A place they could live undiscovered while the fires of war swept the lands.

He turned onto his belly and tried to ignore the sensation, but the tension only built. He sighed, turned onto his back, and looked up, catching two gray orbs glittering just outside the ring of orange firelight.

Ice water flooded his wrists as he yelled, gripped the unburnt end of a log in the fire, and tossed it toward the glittering orbs, sending sparks hissing.

The orbs disappeared, and there came a grunt, and the sound of a body tumbling through the darkness, proving itself more than ghostly vision.

Jade awoke, and Noah twisted and said, "Who's there?"

Elina was already on her feet, unsheathing her dagger as Lamech found the figure, clutched its cloak, and pulled it into the light so he could see its face.

Lamech's jaw dropped, and he let go, rubbing his face to make sure he wasn't dreaming. "What?"

The old man before him nodded with gray brows bunched with worry at the dagger in Elina's hand. "Yes. You know me." The voice was the very same Lamech had known his entire life, even as he knew it could not be.

"Lamech," Elina said. "Who is this? Shall I cut him?"

Lamech raised his hand. "Wait." To the old man, he said, "Am I dreaming?"

"No, you are not dreaming. Feel me." He held out his arm, and Lamech clutched it and felt his breath thicken. There could be no mistaking it.

His father had found them.

But how? How could Methuselah be here, countless leagues from where they last saw each other? And in the middle of the wilderness untouched by human feet? It made no sense.

Lamech wiped blurry eyes, struggling to choose what order in which to ask all the questions that dashed through his mind. "All this time, I thought you were dead. They burned our home. How did you survive? And how—"

Methuselah raised his hand to silence him. "As you can see, I am not dead, and so you have no reason to be upset. I did not come only to disappear and leave your questions unanswered. There will be time enough for conversation in the days ahead. But I am old, curse it, and weary, not to mention parched from an arduous journey. Also, you singed my cloak when you tossed that log at me." He grabbed the burnt fibers and scowled, sucking his teeth.

"I—certainly, I'm sorry," Lamech said. "Elina, could you fetch my father some water?"

Elina sheathed her dagger reluctantly and did as she was told, though not before eyeing Methuselah with supreme distrust.

Methuselah returned her stare and, once she was gone, mumbled, "You have some taste in women, son."

"After you drink," Lamech said, "you must explain how you found us."

"All in time," Methuselah said, but his gaze now landed on Noah, who was staring at him. Jade kept glancing between Noah and Methuselah, as if wondering if they truly were kin. Lamech couldn't fault her. Methuselah's beard and hair were extremely long, heavily matted, and stained with all manner of refuse. Lamech would be surprised if his father had bathed in the last decade.

Methuselah nodded at Noah. "This is your son, Noah?"

"Yes," Lamech said.

"I don't know you," Noah said. "Who are you and how do you know me?"

Methuselah chuckled, a popping wheeze. Elina returned with a wineskin and handed it to him. "I'm your father's father," Methuselah said. "And I was present when you were born. Well, almost." He tipped the wineskin and drank his fill, then wiped his mouth and tried to return it to Elina, but she had already resumed her spot behind Lamech. Methuselah shrugged and set the wineskin on the ground before sitting cross-legged and extending his hands toward the fire.

Lamech hoped his father would say nothing of Adah. Noah had been interested in hearing about his mother for years, and Lamech suddenly realized the danger in Methuselah spending too much time in his son's presence before he and Lamech conversed in private.

Thankfully, no one said anything, though Noah now observed Methuselah with near manic intensity. Methuselah rubbed his face, yawned, and lay on the hard ground with his eyes closed.

Lamech cleared his throat. "Father?"

"I changed my mind," Methuselah said. "We'll talk tomorrow."

Noah chewed his cheek and examined Methuselah as if searching for bits of information to extract from his wizened features. Elina stayed sitting and seemed calm enough, but Lamech did not miss the glint of the bejeweled dagger between her fingers.

Lamech motioned for Elina to follow him, and they walked outside the light of the fire—just far enough so that the children could not hear them speak.

Elina kept her eyes trained on Methuselah and whispered, "We can't let him stay here."

Lamech balked. "And how do you propose we get rid of him?"

"You know how."

Lamech's voice deepened to a near growl. "He is my father, Elina."

"What does that change?"

"Everything."

"It doesn't change that his being here is proof that we are in serious danger," Elina said. "That we were never as safe as we thought. And you're hiding something from me, aren't you?"

Lamech ran fingers through his beard, but couldn't deny it.

"No one was supposed to be able to find us," Elina said. "I don't care who he is. I don't trust him. And now I don't even know if I trust you!"

"I don't know what's going on any more than you do," Lamech said.

Elina studied him carefully. "If that's true, just ask yourself, is there too much purpose for this to have happened by chance?"

"It worries me too. But he said he would explain himself. We must give him the chance to do so."

"And yet he refuses to speak," Elina said, and her grip tightened on the dagger.

"Don't be unreasonable. He will tell us in time."

"And if he refuses?"

Lamech paused. "We will discuss options if the circumstances arise."

"This doesn't feel right."

"Am I supposed to trust your feelings over my own?"

"If I made a habit of disregarding my sense of danger, you and Noah would have been dead long ago."

"What are you implying?"

"You think you're the only one who's protected us? That I do nothing when I sneak off in the evenings?" She spit on the ground and smeared it with her toe. "That old man knows something we don't. I don't like being exposed, Lamech. I've fought all these years to stay to the shadows, and yet that man, merely by showing up here, has made a fool of us both."

"Yet I'm the only one blinded by emotion?"

"Don't be a fool." She grabbed the chest of his robe in her

fist and pulled him close. "If he doesn't explain himself tomorrow morning, he will be dead before the sun sets."

Lamech pried her fingers away and said, "How would his death help us? He is my father, and he has no reason to harm us. If he has been sent by others, how does that change whatever danger we might be in? Furthermore, why would anyone send my father here? They would know we would become suspicious, so how could it help them?"

"I don't know," Elina said, her voice overloud. She paused, realizing the children might have heard, then continued in a whisper, "Whatever is happening, it isn't good."

"Let's hope you are wrong," Lamech said. "But for now, you will trust me, and say no more. Just let me handle it." He made his way back to the fire and lay down, trying to quell the sensation that the world was spinning. After a while, Elina returned, and Noah lay down as well.

Then Methuselah began snoring, and Lamech was fairly certain the only one who slept through the night was his father.

Chapter 34

Noah woke the next morning to the red light of sunrise striking his forehead. His first thought was of the strange man he'd dreamed visited them in the middle of the night. The second was of the mannequin he'd stuffed beneath his covers.

He pulled out the mannequin, thinking it looked like the man in his dream. The others were already gone, so he stuffed the mannequin under his covers, and rose to wash his face in the cold stream behind their home.

As he turned the corner, he saw the man from his dreams talking with Father in hushed tones, and his veins filled with enough chill water to wake himself a thousand mornings to come.

The old man nodded toward him, his ancient face crinkling into either a grimace or a smile. He couldn't tell which, for matted facial and head hair obscured everything but his eyes and the bridge of his nose. Noah nodded politely, turned, and called, "Jade?"

"Jade went with Elina to gather firewood," Lamech said. "She'll be back soon."

Noah nodded again, noticed how the old man watched him. "What are you looking at?" Noah said, and the old man shook his head.

Noah left and returned to sit on his bedding, pulling out his mannequin a second time, though it failed to keep his mind from the newcomer.

Could it be true? Was that old man really his grandfather? He wiped his eyes to relieve them of the strange pressure building behind them.

The old man and Father were talking as if they had known each other for years. Perhaps it was true, and he hadn't dreamed his coming the night before. Only it seemed so strange. Father had been convinced no one would ever find them. That was why they lived so deep in the wilderness, and daily struggled to live.

"Because the world is burning," Noah intoned. "And the thoughts of men are only evil continually." That was why he and Jade had to live here. So that they could be different. Because the Others were evil, but they needed to be good.

Only he had never felt evil, so how much danger could there really be in living near the Others? He would never let them change him. How could they? He didn't believe it possible, and neither did Jade. It was one of the few topics that both consistently desired to talk about, so they fell to discussing it frequently. As of yet, he and Jade had been given little choice to see any Others to judge for themselves what danger might lurk in their hearts.

Now one of the Others had found them. It didn't matter if he was Noah's grandfather. The man's physical exterior was as vulgar as Noah could imagine, so if this man wasn't evil, who was?

No matter what happened, Noah knew he had to get the old man alone. He chewed his bottom lip, walked the little mannequin back and forth, and said, "Do you have a heart of flesh or stone?" He pulled back a bit of the bark, clicked his fingernail on the stone, and smirked before shoving it back under his covers.

Chapter 35

Lamech stood by the stream with Methuselah. After Noah stumbled upon them looking for Jade, Lamech felt his shoulders tense and took care to make sure Noah walked far enough away before continuing in a low voice. "Just don't speak about anything having to do with Adah."

Methuselah eyed him cautiously. "You still haven't forgiven me, have you?"

"Don't be a fool, Father. This has nothing to do with you."

"Doesn't it?"

Lamech shook his head.

"You've done the boy wrong if you've withheld knowledge of her for all these years."

"You will not come here and tell me how to raise my son," Lamech said. "Where have you been all these years?"

"I didn't explain myself last night because I knew you wouldn't sleep once I told you."

"I didn't sleep anyway," Lamech said.

"You really are paranoid, aren't you?"

"And your snores shake the earth."

Methuselah laughed. "Just wait until you've lived another century. Sleep doesn't get any easier. You just learn to let go a bit better."

"How did you find us?"

The glitter in Methuselah's eyes dimmed, then became shaky wetness. "It's not a happy story. When the devils burned our home, they took me alive, bound my hands and legs, and threw me in a bamboo box on a wagon. We drove for what seemed weeks, and finally arrived at a city I'd never seen, where they threw me in a pitch-black dungeon beneath a hideous tower. There they shackled me to the wall with black iron."

"How long were you held captive?"

"They said I had been in there ten years, though it felt like a lifetime. I can't begin to explain the madness of the endless dark. A few days and your thoughts simply end. A few years?" He shook his head.

Lamech stared at his father, letting the meaning of his words take root. "How did you escape?"

"They let me go."

"What?"

Methuselah's gray eyes flashed as he poked Lamech with a meaty finger. "And all so that I would come live with you and that boy you've been neglecting."

Lamech blinked, thinking of the dreams from so long ago, of Adah's fear of being found. He wondered at the little she'd told him and desperately wished he had asked her more, because all she'd said was that she had been held captive and beaten.

Had Methuselah been taken to the same city where Adah had been imprisoned? Maybe even held in the same dungeon? It seemed too strange to be unconnected, for both had found freedom, and if what Methuselah said was true . . .

"Why would they want you to come to me?" Lamech said.

"Everything those creatures do is backward. They capture women, strip them, and throw them in dungeons, but not for the reasons you might think. They do not marry. Instead, they force normal men to impregnate them. Then the God-King touches them. He does something to the women's wombs, and at birth, they take the children from their mothers, but they are not normal children. The babies have horns and are inhabited not by human spirits but by the spirits of devils. And the women who are unfit for bearing children are bled so that the devils can drink their life like wine." Methuselah grimaced and swallowed hard, wiping his watering eyes.

"But you're a man, not a woman."

"I think I was the only man in the entire dungeon."

Lamech ran his hands through his hair and paced to quiet the anxiety rising through his limbs. "Why did you come here? Were you followed?"

"I didn't bring them to you."

"How do you know that?"

"Because they brought me to you."

Lamech's anxiety climaxed, and his vision dimmed. "What are you saying?"

"When they brought me out of the dungeon, I was given a week for my eyes to adjust to the light. In all that time, they treated me with as much kindness as we would treat a king visiting from another land. When I finally received an audience with their leader—he calls himself the God-King—he told me exactly where to find you, and fitted me with supplies before bidding me luck on my travels."

"That was it?"

"That was it."

Lamech pulled at his hair and the skin of his throat. Father was right. It didn't make any sense. "You're sure the ones who captured you are the ones who released you?"

"The horns are difficult to miss."

Lamech swallowed and nodded. "That they are."

"You must believe me. I had to come, if only to know that . . ." Tears welled in his gray eyes. "To know that you and my grandchild were still alive. What do I have left but you and that boy?"

Lamech set his hands on his hips and kicked at the dirt.

"Think on it, son. If they really knew where you were living, what danger could I bring by coming to you? And if they lied to me for sport, what could I lose by playing the fool? I lived ten years in absolute darkness. The bitter weather, the difficulties I faced on my travels, they returned life to a dead man. For once, I was free, and maybe, just maybe, so were you." Methuselah threw his arms around him and wept into his shoulder, and Lamech broke. "I hoped you'd stayed safe, and you have."

He smelled the years of filth on his father, the layers of rancid sweat and dust and mold, and thought of the last decade without him. He had missed him, even as he had grown to hate and love him the more, though he hadn't realized it so completely until that moment.

"I love you, son," Methuselah whispered. "You're all I have in this world."

"I know, Father. Now that I have Noah, I know."

When they released each other, they wiped their eyes and parted ways, Methuselah to the stream, Lamech to his garden.

Chapter 36

Noah stood as he heard footsteps and Jade's voice soft and close. He wanted to know what Jade thought of his arrival almost more than he wanted to talk with the old man. But as Jade rounded the corner trailing Elina with a bundle of branches in her arms, she avoided his gaze.

"Jade," Noah said, but she raised her chin and pressed her lips together as if fighting the urge to speak insults.

"Noah," Elina said, "do you know where your father is?"

"He was speaking with that old man behind our home," Noah said. "But I haven't heard them for a while."

Jade dropped the kindling in a pile while Elina fed some of the larger branches into the small fire they tended day after day to purify water and cook meals. "They're not there," Elina said. "Our visitor is at the stream."

Jade was standing with her arms folded, staring at the wall to avoid Noah's gaze. He approached, but she turned to avoid him again. Noah felt indignation surge through his fingers as he walked to his bedding to find the little mannequin he'd made the previous day.

Thrusting his hand beneath the covers, he retrieved the figure, spinning it to make sure it was suitable. Satisfied, he brought it to Jade. She looked at it quizzically. Then, when he pushed it toward her, she wrenched it out of his hands and forced a laugh. "You think I'm a child, that I would play with this?" She threw it into the fire and turned her chin up at him again.

"Jade!" Elina said. "Why did you do that?" She grabbed a stick and flipped it out of the fire, but the heat had already twisted the bark and arms.

Noah looked down at the mannequin and, despite himself, felt a burning behind his eyes. He kicked it back in the fire and said, "No, she was right. It belongs in there."

Elina examined him as he turned out of the shelter toward the stream, swiping the moisture from his face and hating himself for crying. He didn't know why Jade was being so cruel, and he told himself he didn't care. He would find the newcomer and speak with the man alone. And he wouldn't tell Jade what they talked about. Not until she apologized for the way she'd treated him.

When he found Methuselah bending toward the stream, cupping water and letting it run through his matted hair, the old man ignored him.

"You claimed you knew me before I was born," Noah said. "That means you knew my mother."

Methuselah stood and gauged him, water dripping from his ears, gray eyes pooling with centuries of experience. "If you want to know about your past, ask your father."

"I asked you." Noah stared, willing the intensity of his gaze to press the man's words free.

Methuselah smiled. "If your father won't speak to you about your past, why would I?" He waved Noah off and said, "Leave me in peace."

Noah turned and searched for Father, but couldn't see him for the hills. "Where is he?"

"He was walking toward the garden earlier. If he—"

Noah trudged off, not waiting for the man to finish. He felt as though the fire that burned the mannequin's arms now burned within his own. His fingers clenched into fists, and as he crested the first hill, he spotted his father bent as if whispering to his plants. "Father," he said, and Father glanced up and smiled until he caught Noah's expression.

"What is it?" Lamech straightened and wiped the dirt from his hands.

"Why can't I speak with the old man?"

"I never said you couldn't."

The sun bore down until it felt like a physical weight as Noah took a deep, shaky breath. "Why do you always lie to me?"

"What are you talking about?" Lamech said.

"Do you think I'm just a child? That you could fool me?"

Lamech examined Noah carefully. "You are a child, but you are no fool."

"What was my mother's name?"

Lamech's face paled.

"Why do you refuse to talk about her? I just want to know who she was. Sometimes I imagine that I feel her hand brush my arm. But in my dreams, her face is clouded, and always she disappears, and I search and search and cannot find her." Despite himself, tears blurred his vision, and he cleared his throat.

"Son, I—" His voice caught, and he shook his head.

Father's face was so pale and flat that Noah wanted to strike him. He balled his hands, ground his teeth, and said, "I hate you! I hate you and Jade and Elina, and that old man too!" He turned and walked into the forest, continuing until each breath felt like a thorn in his side, and he collapsed, his body wracked with sobs that came from he knew not where.

Chapter 37

Lamech watched his son disappear and felt a sickness chill the base of his abdomen. Noah's words repeated in his mind, and each time pierced him further. *"I hate you . . . I hate you . . . I hate you!"*

Footsteps approached, and a hand lighted on his shoulder. He turned to see Methuselah's gray eyes. They drooped at the corners, as if weighed down by all he had witnessed in his many years. "Why don't you just tell him?"

"Because it would only make him worse."

"You don't believe that."

"He's been kept from knowing his entire life, and so long as he's kept his mind occupied, he's been well."

"How do you know? Can you feel what he feels?"

"I know my son. Or does a father have no intuition?"

Methuselah snorted. "Of course you have intuition. But it is obviously stilted by your desire to justify lying to the boy his entire life."

"I've not lied to him."

"Noah is hurting because you told him he can't know his mother. You and I both know that's not true."

"How could I tell him and watch the pain bleed from him as it did me?"

Methuselah's eyes flashed and lifted with sudden understanding. "I see. You kept the truth from him, not for his sake, but for your own. Because you can't bear to speak of it."

"How could I let him feel what I felt when Mother was taken from us? Better that he forget her."

"He cannot forget. Who does he have besides you and a woman and girl who aren't his blood? You've already taken the world from him. All he wants is to be given the opportunity to name what's missing."

Lamech ran his hands over his face and looked at the cracks lining his knuckles stained with dirt. The world was filled with toil. How could Noah ever be free from the struggle? The endless scrape of knuckles against earth? When would they ever find *rest*?

"You forget," Methuselah said, "that such a desire is rooted in our bones. Noah can no more part with thoughts of his mother than forget his own name. A child should have parents. But when you deny him the remnants of his mother, you push him to deny you, as well."

Lamech thrust his fist into his palm. "What choice do I have? Nothing will ever satisfy him! 'I am sorry, Noah. I let your mother die.' How could that make him love me?"

Methuselah lowered his voice and tapped his temple as if he knew the remedy to Lamech's problems. "Do you remember when your mother died, how I tried telling you she was only sleeping, that she would wake eventually?"

"How could I forget?"

"How did you feel when you realized your father would lie to you?"

Lamech met Methuselah's gaze.

"I regret a lot in my life," Methuselah said, "but that moment, when I saw your eyes strip me of pretense . . . I regret that moment more than most."

"It seems your lot in life is to tell me to not be like you," Lamech said.

"So be it. You'd be wise to listen."

"What if he doesn't understand the reasons I've kept him from knowing about her?"

"You can't control anyone, least of all one so fiery in spirit. If you have good reasons, he will understand, eventually. If you don't, take responsibility for your mistakes. After all, you are his father. You can't be a father and not make mistakes."

"What if he refuses to forgive me?"

"If you say nothing, you guarantee his hatred. Your only hope is to hold to the truth."

Lamech held his throbbing head between his palms. "I can't do it."

Methuselah sighed and rubbed his eyes. "What evil could come from him knowing about his mother?"

"Pain."

"Pain is not evil. Evil resides in the hearts and attitudes of man, not the forces of nature. And pain is like the heat of the sun, or the cold of the night. No father can keep his child from it. And we are never asked to. Your duty is to help him overcome it."

Lamech chewed on his fingernails and thought back to the endless years alone in the mountains, of the gnawing ache of his mother's absence that still throbbed in the dead of night when his soul was split by the gleam of stars. "How can I help him overcome what I never could? I still mourn the loss of her. I don't know how to get past it any more than he does."

"If pain is truly what you fear, remember that loneliness is the greatest of pains, and the only remedy for loneliness is love. Be there for him. Listen to him and tell him of your pain. He is not just a boy. Noah is a man in the making, and, like you, every bit as deserving of respect."

Lamech took a deep breath and, after running his fingers through his beard, said, "You must have thought a lot in that dungeon."

Tears fell from Methuselah's eyes as his cheeks swelled with a smile. "In such darkness, I could hardly think. Now, I finally feel alive again. Breathing all the breaths and thinking all the thoughts I would have thought in all those many years." He reached and hugged Lamech fiercely. "It was the memory of your face that got me through it. The sense of my love for you. And how I failed you. I am sorry."

Lamech wept on his father's shoulder, hugged him, and said, "It's okay. I'm sorry too. I see now how difficult being a father is."

Chapter 38

Noah wept until his emotions seemed puddled at his feet. He stared at the wet dirt, a dull sense of loss replacing the fire and pain. He sniffed, and a twig cracked; he spun to see Father standing not fifteen paces off.

Lamech nodded in greeting.

Noah averted his eyes and wiped his hands on his rough tunic. Lamech approached and crouched beside him, but Noah couldn't look at him without feeling bile rise to the back of his throat.

Several long breaths passed between them. Bodily rhythms offset, tenuous. Father sighed and said, "Your mother . . . you are just like her."

Noah's throat tightened anew. Now that he'd heard Father speak, he wasn't sure if he wanted him to continue. What if his mother wasn't as he'd hoped? What if, as he so often feared, she had left him because she'd never loved him at all?

"She was headstrong, fiery, and intelligent," Lamech said, and Noah felt his breath seize. "You have her eyes, and her hair and hands. The shape of your shoulders is perhaps a mix of hers and mine. Her name . . . her name was Adah." Lamech paused, wiped his face, and sniffed.

The thought of Father crying angered him, because he knew it was only motivated by selfishness. Lamech was only telling Noah what he deserved to be told years ago because Noah had told his father for the first time in his life that he hated him.

Still, to hear his mother's name. *Adah.* His mind passed over the syllables like a hand over smooth river stones.

"Do you want to know what happened to her?" Lamech spoke the words as if wishing he could take them back.

Noah clenched his teeth, rubbed his burning eyes, and said, "Yes."

Lamech took a deep, stuttering breath, and began, "I found her in the mountains . . ." And he explained how he had nursed her to health after she had been held captive and beaten. How her family had been destroyed by the Others, and how she had fled to find safety. Then how Lamech and Adah married, and Noah had grown in her belly. They planned their future, soaking up each moment together as onyx soaks the heat of the sun.

Noah listened to every detail and had to remind himself to breathe. Even what little Father shared seemed to peel back Noah's ribs and slice through his soul. The pain was unbearable, but for once he felt she was with him, and he would endure anything to sense her nearness.

"But," Lamech said, and his smile crumbled, "days before we expected you to be born, the Others found us in the mountains, beat Adah, and burned our home. I killed them, and she succeeded in bringing you into this world, but doing so spent her, and she died from the wounds she had received from the Others." Lamech wiped his eyes and rocked. "I buried her, took you into the village, and found Elina, who agreed to feed and care for you as I could not. We traveled for months, and nearly perished, for the Others followed us. So we kept moving until you grew older and we realized that the only way we could keep you safe was to live apart from the rest of the world." Another long pause. Lamech wiped more tears. "Son, I . . ." He did not finish.

Noah stood, body trembling, chest smoldering. "What did her voice sound like?"

Lamech stared at Noah, then stood and gazed through the

trees as if conjuring the memory of her. "Low and warm. At times, I thought it silk washed in the colors of sunset."

Another stab of pain, followed by a flood of warmth. "Did she like turnips?"

"I never knew."

"Did she sing?"

A nod. "She could be unpredictable, like you."

Powerful emotions clutched his throat. His breathing sped, and he felt a sudden rush of excitement. "Was she good at making things?"

"I'm not sure where you got that talent from. Certainly not from her."

Noah frowned. "Was she good at anything?"

"She was a good mother. And wife. And a valiant friend."

"That doesn't sound very impressive."

"Most of what's valuable in life doesn't sound impressive."

"Was she kind?"

"Of course. And beautiful. Astoundingly beautiful."

Noah closed his eyes and let a slow breath escape. "Describe her."

"Small, rounded cheeks. A gentle chin and nose. Eyes as large and bright as a deer's. Hair shoulder-length and thick. Neck slender and long. Dark brows. Full lips that spread into a smile that could steal a stranger's breath."

"Did she smile often?"

"No. But that only made the gift of it more meaningful."

"I like that."

"What?"

"I like her." Now the tears overwhelmed him, and he sunk to his knees and wiped his face once. Twice. The pain flowed unstoppable, and he held his face in his hands. With each sob came a ration of satisfaction, like the closing of a bitter circle. He whispered her name, "Adah," his mind focused on the picture Father's words had painted. He loved her as he hadn't loved anyone or anything. And he missed her and wished that he could be with her.

But no longer did he feel a shame for his past, but a glorious pride, and a fury at those who had stolen her away. For now he knew that she had never abandoned him. That instead he had been robbed of what might have been.

Father bent and scooped him up, and he clung to Father's shoulder and screamed because he could do nothing else. The fibers of Father's tunic scraped his wet, swollen eyelids. The trees seemed to spin and whisper words of comfort as they bent over him, their knotted faces filled with compassion until the clouded sky replaced them and he closed his eyes and felt bedding against his back.

The pain waned, and in its wake crept a sense of purpose. For years he had wondered what destiny awaited him. Now, he thought maybe he knew.

He would find the men who killed his mother, so he could cull the longing that burned just beneath the skin of his chest. He imagined that if he pressed his ribs hard enough, he might snuff the flames, but each year had seared further, until he feared that by the time he reached adulthood, naught would be left but a blackened soul.

Chapter 39

Lamech left his son in their small home, walked to the stream, and waded thigh-deep to let the chill water cool his bones. The tears bled dry, forming a salty residue that stiffened his cheeks, and Methuselah approached again.

"I fear for him," Lamech said to Methuselah. "A darkness haunts him, and I'm reminded of my dreams. Long ago, you said that sorrow was coming. I only fear it might grow greater and shatter what family we have left. The world is changing. Those devils have swept the nations, and the few men left are bent on evil. What hope remains? What future might Noah lay hold of?"

"Instead, you should ask yourself what hope isolation offers."

"Survival."

"Better that he die struggling to heal than to live hollow and afraid."

Lamech turned and examined his father.

"He doesn't belong here," Methuselah said. "You tried to keep him safe, but that boy is wounded. If you keep him isolated, you will only delve deeper scars."

"You've not seen what I've seen, Father."

"Refuse!" Methuselah's face reddened, and his beard shook. "I've lived three centuries, ten years of which I spent in the dungeons of the demons you fear. I have seen the devastation they wrought to our kin, hardly recognizable under the tyranny of fear. More, I have seen you grown into a man. If a darkness hunts Noah, who are you to stop it? Do you command the sun and moon, that you would make them shine on him alone?"

Lamech trudged ashore, his legs splashing the stream. "He is my son, not yours. I told him of his mother. What else would you have me do?"

"I would have you wake to the fact that your methods are flawed."

"And yours weren't?" Lamech said. "You kept me in the mountains for years. Never spending a thought for my wounds. Like a bleeding wolf, you cowered and licked your scabs open year after year."

"And now you follow suit, cloistering your son in an empty copse. There is nothing here save the sounds of growing trees and the sun's rays beating the dirt. Such irony in your words, for I criticize only your repetition of my mistakes. I never claimed perfection."

Lamech walked past him and kept going.

"He should be with others," Methuselah spoke to his back. "He needs friendship and community. You will never be enough for him, and neither will that woman or her daughter."

Lamech ignored him until he reached the garden, and then the forest, where he found a suitable space in the shadow of a gophar tree, whose massive limbs stretched wide and held leaves the size of a man's head. He leaned against its trunk and closed his eyes, no longer feeling secure in his beliefs.

From the beginning, he had questioned his intuition to hide Noah, and Methuselah's appearance only added layers of dissonance. Lamech still feared danger might find them, but now he also feared Noah might run away.

If Noah purposed in his mind to leave, and Lamech could not stop him, how prepared would he be to survive the world he'd find?

Lamech tried to see the sky through the canopy, but it was too thick. He wanted to find the stars, to be offered some sense of dimension and distance so that his perspective might be righted. He felt too isolated, and yet he had forced isolation upon himself, trusting in detachment to provide what he could not.

And now he couldn't shake the sensation that something was terribly wrong.

He sat for hours, mulling over the same thoughts until he thought he might go mad. Eventually his emotions waned and his exhaustion grew. He closed his eyes and felt himself drift, but instead of finding rest, a dark dream rolled over his mind like a mountain.

He opened his eyes to a black sky filled with foreign stars. A shadow approached and obscured his left shoulder. "It has been long," the shadow said, "but you must not speak. Not since we last met have you been in such danger. The man who has come to you, whom you call father. You must not listen to him."

"What do you mean?" Now that deadly chill approached, and with it a rush of anxiety.

"Hush!" the shadow said. "Did I not warn you not to speak?"

Lamech knew somehow that if the approaching chill engulfed him, and those fingers that seemed to materialize from the cold grasped hold of him, he would be torn asunder.

"I have much to tell you, but our enemy has found us. Quick, you must flee. Take Noah and run. They are coming!" The shadow thrust him away, and the dream dissolved, leaving Lamech shaking alone beneath the gophar tree, hoping against hope that what he'd experienced was a lie.

Chapter 40

Noah woke to Jade prodding him, whispering, "Are you sick?"

"Of course not," Noah said and rolled away, trying to fight the tightness in his throat, the desire for her hand to warm his side.

"Sorry, I thought . . . I thought that when your grandfather came, you wouldn't want to spend time with me anymore. The thought of it made me angry with you."

"Are you a fool?"

She bit her lip. "Here," she said, and held out the burnt mannequin. He took it, felt its crumpled, blackened limbs, and raised himself on one hand.

"Mother saved it after you left," Jade said, and looked down.

"She should have left it." Noah dropped it between them.

"I thought you would want it back," Jade said.

"I don't want it."

"Oh," she said, and played with the fray of her tunic.

Noah felt a mounting desire to leave. Jade was acting strange. No insults. No haughty disposition. No sneer.

She crossed her legs and glanced around before whispering, "I know how you feel."

"What?"

"I don't have a father."

So she hadn't come merely to apologize for throwing his mannequin in the fire. She wanted to know what happened. "Having a father isn't so enjoyable," Noah said.

"At least your father wants you."

"Why wouldn't he?"

Jade looked away, her cheeks reddening for the first time that he could remember.

"Jade?" Noah said.

She touched the distorted mannequin and said, "Not long ago, I asked Mother where my father was." Her lips quivered, and Noah waited, not daring to prod her.

Jade took a deep breath. "She told me she had never married. Never loved any man. But her brother had forced her to become pregnant with me."

Noah felt his stomach drop as he leaned closer, trying to catch Jade's eyes though she avoided his gaze.

"He told her not to tell anyone. She promised she wouldn't. Then, after he and the rest of the family were asleep, she killed them. She tried to kill me too."

"What?" Noah could hardly believe what he was hearing. Elina was always cold and distant, but he couldn't imagine her doing anything so terrible. She loved Jade.

But Jade hunched into herself, all the sureness and pride she normally held crumbled to a ruined face brimming with tears barely held.

Could it be true? Had Elina really admitted to trying to kill Jade?

"She failed," Jade said, "and I lived. And she was too cowardly to try again. So, here I am." She shrugged and wiped her eyes.

Noah's face felt immobilized. He didn't know how to respond. He supposed she expected him to be sad for her. And if what she said was true, how could he not? Only it all seemed so unbelievable.

She squinted and said, "After she told me that story, I got sick just like you did today."

"I'm sorry."

She sniffed and gave him a half smile. "You didn't do

anything." Then she stood and said, "You forgive me?"

Noah nodded, not knowing what else to do.

She took a deep breath and left.

Noah laid and tried to quell the cold, oily sensation spreading through his abdomen. If Elina truly had done such terrible things, she was just as bad as any of the Others.

Had she really murdered her entire family and tried to kill Jade? An innocent baby?

A thought struck him like a hailstone, and he whispered to the burnt mannequin, "Does Father know?"

Chapter 41

When Lamech returned home, he found Methuselah and Elina arguing in front of Jade and Noah.

"Stay your words," Elina said, "before—"

"Before what?" Methuselah's eyes gleamed like quicksilver amidst brush.

"Don't test me," Elina said. "You will leave, and you will take your fear with you."

Lamech tapped the wall to gain their attention. Methuselah noticed Lamech and said, "Your woman disapproves of me."

Elina's eyes narrowed to viper slits. "I am no man's woman, least of all Lamech's."

Methuselah bent back and laughed.

"She speaks truth," Lamech said. "She is not my woman."

Methuselah smirked at Lamech, then at Elina. "Then what is she?"

"She saved my son's life," Lamech said.

"We are family," Elina said. "Noah needed someone to spend his life with."

"So my son found a woman who wouldn't bear him children," Methuselah said.

Elina looked ready to unsheathe her dagger, so Lamech grabbed Methuselah by the arm and pulled him out of the shelter.

Methuselah glared and jerked himself out of his grasp. "What?"

Lamech hushed him and spoke quietly so Elina couldn't hear. "Stop making her angry."

"She physically pushed me out after you left. When I resisted, she commanded me to leave and said I was not welcomed back."

"That's just Elina. She means no harm."

"Means no harm? She nearly cut me last night. The more time I spend here, the more I question where your mind has been. The way she looks at me makes me nervous."

"So you mock her?"

"I'm not leaving. Not unless you come with me. If she needs to stay and can't abide me, then maybe you and I should leave."

"I built this home with my own hands," Lamech said. "I'm not leaving."

"Then fix her."

"Fix your manner." Lamech took a step back and thought about the dream. "Why have you really come here?"

Methuselah frowned. "I already told you."

Lamech took a deep breath and cycled back through everything Methuselah said since arriving. He couldn't imagine how the man before him could be anyone but his father. He sounded like Methuselah, looked the same, moved the same, thought the same. He even smelled the same beneath the layers of grime. He had certainly been thinned by starvation and weathered by abuse, but his identity was unmistakable.

"Your actions are driving a wedge between Elina and me," Lamech said.

"All I want is to be with my son and grandson." Methuselah's voice shook. "To do what I can to keep you safe."

"And if Elina refuses to abide you?"

"She can leave." Methuselah's eyebrows bristled. "Or does she hold greater allegiance than the blood that flows through our veins?"

Could the dark dream simply have been a nightmare? Some strange vision brought on by anxiety and the upheaval of change?

The shadow had told him to flee, that someone was coming. If that were true, maybe Methuselah really had led the enemy to them. But Lamech couldn't just take Noah and leave.

What of Elina and Jade? Elina would never be convinced by something so vague as a dream under a gophar tree. He *could* convince Methuselah to leave, but if the dream was real, then he couldn't trust Methuselah.

"Son," Methuselah said, "why are you looking at me like that?"

Lamech rubbed his face and said, "It's nothing. I think . . . I think it would be best if you stayed away from Elina."

Methuselah spat on the ground and said, "My pleasure."

Lamech held up his hand. "I will speak with her. Elina has had a hard life, and she distrusts men because of it. But if you have spoken the truth at all points—"

"Of course I have spoken the truth!"

Lamech nodded. "Then she will understand. I only ask that you give me time to convince her. Until then, avoid her."

Methuselah looked around. "Where do I sleep?"

"I will give you bedding and erect a shelter."

"You think this is going to take a while."

"I'm certain of nothing anymore," Lamech said.

Chapter 42

Noah watched Elina touch the hilt of her dagger as Lamech spoke with Methuselah outside the shelter. He could hear Father's voice rising against Methuselah's, but could not make out what was said.

Finally, Lamech returned and made for Elina, but Noah seized his wrist.

"Father," he said, "can we speak?"

"Wait until after I've spoken with—"

"No," Noah said.

Lamech raised his eyebrow.

Noah lowered his voice. "Before you speak with her."

Lamech glanced at Elina and seemed to weigh his options. "Very well."

Noah led him out to the stream, far enough from home that no one would be able to overhear. Lamech placed his hands on his hips and looked at Noah. "What is it?"

"First, a question."

Lamech nodded. "Ask."

"What do you know of Elina's past?"

Lamech stared at the rushing water, pursed his lips, and said, "Why do you ask about Elina?"

"Jade came to me after we returned from the forest and told me about Elina. That Elina's brother had violated her, and that

Jade was born because of it. She said Elina had murdered her family because of it, then tried to kill Jade. She failed, so Jade survived. But it's not true. Is it?"

Lamech's face looked as pale as the afternoon clouds. "I . . ." He scratched his temple and shifted on his feet, swallowing hard. "It is true, I think. Though I did not know that she had tried to kill Jade. That surprises me."

Noah felt his innards compress. "So, it is true. Elina is a murderer."

"You must understand, son . . . Elina's life is more complicated than most."

Noah turned from his father.

"Elina's past is not her present," Lamech said. "She has grown past much of the pain of her early years."

"Then why does she treat her dagger with more affection than her own daughter?"

"Elina is not perfect. I knew this when she agreed to care for you. But we had no other choice."

Noah took a shallow, shaky breath. "What have we been doing all these years? You said the Others were violent. Evil. How is Elina any different?"

"Sometimes, when people suffer much, they do terrible things."

"What about the Others? Is that why they kill people?"

"No," Lamech said. "They are different."

"How do you know?"

"Elina is no longer who she was. When a person is pushed to do evil things out of passion, sometimes those evil actions don't permanently damage the soul. She loves Jade, and though she doesn't always show her love, you cannot deny that truth."

"Then why doesn't Jade believe it? She doesn't feel wanted. She even told me so. How could Elina try to kill Jade if she loves her?"

"I don't know, son. There is much I do not know." Lamech's eyes reddened and glistened. "I am sorry. If you only knew . . ."

"Knew what? Have you lied about even more?"

"None of this may make sense to you now. But I hope one day you will see why I brought you into the wilderness. More than ever before, I question everything. Maybe it seems I have deceived you out of spite, but that is a lie. Since the moment you were born, I have loved you more than anything else." Tears fell from Lamech's cheeks, and he wiped his eyes. "I should not have kept you from knowing the world. Just remember that any failure of mine was an attempt to love you gone wrong. I . . ."

Noah glared at his father, hearing his words, yet trusting none. "You've lied to me about everything."

Lamech wiped his face. "Not everything."

Noah turned away and said, "I never want to see you again." Heat singed his cheeks as he walked through the woods, leaving his father behind.

As he went, he tripped on what seemed a jutting root and fell on his stomach. Coughing with the air expelled from his chest, he grunted and spat out the dust his fall churned up. As he looked up, he saw a boot connected to a leg towering upward.

"What—"

A hand grabbed the back of his neck, yanking him up so that he could see the light of a burning torch glistening off marble eyes and two spiraling horns.

Chapter 43

L amech watched Noah leave and, for the first time, sensed the shadowy haze of the dark dream obscure his vision while he stood awake.

Though it was midday, stars flickered in the sky, and he saw his body wraithlike on the ground before him. Approaching the projection of himself on the ground was the shadow he'd grown so familiar with, only now Lamech saw the shadow held the form of a man with sharp features and dark skin.

The shadow dipped, laid a hand across Lamech's face, and said, "The enemy is upon you!"

The deadly, alien chill returned, sweeping across his neck like a lightning storm that tingled his skin from the top of his head to the bottom of his back. With it came that groping, invisible hand, and it clutched his side, its nails like firebrands digging through his flesh.

He screamed, and the sound ripped the dream-veil away. Lamech's throat throbbed. Warm wetness stuck his tunic to his side, and a surge of heat shot down his limbs as he looked down at his side torn open, pouring blood.

He stumbled toward their home, calling for Elina as he noticed isolated flames moving at the forest edge.

No, not flames. Torches in the hands of warriors.

He rounded the corner of their home. Elina was staring at

the forest edge, her gaze skipping left, right, behind, forward. Lamech followed suit, struggling to deny what he already knew.

They were surrounded.

Methuselah returned to the building, his eyes wide beneath thistle eyebrows. "I swear I did not bring them."

Elina's hand was wrapped around the hilt of her dagger, and the blade glinted in the light of the setting sun as she approached Methuselah with eyes aflame.

Lamech caught her by the arm, but she struggled against him, nearly driving the blade through his arm before her eyes caught sight of Lamech's tunic and she stopped with a gasp.

"Lamech? You're bleeding!"

Lamech did not let go. "Give me your dagger, Elina."

Her eyes darted to his side, then to the armed warriors emerging from the forest. Her grip tightened, and she shook her head. "It's his fault, and I'll kill him for it!"

"Where is Noah?" Lamech said.

"I thought he was with you," Methuselah said.

"You lost him?" Elina's voice betrayed concern.

"He must have gotten away," Lamech said, and prayed that it was true.

"Mother?" Jade said, her voice shrill with panic. "Who are those men? And why are they here?"

A one-armed giant entered the copse, yellow horns above yellow eyes downcast, and Lamech felt his knees nearly buckle. What little color remained in Methuselah's face bled away.

For they recognized that demon, the same one who had set their mountain home on fire.

A familiar, boyish cry struck the air, and Lamech swallowed hard and clenched his teeth, fighting a surge of bitter anger.

"What are we going to do?" Elina said.

"Nothing," Methuselah said. He was grabbing nervously at his matted beard, his gray eyes more uncertain than Lamech had ever seen them. "Son, I swear I did not—"

Lamech held up his hand and said, "It doesn't matter."

"What are you saying?" Elina's eyes narrowed. She stepped from one foot to the other, looking like a cornered bull.

The one-armed giant stopped, and his soldiers stood in a

circle about the home. The giant opened his mouth, his voice an earthen quake. "We have the boy."

Elina went motionless. Jade clutched the hem of her garment. Methuselah passed a hand over his eyes.

Lamech swallowed the bile that crept up his throat and said, "We must hurry to meet them."

Chapter 44

The one-armed giant dug his fingers into Noah's neck, forcing him to kneel in the grass beside their garden. At first, when the Others caught Noah partway through the forest, he'd tried to fight. But a single kick to the abdomen and he'd stilled like a trampled leaf.

Now the Others stood in a tight circle around his home, holding torches in gloved hands, despite the sun hovering midway through the sky. The horns on their heads reflected the flames as if their heads were ablaze.

The one-armed giant inhaled, and yelled in a voice so deep Noah's body shuddered, "We have the boy."

Moments later his father exited the house, followed by Elina, Jade, and Methuselah.

The giant's fingers tightened around Noah's neck until his sight dimmed and his body slumped. "Try anything and your son dies," the giant said. "You, woman. I see that knife. Drop it on the ground before you take another step."

Lamech nodded at Elina, who grabbed the handle of the knife and stared at Noah.

"Drop it," the giant rumbled, and his fingers tightened again, forcing a groan from Noah's throat.

She obeyed, and the giant let up.

"Now kneel ten paces from the boy. All of you."

Noah watched as they did as they were told, and the Others bound Elina, Lamech, and Methuselah's wrists and ankles with rope. A fifth grabbed Jade and forced her to kneel beside Noah, though he did not bind her.

Noah met Jade's gaze and mouthed, "I'm sorry," but her cheeks reddened as she averted her gaze. Methuselah's mouth hung open, his hair and beard blowing in the breeze that cut through the copse and rattled leaves.

Father's murderous gaze was set on the giant, and the fire in his eyes struck Noah with momentary pride, though that too was soon swept away by the sound of slow footsteps crunching to Noah's right.

Lamech, Methuselah, and Elina's gazes re-centered on the approaching figure. Methuselah's eyes widened, while Lamech's and Elina's narrowed. Noah tried to look, too, but the giant's fingers held him fixed.

The giant rumbled, "Do you want your family to live, or not?"

A leather-clad man passed by Noah and stopped, facing Lamech, Elina, and Methuselah. Out of the corner of his vision, Noah caught massive black horns sprouting from the newcomer's head, curving two entire revolutions before ending in spines that pointed skyward.

"Well," the newcomer said, his voice low and smooth. "We finally meet." The man turned and looked at Noah with silver eyes set in a dark face. "And for the first time I can examine the child who has caused me so much trouble." He crouched and smiled, his teeth stained as if by wine, breath smelling of copper. "Hello, Noah. Do you know who I am?"

Noah grit his teeth and fought the tears that threatened his vision. He felt like a fool. Like a weak little boy. "You're the devil."

"Yes. That's right. I'm the devil. But my servants call me the God-King."

Noah's eyes widened, and his pulse hastened.

"You should hate me," the God-King said. "Do you know why?"

Noah glanced at Jade, felt the one-armed giant's grip

tighten, and looked back at the God-King, who leaned in until his nose touched Noah's forehead.

The God-King's breath stabbed his eyes as he whispered, "Because I killed your mother."

Hot coals rolled from Noah's chest down to his fingers, curling his fists tight and pressing his feet to the earth.

The God-King pulled back to Methuselah. "If only you would have done what was expected, old man. Then I wouldn't have had to come at all."

Noah's grandfather refused to meet the God-King's gaze.

Elina clenched her fists and jumped to her feet, struggling to stand with her wrists and ankles bound. "I knew it. You sold us to these demons!"

The God-King approached and struck Elina in the face, knocking her flat on her back, bringing a thin trail of blood from her nose. "Wrong. He was supposed to bring Noah to the city. He did not. It's a pity Lamech didn't listen to the warnings he received. Maybe then you all would have survived."

Elina moaned and rolled to her side, searching Lamech's face. "What is he talking about?"

Lamech's cheeks lost their color. "You know about the dreams? So they're real?"

The God-King grabbed Elina by the hair and dragged her screaming to the space between Noah and Lamech. "Of course they're real."

"Stop!" Jade said, but the soldier behind her smashed his palms into her ears.

"Now we must begin," the God-King said, his silver eyes so cold as to be inhuman. His stained teeth flashed in the light of a day too normal to contain such horror. "You hate me, boy, but not enough. You must hate me more, and more, until hatred is all you know."

"No. Please, don't hurt her," Jade mumbled, lips thin and shaking.

"Oh, don't worry," the God-King said. "I'll only hurt her a little." He motioned toward the giant and the soldier who held Noah and Jade. "Release them."

Noah felt the giant's hand withdraw and saw Jade's captor

release her. Neither Noah nor Jade were bound, and he began to wonder if they might be set free.

Only that made no sense.

The God-King retrieved the knife Elina dropped in the grass and pressed it to her throat, all the while keeping his silver eyes on Noah. "I am not here to kill you, Noah. No, I expect you will live a very long life. Many, many years may pass before you see me again, and by then, perhaps today will seem a distant dream. Maybe, even, you will fancy that it never happened. But please, promise me that you will never forget what I show you today."

Noah nodded, refusing to let the emotions that shook his body come out in a whimper.

"Good. When I tell you to run, you and your friend will run as far and as long as you can, and you will never try to find your family again. If you do, I will kill them, and in worse ways than you could imagine. But first . . ." He smiled at Elina and pulled the blade through her throat.

Her body crumpled, and for a moment Noah caught the shimmer of red gushing from her neck. Jade screeched, but the God-King had already crossed to Lamech and held the knife to his throat. "Run," he screamed. "Run! Or I will kill your father and your grandfather too!" His eyes were stretched wide, silver serpentine bright.

Jade fell forward, but Noah caught her, raised her onto his shoulder, and hobbled as quickly as he could into the forest and beyond, screaming, weeping, shaking.

Trying to block out Jade's voice calling her mother's name.

Chapter 45

L amech watched as Noah and Jade ran away and disappeared behind the cover of trees. Elina blinked up at him, tears spilling down her cheeks and mixing with the blood pouring from the deadly wound.

Sickness bubbled out of his stomach, and he bent and nearly vomited, steadying himself on bound hands.

"No," he said, gasping for breath. "No!"

He could not believe what he'd seen. Birds still chirped in the boughs of trees too familiar. The vegetables in his garden still soaked up the rays of the midday sun. His house still sat open, inviting.

And Elina's life flooded the soil.

He knew she was dying, and yet it seemed a distant lie. As if all were just a terrible nightmare, and he would soon wake. But no matter how hard he struck his palms into his eyes, the vision of her broken and bleeding on the ground refused to leave.

The woman who nursed Noah as a child and saved Lamech's life more than once.

Elina. My friend. My family. Murdered. And for what?

The God-King cleaned Elina's dagger with a dirty rag and examined its hilt before slipping it into his belt. "Berubbal." He snapped his fingers and the one-armed giant knelt. "Take the prisoners back to the city, but do not throw them in the dungeon. They will live in the guardhouse beside my temple. You will order guards to keep a close watch and make sure they never escape. Make sure they live a comfortable, long life."

The giant's yellow eyes narrowed on Lamech, and a sneer hooked the corner of his mouth. "Understood."

Berubbal bellowed for the soldiers to bring the prisoners back, and violent hands grabbed Lamech's arms, yanked him to his feet, and dragged him toward the forest. Lamech turned to stare at Elina's broken body left in the open, and he wept for her as the boughs of the trees obscured his vision, and the soldiers carried he and Methuselah on.

They were brought to a wagon yoked to bulls and forced into cages in the back. He assumed he and Methuselah were kept separate so that they could not aid each other, but they were so tightly bound and cramped in the cages that they could barely shift at all.

Three soldiers climbed into the drivers' seat and drove the bulls onward through the forest onto a dirt road pointing north. Lamech and Methuselah lay silent in their cages for hours. At sunset, exhaustion throbbed through Lamech's body, and he closed his eyes and strained for the relief of sleep.

Instead of sleep, the dark dream forced itself upon him one final time as the pain in his knees and back faded to the bright pricks of stars in a black sky, and the approach of a dark shadow that knelt beside him.

"Why do you haunt me still?" Lamech whispered. "I failed, and Noah will die for it."

"No," the dark figure said. "Noah is alive."

"Not because of me."

"You never had much control to begin with. Who among us does?"

Lamech felt his mouth contort with emotion, saw the twinkling stars wobble. "What was the point of all this?"

"You kept him alive all these years. But now, you must release him. He must find his way without you, for he has been taken beyond your reach."

For a long while, Lamech kept silent. Desire for his son, deeper than the deepest ache, opened a chasm within which all reason fell, and he could grab hold of only one simple thought. "What will happen to him?"

"I do not know. But there is hope, for I have been sent to take care of him."

"By who?"

"By the same One who brought me to you."

"Who are you? And who sent you? I have listened to you all this time, for your words have spoken truth. But truth may be used for good or for ill, and I have seen naught but bitterness and loss since you visited me."

For the first time, the shape stepped in front of him, and Lamech saw the dim light of the night sky shine across dark eyes and dark features harshly wrought. He recognized him immediately, but could hardly believe it.

It was Enoch, his grandfather who had disappeared all those years ago.

Lamech blinked. "You? How? And why my son?"

"The Almighty chooses whom he will. His depths are a mystery beyond our comprehension. But where the Almighty gives burdens, he grants the strength to shoulder them. He has sent me to raise your son up in the way he should go. In addition, the Almighty has woven a protection around your son, so that the enemy who hunts him might never spill his blood."

"You knew this would happen?"

"No. Not fully."

"If the Almighty could protect him, then what was the point of you warning me all this time?"

"The battle is not for your son's body, but for his heart. The Almighty has given him physical protection since before he was born, but his soul has always been exposed, and all this time you have been tasked with protecting it. The God-King knows this. That is why he strove to separate you. If the God-King kills your son, he will undo his own ambitions. But if he corrupts your son's heart, he will find victory. That is where our danger lay. Why do you think I have struggled to warn you all this time? It was not to keep Noah from being killed, but to keep *you* safe, and to keep the two of you together. I saw much danger in you two parting, for I know all too well the damage wrought by the divide between father and son. But we are past that now. And we must trust in the Almighty and the decisions your son is destined to make."

"What, then, is expected of me?"

"Your story, for now, has parted from his. We all think of ourselves as the center of some grand story. But Noah is the center of this one, and you were his helper. Maybe you will have the opportunity to see your son again. I do not know, for much is hidden from me. But I would urge you to seek the Almighty, and to pray for your son's soul. For you may be certain of one thing: the fate of the world rests on his integrity."

Then the dream dissipated, the strange stars blending to a dirty bamboo cage.

The sun rose. Then set. Then rose again.

The wagon traveled for days, weeks, months, until they arrived at the city Lamech would come to call home.

But he knew it would never be more than a prison.

PART V

Noah

"The LORD saw that the wickedness of man was great in the earth, and that every intention of the thoughts of his heart was only evil continually. And the LORD regretted that he had made man on the earth, and it grieved him to his heart."
—Genesis 6:5–6

Chapter 46

Noah's heavy, cold breaths slapped the leaves as he stumbled forward beneath the weight of Jade. Gnarled branches scraped his skin, dripping warm redness across his raised skin. He couldn't hear anyone following, but that didn't matter. He couldn't stop.

"Run or I will kill your father and your grandfather too!"

"I'm running," Noah said, and fought to keep his trembling under control.

But Jade twisted in his arms and screamed for Elina, and Noah lost balance, slid in the mud, and toppled. He tried to catch her, but she landed on his arm and popped his shoulder. He rolled her off and forced his arm back into place, screaming with pain.

"Mother," she said. "Mother? Where is she?"

Noah felt a surge of anger as he fumbled to his knees and grabbed Jade by the shoulders. "She's gone, Jade."

"They took her away," she said. "We have to go back to her!"

He shook her. "She's dead."

"No, she's alive!"

"She's dead! They killed her, and we'll never see her again!"

Jade's eyes shone. For a moment, he thought she would insult him. Then, to his surprise, her lower lip jutted, and she wept. The response was so infantile that for a moment he merely blinked and stared.

He softened. "I'm sorry. I shouldn't have said that. I didn't mean to scare you." And he pulled her close and let her clutch his tunic and soak his chest.

He sat rocking her, rubbing her back, whispering, "You are safe, Jade. I will keep you safe." And he wept for the fear and the pain and the horror. "But we have to keep going."

She shook her head and moaned.

"We have to keep my father safe."

She pushed him away. "And what about my mother?"

Noah stood and lifted her by the arm. "Come."

They continued as quickly as they could. After a while, it seemed they heard men speaking, and the clanging of metal chains and the snort of beasts.

They huddled under the cover of evergreen branches on a bed of brown needles that poked through their clothing.

The voices disappeared, but they stayed hidden, breathing as little as possible until they were sure they were alone. Then they stood and continued, more careful of what twigs and dried leaves they stepped on.

As time rolled on, and the light faded, they continued. Jade spoke of how much she thirsted for water. Noah desired the same, for it had been many hours since they left Lamech and Methuselah behind, and the nervous energy that before sped them along now bled into exhaustion. Every muscle in Noah's body felt swollen and weak. When he held his hand in front of his face, his fingers shook, and when he tried to support Jade, his arm moved as if half-listening.

"We can't stop," he said.

"What?" Jade said.

He shook his head and prodded her on, but she slowed.

"Jade," he said, "we have to keep going."

"How could they know if we've stopped?"

"How could they find us to begin with?"

"Because your grandfather brought them to us."

"We don't know that. Besides, it doesn't matter."

"Yes, it does," Jade said. "I can't take another step." She

pointed, and Noah had to squint to see the mouth of a small cave in the dim starlight that peeked through the forest canopy —an ambiguous absence of light rather than an actual shape.

Noah knew they should move on, but he was so exhausted he didn't think he could. Not if he must convince both himself and her.

He had no idea what animals they might encounter in the absolute dark of the cave. Then again, what animals would they encounter wandering through the forest at night?

Noah and Jade weren't hunters. They were fool adolescents fleeing from pain and fire and the threat of death.

Weaponless. Aimless.

"I'm laying down," Jade said, and stumbled into the cave.

Noah made to resist, then leaned toward the cave, now taking one step, now two, until he entered.

The cave floor was hard and cold and uncomfortably moist. He looked around, brushed the stone, and sat stiffly. "Very well. But as soon as the sun rises, we move."

The opening was no more than a small cove that ended a dozen feet into the rock face. After Noah inspected each crack, trying his best to refrain from yelping as his fingers squelched pockets of molded stone, they lay together, closed their eyes, and huddled for warmth.

Each time Noah approached sleep, Jade moved, startling him awake. Once, he shot up and held his breath, glancing around.

"What are you doing?" Jade asked, her voice groggy and irritated.

"You keep waking me," he said, more to cover his fear than anything else.

"I'm uncomfortable," Jade said.

"You were the one who wanted to lay in the cave."

She grumbled again and elbowed him, so he scooted away and tried to sleep without her.

But long after he thought her asleep, she spun toward him and pressed her face into his neck, crying softly, forcing a hollow ache through his chest.

He ran his fingers through her hair and focused on the

warmth of her breath on his skin. He'd never considered Jade as anything more than a friend, and the thought of attraction toward her at any other time would have drawn a disgusted groan.

But in the lonely dark of that small cave, and the pain of a loss too terrible to bear, he found her touch so comforting that he couldn't remember falling asleep.

And even after he woke to the warmth of a fire crackling near his feet the next morning, he thought himself dreaming, for her arms were entangled in his.

For nearly an hour, he didn't even look up to see the strange man who watched them through the acrid smoke.

Chapter 47

Whoever built the fire now poked the logs with a blackened stick. Noah raised his head and examined a bent old man with gray eyes and hair and beard. His back was stooped over a pan on the coals cooking sizzling cakes.

Jade's breath paused, and she jerked upright and met the stranger's gaze. The stranger did not smile, so Jade scooted deeper into the cave and hugged her knees, eyeing him with caution. "Who are you?" she said.

The stranger ignored her and placed more patties into the pan.

Noah scooted next to her, a mixture of fear and curiosity pinching the corners of his eyes. Jade leaned toward him and whispered without taking her gaze from the stranger, "Where did he come from?"

Noah shrugged and whispered, "He was here when I woke."

"Did you see the way he looked at me? Mother told me once about—" She stopped and pressed her mouth into her forearm.

Noah didn't want to talk about Elina any more than Jade did, so he said, "We can't just sit here waiting for something to happen. We've already wasted time. Look how high the sun is."

He stood, but Jade grabbed his arm and said, "Don't!"

He shook her off, but as he walked toward the man, he

struggled to swallow the saliva pooling in his mouth. Something about the way the man glanced up as Noah approached made him feel vulnerable, as if those gray eyes could pierce a mountain. "Who are you?" Noah said.

The man's eyes roamed Noah's body, then returned to the food in the pan. "You looked cold."

Noah waited for more, realized the man wasn't going to give it. "Where did you come from?"

For a moment, the man seemed to care about nothing other than scraping burnt food from the pan and popping the crisped pieces into his mouth.

"Hello?"

"Eh?" The man turned and licked the excess from his fingers.

"Who are you?"

"You don't even recognize your own family?" The man shook his head and clucked his tongue. "I'm your great-grandfather," the man said.

The man's words sent Noah's vision spinning. Lamech had once told him his great-grandfather had disappeared. That he had been gone for countless years. "What?"

The old man bent toward him and yelled as if Noah were partially deaf. "My name is Enoch. God sent me to teach you the Old Way."

Noah blinked, looked at Jade, who still hugged her knees and stared at the man. Noah returned his attention to Enoch. So many strange things had happened the past few days that for a moment he actually wondered if the man really could be Noah's great-grandfather. He certainly looked as if he had spent the past century in the wilderness. "If you're my great-grandfather, how did you find us?"

"God sent me."

"Why now and not several days ago?"

"You need me now," Enoch said.

"And I didn't before?"

"Sometimes what you think you need and what you truly need are irreconcilable."

But Noah thought that if the man's God could have sent

someone to help them, surely he could have saved Elina. And now Lamech and Methuselah were captured, and Noah and Jade had been forced into the wilderness. If this man was his great-grandfather, and God had truly sent him, Noah needed no more reason to hate both.

Enoch pulled the pan off the coals. "You are young, and ignorant, and filled with passion."

"And you are old and insane."

Enoch laughed. "We'd best remedy your attitude before we get to the more difficult parts of your training."

"What are you talking about?"

"The Old Way."

"Whatever that is, I want nothing to do with it."

"Yet you're still standing here, talking with me."

Noah suppressed the urge to slap him.

"Do your cares supplant God's will? Who can refuse him?" Enoch swept his hands to indicate the grass and trees and sky and fire.

"Thank you for the fire, but we're going now." Noah motioned for Jade to follow as he turned to continue through the woods.

"Aren't you hungry?" the man said, and used his tongue to dab the corner of his mouth.

Noah glanced at Jade in time to see her gaze locked on the food in the pan. "Come on," he whispered, "we need to go." And he grabbed her hand and pulled.

"If you leave now," the man said, "Lamech and Methuselah will die."

Noah fought to still the burning that welled up in his chest. He raised a hand to press the flesh that singed, and fought to quell the shiver erupting at the base of his back.

How did he know those names?

"All those who would come after you—your future children, your future friends," Enoch said. "All of them will disappear unless you learn to walk with God. He will fulfill the desires of your heart."

Noah's voice came cold and quiet. "What do you know of my heart?"

"More than you could imagine."

Noah considered Enoch a moment. There was something about the conviction in his eyes. No insanity. Just a clear confidence housed in a rickety frame weathered by age and beaten by the winds of time.

Enoch took a long breath. "When you lie alone at night and think of the longing in your chest as a burning, you think that the fire would have been quenched had your mother not been taken from you. But you only lie to keep the pain at bay." Enoch approached, nostrils flaring as his voice softened to a near whisper. "Adah could never quench the flames inside you."

The skin of Noah's face chilled like a stone in snow. "How do you know her name?"

"It does not matter. Nothing matters but your heart. Don't you see?"

"All I *see* is a man I don't know who speaks of things he can't understand."

"If your mother had been with you, your longing would have taken another form. She could never heal you, Noah. Neither could your father. Or Jade, for that matter."

Jade shifted beside him. "How do you—"

"Only God can quench the burning in your soul. Drink of his water, and you will thirst for nothing. Come, I know you are hungry. At least stay long enough to eat what I cooked. Perhaps then I can explain myself better."

Jade consulted him with caution in her eyes, then inched forward. "What did you make?"

Noah squeezed her wrist. "No. Don't eat it."

Enoch smiled and said, "I cooked some cakes sweetened with dates."

Jade's expression melted, for it had been over a day since either of them had eaten anything.

Jade crouched beside the pan, where Enoch indicated, and popped little bits of the cakes into her mouth, moaning with each bite. She beckoned Noah close, and he approached and sat, taking no food despite the ache in his stomach.

"You don't trust me," Enoch said.

"Why should I?" Noah said.

Enoch nodded. "What do you want to know?"

"How did you find us?"

Enoch regarded him and said, "Maybe we should start with an easier question."

"We start where I want, or I'm leaving."

Enoch nodded, bit his cheek, then pointed at the food, "If you aren't hungry . . ."

"Go ahead," Noah said, and dug his nails into his legs.

Enoch ate nearly a third of what was left in the pan and left the rest for Jade. "How old is your father now?"

"What does it matter?"

"It would help me answer your question. Also, do you know where we are?"

Noah shook his head. Enoch looked questioningly at Jade, who swallowed a bite of the food and shrugged.

"To be honest," Enoch said, "I don't have any idea either. In fact, I don't know where or *when* we are."

"What do you mean?"

"I seem to have lost track of quite a span of years."

Noah didn't know what that meant, but marked it as another warning.

"According to my reckoning," Enoch said, "your father was still young and without a wife. At least, for me, it was yesterday. For you it was a lifetime, and more."

Noah stared blankly, fighting the urge to topple the pan and claim the man insane. "That's impossible," he said.

"With God, all things are possible. In time, you will come to believe this too."

"How did you get here?"

"God."

"That means you don't know how you ended up here, yet you believe you have somehow appeared in a foreign land many years after the time when you were alive. Correct?"

"Correct."

"Then how did you know I was in need?"

"Why else would God bring me here?"

Noah rubbed his head.

Enoch chuckled. "The Almighty is quite a mystery, isn't he?"

"You have lost your mind. You're insane. You're making everything up."

"Then how do I know your entire family?"

Noah took a deep breath to settle the shaking, and judged how close the nearest jagged stone sat.

Enoch looked at Jade, a slight smirk curving his mouth. "If I were one of the devils, I would have killed you already. The food would have been poisoned, and yet I ate it myself. More than that, I certainly wouldn't tell you about the Old Way."

"Why not? The Others let us go. They didn't try to kill me even though they had the chance. Why should I believe that you would behave differently? Whatever they have planned, you could be helping them."

"The Others? Is that what you call them?" Enoch nodded. "An appropriate name. But I was speaking to Jade. Of course they would never kill you. But that is only because they seek to damage you worse than death." Enoch's neck reddened and his eyebrows crouched over gray eyes flashing like spears. "Make no mistake, the God-King desires nothing more than to be worshipped. His goal is to purge the Old Way from the minds of men. To make them forget who and what they are. To turn humanity into a race of animals—beasts chained and pitted against one another until all their thoughts dissolve into madness. Before God took me, my fellow followers of the Old Way had been working to resist him."

"Why would he want that, though?"

"Some say he himself is only a tool—an instrument played by a master Musician. For what purpose, only God and the Enemy know in full detail. And they will not say. Some mysteries are not for men to take hold of. But I have thought long and think I know enough to define our danger."

Jade had stopped eating, and Noah noticed the forest seemed to have hushed as if to hear Enoch's words.

"From the beginning, the Enemy has envied our birthright," Enoch said.

"The Enemy?"

"He was once a mighty servant of God. Neither man nor beast. Something Other—again, a good description. Then, like a bolt of lightning, he was cast from the heavens, and his form was forever marred by the descent so violent." Enoch gazed at the sky as if he could see the scene before his eyes. "Some say that he stumbled over humankind. That it was for lust of us that he fell."

"I don't understand," Noah said, and glanced at Jade in time to see her mouth a small circle beneath half-moon eyes.

"God created us to master the physical world," Enoch said. "To mirror the Almighty's glory in the world he created. Before he formed us, the Enemy held the highest position of honor among the Almighty's servants. Afterward, he and his brethren were commanded to bow to us. But they were not given the ability to experience the world we so freely enjoyed. And so, as the tale goes, the Enemy lusted after our bodies, and determined in his heart that he would steal them and usurp our position. For he wanted to be like God, as we were like God, and to gain ever more servants."

Noah's hands clenched his knees.

"How could he do that?" Jade said.

"If humankind were to willingly give up their position, the Enemy might take it. And so he has bent every thought toward that end—toward perverting humanity with the intention to destroy us from the inside out. So that he might steal our very bodies and walk in the skin of men, ruling the world as he sees fit. For if he could not rule us from without, he might do so from within. That is what he has been trying to do. But he cannot kill you, Noah. If he could, you would never have been born, for he can sense you as a predator smells his prey, and there is no place on earth that you could go to escape him."

"The Others," Noah said, "the men with horns. They are servants of the Enemy?"

"Indeed. But they have grown more powerful, more sophisticated. A millennium ago, when the first man and woman still walked the earth, their firstborn son did something terrible. Something that had never been done before."

Enoch paused, scooted the coals with a stick, and removed the pan. "His name was Cain, and he murdered his younger brother. In doing so, some say he birthed a terrible evil that the

Enemy used to gain a greater foothold in our world. They say the Enemy named it the Abomination, and now that Abomination walks about in a body of its own creation." Enoch turned toward Noah and whispered, "And, if I am not mistaken, you have met it."

Noah leaned back, eyes widening. "What?"

"It calls itself the God-King."

"The God-King is the tool the Enemy plans on using to fulfill his plan?"

Enoch nodded. "Have you not noticed the God-King's obsession with you? How he has followed your every step, and yet never killed you?"

Noah squinted, thinking back. Jade's fingers slipped into his, cold and slick.

"He has followed you since you were a babe, and feared you before you were born."

"Why?"

"Because you are the Almighty's chosen one. Destined to destroy the Abomination."

Noah paused a moment, thinking. "You tell wilder stories than my father did to get me to sleep."

"Truth can be exceedingly strange."

"What does the Almighty expect of me?"

Enoch narrows his eyes. "That is not for me to say. He will demand much of you. But he will never demand more than you can give. And in giving, he offers greater reward than you could imagine."

"Reward such as what?"

"Fulfillment. Peace." A pause. "Forgiveness."

The image of Elina falling to the ground, neck gushing red, stabbed his eyes, and he closed and rubbed them to push the images away.

No. Elina's death was not his fault. He refused to believe it.

"He wants to set the world free," Enoch said, "but humankind is enslaved to their lusts. The children of Adam have become nothing more than instruments of the Enemy, incessantly braying like donkeys in heat. Masochistic beasts who forget their own reflection. Tell me, could you abandon them? Could you let them perish in willful ignorance?"

Noah took a deep breath, feeling an invisible weightiness on his shoulders, straightening against it and hardening his expression. "What right do you have to place such demands on me?"

"You sit at a crucible of Time. For no fault of theirs, or yours, or mine. You have been chosen. Not by me, and not by some mystical force. You have been chosen by your very Creator."

"I didn't ask to be chosen," Noah said.

"No one asks to be born. Neither do they ask to die. And yet all must live and meet their end."

"Stop speaking in riddles."

"What I say only seems a riddle because you do not yet understand. But that is your call—to hear the truth and to make your choice. Stay with me and rise to meet your destiny, or leave and abandon yourself and all you hold dear to destruction."

A silence descended, broken only by their soft breaths and the gentle crackle of flames. Noah stared at the coals slowly pulsating, thinking they looked like a beating heart, wondering if his own chest would look the same could he peel back the skin and steal a look.

But he knew he would see nothing but the hue of Elina's throat.

He passed a hand over his eyes, longing to sever himself from the world, to find privacy. All the more because he believed Enoch's words and feared the truth of them.

That I will never be free. Never be alone. Never be able to step out from underneath the weight for fear that one misstep might shatter everything.

In that moment, he believed himself special. That few human beings would ever carry such a burden—even fewer at so young an age.

All his life, both loss and lies had primed him for pain and truth. He had been set apart. A tool. And he hated himself for it.

He gritted his teeth, removed his hand, and said, "I'm hungry."

Enoch nodded and retrieved a bag. "I have some extra food. I will cook it for you."

As Enoch worked, Noah tried to feel nothing, to become nothing. For he knew it might just be the last time he would ever be able to.

Enoch touched his arm, and Noah met his gaze.

"Thank you," Enoch said. "For bearing this burden. God will reward you."

Noah tried not to notice how Jade looked at him with wonder.

He had never felt more alone.

Chapter 48

Noah no longer wanted to speak. Thankfully, neither Jade nor Enoch seemed to mind, for Enoch ignored him while Jade stared at the flames, her face drawn in dark lines pointing downward. As night drew close, Enoch rose and tended the fire, building it to a considerable blaze before laying facedown with his palms stretched upward.

Noah tried to ignore the man, but something about the way he laid there nagged at him. He stood and said, "What are you doing?"

"Praying," Enoch said.

"To your God?"

"Who else?" Enoch said. "A leaf?"

"What do you pray for?"

"I've asked the Almighty to provide us a home. He desires your well-being, so I am confident he will supply it. If not, he will provide some other way."

Noah suppressed the urge to scoff at the convenient escape left in the event that a home didn't grow before their eyes. As much as Enoch's ignorance bothered Noah, if the old man thought praying could make a home appear, Noah would let him.

The sun set, and cold crept close, beating the fire with bitter gusts. Noah touched Jade's shoulder, but she shrugged away.

"Jade," Noah said, "I—"

"I don't want to talk."

"I wasn't trying to talk. I only wanted—"

"Just leave me alone."

He stared at Jade's profile, then stood, kicked dust into the fire, and walked into the cave to sit with his knees to his chest.

Enoch was still praying, his mumbling just soft enough to remain indistinct beneath the crackle of flames. Jade rested her forehead on her arm, face hidden, sniffing tears.

He scoffed, hoping it was loud enough for her to hear. If she didn't want his comfort, she shouldn't cry about it.

Then again, even as he stoked his anger, he knew he hadn't been trying to help. Only trying to comfort himself.

He recalled her hair slipping between his fingers and felt a rush of desire so strong he nearly returned to her. He imagined her pressed against him again. The smell of her, the feel of her breath on his neck.

A gust of chill wind slapped his cheek, and he cleared his throat, refusing to acknowledge the rush of warmth to his neck.

How could he forget her misery for his own desire?

And since when had he ever desired her?

Enoch rose and turned toward the brush, and Noah was surprised to see a man with dark skin emerge from deeper in the forest. The newcomer stopped and nodded at Enoch, who returned the nod before urging Jade and Noah close.

Noah stood, dusted off the backs of his legs, and approached. The man was thin and careworn, but his smile was kind.

"Hello," the newcomer said.

"Hello," Noah said.

The man bowed to Enoch. "The Almighty told me I would find some of his children in need."

Enoch's gray eyes grew grave. "We are indeed in great need."

Noah scoffed and smirked at Enoch. "You think we're fools?"

The newcomer ignored Noah and continued speaking to Enoch. "My home is not far. But there are wolves about.

Come, stay with me this night, and I will give you food and drink."

Noah folded his arms.

Enoch grabbed up his pack, kicked sand onto the fire, and asked the man to lead them. The path was dark, but the man knew his way and warned them of dangerous footing.

Even in the dark, Noah could tell something was wrong with Jade. She walked as if dreaming awake, head hung, shoulders slumped, each step dragged through the brush. When Noah tried to touch her, she jerked as if his touch burned. Frustrated, he tried to focus on the quiet words Enoch and the newcomer exchanged.

"My name is Barak," the newcomer said. "Tell me where you come from, and where you are traveling?"

"I come from foreign lands and distant times," Enoch said. "My goal is to teach the boy to continue in the Old Way beyond us."

"Beyond?" Barak glanced back and, when Noah met his gaze, looked away and quieted so that Noah couldn't hear what he said next.

Enoch chuckled, glanced back at Noah, and nodded. "Indeed."

"A darkness has been growing," Barak said. "The Enemy grows furious at some unforeseen twist."

"I have sensed it, too, but could not tell how recently it had grown."

"It's grown for many years. Yesterday, it reached its pitch. Birds fled. Squirrels and rabbits hid themselves. I found two deer slaughtered by one of the cats native to this region, yet the beast did not eat them." Barak caught Enoch by the arm as the old man stumbled. "Watch for those. Their roots grow above ground."

"Do you live alone?" Enoch said.

"Yes, though I first came here with my wife."

"I am sorry," Enoch said.

A sigh. "She rests now in the arms of One greater than me." Barak quieted so that Noah nearly couldn't hear him say, "Where sickness can no longer reach her."

"Why do you live in the wilderness?"

"Persecution. Most of my fellows were slaughtered for following the Old Way."

"Did you flee out of fear?"

Barak shook his head. "If not for the Almighty's command, I would have stayed. But my wife . . . had a difficult time."

"The sickness?"

The man nodded, then pointed and said, "Here we are."

Ahead loomed a dark mass hugged by tree branches. Through cracks in walls Noah saw a soft, golden glow. As much as he couldn't believe this shadowy building offered safety, he found himself longing for the comfort of close walls, a full stomach, and the warmth of family.

But his family had been torn away. Elina had been murdered, and he and Jade had been forced to flee alone, mere children in the wilderness.

He believed Father's claims now about the Others. That the world really was filled with violence and populated by men whose thoughts were only evil continually.

But he'd believed too late. Before, he couldn't trust people to be evil. Now, he trusted none to be good. All his life he'd been lied to, and now he wondered what he could ever truly believe.

He did not want to be special, and now, under the cover of darkness, he doubted his ability to be such. He wanted nothing more than to be a normal boy with a mother and a father and an uninteresting life. To grow into adulthood, become a builder, and enjoy relaxing in the afternoon sun, or waking to view the sunrise.

But he would never be able to devote himself to simplicity. Because all his life had been a slow darkening. Without knowing it, he had fled unseen enemies. Now he'd met the devil's weapon, and found it aimed at the flames burning beneath the skin of his chest.

But he would survive.

And Jade?

He struggled to see her face in the little moonlight peeking through the branches. As much as he wanted to trust Enoch and

Barak, he believed Jade the last of his family. The only one he might be able to trust.

But Elina had been murdered, and now Jade acted strangely. Had Enoch's words made her think he was responsible for her mother's death?

Barak moved up a small incline toward the door, released the latch, and swung it open, revealing an interior with a low ceiling lit by candlelight. He passed within, beckoned them to follow, and Enoch went first, followed by Jade and Noah.

Barak locked the door behind them.

Chapter 49

The first thought that struck Noah was that Barak was no builder. The home did little to keep out the cold, because when the wind intensified, the chill lanced through cracks in the logs sealed only partway with black resin. He stared at their construction, wondering how the walls stood at all. Then he approached the corner and saw hidden grooves Barak had used to notch the logs together, achieving remarkable sturdiness without visible support.

So, maybe the man knew a few tricks. The home certainly would offer safety from wild animals, but it was smaller than it appeared, and no more than a simple square box. In one corner sat a pile of animal skins. In a second lay utensils and dried fruit with herbs hanging above cooked meat and vegetables laid beside pitchers holding water and rice. Candles burned on knee-high tables haphazardly hewn from what appeared to be fallen trees. Along one wall sat a row of bins filled with knives, hammers, traps, netting, and rope. Across everything rested a layer of soot and the marks of frequent usage.

Jade crossed to the animal skins and lay on them, curling inward and closing her eyes as if to block out all the truth in the world. Barak frowned and approached the pitcher, grabbing three stone cups and filling them for his guests.

Noah thanked him and drank deeply, asking for two refills

before the madness of thirst waned. Enoch followed, but Jade would not respond, so Barak handed Noah the cup and bade him offer it.

Noah did as he was asked and knelt beside Jade, softly nudging her.

At first, she did not respond. When he grabbed her hand and kissed it, he said, "Jade, you must drink at least a little."

She raised her head, took the cup, and sipped once before setting it on the ground and pulling the animal skins over her head.

Noah returned and mirrored Enoch and Barak, who sat crossed-legged beside the table and bent forward in quiet conversation.

"Warriors passed through the forest yesterday," Barak said.

"I know nothing about them," Enoch said.

"I tracked them," Barak said. "They seemed to have captured two men. I can't ensure you're safe here."

"We shall stay for as short a time as we can," Enoch said.

Barak pointed to the empty cup in Enoch's hand and raised his brow.

"I am satisfied, thank you," Enoch said.

"Then you are hungry." Barak stood and gathered what appeared to be dried fruit. He took the top off a small container and retrieved three flat breads. After placing the food on the table, he refilled their cups with wine from a skin at his side.

Noah tore the flat bread and grabbed a dried apricot. The bread was bitter, but the fruit masked the bite. Soon the gnawing ache of hunger diminished, and the fog in his mind cleared.

"Thank you for your hospitality," Enoch said. "May the Almighty bless you for your generosity."

"Servants serve," Barak said.

"And faithful servants are well rewarded." Enoch wrapped a ball of dried fruit in the flatbread before dipping it in wine and taking a bite.

Barak tipped his head Jade's direction and quieted. "Is the girl ill?"

Noah cleared his throat. "She lost her mother yesterday."

Enoch stopped chewing.

"The devils cut her throat." A shudder began at the base of Noah's neck and rippled down his spine, raising the hairs on his arms. "And the captured men you saw were my father and grandfather."

Barak's jaw muscles tensed. "Then you deserve peace." He stood. "I will return late. Sleep where you find comfort. The food you find is yours. Only do not touch my trapping supplies. They are difficult to replace."

Barak unlocked the door and left, and Enoch stared long at Noah.

"Why stare when you could speak?" Noah said.

"I am sorry," Enoch said. "I did not know what had befallen you. My son and grandson . . . were they injured?"

Noah shrugged. "They were alive when I saw them last."

Enoch nodded and pushed away from the table. Folding his hands, he pressed his fingers to his lips. With eyes shut, he rocked back and forth, humming a low melody.

Noah could take no more of the man's religion, so he stood and left Enoch to his rituals to see Jade, who stiffened at his approach. Sometime soon, Enoch would sleep, and they would have the opportunity to leave.

Noah could not abide the thought of being chained to some religious relic. He couldn't imagine being what Enoch wanted him to be. He just wanted to leave so that he and Jade could find their way back to Father.

The longing for Lamech's voice lodged in Noah's throat, bringing a sickness to his belly and a burning to his eyes as he lay beside Jade, ignoring how she whimpered when he turned his nose to her hair, letting the burning in his eyes wash his face.

The flames grew, and as he waited for sleep, he clutched his breast, fearing that just beneath his skin lurked a demon devouring him from the inside out, gnawing through the marrow of his bones.

I must drown it, he thought. *I must drown it in a flood.*

And so he shed enough tears to do just that.

Chapter 50

Half of the candles burnt themselves dark before Noah woke to Enoch snoring. Wind twisted the cabin and pressed the logs to groan. He didn't remember falling asleep, but Jade's head rested on his chest, and her arm lay across his belly.

He leaned up slowly, holding his breath. Jade's arm slid off, and he pressed a hand over her mouth, shushing her awake. Her eyes flashed, then narrowed with irritation.

"What are you doing?" she said after he released her.

"Don't wake the old man," he whispered.

"Why not?"

"We have to get out of here. We have to find my father."

Jade glanced around the home as another blast of wind struck. She clutched the coverings closer.

"You know we can't stay," Noah said. "You heard Enoch. He wants to turn me into his apprentice."

"You don't believe him."

"I'm no savior."

They stared at each other for several moments before Noah stood, carefully creeping to the food, gathering dried fruit and bread, and tying it in a cloth satchel. After securing the food to his belt, he crossed to the toolboxes and retrieved a long knife.

In the middle of the room sat two candles still flickering,

sending just enough light to illuminate the rise and fall of Enoch's back beside the table. Noah slid the knife carefully into the belt of his tunic and followed the wall on tiptoes past Enoch's sleeping form.

When he reached the door, he turned back to see Jade standing atop the animal skins. He was too close to Enoch now to risk warning her to keep quiet, so he kept on.

Each scrape of his foot sounded a hammer blow. Noah felt his pulse thump in his throat, then his ears as he reached, fingers slipping over the handle of the door.

Enoch's snores skipped, then deepened once more.

Noah pushed against the door, exited, turned, and shut it behind him.

The canopy was thick, and he searched for the night skies to find his bearings.

As he did so, the door creaked, sending a shock of fear up his throat. He slid into the shadows and pulled the knife from his belt as a dark shape emerged from the home.

It was too small to be Enoch, and as the door swung shut, he approached and slipped the knife into his belt. "You woke him for sure."

"I checked after the door creaked," Jade said. "He's asleep."

"So . . . couldn't stand to be alone?"

"Stop speaking to me like that," Jade said. "You've been angry toward me ever since we woke."

"And you've ignored me since Enoch came."

"I haven't been ignoring you."

"Right," Noah said. "That's why you wouldn't look at me, or respond to anything I said."

"What do you expect?"

Noah clenched his jaw. "I don't know. I feel . . . when we were in the cave, I . . ." He cleared his throat. It was pointless to talk about the desire that had erupted within him. Besides, how could he put it into words? "We need to get moving before Enoch realizes we're gone."

She grabbed his hand. "Noah . . ."

He tried to ignore the skewering in his chest, the ache he

saw mirrored in her eyes. "I miss Elina," he said. "I miss them both."

The wetness on Jade's cheek shone in the forest-dappled starlight. Even in the dark, he could tell she was shaking. "Will it ever stop hurting?" she said. "I've felt I would die these few days, but I haven't, and I'm too scared to die."

"Whatever happens, we can't give up," Noah said. "It's what they want. But I won't do it."

"What's wrong with you? Why don't you want to die?"

Noah turned away and said, "We have to hurry."

The door creaked again, and a deep voice rumbled, "Hurry to your death?"

Noah jumped as he caught sight of Enoch standing in the doorway, candlelight casting a dusty halo about his head, obscuring his face in shadows. "For that is all that will meet you."

"You won't stop us," Noah said.

"No?" Enoch stepped into the moonlight. "Do you know how to navigate the wilderness? Could you save your family?"

Noah's hand slid over the handle of the knife, but he dared not draw it. Not yet.

Jade fidgeted beside him. Likely wanting any excuse to return to the house and hide under the covers.

It made him hate Enoch even more.

"Come back inside." Enoch's back bent, and he looked his age. "I've endured enough of your foolishness."

"I'm not coming back."

Enoch waved him forward. "You are just a child."

"I'll do it."

"Or die trying."

"Either would be better than what I feel now."

Enoch quieted. "I know. That's why you are standing with your hand on a pilfered knife. And I, an old man, am awake fighting back pain when I'd rather be asleep. But you already know you would be a fool to leave. Even more so if you took Jade with you."

Noah drew his knife. "Are you trying to make me hate you? I don't trust anything that comes out of your mouth."

"Hate is a symptom of stupidity. Distrust, however, is a symptom of being lied to. Tell me. Have I lied to you?" Enoch paused, waiting for a response. When he received none, he chuckled. "Yes, you know I have spoken openly. And yet you hate me for it. Let that give you pause."

"You claim to speak truth, but you can't prove a thing."

"I already told you that I only guess most of the story."

"What, then? You would have me stay and lie prostrate until the devils come and slit my throat like Elina's?" Noah's face reddened, and his knuckles ached against the metal. "You would have me give up? Let them take my father away, just as they took my mother away, and everyone else I ever loved?"

"Not everyone," Enoch said, and pointed at Jade. "She is still with you. And she loves you. Trust me, I was not sent so that you might love me, or so that I might replace your father. I was sent to teach you the Old Way, and that is all. That is what I care about."

Noah spat on the ground and smeared it with his sandal.

"The choice is yours," Enoch said. "Stay and live, or leave and condemn us all to death." He ascended the stairs to Barak's home and said, "I am going to sleep. Be quiet when you return."

And he slammed the door behind him.

PART VI

Noah and Jade

"When Enoch had lived 65 years, he fathered Methuselah. Enoch walked with God after he fathered Methuselah 300 years and had other sons and daughters. Thus all the days of Enoch were 365 years. Enoch walked with God, and he was not, for God took him."
—Genesis 5:21–24

Chapter 51

J ade slid away from Noah, the bond of mutual suffering broken by the shadow cast by Enoch's words. Once more the old man had illuminated the difference between him and Jade.

"I'm sorry," Jade whispered as she shuffled to the door. She opened it carefully, and this time it didn't creak when she slipped inside and left him alone.

He slid the knife into his belt and gripped his forearms to still them, but he shivered neither from cold nor fear.

Ever since the God-King spilled Elina's blood and took Father away, hatred had been the only true force in Noah's life. He hated the Others for what they'd done to his family. Hated his mother for dying. Hated his father for lying. Hated Jade for changing. Hated Enoch for his demands.

Noah desired nothing more than to rediscover the trail the Others left, follow it, and find his father so that they might be reunited, the world be damned.

But as much as he distrusted Enoch and thought the man inflated by his own words, he was right about one thing. Noah would never make it through the wilderness alone.

Even if, by some stretch of good fortune, he survived, what would he do when he came upon his father captured by the Others? He'd been powerless to save Elina.

He'd be just as powerless to save his father.

And so he hated himself most of all. Because he couldn't save anyone. Yet Enoch placed the mantle across Noah's shoulders and bid him carry the weight of the world.

He closed his eyes and counted to release emotion and allow his mind to drift, as his father had taught him all those years ago, so that anything might replace the inferno raging in his chest.

The heat lowered, settling in his belly like blistering ash, coiling and cooling to an oily sickness. Rage made way for reason, and he settled for the only decision that would give him a chance at a better life.

He would stay. Not because Enoch said he should, but because he knew his own plan had been impossible from the beginning.

He shivered at the realization that it was the burning he felt that nearly made him throw his life away. And for what? If he did not find a way to suppress it, he feared it would consume him.

But how could he be rid of it? It had stalked him his entire life. More than anything, he longed for peace, for a settling of the burning. He hoped the Old Way was the key, even as he balked at the possibility.

He returned to Barak's hovel. The candles had all been blown out; he heard Enoch snoring beside the table and just barely made out Jade's form on the pile of animal skins. He said nothing as he sat in the corner, hugged his knees, and rested his head.

Hours later, Barak returned quiet as a bat, barely a rustle of cloth as he locked the door and reclined to sleep.

Only then did Noah relax, his bones achingly stiff. He sprawled out several feet from Jade on the knotted floor, where he spent the rest of the night caught between fitful nightmares and waking fear.

...

In the morning, Noah woke to Jade rustling the covers and

Enoch mumbling prayers. Barak was gone, and from outside came a rhythmic thudding. Noah's face flushed as he realized someone had removed the knife and satchel he'd stolen and arranged the bag's contents on the knee-high table.

Noah stood and said, "What is Barak doing?"

"He is preparing firewood," Enoch said.

Noah sucked his teeth and tried to avoid looking at the food on the table.

"Eat," Enoch said. "Barak is not angry you tried to steal food. He already offered what you took, save the knife. And you returned that."

Noah sat cross-legged before the table and ate, knowing he must consume as much as he could to fight the sickness that tightened his throat. When he finished, he stood and gathered water in a cup.

"Follow me," Enoch said.

Noah downed the water and followed him through the door.

Behind the home, Barak stood with his axe in hand and paid them no mind as they passed. Enoch neither prayed nor spoke, though he took uncomfortably wide strides, forcing Noah to rush. As they passed under a low tree branch, Enoch snatched a leaf and continued.

The old man seemed to take turns with no more guidance than whichever path was the easiest—now turning left to avoid thorns, now descending a ferny valley to avoid a rocky hillside, all the while nearly going in circles. When given the choice between a bog and a hill, he ascended the hill and sat at the top, laying the leaf on the ground before him.

Noah sat facing him and mirrored the man's crossed legs. "So," Noah said, struggling to excise the disdain from his voice, "when does my *training* begin?"

"It began more than a day ago. You've done nothing but fail, which is precisely why we are sitting on this hill."

Noah reached for the leaf, but Enoch slapped his hand hard enough to drive an ache through his bones. Noah scowled and rubbed his knuckles.

"Don't ruin my illustration."

"What are you talking about?"

"That leaf is you," Enoch said.

Noah stared at it with one eyebrow raised.

"You have been snatched from where you belong," Enoch said, "severed from the roots that would otherwise nourish you. Just like this leaf, the longer you remain separated from your beginning, the more you will deteriorate, until you can no longer fulfill your purpose."

"And what is my purpose? To save the world?"

Enoch rocked back as if Noah had struck him. "Of course not. What gave you such a ridiculous idea?"

"You did, you old fool."

"If you fail, the world will be destroyed, but you were never tasked with saving it. No man ever will be, save one, and you are not him." Enoch reached toward Noah's forehead, but Noah struck his hand away.

Enoch caught Noah by the wrist and squeezed. "I may stoop as I walk, but it would be many years before you could hope to best me, even with a weapon in hand."

He let go, and Noah stood and turned away as much to hide the heat rising to his face as to avoid looking at Enoch any longer. He hated how the man's eyes probed. How his bent posture held a strange confidence. It reminded him very much of Methuselah, and of his father.

"Sit down," Enoch said. "I wasn't finished."

Noah turned and lifted his foot to kick sand into Enoch's face, but one look at the man's expression stopped him. He growled and sat back down hard enough to send a bit of grit into Enoch's teeth, then folded his arms and glared. "Get on with it."

"Do you know how we came to be on this hilltop?"

"You led the way," Noah said.

"I'm looking for the symbolic answer, not the obvious one. Apply your mind and answer appropriately."

Noah took a deep breath and let it out slow, consciously willing his fingers to relax. "We took the easiest paths."

"Wrong. We took the *less difficult* paths."

Noah couldn't stop the incredulous chuckle that escaped his throat.

"Think about it," Enoch said.

"I did."

"The difference resides in the attitude."

"Are you trying to tell me I like the easy way?"

"You may be foolish, but you're not lazy," Enoch said. "When tasked with getting from one cliff to another, rather than climb or search for a hidden path, you would rather jump to your death. The Old Way is neither the easiest nor the most difficult path—or in your case the impossible one. The Old Way is the *less* difficult way, though it often doesn't appear so."

"I'd only jump off a cliff if I saw no other way."

"Exactly. Which is why I have been sent to you. You are brash. Impetuous. Easily angered and disturbed. You face an enemy beyond you, forced into an impossible situation."

"You're the only one who's disturbed," Noah said. "Just tell me what the Old Way is so we can be done with this."

"The Old Way is not some principle of carpentry. It is a life-style. You can only understand it as you live it. I am not here to teach you concepts so much as to equip you emotionally and spiritually so that you might *experience* the Old Way and allow it to transform you."

Noah considered that. "This isn't going to be quick, is it?"

Enoch chuckled. "What is Time to the Almighty?"

"Will the Old Way help me reconnect with my father?"

"I don't know. Perhaps. Maybe not. It hardly matters."

Noah tore up the grass and tossed it to the slight breeze cresting the hill. The blades shone as they spun, reflecting the sun, scattering light as they scattered themselves. "How am I supposed to know which paths to choose? Is it just some random dance?"

Enoch lifted the leaf between his thumb and forefinger, twirling it before his eyes. "If you walk with the Almighty and daily seek his face before anything else, he will speak to you." He blew on the leaf, sending it fluttering in a new direction.

"What if I don't understand him?"

"He wove you with his own Word. He knows how to speak so that you will understand."

Noah stared at his hand, subtly stained green by uprooting

the grass.

"You are displeased?" Enoch said.

He could not remember the precise moment the burning returned, but nonetheless it was there, spreading through his chest. "I must leave my family, my dreams, and my desires to sit on a hilltop and follow an imaginary being that I don't believe exists. And every important choice for the rest of my life must be defined by what makes me the more perfect person you and this invisible being expect me to be. Correct?"

"Hardly."

"What am I missing?"

"In worshipping the Creator who made you for his own good pleasure, you will please yourself."

"The last thing I want is to please your God."

"That's because you do not know him yet."

"Do you know what it's like to never know your mother? To have your father torn away? To see the only woman you ever called family murdered in front of you?" The burning rose to the backs of his eyes.

Enoch's voice settled. "No, child."

"Then you have no right to tell me what I want. Because the only thing I desire is to kill the God-King like he killed Elina and my mother."

"You think that will satisfy you?"

"I do."

"And what happens once you've succeeded and the ambition gives way? What will be there to greet you?"

"The drive to find the rest of the Others and do the same to them."

"You are not special in your pain. Your ambition is not driven by the loss of your family, but by something deeper and more primal. We are all born forgetting our Creator, and life is but a long discovery of his goodness. Pain, many times, is the pathway that teaches us. In time, you will see. I pray sooner rather than later." Enoch rose, set his hands on his hips, and popped the bones in his back. "That's enough for today," he said. "Your training will resume tomorrow. I need to spend more time in prayer before we continue."

Chapter 52

J ade squeezed her eyes shut, but no matter how hard she tried, sleep eluded her. She only wanted to return to dreaming so that she might steal another glance at Mother's smiling eyes.

She thought she had known pain until she saw her mother murdered. Now, each moment that slid by seemed a little more of the stuff of life lost to the dust.

She rolled to her side and saw a white lily laid an arm's length away. Barak had offered it nearly an hour earlier. She knew the flower's form held beauty, yet could no more feel its beauty than she could feel her mother's hand on her shoulder.

However, all of Elina's mistakes and loveless distance now seemed emptied of substance. Jade knew her mother deeply flawed, yet finally, in death, somehow Elina's love had been freed to touch her.

"It's sick," she whispered to Enoch's God. "You're sick." Because if he truly were in control, surely he would know . . . how cruel that is.

The door creaked, and Jade did not look, for she believed Barak returning. Then she heard Noah's voice speak her name. "Jade."

She turned and met Noah's gaze. He stood alone beside the knee-high table. A boy with the weight of the world on his shoulders, and the intensity of manhood thrust through green eyes.

She knew she must face him, even as she'd avoided him these past days. For she could not bear to lose him. She loved him more deeply than ever, but when he looked at her, she heard Elina's screams and felt the pain of that knife at her own throat.

She could endure the pain for a time, but soon it strangled her, until she needed to push him away to breathe more easily.

"Jade," he said a second time.

She looked away as he sat in front of her. She picked up the lily between her first and second fingers, twirling it, studying its curves and silken texture. "You returned quicker than I expected."

"Enoch said we've done enough today."

Jade nodded and broke the stem. Clear fluid oozed from the stem onto her fingers.

"I don't think I can do it," Noah whispered. "Do you really believe what he says is true?"

She folded the remains of the flower on itself and broke it again. "What would change if I didn't?"

A pause. Then, angrily, "Nothing, I suppose."

Jade crumpled the petals in her fist, tossed them away, and lay down again, turning her back to him. She felt she would cry, though she could identify no reason why.

"It's not my fault," Noah said. "What happened to her."

Jade's body shuddered.

"So stop blaming me," he said, and the words pricked her like a thorn in the side.

He stood and exited, slamming the door behind him, making her jump and whimper beneath the covers.

Chapter 53

The next day, Enoch took Noah on another walk. This time, Noah was expected to listen to Enoch's prayers. When it came time for him to mumble assent, he let out an involuntary snort.

"You're being insincere," Enoch said, and stopped them short.

"How can I be anything else?"

"By choosing to be sincere."

"You want me to lie?"

"Repent for not believing, and ask the Almighty to give you the strength to believe."

Noah rolled his eyes, but the old man was watching, so he followed it with a shrug and walked on.

Enoch didn't follow. "I'm waiting for you to say it."

Noah turned back, balled his hands into fists, and spoke each word slowly and deliberately. "Dear Almighty, forgive me for not believing. Make me believe you so that this fool servant of yours can finally give me peace." And he turned and began making his way back to Barak's home.

Enoch followed and said, "Where do you think you're going? We're not done yet. Get back here."

Noah flicked his wrist in dismissal. "Apparently I need to spend more time in *prayer* before we can continue."

...

Later that night, after Noah calmed enough to speak with Enoch, he interrupted the man's evening prayers by asking when they should expect to leave Barak's home.

"I don't know," Enoch said. "That's why I'm praying."

"You've been praying since the sun set," Noah said. "How could you have anything left to say?"

"Because I've not been speaking. I've been listening."

"What has he said?"

"Nothing." Enoch opened his eyes. "Silence can also be a gift. There is great peace to be found in it, if you know what to listen for."

"Right."

"If you sit down, I'll show you."

Noah groaned. "Do you really think I want your training after earlier today?"

"Just hush and sit. You don't have to fake anything. Just sit and listen."

Noah looked toward Jade to see if she was watching, but she was sleeping again, a crumpled heap beneath animal skins, seeking dreams for what life could not offer. Barak had left to hunt for food and wouldn't be back until deep in the night, so Noah had little else to distract him. He wasn't tired, so sleep seemed an impossibility.

He sighed, sat where Enoch indicated, and said, "Fine. But I'm not doing anything weird."

Enoch closed his eyes. "No reason to."

After a long, uncomfortable silence, Noah said, "What am I supposed to do?"

"First, stop talking. Second, focus on the quiet. Let your thoughts, worries, and cares fall into it." Enoch opened one eye and smirked. "Or you can just sit there."

Noah tried to do as Enoch said, attuning his ears to the quiet. After a few moments, the sound of blood rushing to his ears intensified, followed by the deafening ring of silence.

Silence is nothing. What's the point of focusing on nothing?

Is something supposed to happen?
I don't hear any voices.
Apparently neither does Enoch.
He said I'd feel peace, but I don't feel any peace.
Father is gone.
Elina is gone.
Jade is angry at me.
Stop. Try to focus on the silence again.
Okay. There it is.
Right beneath Enoch's loud breathing.
"It's not working," Noah said.

"Of course not," Enoch said.

"What am I doing wrong?"

"Nothing."

"Nothing you say ever makes sense."

"You don't have the strength to do it right."

Noah slapped the floor. "Then why did you tell me to try?"

Enoch opened his eyes and stared at Noah with such intensity it sent a shiver down his spine. "You couldn't be born on your own. You can't breathe on your own. You can't live another day on your own. You think you want justice, but if justice were allowed, you would be slaughtered with the rest of us. You are nothing special, save that you belong to the Almighty. That you were formed to reflect his glory, the same as the rest of us. Our purpose is to worship the Almighty, and to offer everything we have to him. It is only when we offer up our will to the Almighty and declare that we can do nothing apart from him that we will be able to do anything but die."

Noah scoffed. "Then how can I deny the Almighty's existence?"

"He gave you the strength to do so," Enoch said.

"How does that work with what you just said?"

"The Almighty gives you the choice to deny him to intensify the meaning of choosing to love him. If that makes no sense to you, think about if Jade could choose nothing but to love you. Wouldn't her love become meaningless?"

"You never speak this straightforwardly. What else are you trying to get at?"

"You should expect yourself to hate the Almighty, because that is your nature, just as it is my nature. We must die so that he can live. We must sacrifice our will, our lives, everything, and petition him to give us the strength to love and choose him. Only then will we live out our destiny. Only then will we find peace. But I promise you this—the peace, joy, and hope that you will find by walking the Old Way cannot be stolen. The Old Way is sacrificial. Death is the ultimate fear, so if you've already died, your fear dies with you. That is why I spend so much time in prayer. That is why I sit here listening to the silence. Because I can throw all my selfish desires and ambitions and sin into that great abyss, and out of it comes nothing. Then, after I am emptied, the Almighty pours himself into me, replacing every dirty, broken part with wholeness. He restores my soul." Enoch's eyes shone as he said, "That is the Old Way. Believe and be whole or reject him and die a thousand deaths."

Noah leaned back, only now becoming aware of his fingers clenching his tunic.

"Now," Enoch said, and closed his eyes, "if you'll excuse me, I need to finish praying."

...

Over the next week, the days fell into a familiar pattern. Noah would wake to the sounds of Barak working outside. In the mornings, Jade refused to speak, so Noah would accompany Enoch on his walks and listen to his ramblings.

Enoch told stories of ancient times. Of the beginning of the world and the first years of humanity.

At times, Noah was certain the man was insane. At other times, Enoch's words struck a chord so unexpectedly profound that he wondered if the man truly did know the world's deepest secrets.

In the afternoons, after Enoch and Noah returned, Jade would speak, though in a stilted, limited fashion. Noah would tell her of his training, his doubts, and all he nearly believed.

Jade would nod and agree, but she never spoke as she used

to. Her haughty laugh and glittering eyes had been stolen, along with the rest of the life Noah had known.

Ten days after they arrived at Barak's home, Enoch declared that they must go to the city. When asked why, he replied, "The Almighty spoke."

"When will we depart?" Noah said. "And will we return?"

"We will depart tomorrow morning. I do not know when we will return, or even if we will. Barak will accompany us, for he needs to replenish his supplies. Beyond that our way is unknown."

And so they prepared for their journey.

Chapter 54

"Time to leave, Jade." Enoch's voice came soft, yet firm.

Jade felt for the burnt remains of Noah's mannequin, that final memento still left of their former life, and hid it in the folds of her dress.

"Are you ready?" Enoch said.

Jade stood and nodded, then followed Enoch into the harsh sunlight. After countless days huddled in the dark of the shack, the world seemed oppressively large. Noises came foreign, half-remembered like songs in a dream. From the patter of Barak's sandals, to Enoch's heavy breathing, everything seemed louder than she remembered.

As they went, she sidled up to Noah, who lagged behind the others. She drew out the remains of the mannequin. "Here," she said, and offered it to him. "I thought you would want this back."

He stopped midstride and stared at the object. Taking hold of it, he brought it to his lips and kissed it before stuffing it in his tunic. "You had it this whole time?"

"It was all I thought to grab. Mother . . ." She rubbed her neck.

"I understand," Noah said.

"Can I tell you something I've not told anyone else?"

Noah nodded.

"After everything that happened . . . I feel that my mother truly did love me. But part of me thinks that it only feels that way. That it's only true in seeming."

Noah shook his head. "Don't let the Others make you doubt. She loved you, Jade. She never left you."

"Then why is she gone?" Jade said.

"We have to move on. Otherwise, how could you pay the Others back for what they did?"

She looked into his eyes and saw in them the strength she longed for. "How can you just push it aside?"

"I'm not."

"Well, I'm trying to, and I can't. When I sleep, I see her. When I wake, the pain just strikes deeper. I try to sleep again, though I know it will make it worse, because I can't bear to breathe without her."

"I know," Noah said. "And I would feel the same, but for the fact that the ones who did this are still alive."

Footsteps grew as Barak and Enoch approached. Enoch raised his brow as he neared them. "Why have you stopped?"

Noah looked toward Jade, who redirected her gaze to the ground. "I needed to rest for a moment," Noah said.

"Next time, warn us. We didn't know where you had gone."

"Sorry," he said. "I'll speak up next time."

Chapter 55

The village was a huddle of thatched huts interspersed over rolling plains farmed by its inhabitants. As they approached, Noah saw no farmers in their fields. He wondered why, for the weather was fine and the season ripe.

Before they entered the village, Barak stopped them and whispered in Enoch's ear. At first, Noah thought it a passing remark. Then Enoch whispered into Barak's ear.

Jade bent toward Noah. "Why have we stopped?"

Noah hushed her to catch Barak's words, but the man was too quiet. Enoch nodded, then addressed them. "You will cause no trouble when we enter the village. You will speak to no one, even when spoken to. Let Barak and I handle any issues that might arise. No matter what, do not let yourself be separated from us. Do you understand?"

Noah suppressed the urge to groan. "We understand."

"Barak needs to purchase supplies. Now that we're here, he thinks today was a bad time to visit. Nothing can be done about it, and there's no reason for us to hide the potential danger from you."

"What do you mean?" Jade said.

"I hope Barak's fears prove unfounded, but if you do as I say, you should be safe. Just remember to stay near us and speak with no one."

Noah nodded. Jade bit her cheek. Barak and Enoch trudged on.

As they entered the village, the way grew easier. The grasses were replaced by dirt paths hardened from frequent travel. No children played outside the houses. No men or women stood in open doorways.

Deeper in the village, they heard great revelry. Within the distant laughter laid a shadow that, combined with Enoch's warnings, gave Noah a sense of dread rather than excitement.

They rounded a high fence that surrounded the market, and in the center stood a wooden platform. Naked women lined the platform with shackles on their wrists and necks, each woman linked to the next. And the chains were held by a pair of Others whose horns reached toward the sky.

Men gathered around the platform. Some drank amber liquid from flasks. Others jeered at the women and laughed. A select few stood aloof, arms folded, scowls plastered under dark-rimmed eyes. On the outskirts stood the market booths.

Barak led Noah and the others to a booth that held tools both wooden and metal. The tool merchant refused to meet Barak's eyes. When Barak chose what he wanted and slid the money toward the merchant, the man whispered, "You should leave. That one on the stage is eyeing the children."

Jade's face paled, and her fingers shook as she clutched at her dress as if to keep it from being torn away. She craned her neck to see the Others on the platform, and stilled.

Noah followed her gaze toward a trio of women being led down the stage to a short, fat man who stumbled from too much drink. The Other leading the women handed the little man the chain in exchange for a lump of gold. The little man pulled out a whip and snapped one of the women in the face. She cried out as a red line thickened and dripped blood down her neck.

Noah felt as if someone had struck him in the throat. Who were these men? How dare they abuse the women like that? "What are they doing?" Noah said. "And why are we doing nothing to stop them?"

Enoch grabbed Noah's shoulder and whispered, "Don't."

"Are they selling people?"

The little man jerked the chain and forced the women he'd purchased down an alleyway, whipping them as he went.

"No," Noah said, bitter tears rising as he thought of Elina and Lamech, and then of his mother. The very acts being perpetrated before him were the source of his life's greatest horror. He tried to count the women, seeing them anew as broken families, but lost count as he noticed the Other who had sold the women staring at Jade.

Jade fainted, her body crumpling to the ground as the fat man and his newly purchased trio disappeared around the bend. Noah stood dumbfounded as Enoch dipped and lifted Jade, patting her cheeks to wake her. Barak, too, dipped to her level and spoke her name, but she did not wake.

After one more glance down the alley where the little man disappeared, Noah wrenched a fishing spear from the booth and sprinted after him.

"Don't!" the merchant said.

But Noah was gone, intoxicated by the cool air rushing through his lungs as he stretched his legs further, faster. Heavy footsteps gained on him, and he glanced back just long enough to see Barak, whose gaze was set like coal in a mountainside.

No, Noah thought. *I will not fail. Not this time!*

Rounding the corner and increasing his speed, he found the fat man forcing the women against the wall of a building so that he might beat them. Already, the women were cowering, weeping, bleeding from the lash of the whip.

Noah paused for a fraction of a moment, frozen by the sight of them so vulnerable, so exposed. Then the man thrust his knee into the first woman's abdomen, and Noah's grip tightened around the spear, his vision contracting. The burning rose in his chest until it seemed his hands had been thrust into flames, and he dashed down the alley, raising the tip of his weapon and bracing for impact.

The fat man glanced up and narrowed his eyes just as Noah plunged the tip of the spear through his side. The man bellowed like a wild boar, and the women collapsed over each other and screamed. The weapon slid through the man's ribs, and Noah lost his grip and collided with him.

As they tumbled over each other, Barak swooped down with hands like steel and breath like a lion's. He lifted Noah off the ground and slammed him into the building, knocking the air from his chest.

Noah crumpled into a heap next to the cowering women, and Barak spun and slammed his heel into Noah's head, sending a covering of blackness over everything.

Chapter 56

J ade woke to Enoch's wrinkled fingers spreading her eyelids. His bright eyes peeked through a mess of tangled hair and probed her, questioning. She moaned and turned away, noticing that she leaned against a wooden wall, and above her hung a thatched awning.

"Can you speak?" Enoch said.

"Yes," she whispered. "Where is Noah?"

Enoch huffed. "He stole a weapon from the merchant and ran off to pursue his obsession."

"What—"

"No time for questions. Barak will take care of him. We must leave with all haste. The merchant was furious, but he has no desire to see a child fall into the hands of the slave drivers. And neither do I."

Enoch pulled her up, and she didn't even have time to dust herself off before they were off again at a faster pace than she'd thought Enoch capable of. They skirted the outside of the village and made their way back in a different direction than they arrived.

"Where are we going?" Jade said.

"Barak's home is no longer safe. We return to the cave where we first met."

"And after?"

"We part ways."

The ground seemed to melt beneath her, and she stumbled and nearly fell. "With Barak? Or with you?"

"I do not know," Enoch said.

Jade looked away and thought back to what had happened in the village. When she'd caught the Other staring at her, she saw it happening all over again. The way they jerked those women around like dogs on chains . . .

"I'm sorry you had to see that," Enoch said. "You have no reason to feel shame."

"I never knew . . . I mean, Mother told me of things like that. I just . . ."

"It is hard to believe that men can be so filled with death that they might rob others of life. But it is the truth. Under the leadership of the ones you call the Others, they have murdered followers of the Old Way. Through the pressure of fear and violence, the Others changed our world in ways unimaginable—even after what you saw today."

"How could anything be worse than that?"

"I could not even describe the depths of man's evil without feeling remorse for darkening your imagination. But we should not be surprised. The heart is desperately wicked, even more so when lost in the sounds of separation. They have not the tools to peer through the veil, because the tools were never theirs to own. They have grown too proud to bend their knees to the One who holds authority over life and death."

Jade fell silent. The rolling plains gave way to forest once more, and Enoch led them in a new direction.

"You have no idea how strong you are, Jade."

Enoch's words sent a shock through her chest.

"Loss is to the soul what a spear is to the body. You've been skewered, yet still you live. It is a testament to the strength of your heart. God knitted that strength into you, for you and for Noah."

Tears came unbidden. She slowed as her eyes burned and she lost view of her path.

Enoch matched her pace. "You and Noah are deeply wounded. A man with a wounded back does not have the ability to treat himself. Another must do it for him. Do you understand what I'm saying?"

Jade nodded and wiped her cheeks.

"You were born for each other. You cannot heal him, but you can tend his injuries. Without you, he will fail. Together, I believe you will be given the opportunity to grow. You already love each other. It is little more to be bound in marriage."

The tears increased and scattered.

"He is all the family you have left," Enoch said. "It may seem odd to you now, but you will grow to love each other in more ways than one." Enoch stopped and placed his hands on her shoulders. "I am proud of you. And I count it a blessing to have known you."

"Thank you," she said.

"Now, wipe your tears, and let us get back to the cave."

Chapter 57

Noah awoke to the sensation that his skull had been split. He was jostled back and forth, and could hear the metallic shift of long grass on leather. Several of the blades scraped his arms before he realized someone had thrown him over their shoulder.

He cried out and slid off, landing hard on his side. As he struggled to his knees, he looked up to see Barak's face lower into view. Noah lashed out and scrambled back, but Barak clutched his tunic and shook him. "Stop! I'm trying to help you."

Noah grabbed the man's wrists and attempted to force them away, but Barak was strong. "Leave me alone!"

"And let the Others kill you?"

Noah paused, confused.

"If we don't hurry, they'll find us." Barak pointed to the forest a stone's throw away.

Noah stood, chest heaving, and tenderly touched his head, where he found a lump covered in crusted blood beside his right eye. The place where Barak had kicked him. His back throbbed and resisted bending, and as he looked around, the thought struck him that the village was gone, and so were Enoch and Jade.

He couldn't trust Barak after what Noah had done. Still, they were exposed, and after what he'd done to that man in the village, certainly someone would try to chase them. He dusted himself off and jogged to the tree line, careful to keep his distance from Barak, who set his back to a tree and indicated Noah should do the same. Noah stood instead with his back to a bush and glared.

"I apologize for striking you," Barak said. "After you went after that man in the village, it seemed you'd gone mad."

"You threw me against a wall and kicked me in the head. Where is Jade?"

"She is safe. Enoch tended to her after she fainted."

Noah closed his eyes and took a deep breath. At least he could trust Enoch to take care of her. Though he had thought he could trust Barak as well.

"I was yelling for you to stop before you attacked that man," Barak said. "The only reason he saw you was because he heard me."

"Why should I believe you?"

"I don't care if you believe me. We have to get you farther away before the slavers find you, or the men from the village tell them where you might be. A few saw you run after that man."

Noah closed his eyes and willed his chest to stop thumping. His next words came as a bone-dry whisper. "Did I kill him?"

"He won't survive."

Noah let his breath out slowly. "Good."

"Do you understand nothing?"

"I understand that I did what you lacked the courage to do."

"You put us all in mortal danger," Barak said.

"Do you want to know what I think? That the world is the way it is because everyone is like you—afraid."

"I wasn't afraid to give up everything to follow the Old Way," Barak said.

"Does the Old Way demand you ignore those women?"

"It wasn't easy for me to turn my back to them."

"Liar."

Barak chuckled bitterly and shook his head. "I was like you once. To me, the future was filled with possibility. If I met an obstacle, I overcame it. Then I watched my friends slaughtered. Afterward, my wife died a slow and excruciating death. And do you know what I learned? That I could do nothing."

"I did something today."

"So did I. The Almighty told us to keep you safe, and that is what *I* have done. Or would you like me to let them find you, and slice your body open from top to bottom to let your innards dangle while you struggle to breathe? Because that's what they did to my friends. Men and women faithful to the Almighty. Or how about if I let them cut Jade's wrists and catch her blood in goblets to drink?"

"Why should we ever ignore atrocities? When does it ever make sense to let innocent people be slaughtered?"

"Noah," Barak said. "You hate those men because you believe all life to be sacred. But today, you took a man's life. Who gave you that authority?"

Noah touched the wound on his head. "If I hadn't killed that man, those women would have been killed."

"You didn't change their outcome."

"How do you know?"

"Because that's the way it works. They were shackled. Did you free them? They were naked. Did you clothe them? They were frightened. Did you offer them courage? Even as I carried you away, I heard the slavers coming. Do you want to know what those women did?"

Noah turned away.

"Nothing, Noah. They just sat there. Waiting."

"What's your point?"

"Who can determine when a person should die? God does not give us the authority to make that decision, for he is the only one who can bring life back to what has been destroyed. There is only one Judge, and if you try to become him, you will only reap judgment upon your own head tenfold."

"I'm not evil, like them."

"Yes, you are, Noah. We all are. That's what you don't understand. The only righteousness that exists in the world is God's. Search your heart and you will know it to be true. Stop trying to be God. Instead, strive to be *with* him. Let him make you righteous. Let him bring about justice as only he has the wisdom to do. Let him decide who must live and who must die. If you refuse, your desires will control you, just as they did today. And, eventually, they will destroy you. Along with everyone and everything you love."

Chapter 58

Enoch and Jade reached the cave, and Enoch gathered sticks and dry brush to make a fire. Piling the brush on a split log, he pressed the end of a stick into the kindling and used friction to heat the fibers until they smoked. He bent, cupped his hand about the smoke, and breathed the tongue of flame to life. "They're about to arrive," he said, and added sticks.

"How do you know?" Jade said.

Enoch pointed just as Barak stepped through the brush. The man walked to the fire and sat, but Noah did not follow.

"Where is he?" Jade said.

Barak ignored her.

Jade strained her eyes to peer through the darkness, yet saw nothing.

Turning to Barak, she wondered if the man could have failed to bring Noah away. Or worse, if Noah could have been captured. The thought made her throat seize.

A stick cracked in the distance. Slowly, through the leaves, a shape emerged.

Noah.

Jade passed a hand over her face and wondered at the relief she felt. Wasn't it only days ago she believed Noah the reason for her suffering? Yet she felt in that moment that she would do anything to not be separated from him.

"We took the cautious route," Barak said.

"Do you believe we are safe?"

"For a time. The way is riddled with tangled brush and rocky hillsides. Not even a master tracker could find us so quickly."

Enoch nodded and motioned Noah close. "Sit beside me. We have much to take care of, and too short a time."

As Noah walked to the fire, Jade watched the orange glow of the flames flicker across his features and wondered if, for the first time, she saw him true. His steps bordered violence, and behind him the fire casted shifting shadows.

"Jade," Enoch said. "Join us."

Jade approached Enoch, but he stopped her. "No. There." He motioned next to Noah, and Jade pushed her hair back, and sat beside him.

"I have prayed," Enoch said, "and the Almighty has spoken." Enoch grabbed their wrists and crossed them. Jade felt the warmth of Noah's wrist against hers and struggled to keep her vision from spinning. Noah turned his gaze on her, and the breath drained from her chest as Barak pulled out hemp rope and tied their wrists.

"Noah," Enoch said, "do you commit yourself to Jade?"

Noah searched Jade's eyes, parted his lips as if to speak, yet remained silent. Uncertainty clouded his eyes, and for a moment Jade wondered if he would refuse. Finally, he nodded. "I do."

"Jade," Enoch said, and her body trembled. "Do you bind yourself to Noah?"

"I do," she said, for what else could she say? The ritual they performed seemed a distant dream, as if she knew it to be the consummation of what had already taken place.

Had she mistaken the pain of bitterness for the ache of love all this time? For once, she thought she understood the love her mother had felt and failed to offer. And she realized her mother's fractured abilities stemmed from her own unique pains. Tears came to her eyes as she mourned her mother's hurts, and as the love in Noah's eyes sealed them.

"You were right," Jade whispered.

"Of course I was," Enoch said.

Noah glanced at him questioningly, but Enoch waved him away.

Then, as Barak loosened the tie around their wrists, Noah wove his fingers into Jade's, and she realized she'd never felt more at home.

Or more vulnerable.

When Enoch spoke his next words, the thrill in her chest gave way to panic.

"Now, Noah. It is time to choose how you will die."

Chapter 59

Noah was still reeling from Enoch's words when Jade's nails dug into the skin of his hand. "What do you mean?" she said.

"I mean," Enoch said, "that every event in the past century has led toward this one decision: either Noah will reject the Almighty and, with the rest of humanity, die before sunrise, or he will choose to walk the Old Way, and in doing so will postpone the Almighty's wrath."

"Do you mean to claim people will die because of my lack of faith?"

"Of course not," Enoch said. "The Almighty is going to destroy them, regardless. Humanity has rejected him, and the God-King's seed has poisoned the human race. Soon, there will not be a single person left on the planet of pure lineage."

Noah said, "Wait, what do you mean by—"

Jade's eyes widened to twin moons. "The women?"

Enoch's eyes seemed to sink into his skull. "The Others have taken only women from every village they plunder because the God-King has the ability to change the womb so that every child conceived might be born soulless."

Noah laughed. "That's not possible."

"It is no laughing matter," Enoch said. "His power forces children to be formed into hollow shells. Just alive enough to keep a heart beating, yet far enough from human to never be given a soul. Bodies meant to be filled by the Watchers."

"The Watchers," Jade said. "Who are they?"

"The Others. Word of the Watchers has been passed down generation by generation, even back to the first generation. Because before the first child was born to human parents, the first man and woman were deceived by the Prince of the Watchers, the one who calls himself the Light Bringer. Followers of the Old Way have never forgotten."

"So," Noah said, "what must I do?"

"Make your decision."

"But there is more, isn't there? I can see it in your eyes."

"Indeed," Enoch said, and his voice sounded like steel on a whetstone. "For the Almighty finally revealed all that I conjectured, and more. Because of what you have done—because of your unbelief—my time with you ends today. The Almighty has another task for me. One that demands I leave. However, before I go, he has offered you the rare opportunity to meet him in physical form."

"And if I say no?"

"You should say no."

A pause. "I should?"

"To believe without seeing would be far better than to see and disbelieve."

"You think I won't believe even if I see him."

"To whom much is given, much more is required. It would be better for the God-King to have flayed you alive than for you to reject the Almighty after knowing him."

"And you say your God is loving."

"It is for the sake of love that he would destroy the world and make it new. You forget that without God, man is incapable of love. And the more intensely someone denies God, the more their soul deteriorates, until there is nothing left but darkness within darkness."

Noah considered this as he stared into the flames crackling a mere arm's breadth away. He thought of the burning and rubbed his chest with his free hand while Jade's cold fingers clutched the skin of his wrist. As much as he wished he could be what Enoch wanted, he could not bridge the gap. To believe in the Almighty would demand he deny everything he ever knew. Everything he'd ever hoped for.

In exchange for what? An old man's religious fantasy?

Noah closed his eyes and saw Father's smiling face splattered red. A grin mockingly carved into Elina's throat. The vague form of his mother shadowed by death.

Then Jade's hand twitching against the cold ground.

It was for love of them that he could not believe.

For love.

Noah's eyes snapped open. "You said the Almighty created us. That he knows how to speak in a way we understand."

Enoch nodded.

Noah stood. "Then I've made my choice. I want to meet the Almighty."

Embers popped, and the fire collapsed, sending sparks to the sky in a cloud of smoke. A whisper scraped out of Enoch's lips like bones across the cave floor, "So be it." And with a flick of his wrist, the world swirled away.

...

The colors were so bright Noah shot his arms across his face, but not even that could stop the Light from burning his eyes, until the swirling cloud around him seemed the disintegration of his very being. He tried to yell, but no sound escaped his throat. He tried to move, but there was no substance through which to twist.

A Voice as deep as the earth and as ever-changing and wild as the ocean spoke a Word that sounded like violent Music, and darkness swooped over the Light, pressing his body like a grape in a winepress. Finally, with an ear-splitting crack that sounded like a laugh, he shot forward into swirling blue that churned with bubbles.

Weightlessness buoyed him upward. He twisted through viscous liquid until he breached the surface and slid, spluttering, onto a sand bar so fine he thought it might be ash. A foot splashed into view, and the hairy leg attached to it cast a shadow across his eyes.

"Who—" was all Noah's salted lips could make out, but already he knew, and refused to believe.

The figure crouched and offered him a hand, but when Noah took hold of it, his fingers touched a deep scar on the backside of his wrist. He thought momentarily of withdrawing, but the Man pulled him too quickly to a stand. He nearly fell, but the Man steadied him and laughed, the same Voice he heard in the swirling Light, only its terrifying complexity had been replaced with a low warmth. "Disorienting, isn't it?"

Noah rubbed his eyes and tried again. "Who are you?"

The Man bent forward, a smile spreading across his dark face. "You already know."

A shiver crawled down Noah's spine. He found himself both disappointed and elated. "The Almighty is a man?"

"Well . . . no. And yes. It's complicated."

"Try me."

The Man nodded and said, "But first," and swept his arm to indicate a line of trees laced together like the weave of a shirt, creaking in the wind. "Shall we join them?" the Man said.

They climbed the incline to the trees, and when Noah reached out to touch a tree trunk, it slid aside, opening a path into the jungle. Noah paused at the entrance, the green-scented breeze bringing whispered melodies from within. He held his breath to hear better, though they quieted as if carried reluctantly from the forest. "Where are we?"

"We are near the Shrine of the Song," the Man said.

"And you are my guide?"

A nod.

Noah swayed. Something about the world set his vision spinning. The colors were beyond reality. The Light too bright, the darkness too stark. The smells and taste and touch painfully enjoyable, strange, yet familiar at once.

"You are no longer in the world of humans," the Man said. "The absence of Time plays tricks."

"What do you mean?"

The Man pointed at the Water. "Those are the Sands of

Time. You washed up on the boundaries of Time itself. Without Time to regulate your experience, your soul is overwhelmed. It won't get better while your body lives, so there's really no point in belaboring it. Follow me."

Noah rubbed his temples, bewildered and fascinated as they walked under the leafy canopy. The path lengthened. As they went, the melodies grew until they wove into a great Music. Like the rest of the experiences in that land beyond Time, the Music was larger, more complex, more nuanced than anything Noah had encountered. It set his heart fluttering, and his limbs burning to move deeper into the forest.

They broke through the brush into an open space filled with stone ruins, and the Man lifted his hand and spoke a soundless Word that swept the Music away. A silence fell over them so deep it felt alive, but Noah found himself wanting to hear the Music again.

For the silence to go away so that he might hear those melodies.

"That Music you heard," the Man said. "It is evil."

"What do you mean?"

"I draw your attention to it only to let you know that I will not allow you to hear it again."

"I didn't hear anything wrong with it."

"Did you not feel it tempt you to enter the forest? How it drew you deeper, tickling your ears with strange notes until you smiled without knowing?"

Noah opened his mouth to say that he wasn't smiling but realized that he was. He rubbed the expression from his mouth and said, "If it was dangerous for me to enter this forest, why have you led me here?"

"You will know soon enough." The Man motioned him forward.

Arches, domes, and towers lay half-fallen. Noah approached and examined the constructions with wonder, brushing fingers across porous rock lined with zigzagging patterns of fleshy plant life. The ocean air was further humidified by the grove that, other than the creeping vines and lichen, kept its distance from the buildings, as if the stones poisoned the ground.

"If there is no Time, how do these plants grow?"

The Man smiled. "Your body is being fooled. In this world, the depth of Truth is beyond your comprehension. You see only what representations your mind is capable of grappling with. And so you perceive me as just a man. I am a man. And yet I am also much more." The Man pointed to a black recess in one of the walls and said, "Come, follow me."

They walked to the grim opening tarnished by weather and vine. A few of the stones lay on the ground like fallen teeth, and a staircase tumbled down its throat. The Man hurried down the steps, and Noah entered and found himself in a tunnel with windows every fifteen paces or so, dropping Light like flames into the cobalt shadows. At the end of the way stood a doorway in the shape of a shield with its center pressing toward them in a needlepoint. Forming a circle around the shield was an assortment of letters Noah could not read.

The Man swept his hand from left to right and the door rolled into a dark recess. They continued into an expansive, circular chamber whose walls were formed of polished stone. Ornate script ran along the bottom, and pillars rose like arms to support the ceiling with many hands. A mural spanned the room, and Noah spun to take it in, though its details were obscured by shadows.

The Man motioned him to the mural and lifted his hand. Light glowed at the tips of his five fingers, casting the relief in stark shadows. Countless beings marched in rows, carrying banners and weapons toward a great City. The figure at their head stood above the rest raising a trumpet to his lips. Volleys of light shot out from the trumpet, and the Man traced the rays with his fingers, mouth drawn downward, eyes pooled with sorrow.

"This mural commemorates the Great Rebellion of the Watchers," the Man said. "A failure they hold pride in."

Noah raised his shaking hand to feel the figures on the wall. Here, finally, was proof of the very legends Enoch spoke of, in a land beyond Time, a land filled with things he had never felt, seen, or heard.

"The Watchers were once my beloved children, but they

abandoned their identity to take what was not theirs. So very much like your forefathers," the Man said, and offered Noah a meaningful glance. "Both races followed the one who calls himself the Light Bringer, who wages war against me."

"To what end?" Noah said.

The Man sighed and withdrew his hand. "The Light Bringer said in his heart, 'I will ascend to heaven. Above the stars of God I will set my throne; I will ascend above the heights of the clouds; I will make myself like the Most High.'"

"What happened?"

The Man turned to him. "I cast him into the land of Death, to the far reaches of the pit, and now he seeks to escape his prison through you, Noah."

Noah stepped back. "Me?"

"Why else do you think I have brought you to this accursed place? This Shrine exists to weave every note in the Great Rebellion into a single Music, to unify all the rebellion and chaos in the world into a living Death. And nearly every human being has offered themselves as its instruments. All that is left is for you to give yourself to it and its hold will be complete, for I have risked everything on you."

"But why? I understand that the Light Bringer wants to be freed from prison, but what can he gain if he failed to overthrow you before? And why do you do nothing about it?"

"You asked me before if I was a man, and part of the answer to that question is that I am willing to humble myself and become a man to redeem you and all the others who bray their melodies like donkeys in heat. I frighten the Light Bringer. His primary goal is to stop me from being born to a human woman, and so he steals all the women he can find to twist their wombs and bar my entrance into the world." The Man takes a deep breath, chuckles, and shakes his head. "And you have the courage to claim I have done nothing. I created *you*, Noah. I wove you together in your mother's womb with my very Words. You are my counter-melody, a thread woven through the Music of me, which is being assaulted by the Music of the Watchers even as we speak."

"You risk your success on me, yet give me the choice to deny you, to align myself with the Music of the Watchers?" Noah said.

The Man nodded. "Now you begin to see."

"You are insane."

"I am in love," the Man said.

Noah shook his head. "I don't even know you."

"I know you better than you know yourself, for I formed you in your inward parts, and know every thought you have ever thought, and every thought you will yet come to think."

Noah's face warmed, and he turned away and folded his arms.

"I know of the burning. I know that you think of it often. That you fear it. I also know that you hope I will take it away. That you wish you could believe in me, yet you think that to believe in me you must part with your father." The Man laid a hand on Noah's shoulder, warming it. He cupped his other hand before Noah as if ready to receive from him. "Let me have it."

Noah met the Man's eyes, which shone with emotion as deep as the ocean, as intense as a wave that broke itself on a cliffside. "Have what?"

"Everything," the Man whispered.

His words thrust a stab of longing through Noah that burst a well of tears that bubbled unbidden and fell down his cheeks. He passed a hand over his face and shook his head as the burning returned, coiling at the base of his belly. He clenched his teeth and yelled as he struck his palms against his eyes. "I can't!"

The Man pulled his hand away and nodded. "Not on your own. But I will be with you, Noah. All you must do is humble yourself and draw near to me. Remember that." He motioned them onward, and thrust a second door aside, continuing before Noah could think to say anything else.

Noah hurried through the doorway after him.

The way forward was a long passage down into darkness. The floor was smooth, yet not steep enough to warrant danger. When the way grew too dark to see, the Man lifted his hand and illuminated the way with the tips of his five fingers.

Chapter 60

When Enoch flicked his wrist, both he and Noah disappeared in a puff of smoke that rose and disappeared on the wind.

Jade blinked hard, unbelieving, and turned to Barak, who watched her with quiet intensity. His hand lay on his hatchet, and his expression spoke warning.

"Where have they gone?" Jade said.

"They have been taken," Barak said.

Jade's pulse struck her throat hard. "Forever?"

"They have fallen into the hands of God. But they have not died. Not yet."

Jade pushed her hair behind her ear and took three breaths to clear the shadows encroaching on her vision.

Perhaps this was all a dream. Perhaps she was still curled on the animal skins in Barak's home.

"It's real," Barak said. "The Almighty is teaching us all a lesson in power."

"I don't like it," Jade said.

"It is a terrifying thing to fall into the hands of God. We are just fools to think we are ever outside of them."

Jade stood. "Stop speaking like that. You're frightening me."

"You should be frightened, Jade. Everyone is frightened when they encounter true purpose. That is why my hand sits on my axe. One never knows what another will do when faced with reality. Truth is a powerful force, and to meet it is to encounter the deepest of dangers."

"Do you think Noah will deny what he sees?"

Barak shook his head. "I do not know. Only the Almighty does."

"If the Almighty knows, then surely Noah will accept what the Almighty shows him. Otherwise, why offer it?"

Barak's expression darkened. "A pigeon may think itself safe in its master's hand. If the pigeon obeys, the master will give it freedom. But if the pigeon attacks the master's hand . . . who would suffer it? The Almighty shows kindness to whom he will. But kindness rebuffed is death twice fulfilled."

Jade brushed the dust still bearing the marks from where Noah sat, then the space Enoch had occupied. She turned to Barak and said, "Then I suppose we should pray that Noah chooses rightly."

Barak's hand slipped off his axe, and he nodded, a grim smile momentarily lifting his expression. "Agreed."

Chapter 61

E ventually the path leveled, and the Man led Noah down a long corridor lined with doorways with images burned into their grain. A staircase that led farther down materialized out of stone before them. After descending, they arrived at a beautiful archway gilded in silver and shining like pearls.

Through the archway lay a great basin filled with water that lapped against the sides of its domain like a crooked smile undulating in ecstasy. The Man stopped at the water's edge. "The Light Bringer can only imitate what I do, twisting it to his liking. This water is not the water of life. Instead, it brings only death. It is unfiltered lust. Hollow, empty, intoxicating. Poison to the soul." He opened his palm and breathed out, and the water boiled away, leaving a hollow bowl for them to cross.

Noah followed the Man across, through new hallways and rooms and staircases as the Shrine continued to expand. Finally, as a rhythmic thumping shook the ground beneath them, the Man opened stone double doors to reveal a massive room containing a metal shape.

"This," the Man said, and swept his hand to indicate the monstrosity filling their ears with measured noise, "is the heart of the Shrine. It is the pump of the lifeblood, the percussion in the Music. It is the Metronome."

Noah rubbed his forehead, confused. "How can rhythm exist without Time?"

The Man smiled. "The Metronome is a multiplicity. An anomaly lodged between the layers of reality. Through it, one can glimpse the workings of the Song of the Watchers throughout Time. Come, do you wish to see for yourself?"

They ascended a bridge leading over the Metronome, and Noah caught sight of what could only be described as a bubble set into the Metronome like a great eye, the surface of which was akin to a membrane of oil with iridescent markings shifting constantly.

"What is that?" Noah said.

"That is the Metronome's telescope."

Noah bent over the rail to peer inside, and the telescope expanded until it engulfed his vision. Strange sensations rippled down his back and sides, as if he were being removed and fastened to the Metronome's belts.

Visions appeared within the shifting membrane, and he felt somehow closer to Time, as if a part of him had stepped through the layers that the Man spoke of. But he was incapable of setting both feet in any one Place, and he remained suspended as he viewed a piece of Time here, a scrap of life there.

He watched as gray-skinned people appeared, followed by the Others, whose horns reflected the flames of burning buildings and pyres. The Others heaped piles into a foundation, and the foundation spread until there was no escaping its totality. On it, cruel empires built many black towers, and warriors beat their chests.

Men tortured people with cruel instruments. Women were stripped and abused and slaughtered. Children were thrown into rivers, dashed upon rocks. Flames rose and licked the Metronome's lens.

Then came Water. It filled the foundation until it overflowed like a great basin and washed the world clean, snuffing the burning, ravaging the world, destroying everything.

After the Water receded, the world was empty. Void.

Noah pulled back, stumbled, and fell on his back, breathing hard. "What did I just see?"

The Man crouched over him. "You saw what is meant to be. You saw the sin of man."

Noah passed a hand over his eyes. "You are going to destroy everything you made. Why?"

"To make it anew."

"Is the world so lost?"

"You tell me."

Noah thought of his mother. Of his father. Of Elina. Of the women being sold in broad daylight. Of the unspeakable evil hidden in the dark recesses of the world.

Then, most terribly, he thought of the dark desires burning within his own chest.

"Yes," he whispered, and tears filled his eyes.

"And yet," the Man said, and cocked his head, waiting for Noah to finish.

"And yet our lives must be worth something."

The Man nodded. "I have risked everything to give you a life, and the burden of choice."

"But I can't choose to be whole. I don't know how to."

"Wholeness has nothing to do with your ability." And he lifted scarred wrists so Noah might see them again. "What I plan to do is for the sake of love. I brought you here to show you that I am real. That I have the power to destroy the universe ten thousand times over, and to resurrect it from nothing. For I am the Word. The first Music that will continue past everything. The Beginning and the End, the Alpha and Omega. I am that I am. And you and all the others are just a note within my Song. Even as you try to play a different Music. For you were created to love me. That is all that is expected of you, Noah. Love me more than you love anything and everything else. If you could only realize how my heart yearns for your joy. If you let me, I would take away the burning. I would quench your thirst."

Noah wiped the moisture from his cheeks and whispered, "How?"

"Rest in me. Do that, and you need not fear anything. Not yourself. Not the Others. Not all the pain in the world."

Noah nodded. His face twisted, and his throat ached until he heard himself wailing. "Take it away. I just want it gone."

The Man embraced him, and suddenly he felt himself falling, falling into . . .

A Light so bright he thought it would burn him. But this time, it inflicted no pain. As it shot through him, it took with it every bit of dust, every shifting shadow.

It was a Holy Burning completely unlike the flames that had driven him since he could remember.

What a rush to finally be fully seen. To know that no dark portion inside him could escape that Light, and yet it did not wound him.

It was such an ultimate and unexpected joy that he cried out, "This! This is what I've longed for!"

It all seemed so clear. So undeniable. This goodness, this *Holiness*, was what he was meant for. He would give his life to stay. To taste a modicum of what now engulfed him.

Then, in the space of a single, soundless Word, the Light was gone, and he found himself once again lying on the ground, staring up at a star-filled sky.

"Noah?" a soft voice said. "Is that you?"

Chapter 62

Barak had left shortly after Noah and Enoch disappeared to forage for food, but Jade stayed and stared so long at the spot where Noah's feet scuffed the earth that she nearly didn't believe her eyes when a dark shape materialized on the ground before her. For a moment, she wondered if one of their enemies had come under the cover of night to steal her away.

"Noah?" she said. "Is that you?"

Silence. Jade's cheeks chilled, and her throat stretched tight. The shape moved, and she shuffled back. It turned toward her, a clot of darkness with two bright ovals that gleamed in the starlight.

"Jade?" The voice was familiar, warm, and filled with confusion.

Relief flooded her chest. "I thought you would never return."

"Return? How long have I been gone?"

Jade waved away his question. "Don't worry about that. What did the Almighty show you? Are you all right?"

Noah took a deep breath as if to speak, then paused and let it out. "I don't know what to think."

"You disappeared out of thin air," Jade said. "You were gone for hours. Surely something happened?"

"Certainly. I just . . ."

Jade thought she heard his voice waver, as if he were on the verge of tears.

Noah's next words were the least of a whisper, as if he didn't want to hear himself say them. "I felt him, Jade."

"You felt him?"

"And I don't know if I want to believe that I did."

"Why not?"

"I'm not going to forget about Father."

"Who said you have to do that?"

Noah did not answer.

"Tell me what happened."

Haltingly, Noah explained the burning Light. Then how he had washed up on the shores of Time at the feet of the Almighty, and followed him into the Shrine, where he was shown the world's terrible future.

After he finished, Jade said, "You believe everything, don't you?"

"I think . . . ," Noah said, "that I love him. I know it sounds strange, but if that Light had anything to do with the Almighty, I would die a thousand deaths just to bask in it again. It felt so clean, so pure. For the first time in my life I felt free to let myself be truly known. I never knew how much I hated hiding."

"Well," Jade said, "then maybe we should follow Enoch's advice, after all. Maybe then you'll find the Light again."

Noah slipped his fingers between hers and whispered, "Maybe."

Jade leaned her head on his shoulder and breathed the heady smell of him.

"Jade?" he said.

"Yes?" She lifted her face until their lips nearly touched.

"I'm glad you're here with me at the end of things."

"Me too," she said, as his warm breath on her face sent a chill down her spine. "Me too."

Chapter 63

Noah woke in the cave the next morning to the smell of Jade's hair and the warmth of her chest slowly pulsing at his side. She breathed deeply, slowly. Close-by a fire crackled, and the sound sent him to the day they first woke to Enoch in that same exact spot.

Noah raised himself up on his palm and caught sight of Barak cooking mushrooms and wild onions over the fire.

He wiped his face, mind foggy, and sifted through what had happened in the past few days.

"He's gone," Barak said.

"I know," Noah said.

Barak nodded. "You grew fond of him. Come. Eat." Barak removed the skewers of mushrooms. He tried pulling off one that still smoked, but it crumbled and fell to the ground.

Noah joined him and glanced at Jade.

"She's exhausted," Barak said. "Let her sleep. Here—" He broke the skewer just below the mushrooms and handed it to Noah.

The scent made his mouth water, and the flavor was sharp and the flesh moist.

Barak pulled one knee up and stared at the fire. The lines on his face seemed to deepen as his hair fell, casting flickering shadows across his cheek. "He won't be back," Barak said. "God took him."

Noah paused midbite and lowered the food. "I never thought I would have to say good-bye to so many. The Almighty hasn't destroyed everyone as Enoch seemed to think he would. I think he still plans to. I just don't know when."

"Everyone dies," Barak said.

"But not everyone lives to see their family die. That's different."

"It is." Barak said.

Noah set the skewer on a stone and leaned back, joining Barak in searching the flames.

"What will you do?" Barak said.

"I will pursue him. I will seek the Almighty."

"Then I'll stay with you."

"Does it get easier?"

Barak took a deep breath and exhaled. "A bit."

"But it still hurts?"

"Every moment."

"You still love your wife," Noah said.

"More than life."

"Yet you follow the Almighty."

"God gives and God takes away. Should we accept only good from him?"

Noah ripped up some grass and tossed it in the fire. "Do you sense his presence?"

"Most of the time."

"What about when you don't?"

"I obey his word and seek him. Emotions are fickle. The Almighty is constant. Just because we don't feel him doesn't mean he isn't present."

"Is he here now?"

"All around us."

"Then he knows our pain."

"He bears it alongside us."

Noah nodded, for he believed. After experiencing the Light, he believed it all.

Barak stood and added wood to the fire. He stoked the

embers to churn up the heat and ate one of the onions. In between bites he said, "We can stay here maybe another day. You should get as much rest as you can. Long journey ahead."

Noah agreed, then went and lay beside Jade again. He closed his eyes, searching for the Light. Thirsting for it. Silently asking the Almighty to show himself.

For a moment before he fell asleep, he thought he caught sight of a small glimmer, like a candle flame in a distant cave. It warmed his chest and expelled his anxiety, nesting a little spark beneath his skin.

A totally different kind of burning.

PART VII

Years Gone By

"But Noah found favor in the eyes of the LORD."
—Genesis 6:8

The next morning, Noah, Jade, and Barak made their way south to escape the spreading war.

As they traveled, Noah recited the stories Enoch had taught him. The ancient histories came piecemeal, but he visited them frequently enough that they solidified in his mind, albeit in a simplified form.

What Enoch said of the Almighty came easier. Noah whispered of the Almighty's perfection, goodness, righteousness, and steadfast love until he believed it.

As he bent his spirit toward the Almighty, the gentle spark returned, and each time was like a taste to one starving. He felt the Almighty was drawing him slowly hand over hand. But when Noah attempted to take control of the sensation, it fled. Only when he meditated on God and spoke of the Almighty's goodness did he feel any lasting peace.

Could it be that putting the desire for peace above the Almighty himself somehow offended God?

They traveled on, sometimes resting for days. All the while Noah pursued the Almighty as Enoch taught. Days became months. Months became years, and Noah began to treasure not just how the Light made him feel, but the Almighty himself.

In return, Noah began to find favor in the eyes of the Lord. He recognized it first after subtle nudges led them to go to certain homes to meet kindred spirits that accepted them graciously. After, the sense bloomed into a deep knowing that helped them avoid danger and find solace.

They settled in several valleys but always felt pressed to move on, until at last they came to a small village on a great river unoccupied by the Others.

Noah had grown in both physical stature and emotional maturity. His limbs were strong and lithe. Eyes pooling with deepening wisdom. Spirit calmed by endless prayer.

Jade, too, had matured into full womanhood, and Barak's hair had grown speckled with gray.

...

As Noah dropped to his knees to speak to the Almighty the morning they meant to leave the village on the river, Noah heard the Voice speak for the first time since Enoch left.

"Ask the boat master for work. I have given you gifts. Pursue the craft."

"For how long?" Noah said.

But he was answered with the same silence he'd endured for years. Albeit amidst a boiling sense of purpose that blossomed into excitement. He stood and faced Jade, who watched him with interest.

"Did something just happen?" she said.

"The Almighty says we should stay."

...

Noah met the boat master and asked for a job, but the man was reticent. Noah still looked young, and the boat master was wary of foreigners.

"Let me build a boat for you," Noah said. "Then, perhaps you will know whether you want me to work for you. And you can keep the boat at no cost, whether you hire me or not."

The boat master eyed him, then nodded. "Come to me when you finish."

Noah carved a small fishing boat from a fallen tree in half the time it normally took other builders. He went to the boat master to say he'd finished, but the man said, "You began building after we spoke?"

"Of course."

The boat master snorted. "No one can build a proper boat in so little time. Find work elsewhere."

Noah stood for a few moments, dumbfounded. "At least come see what it looks like."

"Go away," the man said. "You don't know anything."

Noah returned to Jade and told her what happened.

"What?" Jade said, and she left without another word.

A quarter sundial later she returned with the boat master in tow. The man nursed a bruise and flinched when Jade moved too quickly. But when he saw the boat, he dropped to his knees and ran his hand over the wood, examining its construction with the intensity of a careful artist.

He stood and said, "Get it in the river."

They placed the boat on the water, and when the boat master stepped in, it did not sink.

"Hand me an oar!" the boat master said, and Jade tossed one, though he flinched and the oar splashed into the water. After recovering, he just barely reached the oar and began paddling around.

Finally, he drove it up the beach, stepped out, and shook Noah's hand. "Meet me at dawn."

...

The boat master's name was Kenan.

Kenan's first wife died giving birth to their first child—a stillborn. Kenan's second wife was taken by the Others, leaving him childless and alone. In the wake of such suffering, Kenan was a simple man lacking in words, driven by one love and many hatreds. He offered few critiques and even fewer compliments. Though he had many workers, he kept Noah closest, until the others named him the boat master's apprentice.

Autumn gave way to mornings dusted with a fine layer of frost. Noah continued under Kenan's direction from sunrise to sundown. From fishing vessels to ocean cutters with sails on high masts, the work remained varied and interesting.

When Noah saw Kenan using a new woodworking technique, he asked to be taught, and Kenan took as much time as necessary to impart all the knowledge he had.

Still, many of the hours were filled with repetitive labor. Into these moments Noah poured his prayers, and every night he returned home to lay with Jade and explain all he learned before listening to what Jade had learned in her trade as a weaver.

Both excelled at what they set their hands to, and Barak, though quiet as ever, began to teach the locals how to build better nets and fishing tools. The strange little family slowly gained a place of influence in the surrounding areas, until late in the night visitors came to speak with them.

The following spring, Noah found Jade looking out at the flowers in the morning. He was struck by how mature she looked, and couldn't remember when the change had begun. Her eyes, though still sharp, had deepened. Her dark hair lifted in the gentle breeze, and a distance lay across her face. Noah approached and said, "What's bothering you?"

Jade sighed and placed a hand on her abdomen. "I thought that by now I would have become pregnant."

Noah noticed a bud severed and crushed underfoot. Had she been staring at it?

"All I want is a child to call my own," she said. "I see the women suckling their little ones and feel a sense of emptiness. As if a part of me has not yet come to be."

"I'm not sure how I feel about having a child in these times."

"I've known for nearly a year that we're supposed to," Jade said. "You're not the only one who talks to God." And she smiled as she used to when they were children before her gaze fell to the crushed bud, and her expression darkened. "I don't understand why it hasn't happened yet. Do you think I'm incapable?"

Noah wrapped his arms around her. "Of course not. If it truly is the Almighty's will, it will happen in his timing."

"What if he never gives me a child?"

"If he planted this desire in your heart, he will fulfill it."

"Or use it to make me grow more patient."

"Either way, it will benefit you."

She pulled away and wrapped her arms around herself. "I should get going. And so should you. Look at how late it's grown." She pointed to the light of dawn tossing itself over the horizon, gathered up her clothing, and disappeared into their home.

Noah stayed staring at that little crushed bud. He bent and picked it up, feeling a sudden rush of emotion as it rested dwarfed in the palm of his hand.

...

Three years passed. Jade threw herself into her work, as Noah did into his.

Noah no longer needed Kenan's guidance, and nearly always worked alone or directed the other builders. Some days they repaired. Other days they built new. Still more days they spent selling boats to travelers, or driving finished pieces to a nearby port where merchants and workers bustled back and forth.

After delivering a fishing vessel to an old, wealthy fisherman, he heard talk of aggressive expansion in the war. It seemed the God-King was trying to assault one final bastion far to the west, and one of the fastest routes was by river.

A month later the Others arrived at Noah's village and demanded a war vessel capable of carrying three hundred men be built and delivered by the end of the season.

Kenan didn't bother saying it had never been done. He merely nodded, turned to Noah, and said, "Start working on the design. We will need to recruit builders from the surrounding areas."

...

Noah didn't recognize the shift until he heard others murmuring about Kenan not designing the vessel.

As he watched Kenan plane a slab of wood, he felt a strange pride and love for the old man who had first denied him, then embraced him, and now stepped aside without comment. In a way, Kenan felt like a second father, and Noah was thankful, even as he felt the desire for his own father throb.

He wondered what Lamech was doing. If he was thinking of Noah. If he was even still alive. The thought made Noah's hands clammy. He turned back to the parchment on the stone before him and tried to focus, though his mind kept drifting back to Kenan and how their relationship had developed.

Had Kenan always believed so much in Noah's skill? Had that been why he had taken him under his wing? So that he would have a successor? A sort of son of his own?

Noah purposed in that moment to take Kenan aside later that evening to tell him how much he appreciated the man's help. But even as he thought that, and marked an angle on the parchment, the door covering parted, and the sergeant who had ordered the vessel entered and demanded to see the war vessel.

Kenan showed him, but when the sergeant saw the boat half-finished, he drew his sword and rammed it through Kenan's chest.

Noah's pulse stopped. Kenan coughed, splattering red on the sergeant's arm, then crumpled as the sergeant kicked him off and cleaned the blade, sheathing it once more.

Angry tears burned Noah's eyes. Were he holding a tool, he would have attacked. The sergeant said, "Fool," and the word was like a slap to his face. He knew retaliation would only risk the lives of everyone in the village, including Jade and Barak. He stayed where he was, and hated himself for his inaction.

"Finish it quicker next time," the sergeant said, "or I'll kill you next." And he pointed at Noah before leaving.

Noah felt a tingle run from his scalp down to his toes.

...

That day, after Noah and the other builders buried Kenan, they went home.

Noah wept until his eyes nearly swelled shut, thinking of

how his family had been shredded from his life, and of the possibility that he could be stolen away from Jade. He would not allow himself to be murdered for something as simple as angering a soldier of the God-King's army.

After all, he had faced the God-King and lived.

In the days that followed, he returned to work and doubled his pace until the vessel was finished.

He delivered it on time to a captain in the God-King's army at the nearby port. The captain had silver-tinged horns, and an eye for shipbuilding. He examined the construction with wonder and demanded to know who had designed the vessel.

Noah knew that to expose himself would likely mean more demands, so he said, "My boat master taught me everything I know, and he worked with me on the vessel."

"Where is he, then?"

Noah paused, wondering how much he should say. But even as he vacillated, the Almighty warmed his chest with a deep confidence, and Noah spoke boldly. "He was murdered by the sergeant who came to see the progress last month."

The captain shook his head. "For work like this? That's a crime. The sergeant will be executed within a week's time."

And he left without another word.

After that day, Noah never received another request from the God-King's legion. And he praised the Almighty and offered him a burnt sacrifice.

As the smoke rose, Noah heard the Voice a second time.

"The evil ones destroy the flesh of living creatures with impunity. And the Watchers have taught many to eat the flesh of human beings. But never have I given the flesh of living creatures to men for food."

After, Noah considered how never had he seen Enoch eat meat. And neither had they ever eaten meat around him. So, of course, he had never told them of this mandate of the Almighty. And Barak was faithful, but he was no prophet, and had grown up among heathens and only received a portion of the teaching that Noah had.

Noah spoke with Barak and Jade, and from that day on, they abstained from eating meat, and word of their way of life spread, until others asked in secret to be taught the Old Way.

...

Years turned into decades that turned into centuries.

Their village grew to a small port town bustling with activity, and all that time the Almighty sealed Jade's womb so that she would not bear children.

Because they lived far on the outskirts of the God-King's kingdom, they had little contact with the Others, though from time to time they received word from abroad.

The God-King successfully conquered the known world, and his servants combed more and more towns for women to be taken to the capital. Word spread that the Others grew more numerous, until they nearly outnumbered human beings.

Still, Noah's little port town was a strange haven far away to the south at the border of civilization. Many in the village had secretly converted to the Old Way, and Noah led them, for he was now five hundred years old and the memories of his past had turned to distant shadows better left forgotten.

However, in the middle of the summer of Noah's five hundred and fifth year, Jade interrupted Noah's work with a smile. "It has happened," she said.

"What has?"

Her smile deepened, and tears shone in her eyes. "I'm pregnant."

...

Nine months later, Jade gave birth to their first son, Shem. Two years later, they celebrated another, Ham, and then Japheth.

It seemed for the next two decades that the family would live the rest of their days in bliss despite the suffering endured by the rest of the world. Shem, Ham, and Japheth took wives and started working beneath their father. Jade had never been filled with more joy or purpose, and Noah claimed it was the blessings of the Almighty.

...

But in all those many years, Noah never forgot what the Man had shown him in that place beyond Time. Over the years, the Shrine had begun to seem more a dream than a reality, but his spirit knew all along that their simple lives would never last.

PART VIII

The Deep Breath before the Plunge

"And God said to Noah, 'I have determined to make an end of all flesh, for the earth is filled with violence through them. Behold, I will destroy them with the earth.'"
—Genesis 6:13

Chapter 65

The end began with a dream. Noah knew he was lying with Jade, whose seamed fingers were intertwined with his, yet the dark of his closed eyelids gave way to Light filtered kaleidoscopic through shimmering blue.

He twisted, bubbles bursting from his mouth, and realized he floated in water. Far below stood jagged peaks, the tops of many mountains. Birds floated past with broken wings. Cattle, splintered wood, men, women, children, and tools churned around him. Lifeless save for the current that swept them along.

Noah blinked and found himself floating high in the sky near sparse clouds, gazing down at a curved mass far below.

"That is the world," the Voice said. *"Tell me what you see."*

Flames glowed red against the dark of night and the empty space above pricked by distant stars. "I see a world on fire."

"I have determined to make an end of all flesh, for the earth is filled with violence. Behold, I will destroy them with the earth."

A bright flash streamed past Noah from the heavens toward the earth, sending bits of ice dust shimmering through the atmosphere before smashing into the ground with a thunderous explosion.

The ground rippled like the surface of a pond struck by a pebble, and cracks erupted in the surface, sending plumes of water high into the air. The earth tipped with the force of the blow, and mountains erupted in smoke and fire. Screams echoed distantly as the hills moved and jagged peaks rose while valleys shifted like woven flax. Ground smashed into ground, and water rose, spilling over everything, snuffing the flames.

The world spun, and the sun and moon traded spots forty times as a haze of ash rose to separate the ground from the sky. The fountains of the deep continued spewing, and rain condensed and fell until even the highest peaks were covered.

"Make yourself an ark of gophar wood. Make rooms in the ark, and cover it inside and out with pitch."

"How should I make it?"

"Make the length of the ark 300 cubits, its breadth 50 cubits, and its height 30 cubits. Make a roof for the ark and finish it to a cubit above, and set the door of the ark in its side. Make it with lower, second, and third decks. For behold, I will bring a flood of waters upon the earth to destroy all flesh in which is the breath of life under heaven. Everything that is on the earth shall die."

"What of my family?"

"I will establish my covenant with you, and you shall come into the ark, you, your sons, your wife, and your sons' wives with you. And of every living thing of all flesh, you shall bring two of every sort into the ark to keep them alive with you. They shall be male and female. Of the birds and animals and every creeping thing of the ground, according to its kind. Two of every sort shall come in to the ark with you."

"How could I ever find so many creatures and get them to obey me?"

"I will command them to come to you when the time is ripe. But you shall also take with you every sort of food that is eaten, and store it up, for food for you and the animals."

...

Noah woke to darkness sweating and gasping for breath. He shook Jade awake and told her of the Almighty's words, of the coming destruction of the world. They rose and offered a sacrifice to the Almighty, and praised him for promising them safety, for having mercy on their family.

"But what about the rest of the faithful?" Jade said.

Noah's face chilled, and his throat hollowed. He'd been so overwhelmed by the vision that he hadn't yet thought of them. "I don't know," he said, and looked again to the smoking offering. "I think that if God would have mercy on us, surely he would show mercy to any who remain faithful to the end."

"But to build such a vessel and fill it with so many provisions will take everything we have," Jade said.

"We have built up great wealth these many years."

"But it will be all-consuming."

"So will the Almighty's judgment."

"It will take hundreds of workers," Jade said, nibbling the ends of her fingers. "Builders. Materials carted from leagues away."

Noah took a deep breath as he, too, contemplated the organization necessary for such a massive task.

"How will we feed them?" Jade said. "Such a construction would demand the expansion of our village. Bringing in tanners to provide leathers. Additional weavers to provide blankets for the cold season. New hunters, farmers, bakers. The scale of such a project is beyond anything that's ever been done before."

"I know, Jade."

"I'm not doubting. Just thinking it through. It will take years. Maybe even decades."

"If the Almighty's will is that we build it alone, we will do so, no matter how long it takes. But I believe he will provide the workers."

"We do already have nearly a hundred shipbuilders."

Noah nodded. "And the respect of many from the larger cities."

Jade bowed again before the burnt offering and let out a shaky breath. "Thank you." She stood, faced Noah, and said, "I will bring the parchments for you to begin designing."

"Shem can contact the port downriver and purchase the first of our supplies," Noah said.

"And Japheth can speak with the village elders to bring in new workers and food. It will be more difficult to convince smiths and potters and tanners to uproot."

"Ham can labor toward those ends," Noah said. "It will take

visiting nearby towns and slowly working toward the larger cities. I'd be surprised if they didn't understand what money they'd earn by aiding us."

Jade smiled. "We've remained in relative safety all these years, and now have access to everything we could need."

Noah smiled back and wrapped his arms around her. "It's invigorating."

Chapter 66

Noah spent weeks designing the vessel as Shem purchased materials and ordered them shipped down-river. Builders arrived day after day and began raising the scaffolding. Food arrived on heavily laden carts between shipments of raw materials pulled by oxen from the port. New workers arrived, and the builders had to erect new homes and buildings for smiths and tanners and potters.

Roads were paved. Dirt pathways trodden smooth and hard from frequent use. Weavers arrived from nearby towns and followed Jade's direction. The temperature was cooling, and at night frost began to creep into the homes, so they made blankets and thick tunics, and coverings for the doorways. They lined sandals with fur, and sewed pockets filled with goose down in the builders' clothing so that they might continue building year-round.

Over the next five years they built the lower, second, and third decks. The scaffolding rose higher and higher, until the ark towered above the rest of the village. Many came from foreign places to see, for word of its size had spread. But with fame came another sort of attention.

As winter set on the sixth year, a dozen soldiers arrived led by a one-armed giant with yellow horns and yellow eyes downcast.

When the demon called for Noah with that familiar, booming voice, Noah's breath was stolen, and he found he could not move.

He remembered as clearly as if he experienced it that very moment, how that same giant had bound and forced him to kneel before Elina, Lamech, and the God-King when he was only a boy.

Jade touched Noah's arm, and he took a deep breath and faced the giant.

"You have grown," Berubbal said. "Tell me, do you remember the feel of my fingers on your neck?"

"Why have you come?" Noah said.

"The God-King desires to know for what purpose you labor on such a spectacle."

"I am building an ark," Noah said.

"I see. But for what purpose?"

"To save my family when the Almighty destroys the world."

Berubbal smiled. "If that is the case, then my lord desires an audience with you."

Noah turned to Jade, who shook her head. "No, don't go."

But Noah could not deny that he felt deep resonance in his spirit. The Almighty had led them this far, and the edges of the village had expanded to double the size in six short years. As Noah noticed the shadow of the ark falling over Berubbal, he felt a growing confidence that what Berubbal demanded was something Noah was meant to do. That he should not fear, but rather be resolute.

Noah embraced Jade.

She clutched him tight. "We can't trust him. Don't you remember what—?" But she choked on her words.

"I believe that the Almighty wills it. And if he does, then I will return."

Jade paused and closed her eyes as if praying. After a moment, her face tensed, and she said, "I believe that. But still . . ."

Berubbal stepped forward. "Don't act as if you have a choice. You, of all people, know how persuasive the God-King can be." And he took hold of Noah and bound him with ropes before leading him to a cart, where they pushed him into a bamboo cage.

Chapter 67

They journeyed for a full month by cart. At night, Noah lay on a bamboo mat. By day, he knelt with his head pressed to the bars. He relieved himself in a bucket received upon request. They fed him with half-cooked rice and preserved vegetables. Water was rationed, and his lips broke and bled for thirst.

All the while, he prayed, asking the Almighty to reveal his plans.

The only answer he received was, *"My grace and mercy are sufficient for you."*

...

As they crested the final hill, the city of the God-King sprawled alight with torches not unlike the flaming world he saw in his dream. Massive braziers had been erected through the streets that wove like arteries toward a black tower at the city's center. The cart wound its way to the tower, and Noah was released from his cage and dragged up countless flights of stairs to lavish living quarters.

He was placed in a room with purple draperies over wide windows and a low bed with silk sheets. His bonds were cut, and the Others left him with the simple command, "Sleep."

The door was locked, and the window looked out to a twenty-story fall. Noah stretched his aching bones on the bed, and after shutting his eyes for little more than a moment, he remembered no more until morning.

...

Sunlight stabbed through the window, and slave girls entered his quarters and bathed him. Afterward they dressed him in lavish clothing and applied balm to his scabbed lips. They served him tea, offered fatty meats, which he refused, then breads, which he ate.

Afterward they left him for several hours alone in his room. When they next returned, they reapplied the balm to his lips and offered more tea and breads. He asked, "What is expected of me?"

But the slave girls only looked away, their mouths clamped shut.

...

Finally, after the slave girls left the second time, a knock sounded at the door.

"Yes?" Noah said.

The door opened to black horns that twisted two entire revolutions before ending in spines that pointed upward. Beneath the protrusions lay a face warmed by youth and sensuality, attached to a body as lithe as Noah's had been three hundred years prior.

The God-King smiled and opened his arms as if in invitation. "My dear Noah. Why don't you join me?"

...

The God-King's chamber was surprisingly simple. In the center sat two cushions beside a knee-high table set with goblets and preserved meats. The walls were bare. The windows unadorned by curtains. Two small braziers burned on either side of the table, casting the feast in stark detail, and leaping shadows on the walls.

The God-King sat cross-legged at the table and beckoned Noah to join.

Noah approached and sat, trying to still his erratic breathing and involuntary tremors.

"Are you hungry?" The God-King motioned toward the meat.

"I eat only what the Almighty has given humans for food."

"A shame that I only prepared meat, then," he said.

"Why have you brought me here?"

"To remind you who I am," the God-King said. "I'm only doing the Almighty's will, you know. Otherwise he would have stopped me long ago." He drank deep from his goblet before setting the cup down, teeth stained red. "That is, if he actually *has* the power to stop me. Either way, the meaning remains the same."

Noah pushed his goblet away.

"You should consider aiding my cause."

Noah's fingers clenched his tunic as he prayed for the Almighty to give him strength.

But he heard no response. He felt no leading. He sensed no strength in his limbs.

"Before this is over, you will bow to me," the God-King said.

"I will never bow to you," Noah said.

"Again, you deny the Almighty's will," the God-King raised his brow. "Tell me why you think he delivered you into my hands."

"To warn you."

"To warn me?" The God-King laughed. "I'm not so blind as you think. His flood won't stop me. I'm too powerful, and you humans are too weak to keep me buried."

Noah blinked, surprised, but attempted to hide it. "You seem quite sure of yourself."

"I know you've been praying. Tell me, has your God spoken since you arrived?"

Noah's face twitched, and the God-King's smile widened.

The God-King lowered his voice to a whisper. "Or has he

left you alone just like he's done with all his previous servants? The ones I flayed open?"

"The Almighty would never abandon me," Noah said, but he couldn't stop a nagging hollowness from widening in his abdomen.

"He's very good at making people believe," the God-King said. "Let me guess . . . he gave you a spectacular vision? Some vivid fantasy followed by an intense rush of joy that brought you to your knees?"

Noah swallowed and spread his fingers to dry his palms.

"Since then, he's led you along with little tastes, but nothing like that first experience."

Noah took a deep breath. "You're a liar. All you do is lie."

The God-King leaned in close, the silver-clasped emerald dangling from his neck into the goblet of blood. "The only lie is the Almighty's claims. He's delivered you into my hands because he doesn't have the power to stop me. And he's not speaking to you right now because he can't. Because I forbid him. Go ahead, request his presence."

Noah shook his head and pushed his dishes until they clanged against the God-King's goblet and plate.

The God-King leaned back and smiled. "Still, here we are. You and me, after all these years. Visiting. It seems like fate, doesn't it?"

The God-King stood and paced behind one brazier, then the next. He clasped his hands and leaned against one of the windows, staring out across the sprawling hills. "I am the god of this world. I own it along with everyone who lives in it. I bid you to remember the grace I showed you all those years ago when I let you and that girl live."

Noah stood as the old burning returned for the first time since Kenan was slaughtered. "You murdered Elina. You murdered my mother and countless others. You destroyed families. You stamped out an entire generation."

"It was a gift, Noah," the God-King said. "Pain sparks growth, and I have always cared most for you. You were ready to live a boring life as a carpenter. Now look at you. You have a whole community who respects you. You've built things no one else ever dreamed of building. Including that ark."

"What do you want from me?" Noah said.

"Renounce the Almighty and bow to me."

"Never," Noah said.

"What would it take, I wonder? Because as much as you'd try to deny it, everyone has their price." The God-King observed him long, then snapped his fingers. A slave girl entered. "It is time to retrieve the gift I prepared for our guest."

The slave girl bowed and left.

"I don't want any of your gifts," Noah said.

The God-King shrugged. "You don't have to take it. You are free to leave right now if you so choose." His smile deepened, and his silver eyes glowed orange in the firelight. "But I know that you will stay, because you cannot imagine what I have prepared for you."

Noah looked at the entrance. He hadn't noticed that the door stood ajar the whole time, no guard present.

Could he really be free to go? If so, what was the point of being tied and thrown into a cage for the entire journey here? So that the God-King could have just these few moments to speak with him?

The God-King smiled. "I won't stop you. Anytime you feel the desire, leave. My servants know you. They will not inhibit you."

"But?"

The God-King laughed. "But nothing. I place no demands —very unlike the Almighty. However . . ." His voice quieted. "After you finish building the ark, if you meet me in the port town downriver from where you live, I will give you one final gift. A gift far greater than what I offer today."

Noah said nothing. Only stared into the flames crackling in the brazier and wondered at how the God-King could kindle such hatred. All these years, Noah thought himself rid of the burning, yet here he sat shaking with the desire to murder the God-King.

Everything that the devil did was strange. Noah knew the God-King was evil, and yet the God-King treated him with apparent kindness and gave him the freedom to leave. Perhaps it was true that the God-King could not kill him, but he felt certain of nothing anymore. And the longer he spent in the God-King's chamber, the warier he grew.

"The reason why I know you will meet me one final time is because after seeing the gift I offer today," the God-King said, "you will not be able to resist. Because what I show you today will make you certain that I hold something very dear to you. Something you've desired your entire life."

What could the God-King possibly have that Noah would care about? What could he have . . . ?

An image flashed before his eyes—the shadowed figure of the mother he never knew, and his fingers tingled and clenched.

No, that would be impossible. Adah died right after giving birth to him. Father had told him so. He wouldn't have lied about that.

Would he?

The slave girl returned with a covered dish and set it on the table before them.

"Go ahead," the God-King said. "Open it, if you dare."

Noah gripped the lid and stared at the polished metal reflecting his face. A sickness churned his abdomen at the thought of what might be inside. Should he open it?

Or should he leave and forget he'd seen anything?

He swallowed hard and thought of the Almighty's silence. Of all Noah wished he himself had done—the inaction he regretted.

If I leave now, I will never know. It will just be one more unanswered question. One more mystery in my past.

He was done with unanswered questions.

His fingers tightened on the lid, and he lifted it, revealing a severed human head, shrunken and slanted, its skin like tanned leather.

"I thought you would want to see your father one last time," the God-King said.

Noah's vision narrowed and blackened at the edges. "What?" His chest heaved, and he looked at the distorted head.

"I know how much you loved him." The God-King knelt

and caressed the severed skull, his voice falling to a whisper. "He died five years ago, so I had him preserved just for you."

Noah fell back. "No. That's a lie. You're lying."

The God-King smiled, those silver eyes nearly red in the flickering glow. "I would have preferred your father to remain alive. But my final gift to you is not proof of death, but proof of life. It is for this reason I know you will come see me—if only to see someone you've longed for all your life."

Noah stood, seeing the distinct markers in the preserved flesh. The shape of the cheekbones, the thinness of his father's lips, now twisted and compressed.

"Aren't you going to thank me?"

Noah passed a hand over his face and turned away, stumbling out into the hallway, down staircase after staircase until he burst into the open city.

He passed servants and Others with horns just like the ones who had murdered Elina all those years ago. The ones who had stolen his family away and destroyed his life. They watched him, but none touched him.

"What?" he yelled, spinning from one to another.

They stepped away from him as he approached.

His pulse sped, and ice flowed down his wrists and ankles. He observed the sky to gain his bearings, then ran off down the streets to escape the city and make his long journey home.

PART IX

The End of the World

"And Noah did all that the LORD had commanded him."
—Genesis 7:5

Chapter 68

Weeks later, still miles from home, smoke rose like a pillar in the sky, and Noah forced himself to look away, to keep his eyes on the path so that he still had time to deny what he already knew. That the village his children had been born and raised in, the same one they'd lived in for centuries and had helped grow from a small community to a bustling town, was burning.

He kept on, and after breaking through the trees to see the ark in the valley raised on scaffolding and awaiting God's judgment, the little buildings beside it smoked, and the streets lay painted in crimson slashes.

Blood. Blood was everywhere.

"Jade?" Noah's voice scraped his throat. "Jade!"

He sprinted down the hillside, slipping in the dew-covered grass, sending him tumbling to his hands and knees, then back to his feet.

He whipped through the streets, coughing with the acrid smoke that churned through doorways and out windows. He covered his mouth with his tunic and breathed, calling for his wife, his children, though none answered.

Bodies lay strewn in the marketplace. Limbs separated from torsos piled across faces grim with death. Familiar eyes motionless and dimmed of life.

His friends and coworkers. People he'd known so long they'd become family. Murdered.

He fell to his knees and threw himself over them as the burning he'd thought culled all those centuries ago flared. A smoldering rage beneath the skin of his chest that rattled his ribs like a bamboo prison.

Amidst the bodies, he found Barak's motionless form. He pressed his hand into his good friend's one final time, and closed his open eyelids.

How could any of what he saw be true? How could this have happened after all this time?

Must he suffer the loss of everything?

"Everything . . ." He turned his face to the sky, closing his eyes in a bitter plea. "They've taken everything. What more, God?"

But God did not answer.

Noah stumbled to his feet and threw a slab of rubble, sending it skittering through the dust. "Don't stay silent. Not now." He shook his head. "Not anymore."

A smoldering pile of rubble shifted, and stones skipped and scattered, sending a small plume of smoke and dust billowing. Noah stood and shuffled through the village toward the ark. Even from where he stood, it towered above the village. He knew the construction should have been finished while he traveled those many leagues, and from afar it seemed it had endured no damage.

As he approached, he heard what sounded like a distant birdcall. He looked up to see a figure on the scaffolding. The figure called his name, and Noah's eyes widened at the familiar hair blowing in the breeze, the long dress and slender figure of . . . "Jade?"

Jade fumbled with something, then set it down and descended the scaffolding quickly, dangerously, her feet slipping.

Noah sprinted underneath her. "Careful! Don't fall!"

But she made it safely and fell into his arms.

Noah kissed her forehead, cheeks, and lips. Oh, how he'd missed her and longed for her touch.

She pulled back and wiped her face, pulling the strands of hair out of her mouth.

"What happened?" Noah said, breathless.

"The Others came while you were gone. They watched as we finished building the ark, and after it was finished, they killed everyone and burned the village."

"Our children?" he said, and grabbed her shoulders. "Did they take our children?"

"No, thank the Almighty. The villagers pushed our children and their wives into the ark and commanded them to stay with the animals. They fought valiantly to protect us."

"The animals? What are you talking about?"

"They came, Noah. Just like the Almighty said they would. They're all in there, waiting. Every beast and bird I've ever seen. It's a miracle, and our children are tending to their needs as we speak."

"Show me."

Jade led him up the ramp through the door into the ark, and immediately Noah was assaulted by thick, earthen smells, and the sounds of snuffling, flapping, and low groans.

In the dim lighting from the open entrance, he saw a lion pacing on the other side of a low wall. A shiver spread down his neck and shoulders.

Jade squeezed his hand and whispered, "They've not attacked any of the other animals. When he led the animals here, he said their mouths had been closed."

"*He?*"

"You know of whom I speak," Jade said and nodded. "I was afraid when I first realized that the Almighty was here among us, but he presented himself as just a man. And he was . . . kind. And gentle. Though he looked very plain. And he led the lions in with the rest of the predators and commanded them to lay down, and they obeyed."

Noah shook his head and offered his hand to the lion. The beast approached and licked his hand. When the wet, velvety tongue scraped his skin, he jumped and pulled back. "Was the Almighty here when the village was attacked?"

Jade frowned. "No."

Noah turned away and looked at the lambs in the pen next to the lions. "How could the Almighty be kind and gentle and command even the most powerful beasts to lay down, yet not save our friends?"

Jade opened her mouth to respond, then pressed her lips together and looked away.

Noah looked at his own hands. "I'm not doubting him. We both know how stained my own hands are, so who am I to criticize the Almighty? But I don't understand him. I can't see how so much wonder and so much pain can be present in the same moment. I don't have the capacity to think of what remains ahead of us, because—" His voice broke, and he struggled to fight the ache. He cleared his throat and swallowed hard. "I miss them."

"Me too," she whispered.

"You swear our children are safe?"

Jade scoffed. "You're a bigger fool than I've ever thought if you think I'd lie about that."

"Of course I don't think you'd lie about it. I just need to see them."

"I suppose it would be best if you did," she said. "They've been worried for you." She led him up the stairs to the second deck, where his children and their wives sat huddled around several large candles and a loaf of bread.

When they saw him, they leapt to their feet and huddled around him, embracing him and kissing him, asking him about his journey, demanding he sit down and eat with them. But Noah pushed them away.

"Thank you," he said. "I needed to see you all, to make sure you were safe. But I need some time. Some space."

"We understand," Shem said.

"Come," Jade said. "If you're ready, let's go back outside."

So Noah and Jade walked hand in hand down the stairs, back out of the ark. They said nothing while they went, for to merely hold her hand in silence was enough.

Noah leaned against the scaffolding and pointed upward. "What were you doing up there?"

"Nothing," Jade said.

"Nothing?"

She rubbed her eyes, which were still red and puffy. "A slash in the wood for every person whose hands built the vessel that would carry us to a new world."

Noah saw her hands shaking, saw the stain of the pitch, and the beginnings of blisters from her painful task. Many—so many —had taken part in building the ark, and now would never see it used.

"Because of me," Noah said, and grabbed at the skin of his chest.

Jade placed her hand over Noah's. "It's not your fault."

He pushed her hand away. "How could it not be?"

She slipped her arms around his waist. "Because I know you. That you are a good man. A Godly man."

He wiped his face and leaned into his wife—the woman who had saved and supported him all these years. The mother to his children, and friend to his friends that now lay dead in the streets.

"You never chose this," she said.

"I didn't."

"Yet what can we do now but wait for what the Almighty has planned?"

Noah remembered the words of the God-King and felt a sickness churn in his belly. The God-King was right. After all that had happened, he knew he had to meet him one last time, if only to find closure and understand why his friends had been murdered. For the Almighty refused to respond to any of his appeals, and it felt necessary after what the God-King had said, as if closing this final circle was the last task the Almighty had given before the end.

If the God-King truly did have someone he cared for, could that mean that the devil had kept his mother in captivity all these years?

How could he leave without at least finding the truth?

He backed away, and Jade watched him, expression growing strained.

"What is it?" she said.

"There's still one last thing before the end."

"The Almighty tasked you with something else?"

Noah shook his head slowly. "The Almighty has said nothing to me in weeks. This is something else. Something different."

And he told Jade all he endured on the long journey. Of the strange audience he received with the God-King, and the "gift" the God-King prepared for him.

Jade blanched at that final detail, and shook her head. "He knew. He knew that he was going to slaughter everyone and burn our village. It was all to send you a message."

"But why? That's what I don't understand. That's why I need to go. Because what if he has . . . ?"

Jade grabbed his face gently, her frown deepening. "I know," she said. "Did you think I wouldn't after all we've been through? After all these years? I need to see this through with you."

"No. It's too dangerous."

"I'd rather die than be separated from you again." She stuck her finger into his chest to punctuate her words. "Never. Again."

Noah considered her. If he denied her such a condition, she would just find a way either to make him stay, or to follow him regardless. "What of our children?"

"The port is hardly half a day's walk. We will ride there. Some of the camels are still tied outside the village. I heard them braying while the flames still raged. Our children haven't stepped foot outside the ark since the Others set fire to the village. They think the ark hallowed by God. And perhaps it is, seeing as the Others never touched it."

"And if we die?"

Jade paused, then spoke as quiet as a distant breeze in the leaves. "At least our children will be saved, and the world will begin anew."

Chapter 69

The wind whipped Noah's hair and beard as they loped atop saddled camels. Jade kept up remarkably well despite the blisters on her hands, her expression locked in deadly concentration, her hands clenched as tight as the skin of his chest. Cool air sent chills down his back as he flicked the reins and yelled the command for speed.

He felt the swirling sense of the end fast approaching. The downward spiral toward inevitable Fate. But he was confused, for the Almighty still refused to speak. Multiple times Noah petitioned the Almighty for guidance, wisdom, anything.

The only answer was silence.

It made him anxious. So instead of think about it, he let his thoughts dissolve to the shadowed outline of the mother he never knew. From the beginning, she had been the source. Without her, Noah would never have been born, and the God-King would never have hunted his family and stamped out so many he loved.

Now he though he heard her voice like distant Music.

Come and taste what fruit the God-King prepared for you, and know.
Was your whole life a lie?

Tears sprang to his eyes as he thought of his father, dead and mutilated. Preserved just so that his skull might be presented as a tool to apply leverage to Noah.

If his mother lived, had Lamech been given the chance to see her one last time? Would Noah finally be able to meet her?

Would he . . .

Hills gave way to riverside. They followed its bends as it cut through stone and soil, until the water spread into a great delta that opened to distant blue and a city built on docks. The Others were everywhere. War ships docked at the port, and warriors stood on either side of the road like sentinels to corral him in.

They whipped past the soldiers with horns and, as the way opened to a broad circle, Noah slid off, and Jade followed. The camels skidded to a stop, just before where the God-King sat in an iron throne in the center of the circle, and backed away, wary of the soldiers.

The God-King stood and beckoned them forward, eyes glittering silver beneath black horns and an iron crown studded with emeralds.

Noah stood his ground. "I have come."

The God-King nodded.

"Show me what you will, or be damned," he said.

"First," the God-King said, "bow to me."

Noah gave Jade a meaningful look.

"Why does he even ask?" Jade said. "He knows your answer."

Noah kicked dust in the God-King's direction.

"No?" the God-King said, and he motioned for two guards who jerked up an old man bent with age. The man's hair was heavily matted, and he was too weak to stand unaided.

The guards shoved the man forward, and he fell with a grunt, breath hissing between yellow teeth, paper skin shaking over bones too sharp.

The God-King walked to the man and lifted his chin with his toe. "Speak, Methuselah. Your grandson awaits you."

Noah pressed the back of his hand to his mouth. "No," he said, and took in the withered figure before him.

Methuselah looked up at him with gray eyes sparkling with life yet drawn downward by the cares of a world too heavy. His beard shook as he rasped, "It's all right, Noah."

The God-King kicked Methuselah in the stomach, and Noah fell to his hands and knees and said, "Stop!"

The God-King looked at him, surprised. "So you do care for him. Well then, you know how to save him. Bow."

Noah dragged his nails through the dirt and spit at the God-King, who lifted Methuselah by his beard, forcing a pained croak from the man's throat. The God-King withdrew a knife and motioned another guard forward.

The guard held both a spear and a burlap sack, and he stopped halfway to Noah and dropped his spear to take up the sack in both hands. In one fluid motion, he loosened the tie and tossed the sack's contents forward.

Decaying bones clattered toward Noah and rolled over his foot. He grimaced and kicked them away, glancing first at Jade, who stared at the bones in horror, then at the God-King, who smiled.

"Behold," the God-King said, and pointed with his knife. "Your dear mother!" Then he dragged the blade through Methuselah's throat.

"No!" Noah screamed, feeling the burning consume his arms and legs as Methuselah's body fell, spewing red just like Elina's had so many years earlier.

He thought of his mother, of his father, of Kenan, Barak, and all the friends he'd ever loved wrenched away. His sight blackened and reddened, and he knew he should stop but refused to remain passive any longer.

He ran forward, grabbed up the spear, only barely aware of the rush of the wind and the blurred figures swirling around him as he aimed himself at the God-King's horns.

"Stop!" Jade screeched, and her voice sent a shock through Noah's body, causing him to stiffen, feet sliding, just barely staying upright as the tip of the spear stopped inches from the God-King's chest.

No one was moving. Not the God-King. Not the guards. Not the soldiers, and not Methuselah, who lay in a pool of red.

What was happening? Why was no one trying to stop him? Why was . . .

"What are you waiting for?" the God-King said, and his voice was cold and quiet.

It hit Noah then, and his throat tightened until he thought he would never breathe. The God-King wasn't trying to make Noah worship him.

He was trying to get Noah to kill him.

Every mystery of his past suddenly fell into place, and he could see why the God-King had sent Methuselah to Noah and Lamech—so that Noah would develop a relationship with his grandfather. The God-King had kept himself from destroying the village Noah lived in these past five centuries precisely so that he would grow to love the people there.

Noah's mother had been murdered, and her bones reclaimed, for this moment. Lamech's skull had been preserved and offered as just another tool to incite rage.

Everything about Noah's life had been orchestrated for this moment, so that the God-King could tear everything away and make Noah bow to rage when he refused to bow to anything else.

Because if the God-King could plant the lust for revenge where the Almighty demanded surrender, would he not be in control? Would the God-King not, in a perverse reversal, become Noah's obsession, his god, and in doing so, defile Noah's heart?

In that moment, the Almighty's single response these past few weeks finally made deadly sense. *"My grace and mercy are sufficient for you."*

He wanted Noah to forgive rather than to bow his head to bitterness.

Noah looked back at Jade, the woman who had walked with him, faithful for so many centuries. She had seen the God-King's true intentions when he had not, and he loved her for it.

But as he returned his gaze to the God-King, he felt his soul slip back into all the hate he'd borne since a child. "You killed my mother." He ground his teeth, letting the rage coil serpentine cold in his throat. "My father. My grandfather. My friends. You took everything."

"Yes," the God-King said. "And I'll take more still."

Noah knew that the God-King planned only to defile him, yet wanted nothing more than to press the tip of his spear through the devil's chest. He could do it. And no one would stop him. Not the God-King. Not the soldiers. Not even the Almighty.

Surely the God-King deserved it more than any other creature to walk the face of the earth.

But the Almighty's words echoed like distant, gentle Music, *"My grace and mercy are sufficient for you."*

And the meaning of those words sent a shudder through Noah's bones, for he finally realized what the Man tried to show him in the Shrine of the Song. The two Musics were at war beneath the skin of his chest, coiled over his soul, slowly strangling him.

How could he show the devil mercy?

Yet how could he disobey the Almighty?

God had led him through the wilderness and kept his wife and children safe. The Almighty had given him everything the God-King ever stole.

Noah's shaking hands edged forward, the tip of the spear finding the God-King's tunic.

"No," Jade said. "Don't do it, Noah. You've seen what he has to offer. Just come away like we planned. The ark is waiting."

"You took everything because I hated you," Noah said. "Because I've hated you all my life."

"And why shouldn't you?" the God-King said.

"My hatred for you, alone, have I kept from the Almighty." He paused, his body convulsing, and his voice quieted to little more than a whisper. "But not anymore. Because now I see." Noah shook his head, stared into the God-King's eyes, and said, "I . . . I forgive you."

The God-King's face seemed to jerk, and he grabbed the shaft of the spear and pressed it into his chest until blood dribbled out. "Do what you've dreamed of all these years."

Noah shook his head. "I won't."

Even as it was all he wanted.

"Do it!"

"No!" Noah wrenched the spear away and threw it for fear of his own desire. Tears came to his eyes as he watched it roll through the dust. "I'm done hating you," he said. "You've taken everything, but you won't take my God from me."

The God-King yelled and reared his head like a ram just as a cry erupted from the crowd, and the circle of guards surged. Noah turned and followed their hands pointed toward the sky where a massive light such as a star slashed across the sky and fell toward the earth countless leagues away, sending a rumble through the ground and lighting the edge of the horizon until it outshone the sun.

Buildings shook, and the Others scattered. Boats rocked in the water, and the earth groaned as the roof of a nearby building toppled.

Jade's hand warmed his arm. He turned and met her gaze as she said, "It's time! We have to go."

He followed her back to their mounts, where she helped him up, then joined him.

And with a snap of the reins and a one-word command, they fled the city to return to the ark.

Chapter 70

W hen they arrived back at the burnt village, water had already overrun the river and quenched the cinders in the rubble. The camels splashed toward the ark, and Noah's children stood just inside the entrance, leaning against the chains they would use to seal the door.

When Shem saw them, he pointed, and the rest waved their arms and screamed for them to hurry. Noah looked behind and saw a wall of water approaching fast. Far in the distance a plume of water shot hundreds of cubits into the sky. Jade saw it, too, and they whipped their reins, but the camels were already running as fast as they could.

The wave continued gaining, snapping trees and thrusting boulders, tossing splinters and foam to the sky.

The camels loped up the ramp and, just as they made it inside, the wall of water rushed by, barely an arm's length below the bottom of the entrance.

Noah dropped off the camel and fell against the wall, thanking the Almighty for how high they'd built the opening.

Shem, Ham, Japheth, and their wives hung on the chains, pulling with all their strength, but the door would not lift.

"It's not budging," Shem said, and a chill descended Noah's throat as the water continued to rise.

He grabbed hold of the chains with them and pulled, but the current was too strong.

"Who is that?" Ham said, and pointed.

There, nearly sixty paces out, a figure stood atop the water. He moved slowly, feet barely brushing the surface of the torrent.

Noah's eyes widened in recognition. "It is the Man."

"He was the one who brought the animals!" Jade said.

The Man stopped several feet short of the door and stared at Noah. His children looked at him, then at the Man, with jaws stretched wide. No one said anything, but Noah nodded, and the Man nodded back.

Then, with a flick of his wrist and a soundless Word, the Man commanded the door slam shut and seal.

It obeyed.

Chapter 71

Noah raced through the ark past low walls and myriad animals. Their mixed scents filled the dark space, and he clamped his hands over his ears as birds screamed and cows and goats complained with the shifting of the vessel as the water rose.

Judging by the violent weather outside, they had little time before the scaffolding failed and the ark was sent adrift.

He wanted to look out on the world one last time before it was forever changed.

He made his way to the top of the third deck, and shoved aside the opening to one of the few windows they'd built into the vessel. The ship rocked and bucked, and Noah was thrown against the wall as the scaffolding broke. The movement smoothed, and Noah felt a rush in his abdomen as the ark picked up speed.

He braced himself against the wall just as Jade and Shem caught up with him.

Noah set his face to the window.

"What do you see?" Jade said.

"Water is everywhere. In the distance, fountains are bursting out of the deep." Rain pattered the ark, and thunder rumbled their throats. "There is a haze in the sky, and the world grows dark."

He shut the window and sat with his back to the wall. Jade joined him, and Shem placed a torch in a receptacle. They jumped as a massive explosion sounded outside, as if a mountain had just struck the earth not a thousand paces away from them. Everything shook, and the animals screamed again.

"What was that?" Ham's muffled yell sounded from below.

Noah struggled to his feet and opened the window again. He searched the horizon, but could see nothing, for the rain was too intense. So he sat, and for several long moments, they listened to the groan of the wood, the rumble of thunder, and the sounds of their family and the animals two levels below.

Even from within, they could hear the rush of the water and the splintering of trees as the world they knew was drowned and destroyed.

But all Noah could think of was the way the Man had looked at him.

Jade's hand alighted on his knee. "What is it?"

Noah shook his head. "He knew. I could see it in his eyes." He covered his face as shame and sorrow quenched the burning that had overtaken him in the presence of the God-King.

"You did it," Jade said. "You made the right choice."

Noah shook his head. "I didn't want to. Even now, I wish I would have done it."

Jade and Shem said nothing.

"Maybe I made the right decision, but in my heart . . . I still resent the Almighty for taking from me what I've dreamed of all these years." Noah quieted, fearful of speaking what he knew the Man had already seen in his heart. "I'm angry with him for not letting me kill the God-King. And I'm ashamed for it."

Jade leaned close, and he leaned into her, body convulsing with the force of his dishonor.

"Hush," she said. "The shame you feel is proof of your love."

"I don't love him."

"Who among us can? You taught me long ago that none of us are capable of loving the Almighty in and of ourselves."

"But I've lived with the Almighty all these years. Still, my heart rejects him. What is wrong with me?"

"You are human. As are we all."

Noah looked away.

"Do you want to know what I saw in the Man's gaze just moments ago? I saw love."

"Don't say that. It only makes it worse."

"I think it is precisely your remorse that shows your faithfulness, that shows that you truly have surrendered to the Almighty, even as your heart won't let you. Just remember that your being here right now is proof that he has already forgiven you."

Noah hugged her harder.

"Emotions are slow to respond. They take time to catch up to our actions. If you don't want to let go, the Almighty will help you do it eventually. Just continue being faithful, as you have."

And so they sat together and listened to the Music of the Almighty as it commanded the destruction of the world and every living creature in it.

All but for one small family huddled in the dark amidst groaning animals in an ark set adrift on violent water.

PART X

Mercy as Judgment and Judgment as Mercy

"For as were the days of Noah, so will be the coming of the Son of Man."
—Matthew 24:37

Chapter 72

The God-King sat on his iron throne as the world bent and shifted around him. Everything had failed, but though the end of the age was upon them, he knew hope was not yet gone—even as his brethren fled.

For he was different. Set apart. Though the body he had inhabited these countless years was about to be destroyed, the spirit of the Abomination within that body could never be excised from the world, for it belonged to the world and was tied to it as men's spirits are tied to the world beyond.

After the waters were gone, the Abomination would find another host. And when it did, it would have its way. It would see its father's plans come to fruition.

"I will not fail the Light Bringer," the God-King said.

Then a crack opened in the ground beneath his throne, and he fell into the dark of the pit, and was smashed to death in the depths.

Chapter 73

The rains and flooding prevailed across the earth for forty days, until the highest peaks of the tallest mountains were covered. They passed over the mountains in the ark, so that Noah knew the mountains were covered to at least fifteen cubits of depth.

All living creatures that breathed air perished on the earth. The Almighty blotted out all life, true to his promise, and after the forty days of violence, the waters prevailed on the earth for an additional one hundred and ten days, until the ark came to rest on a range of mountains cut by the water and raised to bitter peaks.

Noah opened the windows and looked out upon dry ground, and the Voice of the Almighty spoke.

"Go out from the ark, you and your wife, and your sons and your sons' wives with you. Bring out with you every living thing that is with you of all flesh—birds and animals and every creeping thing—that they may swarm on the earth, and be fruitful and multiply."

So Noah and the rest of his family went out. And every beast, every creeping thing and bird, all the creatures went out by families from the ark.

No violence was seen among them, for the Man had commanded them to remain at peace with one another.

Noah built an altar to the Lord and fell down before it.

"Almighty . . . I thank you, and bless you for your faithfulness and mercy. Please, forgive my sin. Forgive me for not desiring you as I should." He paused, and continued in a low whisper. "Forgive me for trying to take hold of vengeance. For resenting you for taking it. Truly, I don't want such a terrible responsibility. I want to love you. Help my unlove."

And when he opened his eyes and looked up, he saw a pure white lamb kneeling on the altar, looking down.

Footsteps approached.

Noah did not move as a scarred hand softly pressed his shoulder.

The Man dipped, kissed him on the cheek, and whispered, "I forgave you before I closed the door."

Then he was gone, and Noah took some of every clean animal and clean bird and offered them as burnt offerings on the altar.

And the Voice said, *"I will never again curse the ground because of man, as happened when Cain murdered his brother, Abel. For the intention of man's heart is evil from his youth. Neither will I ever again strike down every living creature as I have done. While the earth remains, seedtime and harvest, cold and heat, summer and winter, day and night shall not cease. For just as I have blotted out man from the earth, so I will offer a sacrifice whose blood will blot out your sins."*

Then the Spirit of the Almighty descended as a piercing Light above the altar, and from it the Voice continued. *"The fear of you and the dread of you shall be upon every beast of the earth. Into your hand they are delivered. As I gave you the green plants, so now I give you everything. But you shall not eat flesh with its blood. And for your lifeblood I will require a reckoning: from every beast I will require it and from man. From his fellow man I will require a reckoning for the life of man.*

Whoever sheds the blood of man,
 by man shall his blood be shed,
 for God made man in his own image.

. . .

"And you, be fruitful and multiply, increase greatly on the earth and multiply in it."

And the Light rose into the heavens, and in its wake stretched a double rainbow that arced over the mountains. *"Behold,"* the Voice said, rumbling the earth like thunder, *"I have set my bow in the cloud, and it shall be a sign of the covenant between me and the earth. When I bring clouds over the earth and the bow is seen in the clouds, I will remember my covenant that is between me and you and every living creature of all flesh. And the waters shall never again become a flood to destroy all flesh. When the bow is in the clouds, I will see it and remember the everlasting covenant between God and every living creature of all flesh that is on the earth."*

And the Almighty remained faithful to his promise.

The Reason Why This Book
Exists

Although the story you've been reading was crafted with much care and respect toward the biblical text, it is a fantasy intended to entertain readers and stimulate thought. The real history of Noah can be found in the book of Genesis, the first book of the Bible. We know nothing more than what is explicitly stated in the original Hebrew text of that book, and any extra-biblical conclusions I drew in this book are either imaginative interpretations or pure invention.

Modern translations of Genesis differ in their interpretations, limiting the text in some ways, expanding it in others. If you want to read an in-depth examination of the text of Genesis, I have prepared one for you at the end of this section, pulling from myriad sources studied in advance of writing this novel.

However, I think it's time I answer the primary question readers have posed me.

"Why are these books so dark and strange?"

A flannel-graph, Sunday school vision of Noah, his family, and the world they inhabited is useless. Noah's world was a very uncomfortable place to live in, so a novel based on Noah's life is necessarily uncomfortable to read.

I find it useful to envision how these real people might have felt, and what struggles they might have encountered—even if I know this particular vision of them is purely invented.

Noah and his family were real people who lived and struggled through a real world. Their lives have been used for millennia as inspiration to the faithful, and my hope is that the emotional aspects of how the characters were portrayed hold a concrete realism that grounds the reader and offers real meat, even while much of the story is fantastical in nature.

However, the primary desire that birthed this particular interpretation of Genesis 5-9 was the aspiration to show just one potential scenario in which God sending the Flood could be seen as truly merciful. Because doing that demanded delving into speculative waters, I decided to fully embrace the speculative side so that no one would be tempted to believe that it actually happened the way this novel portrays it.

Scholars disagree on how to interpret the use of the word Nephilim in Genesis 6. Were the Nephilim the offspring of demons and humans? Were they the offspring of polygamist men? Were they giants born through a genetic fluke? We don't know, and the endless conjecture and popularity of the Nephilim has done little good. Conspiracy theories, though entertaining, are often a waste of time. Even if they're fun.

The point of the story of Noah and the Flood being included in Genesis 6 is to point toward man's depravity and God's goodness, mercy, and faithfulness.

The thought that took hold of me while researching to write *Flood* was, "If the Nephilim were the offspring of demons and women, what if Satan's intent was to pervert the human gene pool so that the Savior promised in the garden of Eden could never come?"

It would have made the Flood merciful beyond dispute because God sending the Flood would have purified the gene pool and allowed for the redemption of humankind through Jesus.

Mercy through judgment. A theme we see all throughout the Bible, just as we see how mercy can become a sort of punishment.

Again, the point is not that I actually believe the story

happened the exact way I portrayed it—no one really knows what it was like, not even scholars.

The point is that if we can imagine one potential scenario within which God can be seen as merciful for slaughtering nearly all life on the planet, can we not trust that God had good reasons for doing so?

My father frequently asks skeptics, "Do you think you know 10 percent of everything?"

If people are honest, they answer, "No."

Next, he asks, "Well, then do you know 1 percent of everything?"

Again, if they're honest (or at least not perfectly self-absorbed), they answer, "No."

"All right," he says, "then let's just assume you don't know 99 percent of everything. Can't you assume that the answer you're seeking is hidden somewhere in the 99 percent you don't know?"

The point is, who are we to distrust an all-knowing, all-powerful, omnipresent Creator?

I have friends who turned away from the faith because their imaginations couldn't conjure a single scenario in which God could be seen as merciful for sending the Flood.

So I applied my imagination to conjure one such scenario. I hope it's useful.

God will never fit within our understanding. Once we think we have him figured out, he defies us. He demands that we engage him not just with our rational mind, but with our whole person (spirit, emotions, imagination, etc.).

...

Finally . . .

If you believe in Christ, I hope you'll join me in striving to follow him more passionately. If you haven't dedicated your life to Jesus, now is the perfect time to get on your knees and do so. In fact, here's a simple prayer to get you started:

Jesus, you died upon a cross,

And rose again to save the lost,
Forgive me now of all my sin,
Come be my Savior, Lord and Friend,
Change my life and make it new,
And help me, Lord, to live for you.

If you prayed that prayer, welcome to the Kingdom. Your next steps should be to find a Bible-believing church to attend on Sundays, purchase a Bible, and start reading it and spending time praying every day.

Your life will never be the same.

Be blessed. And thanks for reading.

If you want more, go to brennanmcpherson.com to download two free e-books and get a weekly devotional sent to your inbox. Then continue reading this series with *BABEL: The Story of the Tower and the Rebellion of Man,* to experience the rest of Noah's long life.

Study of Genesis 5-9

Introduction

Any serious study of a passage of Scripture demands more than we expect, and leads to more fruit than we could imagine. The following is a brief compilation of some of the most interesting and useful details I came across while digging into Genesis 5-9 and writing *FLOOD*.

We must let Scripture speak plainly, and not get too thrown off by the fact that we will never understand everything.

Proverbs 18 says, "A fool takes no pleasure in understanding, but only in expressing his opinion." And again, "A fool's lips walk into a fight, and his mouth invites a beating. A fool's mouth is his ruin, and his lips are a snare to his soul."

I don't want to be the fool that those passages talk about. So, if you believe anything written here contradicts Scripture, contact me through my website brennanmcpherson.com, so that I can consider whether an adjustment to the text is in order.

When we enter into the study of Scripture, we're called to shed our attitude and tread humbly.

With that in mind, I'd like to begin with a short prayer. . .

God. . . you know our tendencies. Please, forgive us for our pride. Give us the ability to see you in your words, and to understand your truths. Thank you. We love you.

The rest of this section is meant to be read alongside Scripture. So, grab your Bible and let's jump in!

The Intent of Genesis 5-9

The purpose of the story of Noah and the ark being included in the book of Genesis can be seen as complex, but its main purpose is to show God's mercy amidst man's unfaithfulness. Genesis goes out of its way to communicate that mankind deserved total destruction. It also goes out of its way to show that God offered mercy to Noah and his family. Though the book is both poetry and history, its main theme is simple and redemptive.

Now, we know from later parts of Scripture that no one is righteous, "not even one" (Psalm 143:2; Romans 3:10). So, when Genesis mentions that Noah was righteous in his generation, it's not actually saying that Noah was justified by works. Men have only ever been saved by faith through Christ, as Hebrews 11 makes clear.

God forgave Abraham not because Abraham was righteous, but because Abraham had faith in God (Hebrews 11:8-19). We are only saved by faith through Christ (Galatians 2:16; Galatians 3:11; Romans 3:28; Romans 5:1), and faith is made real through action (the book of James). So, Abraham proved his faith through his faithfulness, and God counted it to him as righteousness because Christ's sacrifice covered his sin.

So, Noah was not justified by works but by faith in God through Christ. This is the most orthodox belief in the Christian faith. If you reject it, you reject the Christian faith. And it is powerfully illustrated in the story of Noah and the worldwide flood.

This central focus on God's mercy is also shown in the story's poetic structure. Genesis 6:10-9:19 is a palistrophe (a literary structure that reverses back on itself, so that the first item mirrors the last item, leaving the middle point as the axis). Below is an illustration of the story's structure (it's a bit hard to understand it unless you see it graphically represented and have time to think it through).

1. Noah (Genesis 6:10). 31. Noah (Genesis 9:19).
2. Noah's sons (6:10). 30. Noah's sons (9:18).
3. Ark (6:14-16). 29. Ark (9:18).
4. Warning of flood (6:17). 28. Flood never again (9:11-17).
5. Covenant (6:18-20). 27. Covenant (9:8-10).
6. Food (6:21). 26. Food (9:1-4).
7. Commanded to enter (7:1-3). 25. Commanded to exit (8:15-17).
8. 7 days of waiting (7:4-5). 24. 7 days of waiting (8:12-13).
9. 7 days of waiting (7:7-10) 23. 7 days of waiting (8:10-11)
10. Entering the ark (7:11-15) 22. Raven and dove leave ark (8:7-9)
11. God shuts Noah in the ark (7:16) 21. Noah opens window on the ark (8:6)
12. 40 days (7:17a) 20. 40 days (8:6)
13. Waters rise (7:17-18) 19. Waters abate (8:5)
14. Mountains covered (7:19) 18. Mountain tops revealed (8:4-5)
15. 150 days of rising waters (7:24) 17. 150 days of abating waters (8:3)
16. God remembers Noah (8:1)

And what is the axis of the story? Point # 16, Genesis 8:1, "But God remembered Noah and all the beasts and all the livestock that were with him in the ark. And God made a wind blow over the earth, and the waters subsided."

God's mercy and faithfulness is the literal and figurative axis of the entire story, around which everything moves.

I don't know about you, but I find that fascinating.

Notes on Genesis 5

Noah's name sounds like the word for "rest," and is related to the word for "comfort." In Genesis 5:29, after Noah is named, his father, Lamech, says, "Out of the ground that the Lord has cursed, this one shall bring us relief from our work and from the painful toil of our hands." In *Flood*, I have Lamech agreeing with this statement rather than being the first to say it, which still fits within the narrative, though likely Lamech was the one to pronounce it—either as a prophecy or as a hope that became prophetically used by God.

This raises the question of whether or not Lamech and Methuselah were godly men. Methuselah's father, Enoch, was obviously a godly man because the text says he "walked with God" (Genesis 5:22-24). But in a world that soon became so corrupt that "every intention of the thoughts of his (mankind's) heart was only evil continually," what were Methuselah and Lamech like?

Methuselah died the year of the flood, and his name means, "his death shall bring judgment." But we don't know if that's because he was a holy man. Indeed, I wonder what sort of impact Methuselah's father's disappearance had on him. Similarly, we are given no clear information on who Lamech was, or how he raised his child in such an oppressive and violent world, though we do know that Lamech died several years before the flood.

And what happened to Enoch when he was taken? Hebrews 11:5 claims that Enoch never saw death. He is only one of two people in all of history who we know never died. Some Christians (even as early as 200 A.D.) have hypothesized that Enoch and Elijah might be the two prophets seen in the book of Revelation. Of course, I left *Flood* open for that possibility, and even had God using Enoch to speak into Noah's life and show him the Old Way.

Another strange idea I took note of in Genesis 5 was that Noah turned 500 before he sired Shem, Ham, and Japheth. Did he have other children earlier on who were murdered and therefore not mentioned? If not, what took so long? 500 years is a LONG time to have no children. And if he wasn't married for all that time, why did it take him so long to get married? Who was his wife? What was his wife's name? What was she like?

The text offers no clear explanation for any of these questions. That's why, in *Flood*, I imagined that perhaps God had closed Jade's womb for all those years as a form of mercy, to keep their children from being too exposed to the evils of the world they lived in.

I hope, by now, that you'll begin to see the difficulties in converting the book of Genesis into fully fleshed-out fictional tales. It's like being given a fossilized tooth and being demanded to accurately re-construct the creature's movements and personality at the time of death.

And yet, what an opportunity to muse about God's goodness, and the mystery of his ways!

Notes on Genesis 6-9

Genesis 6 begins with one of the most notoriously difficult and uncomfortable sections in all of Scripture. The difficulty here lies with defining who "the sons of God" really were.

Some commentators hold that the sons of God were normal men who had fallen into polygamy and other perversions, like we see with a different Lamech mentioned in early Genesis (a descendant of Cain; Genesis 4:23-24).

Other commentators hold that this portion of the text is some sort of strange mythological fragment. But I believe this is a ridiculous and perverse idea that should be flatly rejected by every Christian.

Other commentators believe that the "sons of God" were the Godly descendants of Seth. But this doesn't make sense because the Nephilim are portrayed as being forces for evil.

Still more commentators believe that the "sons of God" were fallen angels. This is a very old belief strengthened by the usage of the same term ("sons of God") in reference to fallen angels in Job, and elsewhere in Scripture.

We don't know what the Nephilim were, and it matters little. But, if you're interested, I lean toward the final (and possibly the oldest) belief that the sons of God were fallen angels who somehow perverted the human race—either through possession, or some other means.

In *Flood*, I picture a way that demons could manipulate the genetic makeup of the human race to make human beings into shells through which the fallen angels could walk about in physical form and experience and rule the physical world. It fits within the text, and is in line with further scriptures that hint at the fall of Lucifer.

Still, any conclusion drawn is mere speculation and shouldn't be focused on other than for the purpose of further solidifying the fact that the human race had deteriorated beyond the point of return.

There was no conceivable way that the human race could be turned around because they had rejected all of God's invitations to do so. In a sense, the entire world had committed irreconcilable blasphemy. Mankind flatly refused to be redeemed. And because of mankind's total rejection of God, he needed to purify the world.

This is an act of mercy because humanity was in a downward spiral toward total self-destruction. Through punitive judgment, God could bring one faithful man and his family through to a new world for a sort of cosmic re-set.

By doing this, God could do away with the immense suffering the world was enduring, and bring joy and peace back to the world.

We know from the text of the Bible that goodness comes only from God. So, the more godless a world is, the less goodness there is in that world, until there is no goodness left at all.

God was not committing genocide with the worldwide Flood, but rather doing away with dead plants and tilling the soil to bring forth good fruit.

Even still, God grieved over the deterioration and destruction of his beloved children and creation (Genesis 6:6-7).

Noah found favor in the eyes of the Lord because he loved God and had faith in him, as his great-grandfather Enoch did. Indeed, in Genesis 6:9 we even see that Noah "walked with God," the same phrase used to describe Enoch's relationship with God.

Directly after this point is where we enter the "palistrophe" literary structure that details the destruction and renewal of the world, patterned after the Creation story in the earlier chapters of Genesis.

Noah is portrayed as a sort of second Adam, the new father

of all living men and women. Both Noah and Adam bear three children, one of whom turns out to be wicked and debased in mind (Cain and Ham). Noah lives in complete harmony with the animals while on the ark, just as Adam lived in complete harmony with the animals in the garden of Eden. The wind blowing away the waters in Genesis 8:1 recalls the Spirit of God hovering over the face of the waters in the Creation account. The wording of the divine blessing in 9:1 mirrors that of 1:28, and the genealogical lists in Genesis 10 even mirror those of Genesis 4, both tracing all of mankind back to a single ancestor.

There are countless global catastrophic flood legends in nearly every major culture in the world. However, one of the largest elements that sets Genesis 6-9 apart from every other flood legend is that in Genesis 6-9, God deliberately decides to save Noah and show he and his family mercy. This is not the case in the other flood legends.

There are many other unique points that make the Genesis narrative exceptional, such as that only Noah's family was saved. In many other stories, builders were also saved, along with other friends or relatives.

Only in Genesis do we see such a focus on a single family being the source of every culture and people group on the planet. Indeed, it's a major theme that again hearkens back to the story of Adam and Eve.

A full exploration of the distinctive features of the story of Noah and the ark has been conducted by many others. Suffice it to say that we can be confident that the Genesis narrative is not a derivative of another story, but is in fact a fully independent story of which other stories seem to be derivatives.

One extremely interesting note on Genesis 6:9 is that when God declares Noah to be righteous and blameless, the Hebrew words used are tsaddik and tamim. Tsaddik is a legal term that describes someone who has been judged "in the right." Tamim is a word mostly found in ritual contexts. It refers to a sacrificial animal without blemish. So, through the poetic language used to describe Noah, we see God judging Noah's behavior, offering him mercy, and painting him as a foreshadowing of the unblemished Christ (who, interestingly enough, is referred to as "the last Adam").

In the following sections (within the palistrophe), we see a lot of repetition. The word "corrupt" occurs 7 times in the narrative to portray the totality of the world's depravity. God speaks directly to Noah 7 times to drive home that God speaks directly to individuals, rather than being an impersonal God. The re-creation of the world is poetically re-inforced by 7 repetitions of "to make" in God's instructions for building the ark, and another 7 times in connection with the waters abating. The word for ark ("tevah") is also repeated 7 times in the instructions of how to build the ark, and another 7 times while the water is abating. The term implies a craft without any sort of navigational aid, stressing mankind's total dependence on God. And let's not forget that we see the clean animals appear in pairs of 7.

Pointing back to the palistrophe structure, Genesis 7:17 and Genesis 8:6 both mention a 40 day period. 40 is a symbolic number in Scripture that is often connected with purification and the purging of sin. It's used for that purpose here, as well.

Gopher wood was likely cedar. Many modern scholars prefer to interpret it as "cypress" because of a similarity in sound in the Hebrew words, and because it was widely used in shipbuilding for its resilience.

In Genesis 7:16, the text takes special pains to show that Noah was shut in by God. In the Mesopotamian flood myths, Atrahasis and Utnapishtim closed the door themselves.

The actual cataclysm is given very little description in the narrative. However, we have scientific support these days that the global flood actually could have happened. In particular, there are a group of serious scientists called Logos Research Associates who have devoted themselves to studying theories moored in a biblical worldview. I had the fantastic opportunity to spend an entire afternoon with one of their geologists, Dr. Steve Austin, who worked on a pioneering theory called the Plate Tectonics Model: http://static.icr.org/i/pdf/technical/Catastrophic-Plate-Tectonics-A-Global-Flood-Model.pdf

The paper cited above is filled with scientific jargon that I won't get into here. Reading it raised a number of questions, and Dr. Austin was kind enough to answer them all, even going beyond to help me understand some additional forces they've mused over since writing the paper.

Essentially, the paper pictures a single, violent event (such as a comet striking the earth) that set many forces into motion, resulting in an enormous amount of heat and energy being added to the globe, a conveyor-belt like motion in the crust of the earth itself, volcanic eruptions all across the globe, subterranean water bursting through the crust of the earth in mile-high plumes, and massive rains for many days. The majority of the water would have come not from the rain, but from underground.

Noah and his family were shut in the ark with extremely limited visibility. So, as the floodwaters receded, they needed a way to tell if the waters were actually gone before opening the door.

In ancient times, sailors took birds with them to have a way of telling how close they were to land. After the waters receded, Noah first released a raven, and then a dove three times at 7 day intervals. Interestingly enough, God is portrayed in the Bible as *three* persons in one; 7 is (once again) the number of perfection; and in the New Testament, we see God's Holy Spirit descending on Jesus as a *dove*.

When the dove returns the second time, it brings back an olive branch—symbolic of God's blessings of regeneration, abundance, and strength.

Finally, when God calls Noah and his family out of the ark, we see Noah offer a sincere and wholehearted worship offering to God, who is pleased by Noah's act of love. And God promises to never again destroy the earth with a flood.

This is where God points to the rainbow and suddenly layers it with meaning by saying it's proof that he'll never again flood the earth.

Just the Beginning

As many notes as were made here, it's just the beginning of the depth of meaning retained in the original Hebrew narrative of Genesis 5-9. I hope that this has, in some way, inspired you to read the Scriptures with new lenses, and to dig deeper into the text of sections you thought you knew everything about! It certainly has done that for me.

Blessings, and thanks for reading!

...

If you want more, go to brennanmcpherson.com and sign up for my weekly devotional. If you do that, you'll receive two free e-books sent to your email!

Continue the series and read about
the rest of Noah's life in BABEL.

Go to brennanmcpherson.com to buy BABEL: The Story of the
Tower and the Rebellion of Man.

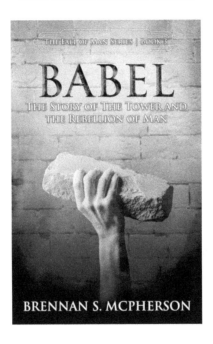

Available on Amazon and elsewhere in e-book, paperback, and
audiobook formats.

Acknowledgments

Thank you, Jesus, for your forgiveness. I pray that you'll help me forgive as you've forgiven, so that I myself won't be disqualified when the race is over. Thank you for my wife, Anna. My daughter, Willow. My super-cool editor, Natalie Hanemann. All my early readers and supporters. Josh Meyer, for his help and expertise. And my parents for raising me and showing me the Old Way. It's been an amazing journey. I can't wait to see what lies beyond the bend. . .

CPSIA information can be obtained
at www.ICGtesting.com
Printed in the USA
BVHW042153080720
583307BV00014B/364